TEMPT ME

UNDERBELLY CHRONICLES BOOK THREE

TAMARA HOGAN

DEDICATION

Many thanks to Brenda Whiteside, Susan Sey, Carolyn Crane, and my blogmates at The Ruby Slippered Sisterhood for continuing friendship, wise counsel, and always having my back. Virtual high fives to my awesome beta readers Rebekah and Sheronda. Special thanks to Patty, for providing such a friendly place to write, and for keeping me caffeinated.

Last but not least, perpetual thanks to Mark—for holding down the fort, for herding the cats, and for the gift of guilt-free time.

THE UNDERBELLY CHRONICLES

Taste Me
Chase Me
Touch Me
Tempt Me
Enthrall Me
Intoxicate Me

THE UNDERWORLD COUNCIL

Incubus: Elliott Sebastiani *
Second: Antonia Sebastiani

Siren: Claudette Fontaine
Second: Scarlett Fontaine

Were: Krispin Woolf
Second: Jacoby Woolf

Vampire: Valerian
Second: Wyland

Valkyrie: Alka Schlessinger
Second: Lorin Schlessinger

Humanity: (vacant)
Emeritus: REDACTED

Sec/Tech: Lukas Sebastiani
Second: Jack Kirkland

* President

CHAPTER ONE

"Well." Banner tapped the papers into a neat stack with obvious reluctance. "I believe everything is in order."

Bailey glanced at the conference room door, her foot bouncing under the table. Everything had been 'in order' since she'd scribbled her signature on the last of the documents Banner had placed in front of her almost ten minutes ago. Before the meeting, she'd kicked off what she hoped was the final series of tests for a security enhancement, and she was anxious to see the results. Sebastiani Labs was getting hammered by malicious incursion attempts, and she had no idea why.

But it wasn't every day that a girl was released from probation.

"A question, if you will."

Yes, there it was—another stolen glance at the heavy security door leading to the working areas of Sebastiani Security. Banner had used every technique at his disposal to drag this meeting out, and it appeared he wasn't quite finished yet. Jack Kirkland, the company's managing partner, her lawyer, and her best friend, had complied with Banner's request to hold this meeting at Bailey's place of employment, but there was no way he was getting behind that closed door. Nope, upon Banner's arrival, Jack had politely escorted him to The Goldfish Bowl, the no-privacy, glass-walled conference room right next to the front entrance. The meeting location had the added side benefit that Banner would be tormented looking at what he couldn't have.

Jack could be nasty that way. Bailey heartily approved.

Under the table, Jack nudged her foot. She hadn't responded to Banner's question. "You can ask." Not that she'd necessarily answer.

"Over the last decade, despite your criminal conviction, you've become one of the most highly-regarded computer security and penetration analysts in the business. You've had your choice of contracts, and named your own price. Why did you close your consultancy to work for someone else? To work…here?" Banner indicated the sterile conference room and looked out the window overlooking Washington Avenue. Across the street, Sex World was doing nice lunchtime business.

Her former clients had been happy to pay through the nose to have a notorious hacker-gone-good break into their computer systems and point out areas of weakness, but infamy wasn't all it was cracked up to be. She hadn't realized how valuable anonymity was until she didn't have it anymore. *Anything you say can and will be used against you.* "I needed some downtime," she finally said. As answers went, it was an honest one, but nowhere near the truth. The servers behind that generic steel door stored a secret that, if exposed, would rock humanity to its foundation. Protecting it took her entire arsenal of skill.

"Well. Congratulations, Ms. Brown." Banner glanced up at the security camera mounted in the corner where wall met ceiling.

"Thank you." It was Dr., not Ms., as the officious weenie damn well knew, but she didn't bother to correct him. After spending over a third of her life under his supervision, after years and years of similar razor blade slights, her so-called corrections officer was minutes away from officially walking out of her life for good. Unofficially, she knew she'd be under surveillance for the rest of her natural life, but at least there'd be no more mandatory monthly meetings spent examining her online activity—the activity she allowed him to see, at any rate. None of her carefully planned test transactions had shown up on Banner's odious report, and her work here seemed to be off his radar—for the moment, anyway. She half-listened as Jack, with his lawyerly attention to detail, arranged to have all monitoring software removed from Bailey's personal computers—a formality, since she planned to wipe the hard drives and donate all of them to charity at her earliest opportunity—but she appreciated Jack busting Banner's balls on her behalf.

She recognized the bulldog expression on Banner's face. She was a mystery he hadn't solved, a case he hadn't really closed. Her very presence here drew too much attention to her friends, and the secret they all protected.

She was going to have to quit, for everyone's good.

Finally, Jack rose from his seat at the head of the oblong conference room table. "Thank you, Mr. Banner." Banner stood, and the two men shook hands one final time. They'd all been dealing with each other for over a decade, but no one had lapsed into familiarity by using first names.

Banner tucked the documents in his briefcase and carefully locked it, and Jack wasted no time escorting him out of the conference room, through the lobby, and to the front door. She followed the men. Who would see the documents she'd just signed? Where would they be filed? How high up the chain of command would they go? It would be *so* easy to find out. She'd mentally executed the hack so many times that the route was engraved on her synapses, but she'd restrained herself. It had been hacking, and a distinct lack of restraint, that had gotten her into this mess in the first place.

As Banner extended his meaty hand for her to shake, the basement door flew open. Lukas Sebastiani, wet-haired, wearing jeans and a T-shirt, and bleeding from a small cut above his left eyebrow, stopped short. Chico Perez, his lieutenant and favorite sparring partner, followed closely behind.

On four legs.

Shit.

Banner's eyes lit. "Mr. Sebastiani! I was told you had an unavoidable conflict at this time. What a stroke of luck." He approached Lukas, extending his hand. "Andrew Banner. I'm Ms. Brown's corrections officer."

Lukas frowned down at him. "It's Dr. Brown."

Banner cleared his throat. "Yes. Quite. Very nice to meet you. And what a beautiful animal you have there. Such a glossy coat, and so, um, large. I don't recognize the breed."

"He's…an unusual cross."

Chico lifted his upper lip ever-so-slightly, exposing the tips of his gleaming white canines. Banner took a big step back.

Smart man.

"We work long hours here," Lukas said. "Many of our employees bring their pets to work."

Bailey fought to keep a straight face. Chico would make Lukas pay for that comment—but then again, maybe he already had. The cut above Lukas's eyebrow looked suspiciously like a tooth nick.

She glanced pointedly at the wall clock. "I need to get back to work."

"Always so industrious." She had to give Banner credit; not the slightest bit of sarcasm twisted in his voice, but she knew it was there. "Good luck to you, Dr. Brown. I hope our time together has been instructive."

It had. The time she'd spent under his surveillance had honed her already-prodigious skills to switchblade sharpness. "Are we done here?"

He nodded.

Game on. They both knew it.

Lukas finally shook Banner's hand—Banner visibly winced—and then personally escorted him through the tempered glass doors to his car, impervious to the snow falling on his bare arms. Chico, loping at Lukas's side, might have had something to do with how quickly Banner scurried behind the wheel of his nondescript gray four-door sedan and closed the door behind him.

"Free at last!" Jack lifted her off the ground and gave her a hug. Face to face with him, her Converse-clad feet dangled over a foot off the ground. "Congratulations!"

"Free? Right." Her lungs felt shrink-wrapped. It was hard to speak. "I'm giving notice."

"What? Declined."

"Jack, surely you can see—"

"Declined," he repeated. "That's fear talking. I'm not setting you down until your brain kicks into gear again."

"Damn right it's fear talking! Christ on a cracker, Jack, he's more curious now than ever. At least when everything was official, we knew what he was up to. Now we don't know *who* the hell will be watching me, how, or from where."

"We'll deal with it." His arms tightened, his voice softened. "Bailey, we'll deal with it. Don't forget where you work."

"What if my precautions fail?" So far, her security suite was doing the job, but the digital gauntlet protecting Sebastiani Security, Sebastiani Labs and Council_Net took constant focus and attention. She couldn't remember the last time she'd slept through the night. "What if someone finds a loophole I haven't considered? What if someone penetrates? I have to protect against every possible vulnerability, every single day, but someone else only has to find one way in. Once. What if I can't...?" With a heavy sigh, she let her forehead drop to Jack's wide, suit-covered shoulder.

She was...so tired.

"You need a break."

"You're kidding, right? I'm months behind on the data archiving project, and I haven't begun to figure out a safe way to crack the tech unit Lorin found at the Isabella dig last summer." She lifted her head. "I still don't know how—or even whether—it latched onto Sebastiani Labs' network, and if it did, what kind of hole it might have created. I'm—"

"Overworked. Exhausted. Bailey, you know the signs of burnout as well as I do."

"I'm okay." *I have to be. There's too much at stake.* She tapped his shin with her round-toed shoe. "Put me down." After he complied, she walked to the security door, slapping her hand against the biometric pad mounted at its side. After a short wait, her handprint was scanned, the status indicator switched from red to green, and there was a barely-audible click as the lock disengaged. She yanked the heavy door open, throwing her full body weight behind it. Jack followed closely behind.

After the funereal silence of the lobby, the sounds of Sebastiani Security's busy first shift hit her like a blast furnace. Dozens of workers either sat or milled about, chatting with clients and each other, accompanied by the clatter of keyboards. She could hear trash talk from the Nerf basketball game underway in the back. Someone had recently made microwave popcorn. The luscious aroma made her stomach sting.

Lukas caught up with them, nodding hello to the vamp who'd just walked out of the break room with a bag of blood clapped to his teeth. "Jack, can I have a minute?"

Jack hesitated.

"Go." Bailey waved a hand toward Lukas's office just down the hall. "I'm fine."

Lukas shot her a look. "Don't do anything stupid."

She sighed. It was useless to try to hide her emotions from an incubus, especially one of Lukas's skill. And he was right. She had to think things through, assess the real risks, in a calm and rational manner. "I'm just going to grab a drink, then go back to The Bunker."

"Good. Who knows what kind of shenanigans Antonia's gotten into while you've been gone?"

"What do you think she's going to do, start a game of Global Thermonuclear War?"

Lukas's bloody eyebrow jerked.

"Joke," she quickly assured him. "Just a joke. Haven't you ever seen *War Games*?"

"No."

"Gap in your cultural education. Great movie." She shooed them with her hands. "Go. Meet. I'll see what she's working on."

Lukas rested his big hands on her shoulders, leaned down, and kissed both of her cheeks. "What would we do without you?"

Ooh, dirty pool. "Go," she whispered around the lump in her throat. As soon as he and Jack disappeared into Lukas's office, she whirled.

Antonia really could have gotten into anything.

Weaving her way through the maze of cubicle walls, she approached The Bunker, her unquestioned domain, slapping her hand on yet another security pad. The Bunker was a warm, windowless room, with monitors crawling up the walls, and CPUs jostling for space on every flat surface. Racks of switches and routers, the backbone of Sebastiani Security's and Council_Net's computer network, blinked and grooved behind another set of secure doors across the room. And there, sprawled on the futon where Bailey slept most nights, was Lukas's seventeen year old sister, Antonia—bare-footed, devouring a bag of popcorn, and flipping the pages of the big honkin' binder overflowing her lap.

Bailey glanced at the bookshelf mounted over the computer she typically used when working on The Shredder, the encrypter/shredder/jammer that kept her—their—work on the down-low. There was a gap where the hard copy backup of her code and script usually stood, but at least Antonia wasn't at a keyboard. By the look of the bright tabs jutting from the thick stack of accordion-pleated paper lying on the floor next to her ratty flip-flops, Antonia had already finished the assignment Bailey had given her before leaving to meet with Banner.

In some ways, Antonia reminded her of herself at the same age—towering intellect, boy crazy, her judgment and control still very much works in progress—but in other ways, the young succubus had already outpaced her own dubious achievements. Antonia was the youngest member of the Underworld Council, the ruling body secretly governing the planet's non-human species. Antonia had recently assumed a seat representing the incubi and succubi alongside her father, Elliott, freeing Lukas to focus on security and technology risks with Jack as his Second. In the short year she'd worked at Sebastiani Security, Bailey had been drawn into their covert world to such a degree, and had attended so many Council meetings as a technology resource, that Valkyrie Second Lorin Schlessinger had recently joked they should stop looking for candidates for the Humanity seat and have Bailey fill it instead.

The very idea made her shudder. She and Jack might be the only two humans alive with confirmed knowledge that "first contact" had occurred eons ago, but she wasn't about to become any more enmeshed in the Council's activities than she already was.

"Hey there," Antonia called out.

"Hey." As Bailey approached the futon, she fought an urge to snatch the binder from Antonia's hands. "Whatcha doing?"

"I finished the analysis you asked me to do, and then I…got bored." Antonia burrowed into the bag of microwave popcorn with her tiny, black-nailed hand. "That probation dude looks like The Banker from Monopoly. And that suit? Way too expensive for a government employee to afford."

"How…"

Antonia gestured to a nearby screen, displaying the now-empty conference room where she and Jack had met with Banner. "Anyway." Antonia kicked into a seated position on the futon, picked up the pile of paper from the floor, and patted the seat at her side. "I think I found something. You know, this would have gone a lot faster if I'd been online—"

"You know the rules." One of the conditions Bailey had put in place when Antonia asked to study with her was that some internet back alleys were off limits, and the hacker bulletin board Bailey had printed the message log from was one of the darkest and nastiest. Antonia's technical skill was growing at an astronomical rate—she had a real gift for scripting languages—but Bailey saw no reason to tempt fate.

"Yeah, yeah. So, the incursion thingies that have been going on at SL all week?"

She nodded. There'd been a noticeable uptick in the number of malicious incursion attempts at Sebastiani Labs. Her countermeasures had held thus far.

Antonia picked up the pleated, tabbed paper. "I think someone on this board claimed responsibility."

"What?" Publicly discussing hacks, especially failed hacks, was akin to sprinkling yourself with loser dust.

"And look at these handles. Puh-*leeze*."

Bailey dropped onto the futon, leaned over, and read. *BowDownBitch. JaCKhaMMer. SnatchMaster3000.* She didn't bother rolling her eyes. The casual misogyny had been fathoms worse when she'd been Antonia's age.

"Like this guy's ever *seen* a real snatch," Antonia muttered as she flipped pages. "Anyway. Here's this Coyote, and he mentions you. You're The Queen Bee, right?"

Her stomach dropped like a free-falling elevator.

"He doesn't seem to have the same sexual compensation issues these other guys do."

"Nope." Wyatt Cooper had always been supremely confident of his skills in the bedroom, with good reason. *Wyatt. Wylie. Wily. Wily Coyote. Coyote.* Damn him for using the nickname she'd given him as his goddamn handle.

Dreamy and wicked-smart Wyatt Cooper, with his Black Irish coloring, his sharp-featured face, his irresistible scent, and eyes as blue as the deepest loch, who'd asked her to be his lab partner "because she brought brains *and* looks to the party." Bailey shook her head at her youthful naiveté. Years younger than her fellow grad students, socially stunted and starved for validation, she'd fallen into his lap like a ripe plum.

Look where it had gotten her.

She skimmed the messages further down on the page. "Ah, shit." No wonder there'd been a noticeable uptick in malicious activity against Sebastiani Labs. Wyatt had doxed her, published her place of employment, on one of the most notorious hacker bulletin boards in existence. She could only surmise that his own coding skills hadn't improved over the years, else he wouldn't have put out the call for help. "But…help with what?" she murmured. "What's your game?"

The security door beeped. Lukas entered, followed by Jack. "Hi, guys," Antonia called.

Both of them showing up in The Bunker at the same time, so soon after their private huddle? She wasn't going to like this.

"Hey, Sprout." Lukas came over to the futon and scrubbed his knuckles against his younger sister's head. Antonia batted his hand away, kicking at his huge body with her tiny bare feet. Despite the horseplay, Bailey noticed that Lukas protected his gonads.

Did they have any idea how much she coveted their easy physical affection? Did they appreciate it?

"Aah!" Antonia shrieked, wiggling and kicking as Lukas tickled her. The binder she'd been looking at slid off the futon, falling to the floor with a thunk.

"Okay, enough." Bailey elbowed in to the melee to rescue her precious code. "What do you guys want?"

"Personnel issue." Lukas winced as Antonia's sneaky heel tagged him in the kidney. "Can you give us a minute, Sprout?"

"Like there's anything you can't say in front of her." Actually, Antonia staying might even the odds a bit. She had a feeling she was about to be tag-teamed.

Lukas simply waited, ignoring his sister's wounded-doe gaze. Antonia finally sat up with a huff, gathered her belongings in very slow motion, and at long last stepped into her flip-flops. "I guess I can use the time to study," she pouted, reaching for the binder.

Bailey held on tight. "The binder stays here."

Antonia heaved a put-upon sigh. "How about the popcorn? Can I take the popcorn with me?"

"Be my guest." Her stomach would rebel if she tried to eat any herself. She gestured to the report. "Good work on the analysis."

With a final theatrical sigh, Antonia trudged from the room, each step snap-snap-snapping with accusation.

Lukas glanced at Jack, then back to her. "We really do have a personnel issue to discuss with you."

She didn't have personnel. She didn't manage anyone. She worked by herself; that was the deal. Glancing at the new flat-screens she'd recently installed above her main work area, she bit her lip. "Am I spending too much money? I know I—"

"—need some downtime," Jack interrupted. "You haven't taken a full day off since you started working here." He crooked a thumb at the futon. "You never go home."

Bailey's jaw dropped. "I can't take time off now. Wyatt doxxed me."

"Wyatt Cooper?"

She handed Jack the pile of paper. "He claimed responsibility for the failed hacks against Sebastiani Labs, put out a call for a virtual army, and also revealed where I work."

Jack shook his head as he paged through the messages. "I see he hasn't acquired any new brain cells since he let you take the fall," he said with disgust.

She shrugged. It was an old argument between them. Jack, her defense attorney at that time, hadn't understood her decision not to drag anyone else into the mess she'd made. He still didn't. "The design and code were mine," she replied.

"And he modified it, and tried to use it in a way you never intended. He manipulated you, Bailey. Played you like—"

"Enough," she snapped.

Silence hummed. "I'm sorry." Sighing, Jack jammed a hand through his short blond hair. "You didn't respond?"

"Of course not."

"He's been obsessed with you for years. Take a couple of days off and let him stew a little while longer."

"What would I do with a couple of days off?" See friends? Spend time with her loving family? Her friends and family were *here*—and Wyatt had just threatened everyone and everything she held dear.

"Just a long weekend," Jack urged. "Get some rest, recharge your batteries. Then we can deal with Wyatt Cooper once and for all."

Jack sounded like he wanted to squash Wyatt Cooper under the sole of his Hugo Boss shoe. *My hero.* "Now's a really bad time, Jack. I need to run a diagnostic on—"

"Bailey." Lukas's voice snapped like a whip, and his nostrils were twitching up a storm. "You're running on fumes. You live on pizza and Red Bull. I can taste your freaking stomach acid from here."

She dropped the fist she'd unconsciously raised to her burning stomach. "Sorry."

"Don't apologize, just take care of it. Take care of yourself." Lukas reached into his back jeans pocket and pulled out a tube of antacids. "Here. I have more in my office."

She knew he did. Though all incubi and succubi absorbed emotional energy for sustenance, due to a genetic glitch Lukas tasted emotions as he absorbed them. Some of them tasted pretty nasty.

"Bailey, you're exhausted, and exhausted people make mistakes," he said quietly. "Don't make me yank your access."

"What?"

"I'll block your access to the building, and to the network. Don't think I won't."

Cut off her access to Sebastiani Security? To Sebastiani Labs, to Council_Net, to The Bunker? Cutting off her fingers would be far less painful. Work was all she had left.

Damn it. Lukas's threat was largely an empty one—she'd designed their network security architecture, and she certainly knew how to get around it—but...

"I mean it, Bailey. If you don't take care of this, I will."

Lukas didn't play the boss card very often, and despite the degree of autonomy she had, he...*was* her boss. It was his illegible signature at the bottom of her outrageous paycheck. On little more than Jack's recommendation, he'd thrown her a lifeline at a time when her lonely existence had threatened to swamp her, drag her under.

And Jack stood at Lukas's side, not saying a word—which meant that Jack agreed with him, damn it. "Okay. Okay. Let me think." She whirled away, her brain whirring. Cheyenne Winterbourne, Sebastiani Labs' network architect, was fully capable of monitoring things, and would send up a flare if she needed help or noticed anything hinky. Bailey could… supervise remotely.

Hmm. Maybe this break idea had some possibilities. Jack was always after her to delegate more. It was impossible to find time to take on new projects without offloading the old ones first. She could do a lot with two or three days' focused attention, uninterrupted by the emergency *du jour*. She might have a reasonable shot at designing that SysAdmin overhaul, or she could brainstorm ways to access the utterly sophisticated device Lorin Schlessinger had found last summer, buried in an otherworldly box alongside three thousand year old wild rice and paper made of birch bark.

The device that had somehow, inexplicably, connected to Sebastiani Labs' computer network when removed from the box.

Had the unit infected the network in a way she hadn't considered? Everything had tested clean afterward, but tests only tested things you knew how to test. Given their working theory that the tech unit had extra-planetary origins, what she *didn't* know spanned the entire frickin' universe.

Maybe she could actually do what Lukas recommended. Take a real vacation; spend some time away from the keyboard. But what in the world would she do? Shampoo her grody carpets? Clean her bathroom? Sweep her apartment and car for bugs again? She had a towering stack of technical journals to catch up on…

Geez, talk about loser dust. A couple of days off work, and the only things she could think of to pass the time were doing household chores and reading geek mags? She really needed to get out more.

She could call Lukas's sister Sasha, meet her at Underbelly—but only if she knew Rafe wouldn't be there, too.

Rafe. Rafael Sebastiani, as gorgeous as the angel for whom he'd been named, fried her circuits and melted her panties. Her memories of his wicked talents in the bedroom—or in his sister's office, to be precise—bedeviled their every interaction. Since the night they'd slept together over a year ago, Rafe had acted friendly but standoff-ish, like nothing earth-shattering had happened between them.

Just another of his one night stands.

What vile words would her father shout from his pulpit if he knew that sex demons were real? What would The Reverend say if he knew his daughter had not only sinned—again—but had positively gloried in it?

"Here." When Lukas held out a key ring, the jingle startled her from her thoughts. "Go up to the cabin for a couple of days."

"Northern Minnesota in the middle of January? You're kidding, right?"

"The cabin's fully winterized. There's electricity, plenty of hot water, central heat, a fireplace, and a security system. The roads are plowed. All the comforts of home."

"And no internet connection."

Lukas didn't bother to deny it. "You could jack in by satellite if you get desperate, but you could also take a walk. Skate on the lake. Read a book in front of a crackling fire. Drive into town, go shopping, have a massage," he said. "Rafe said he'd leave everything up and running."

She ignored her leaping stomach. "So, he's not there?"

"No. He has a meeting with a client. Why?"

"I know he works up there sometimes. I don't want to disturb him." The last thing she needed was to walk in on a cozy seduction scene.

"The client's in L.A. You'll have the place all to yourself." He jiggled the keychain. "We can hold down the fort here for a few days. Come on, the stakes are too high for you to be at anything less than your best."

Damn it, he knew just which buttons to push.

She flicked her eyes to the colorful tabs Antonia had placed on Wyatt's messages. She wouldn't engage Wyatt directly—every online interaction left a permanent trail that someone, with the right tools, skills and incentive could find and follow—but there was no reason she couldn't do some…covert reconnaissance while she was away from the office. "Okay," she finally said, taking the keys from Lukas's hand.

And she had some thinking to do. Despite her release from probation, Banner was as big a threat as ever. He could never be allowed to discover the secret they all protected.

And if she had to leave Sebastiani Security, and the friends who'd become her family, to mitigate that risk? So be it.

CHAPTER TWO

Rafe stroked a calloused finger over the sinuous body stretched before him—her delicate teacup breast, her supple stomach, the curve of her slippery hip—softly, so softly. "Beautiful," he murmured reverently.

She was Woman, femininity incarnate…and he'd created her with his own hands. *Finally.* Relief trickled through his system, a cool mountain stream.

Stepping back from the table, his clay-slick hands extended in front of him, he assessed the abstract nude. Yeah, the hip proportion was slightly off, but it was pretty damn good for a guy who hadn't seen, much less touched, a flesh-and-blood female hip in over a year. Why had his bitch of a muse finally given him permission to express his burning memories of that night in clay? Maybe he had a chance to save his upcoming gallery show after all.

Nudes. That was the answer. A series of nudes, utter simplicity in line and form. A pale, pearlescent glaze, lit from within like her skin.

He had to get the ideas down on paper before they disappeared into the ether. The sketch pad was by the door, leaning against his duffel bag and some perishables he'd hastily unloaded from the Jeep when he'd returned to the cabin so unexpectedly earlier that day. He'd left before daylight, giving himself plenty of time to drive back to Minneapolis and catch his flight, but with each southbound mile, the odd sense of...wrongness, of disquiet, had grown. A half-mile north of the Cloquet cut-off, he'd flat-out panicked, suddenly certain that signing the contract to design functional art sound systems for The Pignello Group's new nightclubs would be an epic mistake, a fork in the road he wouldn't be able to navigate back from. And miraculously, a wisp of an idea was awakening with a slow, languid stretch. He recognized his muse immediately, a familiar friend he'd inexplicably been on the outs with. Without giving himself time to reconsider, he turned the car around and called his agent, instructing her to call off the deal she'd spent months negotiating on his behalf.

He looked at the nude and smiled. If he needed any more validation that turning down the sound system commission had been the right decision, he was looking at her, stretched out and damp, on the newspaper-protected dining room table.

As he swaddled her in damp cloth and plastic wrap, headlights swept across the west wall. Who the hell...? He hadn't taken the time to close the security gate behind him when he'd driven in earlier, but the private road leading to the cabin was strewn with No Trespassing signs. Couldn't people read? And when had it gotten dark?

He glanced at his sketch pad again. Maybe if he didn't answer the door, whoever it was would turn around and go away, and he could—

The garage door opened with a muffled hum. Whoever had just arrived had the next best thing to a house key. Damn it.

He flicked on the room lights with a nudge of his elbow, and then stalked to the kitchen sink to rinse the worst of the clay from his hands and wrists. He had only himself to blame for the unexpected company. His family thought he was on a plane to Los Angeles, and he hadn't told anyone about his change in plans. Maybe Lukas and Scarlett were sneaking away for a long weekend. Maybe it was Sasha with her latest lover, or his father and Claudette. He glanced at the kitchen counter, where his silent cell phone mocked him. He'd turned it off after letting Brooke and the pilot know that he wouldn't be traveling to California as planned.

Ratcheting back his annoyance, he flipped the switch that would flood the driveway and garage area with light, and opened the heavy oak door. "Wow." Every surface—the pine boughs, the gravel driveway, the electrical wires, Bailey's tiny red clown car—was filmed over with ice, and—

He blinked. Nope, he wasn't hallucinating; that was Bailey's MINI Cooper, all right, limping into the garage as a wicked rain/snow mix spit from the sky and froze on contact. What the hell had she been thinking, driving in such dangerous weather conditions? It was sheer dumb luck that she hadn't skidded off the road, slamming into one of the thousands of lethal, telephone pole-sized pine trees lining the road for miles.

And why hadn't she emerged from the garage yet? "Shit." Ducking back into the cabin, he jammed his arms into his parka, slung a knit scarf around his neck, stomped his bare feet into a pair of thick-soled Sorels, and headed back out. Needles of sleet pricked his face and bare hands as he shuffled across the driveway as quickly as he dared.

Any thoughts he might have had about renting her a hotel room in town until the weather cleared flew out the window. No one was going anywhere tonight.

He'd keep his hands to himself if it killed him.

Entering the double garage, he found Bailey sitting in the still-running MINI, her white knuckles clutching the steering wheel. When he tapped on driver's window, she blinked but didn't move. It took a couple of tries for him to get the car door open— the iced-over handle kept slipping from his hands— but when he finally succeeded, a blast of sauna-hot air escaped. Somehow, the little car's defroster had kept her windshield free of ice.

"Bailey?" No response other than a shiver. *Adrenaline crash.* He glanced down at the gearshift. At least she'd managed to put the car into Park. "Bailey, I'm going to turn the car off now." As he reached for the ignition, his parka sleeve brushed against her down vest, a whoosh of rip-stop fabric. So much for keeping his hands to himself. His traitorous hearing picked up her gasp over the sound of the ice pellets pinging off the garage roof.

He inhaled as her emotional reaction flooded the cab. She was ambrosia. He wanted to swim in her, wallow in her, let her desire for him plane the rough edges off his frazzled libido. But... He waited several silent seconds, and then sighed. Yep, there it was. The guilt chaser.

With Bailey, there was always guilt.

He gently peeled her cramped fingers off the steering wheel. Despite the heat in the car, they were cold as icicles. Now that he had a firm grasp on her hands, he turned her body so she sat sideways on the driver's seat, and tugged her to a standing position. "Come on, sweetheart. Let's go inside."

"Rafe?" She looked at him, blinking owlishly. She wasn't wearing a lick of makeup, and her blonde pixie hair was completely covered by a black knit cap with two tiny ears sewn onto the crown. "I need to leave."

Her words sliced like tiny swords, but the emotions behind them were so much more complex: desire, guilt, sheer panic, and utter exhaustion. "Look at the weather," he said. "Let's go in the cabin, get warm in front of the fire, and figure out what to do. Come on." Closing the car door, he led her out of the garage and into the ice pellets pounding down from the sky. "What were you thinking, driving in weather like this?" he scolded, trying to shelter her body with his. Even through the layers of down, her essence leached into him. He gulped like a parched man crawling on hands and knees to a desert oasis.

Hell. What random cosmic alchemies had conspired to make *her*—an innocent, guilt-ridden *human*—the sole object of his desire? Why wouldn't anyone else do?

"The roads were okay south of Eveleth," she muttered, skating across the driveway with him in a sloppy duet. "Got a late start. Had some work—"

An explosion rocked the night, a blown transformer shooting sparks into the black sky.

"Aah!" Bailey slipped and lost her footing.

He grabbed her. Bobbled.

And they both went down.

*

Stretched out on a supple leather couch, her head nestled in a cloud-soft pillow, cocooned in blankets, Bailey floated slowly to the surface but didn't open her eyes. Rafe's long, hard body spooned hers from behind, his arm slung over her hip. She breathed in slowly, luxuriously.

If he could bottle his rumpled morning scent, he'd make a mint.

Why was she sleeping here, in Rafe's arms? Her memories were…a little hazy. The transformer had blown, startling them both, and they'd slipped and fallen. Sharp pain, shooting up her arm. Rafe had helped her to her feet, and they'd hobbled together to the cabin. She couldn't connect the dots between then and now, lying in his arms, stripped down to her tank top, panties and socks, a water-filled Ziploc bag lashed to her wrist with an elastic bandage. Given that the long legs tangled up with hers were still clad in the same soft sweatpants he'd worn last night, it was unlikely that anything…interesting had happened.

Why was he touching her at all? He usually did his best to avoid touching her. Given her close relationship with his family, she and Rafe couldn't help but see each other occasionally, but when they did, he was distant. Scrupulously polite. Like they'd never—

Sometimes she wondered if she'd hallucinated the best sex of her life.

She'd had other lovers since Wyatt, of course—a few one night stands, and a couple of tepid relationships of such short duration that they hardly deserved the name—but Rafe had short duration down to an art, changing lovers as often as he changed designer shirts. She'd lost count of the number of gorgeous women she'd seen him with at Underbelly. He had a definite physical type—tall, busty glamazons with a yard of hair—but her? She barely cleared five feet. Bras were worn for fun, not function. Her hair, a viciously short pixie crop, was shorter than most men's. He could have anyone he wanted, and God knew she had absolutely no game. Convincing her yearning body that there wasn't going to be a repeat performance had been a challenge, but she'd done it. Burying herself in work, she'd done it.

She bit back a moan as his wicked, talented fingers teased her bellybutton. Now she'd have to start over from scratch.

His body curled around hers in a perfect, hard comma, his pillow-top lips nudging the exposed skin at the back of her neck. She shivered as his long, tawny hair drifted over her bare shoulders in a cool, silky tangle.

No wonder men liked long hair on women so much.

He tightened his arm around her, dragging her more firmly against his morning erection. She shifted her hips, and felt as much as heard his soft groan as he nibbled his way to her ear. Bit her tender earlobe. Time slowed to honey as he delved his long fingers under the narrow elastic waistband of her panties.

Ah, God. She stroked her palm down a forearm laced with muscle and lightly dusted with hair. To stop him? To encourage him? Before she could decide, he found her, slick and hot and wet, caressing her with unerring accuracy and devastating skill. When she spread her legs further apart, he rewarded her with a wicked stroke that sent dark delight glittering through her system.

Even asleep, he knew exactly how to ouch her.

Clawing at the sagging bandage—it was in her way—the Ziploc bag fell to the rug with a soft plop. She clutched his ass, writhing and straining for the release that hovered just out of reach, like a helium balloon on a string.

This was *so* wrong. He was asleep; he didn't realize what he was doing, or with whom. He was an incubus, a sex demon, a slave to his biology. Any body would do.

"Bailey…"

Her name.

"Touch me, babe." He dragged her hand to the hot ridge thrusting behind his sweatpants. The thick, blunt flesh seared her palm like a brand, and he arched into her touch. Muttering something hot and sleepy under his breath, he flexed his hips, pressing his hand against hers—

She gasped as a lightning bolt of pain shot from her wrist to her elbow.

"Bailey? Shit." He sat up, yanking his hand from her panties and swiping sleep-rumpled hair away from his face. "Are you okay?"

How was she supposed to answer that question? "I just zinged my wrist." The wrist connected to the hand that still cupped his… *Sweet Jesus.* She snatched her hand away from his erection. "Sor—"

"No, I'm sorry." His rough voice seemed a half an octave lower than usual. "You twisted your wrist when we fell in the driveway last night." He pushed the blankets back and climbed out from behind her with a graceful extension of long arms and legs. As if waking up with someone's hands on his cock, and with his in someone's underwear, was no big deal.

And it wasn't, not for him. She needed to remember that.

Rafe winced as his bare feet touched the chilly floor. "The fire's almost out. I'll get some heat in here."

All righty then. If he could be matter-of-fact and low-key about this, so could she.

He added some logs to the fire. "I think you just sprained the wrist, but let me check it again now that we have some light. Another ice pack wouldn't hurt." Picking up the Ziploc bag from the floor, he padded to the kitchen, dumped the water in the sink, and opened the freezer. "No light in here," he called. "Electricity's not back on yet." Ice cubes clacked.

"No electricity? Won't the pipes freeze?"

"Not likely. We have three or four cords of wood out back, so we should be okay."

No electricity. She'd come up here to get some work done, and now she'd have to conserve battery power... Crap, her laptops. They were still out in the car, along with everything else she'd brought with her. She shoved to her feet, snagging the cashmere blanket and wrapping it around her like a cape.

"What's wrong?"

"I have things out in my car that shouldn't freeze." And it was hours too late for most of them. After a night spent outside in below-freezing temperatures, the fresh fruit and vegetables were surely beyond help. "Where are my clothes?" Rafe Sebastiani had undressed her again, and she hadn't even been awake for the experience. It just figured.

"Slow down. I brought everything in last night, after you fell asleep. The groceries are put away, your duffel bag's over there in the big bedroom—"

"My computer bag?" She couldn't believe she'd forgotten about her laptops, no matter how badly she'd fallen. Where was her brain?

"The bag's in the bedroom, too."

"Thank you." Thanks to him, her work hadn't been left overnight in a poorly secured garage. She didn't want to think about how many trips he'd taken between the cabin and the car in such treacherous conditions.

He nodded, sealing the Ziploc bag of ice with a pinch and a slide. "You can pay me back with some of that lobster truffle ravioli you brought." He eyed her. "I didn't think Chadden did take-out."

What was that odd twist in his voice? "He had a computer emergency at the restaurant last month. After I fixed the problem, he said he'd feed me for life." She grinned. "I'm making him pay through the nose."

"Well, don't tell him we heated one of his signature dishes in a cast-iron pot suspended over a fire."

Hmm. No electricity meant no kitchen appliances. No lights. No coffeemaker. No hot water for the shower, and she probably reeked. Did the toilet work? Would they have to share—she gulped—a potty pail? Talk about being blasted back to *Little House on the Prairie* times.

Suck it up, dude. There was a wood-burning sauna down by the lake, and an old outhouse out back if she got desperate for bathroom privacy. Desperation was a relative thing. Half-Pint's eyes would pop at the rustic luxury of the Sebastiani family's cabin. Needing the fireplace for light and heat rather than for entertainment put a disconcerting spin on things, but on the other hand, they *had* heat, a pantry full of food and snacks, and most important for her productivity, the case of Red Bull Rafe had hopefully rescued from her trunk.

Potty pail or not, she was snowed in with a sex demon. Her imagination fired with images: the two of them twined together on the colorful braid rug, skin to skin, Rafe's long hair curtaining away the world. Him, roving every inch of her body with an explorer's gusto, and her, discovering exactly which combination of touches made a sex demon writhe.

Yeah, you wish. Rafe's reaction to her touch, not five minutes ago, had been to extricate himself from it as quickly as possible.

"Let's check out that wrist." Suddenly he was standing next to her, nostrils twitching up a storm. His species absorbed emotional energy for sustenance, and discerned emotions as they inhaled. He couldn't help but sense her arousal. She couldn't hide from him, and he couldn't escape it—couldn't escape her, no matter how much he might want to.

Heat scalded her cheeks. She had to get a grip on herself here. But he stood so close that his rumpled T-shirt brushed against her skin as he breathed—deep, luxurious inhalations that expanded his chest and dropped his eyelids to half-mast. Holy Mother, he smelled like sin.

When he touched her wrist, a tiny moan escaped. "Sorry," he said, clearing his throat. "I'll try not to hurt you." Taking her wrist in both hands, he carefully poked and prodded, moving the swollen joint this way and that. She felt his eyes on her face, watching for any wince, any reaction.

When he carefully flexed the wrist upwards, he got it. Another hot streak shot up her arm, making her gasp. "Crap, that hurts!"

"Sorry." He winced in sympathy. "Almost done." Gently pressing his fingertips against her ligaments and tendons, he found the bundle that made her leap with pain. "Sprain. Why don't you go get dressed, and we can get that ice pack back on." He cleared his throat again, looking away. "I'll put some water on for coffee, we can have some breakfast, and then we can plan our day—which, in my professional opinion, means leaving the laptop in the bag. You need to rest that wrist."

"Your professional opinion? Rafe, you're an artist, a sculptor."

"Who's studied anatomy. I think you stretched a ligament, here—" he poked, prompting a gasp with his accuracy "—which makes it a sprain, but if you don't trust my diagnosis, you can have Wyland check it out when we get home."

Not bloody likely. She was hardly Wyland's favorite person at the moment.

"Really, why don't you kick back, take a day off and relax?"

"Work *is* how I relax." She carefully flexed her wrist. At least she hadn't hurt her mouse hand. Between both laptops, she should have about twenty hours of battery power. Surely the electricity would come back on today. She could get a good start on the code, but—

"How about reading a book? Mystery, romance, erotica, horror?" Rafe gestured to the bookshelves climbing the living room's north wall. "I think Antonia left some manga here the last time she came up."

Her thoughts were still snagged on the erotica he'd so casually mentioned. No way would she read erotica anywhere in his vicinity. "I have some technical journals I need to catch up on."

Rafe just shook his head.

Yeah, nerds on parade. How long had it been since she'd read for pleasure? Probably years. "What do you plan on doing?"

He glanced at the dining room table, where something lay shrouded in protective plastic, then back to her. "I need to do some sketching." Suddenly his cheekbones and jaw line looked…sharper somehow.

"So, you can work, but I can't?"

He shrugged. "I'm fine. And sketching doesn't require electricity."

"Don't think I don't see that huge bruise on your elbow." She reached for the corner of the plastic. "Can I take a peek?"

Rafe practically flew to the table to stop her. "No. It's…not done yet."

"I don't care."

"I do. Come back by the fire." With a light touch on her elbow, he led her back to the couch. "I don't know about you, but I could really use some coffee. And some food."

Her stomach muscles clenched, way down low. Watching his lips move, watching him enjoy food and drink with his innate sensuality, would absolutely do her in. "I really should get dressed…"

He dropped his hands like she'd burned him. "Sorry. I'll keep my hands to myself. Despite all evidence to the contrary, you're safe with me." Turning away, he threw a couple more logs on the fire and jabbed at them with a metal poker.

Her cheeks flamed.

"I'm sorry I embarrassed you earlier."

Despite the coverage of the blanket, she felt naked. Exposed. "It was a perfectly natural reaction," she said, trying for a blithe sophistication she was far from feeling. "Once you realized who you were with, you stopped. It's okay—"

"I knew exactly what I was doing, and with whom."

Then why the self-loathing in his voice? Why weren't they still groping each other on that couch?

"I won't take advantage of you again."

"When did you take advantage of me the first time?" she squawked.

"That night at Underbelly."

His scent deepened along with his voice, and she struggled to focus. Backlit by flames, his eyes snapping with annoyance, with a sleep line creased into his cheek and his rumpled hair tumbling around his shoulders, he was sex on a freaking stick. "What makes you think you took advantage of me?" And after practically ignoring each other for a year, how had they suddenly gotten into such dangerous conversational waters? Hell. Too late to ask that question now—and no matter how embarrassing the upcoming conversation might be, it was long overdue. Once he gave her the 'it's not you, it's me' talk, she could put him, and that night, out of her mind for good.

Somehow.

"The night of Scarlett's concert, you were under the influence of incubus pheromones," he said. "I was supposed to bring you up to Sasha's office to get you something to counteract the intoxication, not take advantage of it."

After a pause, she burst out laughing. She just couldn't help it. "You're serious? Rafe, come on. You're an incubus. Surely you can tell when someone wants you."

"Bailey, you're new to our world, but you know the rules. You couldn't consent in that condition." She opened her mouth to rebut him, but he barreled on. "Do you remember what we did? Did you even know who you were with?"

"Of course I do. Of course." As if she could forget. As soon as she'd taken the pheromone intoxication medication, she'd lain back on the couch, raised her lips to his. A hesitation, then a groan from Rafe… All too soon, her pants were on the floor, and he'd filled her, inside and out, over and over again.…

She'd felt oddly empty ever since.

Swallowing with an audible click, she tried to ignore the heavy, frustrated ache still seething low in her abdomen. Stared at him, to find his nostrils flaring and his pupils dilating as he absorbed the need she couldn't hide. Rough edges looked…really good on him. The sweatpants and ratty T-shirt he wore exposed his muscles, showcasing his clotheshorse frame in a much more intriguing way than his designer wardrobe did. Gray flecks of dried clay dotted his forearms, and his bare feet were long and narrow, with high arches and squared-off toenails. Seeing his bare feet against the wood plank floor felt…unspeakably intimate.

He cleared gravel from his throat. "Bailey, even now you're swimming in guilt. In some fundamental way, you don't really want this."

"Are you kidding me?" She choked back her disbelieving laugh, because he looked deadly serious. "Rafe, consent works both ways. I touched you while you were sleeping, and…"

Rafe remained silent, waiting for her to continue. His tawny golden eyes bored into her, making her feel hunted. Exposed.

"Rafe. I'm a preacher's kid and a convicted felon. Guilt is pretty much my baseline emotion." She lifted her eyes to his. "I'm sorry I touched you while you were asleep."

He gestured to his rampant erection. "Does it look like I mind?"

No, it didn't, but… "You're incubus, though. If sexual energy's there, you absorb it, right? Won't anybody do?"

"No."

The moment hung.

"Please look at me," he said, tipping up her chin with his finger.

She couldn't help but comply, and when she did, his expression made her breath snag in her throat. She could lose herself forever in his sandstorm gaze.

"So you're a PK," he murmured. "That explains a lot."

"Huh?"

"Never mind. We don't know each other very well at all, do we?"

Bailey opened her mouth to refute him, but closed it again. He was right. They'd had sex with each other, shared their bodies in the most intimate of ways, but almost everything else she knew about him was second-hand. Was it smart to get to know him better? It was bad enough that her body couldn't quite seem to find the muscular will to resist him. What if she came to really like him, too?

"Scarlett told me that at the beginning of their relationship, she and Lukas made an agreement to use words so Lukas wouldn't misinterpret her emotions," he said. "Why don't we try the same?" He waved an arm at the great room's picture window, opaque with ice. "Why don't we get to know each other better? We seem to have some time on our hands."

The velvet rumble of his voice, his drugging scent, made her stomach flutter. Without her quite being aware of it, she reached for his chest.

Rafe leaned back, out of range of her naughty hand. He inhaled hugely, his eyes drifting closed before he fought them open.

"What?" His scent drifted over, made her eyes blur.

"Pheromones," he gritted out. "So no touching."

"Huh?" She was so confused—and so, so aroused. The strain in his voice tugged at her very womb. "No touching?"

"No."

"At all?" she breathed, eyes on his lips.

He inhaled deeply, his eyes flaring with a desire he couldn't feign or disguise. "You're killing me here," he said on a laughing groan. Turning, he padded to the kitchen in his elegant bare feet. "Coffee first. Then I have to do some sketching. Without touching you. Somehow." He reached down to the front of his sweatpants and adjusted himself.

The frank gesture, so at odds with his typical high tea manners, almost made her moan. God help her, he was even more attractive with his control frayed around the edges.

Pans clanged together in the kitchen.

She bit back a giggle, but it quickly died. Snowed in with a sex demon. How was she going to keep her hands off him?

Knowing he wanted her, too?

CHAPTER THREE

And…action.

"Dang it," Wyatt Cooper muttered as the cutting winter wind tried its best to snatch the door handle out of his grasp. He shouldered into the building's cavernous lobby and stomped the snow off his shoes, juggling a messenger bag, a leather portfolio and an almost empty coffee cup. He'd purposely spilled most of the coffee on himself and the folder on his way in from the parking lot.

The woman helming the huge reception desk looked him up and down as he approached, taking in the wet stain darkening his light blue dress shirt, and the dripping leather folder he carried. "Tough morning?"

He quirked a rueful smile, tipping his head slightly so his bangs flopped onto his forehead. She was a trim, yoga-toned forty, a single mother recently divorced from a man who'd cheated on her with a younger woman. A little light flirting certainly wouldn't hurt. It never did.

"You don't know the half of it."

And she really didn't. He'd spent all night slogging through the hard drive of the computer he'd hired a colleague to steal from Bailey's apartment. She hadn't even bothered to password-protect the thing, and now he knew why. The hard drive was a barren wasteland. Her real work—the good stuff—must be at Sebastiani Security or Sebastiani Labs.

He didn't have the skill to take Bailey on mano a mano, but hopefully others who did would keep her busy for a while.

He straightened, fighting off tiredness. The coffee he'd spilled was his fourth cup since midnight. He didn't pull all-nighters very often anymore, but a legit paying gig was a legit paying gig. The fact that such jobs were easier to come by since Bailey closed her business and dropped off the face of the earth definitely stung.

To find her, in Minneapolis, working for Lukas Sebastiani? There was a much bigger story there. But for now, he had to set his curiosity aside. He had bills to pay.

He smiled—admiringly, not tipping into creepy— at the admin. The contract he'd signed with the company's CIO authorized any and all incursion methods and provided full legal indemnity, but the guy had no clue how little time or actual technical skill it would take for him, or someone like him, to access the company's supposedly secure computer network.

Until someone developed a patch for gullibility, humans were the weakest link.

"Here." The receptionist plucked a trio of tissues from the square box sitting between a desktop printer and a silver-framed picture of a gap-toothed little girl, and extended them over the counter. "Use these."

"Thank you." Taking them, he made sure their fingers brushed, oh-so-lightly. "Is that your daughter? Very cute. How old is she?"

As the woman chattered about her kid, confirming information he'd already gathered during his background work, he used the tissues to wipe the leather portfolio. Opening it, he looked in dismay at the sheaf of coffee-stained papers. He glanced at his wristwatch, then back at the papers, gingerly lifting a document by its stapled corner. Coffee dripped down the cover page and onto the lobby floor. "Dang it. I have a meeting with your CIO in ten minutes, and needless to say, I'm not going to make a great first impression." He looked to the entrance, and back at his watch again, patting the pockets of his messenger bag. "I hope I brought…yes!" He pulled a USB stick out of one of the bag's front compartments. "Could you tell me where the nearest print shop is?"

"No need for that. I'd be happy to print a fresh copy for you."

"Could you really? I'd be your slave for life."

"No need for that." Despite her wry retort, her cheeks pinked ever so slightly.

Their fingers brushed again as he handed over the stick. She cleared her throat as she accepted it, slipped it into one of her sleek laptop's USB ports, and double clicked. "Which document? The PDF?"

"Yes, that's the one." He'd initially considered trying something more sophisticated, but finally decided to go with the ol' tried-and-true.

She clicked again, opening the document—and in less time than it took to spool the document to the printer, the virus slithered into the company's computer network, lying coiled, waiting, and poised to strike.

Gotcha.

What would he find this time? Technical specs for a top-secret product not yet released? Financials? Marketing materials? Patent submissions? Corporate expansion or layoff plans? Cached-up porn that some poor, deluded fool killing time on the night shift thought he'd permanently deleted?

Nothing was ever permanently deleted—not with guys like him around to find it, and to exploit it.

He sighed. He'd abide by the terms of the non-disclosure agreement he'd signed. He kept a firm boundary between his contract penetration work and his…extracurricular endeavors.

A man had to have some standards.

The printer spit three colorful pages into the tray. She plucked them up. "Stapled?"

"Yes, please. Thank you so much."

She stapled the pages together with a clunk and handed them to him, flicking her eyes to his bare ring finger. She subtly cleared her throat. "May I get you another cup of coffee before you go up to the fifth floor?"

"No, thank you. I have to get going," he said with visible regret. Webster, the CIO, had no idea he was here, and he needed to keep it that way. He'd take the elevator up to the fifth floor, but come right back down using the back stairway.

After a pause, she snatched one of her business cards from a nearby holder, scribbled something on the back, and held it out to him. "Please let me know if I can help you in any way."

He took the card with a smile, and with another careful brush of their fingertips, gave her a card of his own. "I certainly will—" he glanced at the cell phone number she'd written on the back before flipping it to the front "—Nicola. What a beautiful name." Still facing her, he took several reluctant steps away from the desk, keeping eye contact. "Goodbye, Nicola. Thanks for your help."

She looked down at his card. "Have a good meeting, Mr. Wallace."

"Please, call me Wyatt."

She colored again. "Wyatt."

He held her gaze for one second. Two. Then he pivoted and walked to the elevator, giving Nicola a final glance over his shoulder.

She was staring at him.

Nicola was really quite pretty, especially when she smiled. She'd be a useful contact to…cultivate.

Yep. A man had to have some standards.

*

He couldn't touch her, so he drew.

Curled in the corner of the couch by the fireplace, sketchpad in his lap, he watched the expressions chase across her face as she worked at the dining room table. If he waited long enough…there. There it was, appearing like clockwork—that adorable rumble strip of annoyance pinching her eyebrows together as she glared, again, at her laptop screen. Not taking his eyes off her, his hand moved with ease, but each scratch of charcoal against the pulpy paper sounded unnaturally loud to him, like a match seeking a spark. After a day and a night spent cooped up together in the cabin, working, chatting, and emphatically not touching, the air felt heavy and combustible.

To him, at any rate. Bailey seemed oblivious, barely speaking while she worked except to utter an occasional, colorful curse. She was racing against the clock—or rather, her laptop's draining battery. Why bother to hide his gaze when she rarely looked up from the screen?

Rafe glanced down at the page, satisfied with his work. The expression studies he'd done were as exquisitely detailed as any he'd done at art school: The delicate whorls of her ears. The huge eyes, framed by dark lashes and slashing eyebrows. The plane of her stubborn jaw, her tiny button nose, and her lips…her criminally neglected lips. The studies wouldn't help him with the sculpture series for his upcoming show, but it wasn't like he could ask her to pose for him, stretched out gloriously nude on the rug in front of the fireplace—

He slammed the door on that line of thought. When would the electric company get the transformer fixed? He thought he'd heard repair trucks at first light, along with road crews laying down their salt/chemical slurry, but he hadn't gone outside to check.

He and Bailey managed to platonically share the big couch last night, sleeping with their heads at opposite ends, awakening this morning with only their lower legs touching.

"You galaxy class bitch." Her voice sounded half-admiring, like whatever she worked on was putting up a damn good fight. He'd heard the same tone of voice from Lukas when a walleye snapped the line rather than swimming into his net.

Her energy changed when she worked; he could sense it from across the room. At the keyboard, she swaggered like the captain of a pirate ship, master of all she surveyed. He'd been wallowing in her energy, fighting the pull of the tide, for hours.

If she brought even a fraction of that confidence into bed with her, he'd gladly go down with the ship.

Across the room, she glared at the screen. Leaned in and snarled. "Don't you dare."

Hiding a smile, he slowly inhaled. Bailey had a temper on her, and he found it…utterly enchanting. Glancing down at his drawing—all eyes and hair, the lower portion of her face obscured by her laptop screen—he smudged the paper with his thumb to create a subtle shadow between her brows, and then picked up his charcoal again. He couldn't capture the precise color difference between her hair and brows, but their arrogant slant? Yeah.

"Don't you dare what?" he asked.

"Crash. Blow up. Shit the bed."

He winced. "There's an attractive visual."

"Yep, there it goes. Gah!" She whapped the frame of the laptop screen like she was clouting someone upside the head, then leaned back in the dining room chair.

"What are you working on that's giving you so much trouble?"

Now he was the recipient of her green-eyed glare. "I've almost got it."

Adorable. "I'll rephrase. What are you working on?"

"I was working on an enhancement to Sebastiani Security and Sebastiani Labs' security suite, but then I got an idea…"

"About what?"

"A possible way to access the tech unit Lorin found last summer. Hard to do without the actual unit, but…" She trailed off, shrugging. "I haven't been able to figure out how to examine it without putting other networks at risk, and Wyland won't release the unit back to me until I do."

Last summer, the archaeological site Lorin and her mother had searched for decades had finally coughed up evidence that supported the legend of their people's extra-planetary origins—and Lorin had fallen in love.

At least one of them was getting regularly laid.

Her eyes narrowed and she pursed her lips, her face settling into the expression he privately called "Evil Genius." He could almost see synapses snap and thoughts form.

A burst of energy hit him broadside.

"Oh. Of course," she muttered. Lifting a finger in the classic 'wait a minute' gesture, she picked up a pen and scribbled something in the notebook sitting next to her mouse. Carelessly dropping the pen, she turned to the other open laptop and banged out something with a ferocious rat-a-tat-tat.

He'd never seen or heard anyone type so fast, or so…expressively. The ebb and flow of her intelligence enthralled him as much as the luscious physical reaction she couldn't hide. Completely focused on her task, she didn't notice that his tarp-covered sculpture had stopped her pen from rolling to the floor.

His cock stirred, stretching behind ancient, soft denim. The fact that she'd unknowingly shared table space with a sculpture of her own nude body all morning was unspeakably arousing.

He was a sick, sick man—and very hard up, if the sight of her tiny fingers banging the keys was enough to almost make him come in his pants. No touching? What had he been thinking? His attack of scruples was painful, damned inconvenient and likely unnecessary, because he knew she wanted him, too.

What was it about her? Bailey was not at all his usual type. She was so small she was practically elfin. If memory served—and it damn well did—her tiny, tip-tilted breasts didn't come close to filling his hand. Her blonde hair couldn't be three inches at its longest, and right now half of it stood on end because she'd been tugging on it most of the morning. A lot of women wouldn't be able to pull off such a short cut, and fewer women yet would have the guts to even try—but the ruthless crop showcased her gamine facial features perfectly.

Compared to her, his previous lovers suddenly seemed ungainly.

His stomach grumbled. They'd shared a light breakfast of coffee and fruit when they'd first woken up, but that had been hours ago. Slapping his sketchbook closed, he stood up and stretched, half-turning so she wouldn't see the wood he sported. "I'm going to eat all that ravioli by myself," he called to her. Her head popped up. "Yeah, I thought that might get your attention. Come on, let's eat."

She saved her work, booted down, and joined him in the kitchen, where they companionably prepared their meal. "Here." Rafe passed her the plastic lid so she could read the note Chadden had taped to the cover, and then scraped the lobster truffle pasta into a cast-iron pot. Though the message was innocent enough—a request that she return the container at some point, along with the dozens of others in her possession, sooner rather than later, PLEASE—the note's salutation made his blood pressure spike.

Chadden called her Tidbit.

His jaw clenched tight. The fact that Chadden had a pet name for her suggested an intimacy in their relationship that he hadn't established—yet. He had to admit the nickname suited her. Tidbit. A tiny, delicious bite.

Perfect.

Rafe glanced at Bailey's delicate neck, swaddled in dusty blue Polar fleece. Had the vampire dared to feed from her? His knuckles whitened around the big metal spoon. Just how far had this little human been drawn into their world? Which acts had she already consented to?

"What should I use to cut this bread?"

Releasing his death grip on the spoon, he walked across the kitchen, where an assortment of knives clung to a magnetic strip mounted on the south wall. Selecting a serrated knife, he returned to the butcher block table, their hips brushing in the tight space. Her energy hadn't changed much reading Chadden's note—a roll of the eyes, a bump of amusement—but it changed now. Her hand trembled slightly as she accepted the knife. The softest sigh. Her breaths, shallow and fast. She stared at his hands like she was imagining how they'd feel stroking her bare skin.

Desire—for him.

He slowly inhaled, her succulent essence twining around his lower spine and pelvis. His cock sat up and begged. Step away. Think. "I'll go put this on the fire," he said, picking up the pot and carrying it to the fireplace.

He felt the weight of her stare as he knelt on the hearth and suspended the heavy cast-iron pot over the low, licking flames. After a pause, she made short work of the crusty French loaf, slicing with almost violent strokes of the knife.

Rafe's eyes drifted shut. All that sexual energy, sublimated. What a waste. Maybe they could—no. He rose from the hearth and joined her in the kitchen again. "It's probably best that we don't let Chadden know we heated his food over a lowly fireplace."

"It will be our little secret."

Her voice was annoyed and aroused—one of his favorite combinations.

"Is there a basket I could put these in?"

He reached to the top shelf, grabbing one of the wicker baskets nesting there. "Here."

While Bailey lined the basket with a paper napkin and transferred the bread, he quartered oranges and arranged them on a plate. Bailey's gaze followed his movements as he added several chunks of dark chocolate, broken off from a wrapped bar of Godiva he'd found.

"You have keyboard hands—piano, not laptop," she mused. "Do you play?"

Did she remember how much pleasure he could wring from her body using nothing but his fingertips? "Sorry, no musical talent at all."

"Too bad. You have a hell of a span, but I imagine it comes in handy when you're sculpting." She snitched a sliver of chocolate, slid it between her lips, and closed her eyes in ecstasy as it melted on her tongue.

Rafe stared, all blood detouring south.

"While we're waiting for the pasta to heat up, will you show me what you're working on?"

He blinked. "What?"

"Can I see what's under the shroud? I've wanted to sneak a peek for hours. I can smell the clay, you know. Loamy, earthy." She walked over to the dining room table where his sculpture lay, plucking at the plastic. "Come on, show me."

"You might regret you asked."

"It can't be that bad, Rafe." She indicated the chest-high abstract bronze displayed next to the fireplace. "Even a noob like me can see how talented you are."

Walking slowly, he joined her at the table. "It's…a work in progress."

She patted him on the shoulder. "My expectations are firmly in the basement. You hereby have permission to suck."

"Thank you," he said wryly. "I can't tell you how much that reassures me."

"Oh, stop with the arrogance already. Critics genuflect before your work, blah blah blah, and I'm sure this piece—" she nudged the plastic "—will be no different."

His stomach felt weighted down, like he'd swallowed rocks. The issue of whether she'd recognize herself as the model was suddenly secondary. Could he stand by while critics and art patrons studied her nude body with appreciative eyes, all the while covertly glancing at every woman in the gallery, trying to figure out who the model was? Or take bets on how often he interrupted his work so he could fuck her?

Screw his artistic breakthrough; his gallery show was toast.

He frantically considered his alternatives. Lorin had offered to model for him back when they'd been sleeping together; maybe she'd… Nah. Lorin had a bondmate now. Mild-mannered Gabe Lupinsky would tear off his head and piss down his throat if he suspected that the words 'Lorin' and 'nude' still had an even glancing proximity in his thoughts. Not that the idea would work anyway. For some inexplicable reason, Lorin's warrior princess frame hadn't engaged his muse.

He gazed down at the top of Bailey's bright blonde head. Nope, it had been a pocket-sized human—a preacher's kid—who'd managed that particular feat.

"Rafe? Come on. Let me see." Peeling back the plastic herself, she tugged at the damp fabric swaddling the clay.

"Be careful with that! Jeez." He carefully peeled back the cloth, exposing her figure inch by inch, until she was completely bare. He looked at Bailey. Suddenly her opinion was more important than that of the most well-respected art critic.

She stepped back and perused. Moved closer again. "It's…beautiful, Rafe. Delicate, subtle. She looks…pleased. Sated." She tipped her head to the side, hesitantly extending her hand to the nude. "How do you do that? How can you express emotions in clay?"

He glared at her. "How can you be so goddamn oblivious?"

She froze, deer in the headlights, almost touching the nude's barely-there breasts. Glanced down at her own, camouflaged by fleece.

Her seesaw emotions nearly gave him whiplash. Suspicion. Denial. Wonder. Delight. More denial.

Jesus, she slayed him.

He took a step closer to her, got in her personal space. She swallowed with an audible click. When she finally looked at him, a dawning awareness was shoving the confusion out of the way. "Why did you—"

"Sculpt you? How could I not?" He didn't tell her how long it had taken for his subconscious to give him permission to do so. "I just wish my skill did you justice."

"I…don't look like—" she gestured to the sculpture with an embarrassed wave "—that."

He took half a step closer, until they were standing so close that the air between them vibrated. "Like what? Satisfied? Gorgeous? Yeah, you do."

Though a hot blush stained her cheeks, her eyes went heavy and hungry. The little witch edged closer to him, so close that the fabric of their shirts brushed together. She lifted her tiny hand, rested it against his hipbone with a feather-light touch.

Rafe caught his breath. Maybe she remembered more about that night than he'd thought. The vision of his hands holding her hips in place to receive his thrusts, and hers caressing his in return, was burned into his memory for all time. He inhaled deeply, and the seething, roiling sexual hunger, combined with the scent of her spicy, humid need, nearly clubbed him to his knees.

He eyed the waistband of the navy blue yoga pants that clung so faithfully to her curves. One downward yank and he could taste her again. She'd be slick and wet, and he'd take them both to heaven using nothing but his tongue. With a groan, he tried to reach for what remained of his tattered control. "What am I going to do with you?"

"Whatever you want."

Her naughty whisper drove a spike into the heart of whatever restraint he had left. Before he could react, she reached up with both hands, threaded her fingers into his hair, and tugged his head down, bringing their lips together.

He simply…gorged. She tasted of wonder, and sinful dark chocolate, and he dove in, licking up every bit. It didn't matter that he had to be pumping pheromones like a wildcat oil rig, or that she had to be as influenced by them today as she'd been the night they were together. Her tongue tangled and dueled with his, parrying and thrusting, like she was as starved for him as he was for her.

Her hands clutched his ass, yanking their hips together. She dragged her mouth away from his, just enough distance to talk. "Can we dispense with the no touching rule?"

Each puff of her chocolate-scented breath bathed his face in sweet heat, and he couldn't resist taking another taste. Licking at the corner of her mouth with his tongue, he nipped her upper lip.

Her gasp of delight glittered into him. When she bit back, he couldn't hold back a groan. His cock pulsed, like she'd nibbled him there instead of on his mouth.

"You haven't—" another flick of her agile tongue "—answered my question." Her eyes snapped with frank, unabashed need. With demand.

Damned if his little PK wasn't giving as good as she got. He felt like he'd crawled on hands and knees for miles, finding a miracle desert oasis just before he died of thirst. He could drink from her for days.

He tried to rein in his unruly hunger. Despite her confident touch, the original reason he'd wanted to follow the no touch rule remained firmly in place. He really wanted—no, needed—this to be more than physical, and because of his very physiology, he might not ever have that reassurance. Her clever hands tunneled under his T-shirt, stroking his stomach, and ecstasy flooded his system.

Her touch made him feel…worshipped somehow. Did Lukas feel this way when he was with Scarlett? Was this what—

"Rafe, stop thinking so much," she whispered. "I want this. I want you." She pulled their lips apart long enough to lift her jacket over her head and throw it somewhere.

As he admired the girly purple camisole she'd revealed, the great room lights flickered, then stayed on. His subconscious registered the light, the subtle hum of electronics waking up from a day and a half of sleep. Over in the entertainment center, the vintage VCR spit out a tape with a click. But he was a lot more interested in how the lacy camisole clung to her perfect cupcake breasts.

As he cupped them his hands, he couldn't help but glance at his sculpture. Yes, he'd captured their shape and dimensions perfectly. And now he could touch. Taste.

He'd use every skill in his arsenal to bring her more pleasure than she'd ever known. Make her forget any lover but him. "Bailey—"

The cabin's landline phone rang. They stared at each other, breathing hard.

Four, five, six obnoxious rings. He closed his eyes and dropped his hands.

"When did the electricity come back on?" Bailey murmured, blinking, as the answering machine invited the caller to leave a message after the tone.

"Rafe?" Lukas's disembodied voice. "If I'm getting the answering machine, the electricity's back on. Pick up."

What was that smell? "Shit, the pasta." Their Michelin-star brunch was burning in the cast-iron pan.

Bailey nudged him toward the phone. "He's your brother. You talk to him. I'll rescue the pasta."

Half his weight, and she'd thrown him under the bus without a qualm. "Be careful of your hands. Hot pads are on the hearth." As she passed, he snagged her around her waist, pulling her against him for a soul-sucking, lip-clinging kiss.

"Damn it, Rafe—" Lukas did not sound pleased.

"Grumpy," Bailey murmured against his lips.

"Rafe, damn it…"

"Okay, okay." He took a big step backwards, out of range of those dangerous hands of hers. After making sure she slipped on the walleye-shaped hot pads, he snatched up the blocky portable handset from the end table next to the couch. Antonia frequently said that the cabin was the place where old Sebastiani family electronics came to die. "Hey." He deactivated the answering machine with a punch of a button. "What's up?"

"What the fuck, Rafe. Nice of you let us know you're okay."

Bailey was right, Lukas was grumpy. "Cut us some slack; we were busy. The electricity literally came on a minute ago."

Lukas didn't respond. He probably knew exactly what they'd been busy with.

"Didn't I tell you not to worry if you didn't hear from us for a couple of days?" He'd called Lukas as soon as he'd gotten Bailey settled the night they'd fallen, letting him know she was with him up at the cabin, that she'd injured her wrist, they'd lost electricity, and that he was turning off their cell phones to preserve battery power. Lukas had agreed to pass the word to the rest of the family. The silence grew, and Rafe stubbornly let it. His brother's ability to assess emotional energy signatures long distance was unrivaled, but damned if he was going to fill in the blanks. He and Bailey were adults, and didn't have to answer to anybody but each other.

Lukas sighed. Apparently he was in no mood for a game of Chicken. "Can Bailey hear us?"

Rafe glanced over to the fireplace. Bailey knelt on the hearth, looking bemusedly at the whimsical hot pads protecting her hands. She opened and closed the fishes' mouths several times before carefully lifting the heavy cast-iron pot off the hook. Subtle muscles shifted and flexed as she transferred it to the rock hearth.

"Rafe, can Bailey hear us?"

Rafe fought his eyes away from her ass so he could focus. "No."

"How's her wrist? Did you manage to keep her away from her laptop?"

"The wrist is sprained, and no."

"So much for downtime," Lukas grumbled.

"The swelling's down; we've been icing."

"And her stomach? Has she been rubbing it, scrubbing it with her knuckles? Popped any antacids?"

"What? No, not that I've seen." He glanced at her again. The hot pads now off, she gave the pot a stir with the wooden spoon, then lifted it to her mouth, licking at the Béchamel sauce with tiny laps of her tongue.

Jesus.

Where were his scruples? Because somewhere along the way, he'd decided to do this, scruples be damned. She was an adult, an interesting, alluring woman who knew her own mind, and she seemed to want him as much as he wanted her—impossible, but a man could dream. To take her at anything less than her word would be insulting.

She might be small, but she was definitely no infant. And something about her touch, her carnally innocent kiss, made desire feel shiny and new, something they'd discover together.

"Earth to Rafe."

Shit. "Yeah."

"If she doesn't have an ulcer yet, she's verging on it," Lukas said with a tired-sounding sigh. "She's going to a doctor when she gets home if I have to drag her there myself."

Rafe stared at her. Hard. Though sometimes Bailey and Lukas squabbled like brother and sister rather than employer and employee, Rafe knew they cared for each other deeply. His own feelings about Bailey were nowhere near brotherly, but on the issue of Bailey's health, he and Lukas marched in lockstep. "I'll drag her there with you."

"No, you won't," Bailey called from the hearth, pointing the wooden spoon at him. Somehow, she'd figured out what they were talking about. "Lukas, I can take care of myself."

"Then why aren't you?" his brother hollered back.

Rafe jerked the phone away from his ear. "Lukas, she can't hear you."

"Thankfully," Bailey grumbled under her breath.

Silence hummed on the line. When Lukas spoke, it seemed to be from between gritted teeth. "How are the road conditions?"

"The road crews have been out since early this morning," he replied. "Why do you ask?"

"Someone broke into Bailey's condo last night."

"You're kidding." As soon as he blurted the words, he knew they were wasted. Lukas did not kid—not about criminal activity, at any rate. "Was anything stolen?"

"A computer's gone, but she needs to check the rest of her possessions, see if anything else is missing."

Her computer. To Bailey, having a computer stolen would be akin to someone snatching her child off the street.

"The computer is no loss; it was an old piece of shit she used to comply with the terms of her probation," Lukas said. "Now that she's been released, she planned to donate it to charity anyway. It was stolen before Jack could wipe the surveillance software, so whoever took it might get more than they bargained for."

Bailey had completed her probation?

"Put us on speaker," Bailey demanded, suddenly standing at his side.

He smelled lobster and truffles on her breath. He wanted to watch her tiny, white teeth sink into pillows of pasta, watch her jaw move while she chewed. Eating together was one of his favorite forms of foreplay—

"Rafe? Speaker?"

Damn it. He complied with a punch of a button.

"Lukas. For future reference, having my boss call while I'm on a boss-ordered relaxation weekend is not at all relaxing. What do you need?"

Rafe grinned. Though Lukas was her boss, she was tearing him a new one as well as Sasha or Antonia would.

"Your condo was broken into last night. Your computer is gone—"

She snorted. "No loss."

"—but we need you to walk through, check the rest of the place out."

"Let me check road conditions and give you an ETA." She went to the butcher block island, bypassing the two pre-paid disposable cell phones he'd found in her purse in favor of the prototype mini that most Sebastiani Security employees carried. He'd watched The Wire. Why did she carry burner phones when she had so much secure mobile firepower at her disposal?

Did he really want to know?

Bailey peered at the screen. "Mn-DOT shows the road conditions as passable," she said to Lukas. "I can probably be on the road within an hour."

He couldn't read her expression, but he could sense her emotional pulse: thwarted desire, sexual frustration, and a distinct lack of concern about her condo having been broken into.

Odd...and oddly intriguing. Just one more way she seemed utterly unlike any other woman he'd known.

As Lukas and Bailey made arrangements to meet at her place later that evening, leaving a wide margin for safe travel, he tried to be philosophical about their snowed-in sojourn being so rudely interrupted. It was really for the best. The time-out would give him a chance to think this through.

He sighed. He wanted something serious, something long-term, with her. He wanted what his brother had with Scarlett, what his father had with Claudette. With her.

She definitely knew the score, but were they even playing the same game? Was Bailey simply interested in a stellar lay, or did she sense the possibility of...more?

Did she want him, or would any body do?

CHAPTER FOUR

Bailey glanced in her rear view mirror as she pulled into her condo complex's poorly plowed parking lot. Yep, there Rafe was, following a safe distance behind, signaling his turn. Why hadn't he just continued on to his place when she'd turned onto Hwy. 694 westbound? Now she'd have to invite him in.

Her 1970s-era building overlooked the busy interstate, and like many multi-family housing units built during that time, it was blocky, beige, and completely devoid of personality—unless you counted the tag art adorning the side of the building. The stores in the strip mall across the street had been closed for hours, and a snowplow scraped snow to the edges of the empty parking lot. Next door at the auto shop, a customer dropped off his car for a next-day appointment, the headlights of his waiting ride spotlighting him as he dropped his keys into the slot in the door.

Rafe's navy blue Jeep pulled into the space next to hers. He got out of the vehicle, stretching his arms overhead, and joined her. Wearing jeans, UGG boots, and a soft black sweater, his blond hair tumbling down to his shoulders, he looked like he should be sipping an aperitif at a Swiss chalet, not dodging snow turds in her working class neighborhood.

Rafe Sebastiani had probably never set foot in Brooklyn Park in his life.

He looked around the parking lot with a frown. "Too dark."

"It's perfectly safe. Look, there's a day care center across the street." After shrugging back into the heavy coat she'd removed for the drive, she reached into her tiny back seat, unthinkingly grabbing her heavy laptop bag with her left hand. Pain ricocheted up her arm, and she dropped it back into the car with a hiss.

Budging her out of the way with a nudge of his hip, Rafe picked up her laptop bag and duffel, pretending to stagger at the weight of her computer bag. "This thing weighs a quarter what you do."

With two laptops and assorted peripherals, she knew exactly how heavy the bag was. His estimate was fairly accurate. "You don't have to carry my stuff."

"You're on the road to recovery. Let's not tempt fate." He scanned the parking lot with a jaundiced eye. "Or thieves."

Bailey rolled her eyes. "I've lived here for ages. I haven't had anything stolen—"

"Before today?"

Damn it, he had her there.

"Let's go inside. It's freezing out here." He glanced at his jam-packed Jeep. "The clay should be okay for an hour or so."

So, she had a clay sculpture of her nude body to thank for the fact that he wouldn't be hanging around her apartment very long. The thought sent a shiver through her body that had nothing to do with the weather.

As they picked their way around snow clods, she wondered what they'd walk into upstairs. Lukas had been stingy with the details of the break-in. If her place was completely trashed, she just might consider moving. Her condo was more a storage space than a home, and the stolen computer was Paleolithic, a slow, clunky POS she'd used solely to establish some innocuous online activity for Banner to analyze—set dressing, and now that she'd competed the terms of her probation, the show was over. She silently laughed. If Banner thought he'd gained any authentic insight into her by analyzing her online purchases, he had another think coming. Most of the searches she'd issued, and items she'd bought, had been chosen with mind-fucking Banner as her one and only priority. She'd closed down all the credit cards and accounts Banner had been aware of before she'd left for Lukas's cabin. Any cookies, temp files or other information someone might be able to recover from the stolen computer's hard drive would be useless to a thief.

Lukas was waiting for them in the tiny entryway, taking up so much space that Rafe had to brush up against her to close the outer door behind them. "I saw you pull in," he said, taking her laptop bag from Rafe. "How were the roads?"

Lukas opened the stairwell door, letting more oxygen into the room. While the men talked about road conditions, Bailey started up the stairs. Maybe the overwhelming onion and garlic odor of Miss Ella's famous Sunday hash browns would drown out Rafe's luscious scent.

She didn't know whether to thank Lukas or throttle him for interrupting what she and Rafe had started up at the cabin—because she would have slept with him, for sure. The angel on her shoulder whispered that she should be thankful for the opportunity to think about her actions with a clear head. The devil laughingly informed her that if she'd slept with Rafe, the frustration that had plagued her for three hundred miles wouldn't be an issue.

"How's your wrist?" Lukas asked. "Do you need an X-ray? I can call Wyland, get you an appointment at Memorial—"

"I'm fine," she answered before Rafe could agree with his brother. "So, how bad is it? What am I going to walk into up there?"

"It looks contained. Targeted." When they reached the fourth floor, Lukas opened the fire door. "Jack discovered the break-in. When he came over to remove Banner's surveillance software from your home computer, it was gone."

"Any damage to the door?"

"Locked when he arrived," Lukas said, his footfalls heavy on the thin carpeting as they approached her unit at the end of the hall. "No signs of forced entry."

"Hmm." The fact that someone had acted with such apparent deliberation bothered her more than a shattered doorframe would.

Jack opened her door before she could. "Hey."

"Hi." She walked into Jack's open arms. His hug was home, the only one she'd really had since her conviction, when her parents had oh-so-piously removed themselves from her life.

"Were you able to relax at all?" he asked.

"Yeah." *Liar, liar, pants on fire.* Relaxing was hardly the word she'd choose to describe the feel of Rafe's long fingers on her breasts, but it would do for now.

She backed out of Jack's arms and removed her boots, setting them beside Rafe's on the rug next to the door—

Rafe. Where was he?

Standing in the middle of her pocket-sized living room in his stocking feet, looking at his surroundings with too much interest.

The combo living room/kitchen/dining room was beige and bare—no photographs, no posters, no art. The sagging love seat had definitely seen better days. The hand-me-down computer table, empty now except for a snarl of cords, was barely serviceable. The refrigerator door was papered with take-out menus held by magnets, and there was a stack of unopened Amazon.com boxes stacked along the south wall—the books she'd ordered to screw with Banner's psych profile. She'd planned to donate the books to a local library, but had never gotten around to it. Somehow, the boxes had just become part of the décor.

What did her apartment look like through his eyes?

"Jack, there's nothing in the bathroom—hey, Rafe!" Jenny Williams' face lit with pleasure. "What are you doing here?"

"Hi, Jenny." Rafe hugged the other woman, kissing her on both cheeks.

It took Bailey a second to recognize the emotion slinking through her system: jealousy. Apparently statuesque Valkyrie cops with sleek brown ponytails weren't immune to his sex demon charm.

"Excuse me. I need to make a call." Lukas headed back to the door.

Jenny sighed, stepping out of Rafe's embrace. "Is your brother ever going to be able to look me in the eye again?" Jenny had been part of the team who'd taken Annika Fontaine's killer, Stephen, into custody the night he'd attacked Lukas and Scarlett. Her speed retrieving a portable defibrillator had probably saved Lukas's life.

"Appreciate it while it lasts," Rafe muttered. "Jenny, have you met Bailey?"

"Not officially." Jenny extended her hand. "Nice to meet you, Dr. Brown."

Bailey shook it, her own hand completely engulfed. Jenny had man hands, calloused and capable, and she wore a hammered silver ring on her thumb. "Please, call me Bailey."

"And I'm Jenny. I've seen you at Underbelly a couple of times," she added. "It's nice to finally meet you in person."

Though Jenny wore no uniform or insignia that would draw the attention of human civilians—her trim black pants and blue oxford shirt would blend in almost anywhere—her flat, cut-the-bullshit gaze positively screamed 'cop.' Bailey felt neatly dismantled, examined and reassembled before the short handshake was over.

As Jenny explained what she'd done so far—a cursory search, and dusting the doorknob, doorframe, and computer table for fingerprints—Rafe wandered over to the chipped Formica breakfast bar separating the kitchen from the living room. He perched on one of the second-hand barstools and started snooping through the items that had collected there over time.

Jack sat on the stool next to him.

Crap.

Jenny touched her forearm to get her attention. "Can you walk around with me and check whether any other belongings are missing?"

"Sure." Shooting Rafe and Jack a quick look over her shoulder, she followed Jenny into the sea-of-beige bedroom. After several minutes, she was certain that nothing in the room had been disturbed, not even the dust coating the bedside table. If Jenny was baffled or intrigued by Bailey's living arrangements, she didn't let it show.

"Is there anything on the computer's hard drive you're concerned about? Documents, credit card numbers, anything that could be used for identity theft?" Jenny asked as Bailey made a cursory search of the cabinet under the bathroom sink. Out in the living room, the apartment door opened and closed. Lukas was back, and the guys were talking, but not loudly enough for her to hear what they were saying, damn it—

"Bailey?"

"Sorry. No." Leaving the lightest possible digital footprint was such a deeply ingrained habit that she wasn't worried. "One thing that might interest you, though? There's a surveillance package loaded on the stolen computer."

"Reporting to…?"

Banner. Damn it, they'd have to report the theft to Banner. So much for being done with the odious bastard.

Banner might be able to help them figure out who'd stolen the computer if someone was foolish enough to actually use it, but engaging Banner in any way was risky. Rising from her crouch, she closed the cabinet with a snap. "Nothing missing here, either. Let's go talk to the guys." In the other room, Rafe spoke in a low rumble.

God only knew what he was saying.

Rafe stopped talking as they entered. Lukas, leaning on the postage stamp-sized counter from the kitchen side, straightened abruptly, striking his head on the suspended light fixture. Jack was near the love seat, hanging up her landline phone.

"I notified Banner that your computer was stolen," he said. "I don't want you blamed for any crime someone might commit using the machine."

"Better you than me."

"*Always* me. Do not contact Banner directly. Ever." He joined them at the breakfast bar. "You said it yourself a couple of days ago. His interest in you isn't going to end simply because you've fulfilled the terms of your probation. Nothing's changed."

She closed her eyes. Now that she'd paid her so-called debt to society, she had less freedom than ever.

Would she ever stop paying?

Jenny cleared her throat. "So, just so I'm clear. You don't want this Banner's help to get the computer back."

"No."

Lukas rested his elbows on the countertop. "Send Jack a copy of your report, and we'll take it from there."

Jenny nodded. "Bailey, are you certain nothing else is missing?"

"Not that I can see." During her time as a consultant, she'd pretty much lived in hotels, stopping home only to wash clothes before repacking her suitcase and leaving again. Since starting work at Sebastiani Security, she'd moved pretty much every possession she cared about, plus a healthy stash of cash, to The Bunker.

"Okay. I'll zap both you and Jack a copy of the report. We'll keep an eye out, but…" Jenny shrugged fatalistically.

"Yeah." It wasn't likely the computer would ever be recovered—especially if her suspicions about who'd taken it were accurate. "Thanks, Jenny."

"Do you feel safe here? Do you have a place to stay until the locks are beefed up?"

"We're on it," Lukas said. "Thanks, Jenny."

"No problem." A series of beeps shrilled from the pouch attached to Jenny's belt. Opening its Velcro closure, she snatched up a small black gadget and read, her expression going grim. "Domestic. Gotta go."

Lukas straightened. "Need some backup?"

"Nope. Got it." Picking up her jacket from the floor next to the door, she jammed her arms in with a whoosh, stepping into her boots on the move. "Bye."

The door closed behind her. Jack reached into the refrigerator, snagging a can of Coke. Lukas threw his shoulders back and his chest out, like he was about to enter the sparring cage in Sebastiani Security's basement. Rafe looked…vaguely guilty.

What the hell…

"Wyatt Cooper," Jack stated as he opened the can.

She blinked at his unexpected conversational detour. She should have realized that their thoughts would run along the same track. "Yes. He's likely responsible."

"Outsourced."

"Probably." Wyatt's specialty was exploiting gullibility, and convincing someone else to take the fall.

As she very well knew.

Rafe sat up straight on the barstool—some feat, given how badly the thing tilted. "Who," he asked, "is Wyatt Cooper?"

She stared, mesmerized by the controlled violence in his soft tone. His glorious cheekbones stood out in taut relief. His fingers twitched, like he wanted to hit something.

A sudden wave of lust about buckled her knees.

"How much time do you have?" Jack responded.

"Not tonight," Lukas said around a jaw-cracking yawn. "Let's get some sleep and regroup tomorrow morning." He looked at Jack, then Bailey. "Eight o'clock?"

Jack thought a moment. "Yeah, I'm open."

"Me too," she sighed. She knew her schedule was clear because she'd specifically blocked out the morning to work on some projects that were woefully behind schedule. She sighed again, jamming her hands into her overly-long hair. Personal errands like haircuts and—she flicked Lukas a guilty side-eye— doctor appointments had completely fallen off her radar. Hopefully the doctor appointment would fall off his.

"We don't think you should stay here tonight," Lukas said.

So that's what their low-volume pow-wow had been about. "I hadn't planned on it. I'll stay at The Bunker. My futon's there, there's a shower in the locker room downstairs..."

"I'd like you to bunk in with Sasha and Antonia until we figure out exactly what's going on here."

Stay with Lukas's sisters? They lived in one of the two penthouse units topping the Sebastiani Building, home of Underbelly, Crackhouse Coffee, and God knew what else on the floors between. Antonia had recently moved across the foyer from her father's unit to her sister's. She chattered incessantly about how much she enjoyed her new living arrangements.

She opened her mouth to decline, but then reconsidered. With three Underworld Council members living on the top floor, it was an understatement to say the building had formidable security. Sebastiani Security was just down the street, so her commute to work would be negligible. She'd have access to a 24-hour coffee shop she could walk to in her slippers. In the deep freeze of a Minnesota winter, it was a considerable perk.

Perk. She snorted with laughter at the weak pun. Yeah, it was time to get some sleep.

"Bailey?" Rafe's voice was soft as a feather bed. "Are you okay?"

"Just tired." She couldn't stop from weaving toward him like he was a magnet and her body was composed of iron filings. "Too tired to argue with all three of you at the same time. I'll go to Sasha's." Right now, she didn't really care where she slept, as long as sleep was on the agenda.

What was she going to do to—um, *about*—Rafe? Did she have it in her to simply enjoy him, to wallow in the pleasure he would bring her, without getting emotionally involved?

She needed to think.

"Need anything else?" Lukas gestured to the duffel and computer bag he'd carried. "I'll drop you off, get you upstairs for the night. We'll have to wait until tomorrow to update the security systems to recognize you."

"I'll drive myself. What's already in the bag is fine." Anything else she needed could be picked up tomorrow, once she got to work.

"Didn't you say that Scarlett wasn't feeling well?" Rafe asked Lukas. "Why don't I get Bailey upstairs? I'll swing next door and say hi to Dad and Claudette."

Lukas considered, then nodded. "Thanks."

Jackets rustled, boots were donned, and lights turned off. Following the guys out of her condo, she locked the door behind them, for what it was worth. When she reached the parking lot, she saw Lukas had put her bags in the back seat of Rafe's already-running Jeep. Its bright headlights sliced through the lightly falling snow.

"Ready?" Rafe called from his open window. "Take it slow; these roads are pretty slick."

She nodded and got into her car. The drive downtown would give her time to shore up her shaky boundaries, to get her brain back in gear. If nothing else, having Wyatt ooze back into her life was a great reminder that, when it came to men, her judgment could be very seriously flawed.

✳

The pale winter sun barely peeked over the horizon when Rafe opened Sebastiani Security's heavy front door the next morning. Between dropping Bailey off last night, visiting with his father and Claudette, and unpacking the Jeep when he'd finally gotten home, he felt like he'd barely rolled into bed before he'd had to roll right back out again.

His brother's text, requesting that he attend an 8:00 a.m. meeting, had been his alarm clock.

Lukas poked his head into the empty reception area from the inner security door. "Hey, come on back. We're just getting started."

Grunting a response, he followed. Lukas looked pale, and he reeked of worry. "What's wrong?"

Lukas's glaze flicked upward. "Scarlett's not feeling well this morning." After her sister had been killed, Scarlett had moved from the penthouse unit she'd shared with Sasha into Lukas's loft so he could better protect her. She'd never moved back out.

"Did she pick up a bug somewhere?"

Lukas nodded, rubbing his neck. "Christ, I hate winter. Hang on a sec." Detouring into the break room, Lukas opened the refrigerator, grabbed an orange and an apple, and then closed the refrigerator door with a tap of the heel of his work boot. "There's coffee in the conference room."

"Good."

He followed his brother down the exposed brick hallway, passing Lukas's cluttered office, Jack's neat one, and several small conference rooms. In one of the rooms, a woman scribbled on a white board, wielding a dry-erase marker with rapier speed. Someone was making a phone call in another. When they reached the large conference room in the corner, Jack rose from his seat at the big oval table to connect his sleek laptop to the projector. Sebastiani Security operative Chico Perez leaned against the back wall. Antonia, wearing a sweatshirt that had mysteriously disappeared from his closet last year, sat next to Jack, sipping Diet Coke and nibbling on popcorn, flicking at a screen as she read. And there was Bailey, leaning over the credenza, pumping coffee from a stainless steel air pot with a soft vacuum hiss. She wore a black turtleneck sweater tucked into a pair of black skinny jeans that made the most of her subtle curves.

Bailey's head whipped to the door. The pleasure, the desire she couldn't disguise, flickered over her face momentarily, then quickly disappeared.

The display of mental discipline was…oddly hot.

"What are you doing here?" she asked when he joined her. She wore a pair of those clever fingerless gloves, with a foot of knit fabric bunched at her wrists but leaving her fingertips free for typing. Her breathing was fast and shallow, her pupils were dilated, and she clutched her coffee cup like a lifeline.

Relief bloomed. *I'm not alone in this.* "I don't know yet," he admitted, reaching for a coffee cup. "Lukas asked me to come." When he filled the cup, the glorious scent of Crackhouse Blend filled his sinuses. "How's your wrist this morning?"

"Fine." A pause. "Okay, it's a little sore."

The tips of her fingers weren't puffy or bruised, but who knew what damage was hidden under all that wadded-up knit? "Did you ice it last night?"

She rolled her eyes. "Yes, Dad."

His concern wasn't the least bit fatherly, but now probably wasn't the best time to bring that up.

"Let's get started." As he entered the conference room, Lukas flicked off the lights with his elbow and sat down, gesturing to Rafe to take the seat at his left.

He set the apple in front of Bailey, who'd taken the seat to his right. He rolled the orange across the table to Antonia, who ignored it.

Jack snatched the orange before it hit the floor, and tossed it to Chico. "Let's get everyone up to speed." With a click, the wall-mounted flat-screen woke up, displaying what looked like a message board of some type. "Late last week, a poster named Coyote revealed Bailey's association with Sebastiani Labs on a popular hacker bulletin board. Since that time, there's been a noticeable uptick in malicious incursion attempts. The extra work has kept SL's network staff a little busy this week." Jack looked at Bailey. "Status on last night's attack?"

Bailey stretched her neck. "Countermeasures held."

She'd worked last night? Rafe shot Lukas an annoyed glance.

"Last weekend sometime, Bailey's condo was broken into and a computer was stolen."

As Chico asked questions about the break-in, Rafe skimmed the screen. "You're The Queen Bee?" he asked Bailey.

She shrugged. "I was."

"Cute. Who's Coyote?"

Lukas abruptly stood, glancing at the ceiling again. "Excuse me." He left the room without saying anything else.

"Code Red?" Chico asked Jack. Lukas had the ability to connect a perpetrator to a crime scene by an emotional taste or signature, and was on call to their police force 24/7.

Jack's mini lay silently at his place at the table. "Nothing here."

"Scarlett's not feeling well," Rafe offered. "He's probably checking on her."

"Let's keep going. He'll catch up." Jack clicked a button on the small remote he carried, and the screen filled with a picture of a very handsome man, mid-to-late thirties, with pale skin, twinkling blue eyes, and black bangs that flopped over his forehead. His boyish charisma positively leaped off the screen.

"Coyote is a computer security consultant named Wyatt Cooper. He and Bailey have some history."

Jack's loathing for the guy leached into the room. Sitting in the projector's milky backwash, Bailey's expression was battened down tight, but her emotions roiled like a storm at sea.

They'd been lovers, of course. And he'd hurt her. An unfamiliar, wild tightness made his jaw clench and his temples throb.

He wanted to tear the guy apart.

"Get in line." Chico clapped a hand onto his shoulder before dropping into Lukas's empty chair.

Across the room, Antonia rolled her eyes at the lot of them, no doubt attributing their reaction to testosterone poisoning. Well, she was dead wrong. His sister might be a genius, but she lacked the chromosome necessary to assess the fine nuances of the situation.

It was unacceptable that this *Dead Poet's Society* reject had caused Bailey even one second of pain.

Jack walked through Cooper's educational background, financials, and current residence.

"Minneapolis," Rafe noted with a scowl. "There's a coincidence."

"Now we have to go back in time a little bit." Jack clicked, displaying an old picture of Bailey.

"Must we?" she muttered.

"You know we do."

Rafe stared at the picture. She had the same haircut, was the same height and weight, and wore jeans and a sweater against northern California's fall chill, but she looked…so damn young. It was all in the eyes. She looked brazen, confident, ready to kick the world in the ass—not yet knowing that sometimes the world kicked back.

As Jack described her relationship with Cooper—lab partners in her computer science doctoral program, where their relationship had inevitably turned romantic—Rafe's blood pressure rose. "So, let me see if I have this straight," he said. "Cooper was your lab partner, then your lover. How old were you?"

Bailey's cheeks were as pink as the Braeburn apple Lukas had given her. "Eighteen."

He considered her. "You were in a doctoral program at eighteen."

"I was…precocious."

"Intellectually, yes—but in terms of relationships, you were a babe in the woods, easy pickings."

"I deposed Cooper to help build Bailey's defense," Jack said. "He's a major league asshole, and an expert manipulator."

"Social engineer," Bailey corrected.

"What?"

"His technical skills are average at best, but he's the most skilled social engineer I've ever known."

"What's a social engineer?" Antonia asked before he could.

"A social engineer exploits human gullibility to extract private or confidential information. He or she then uses that information to access data, systems or facilities they aren't authorized to access." She bit into the apple with a soft crunch, chewed and swallowed. "I worked the architecture, design and coding side of our dissertation project, and he worked the rest. The division of labor catered to our individual strengths."

"What was your project?" he asked.

She glanced at Jack, then at the table. "I had an idea for a way to reduce malicious incursion risk against high-value databases—"

"He tried to hack the freaking NSA and left you holding the bag," Jack snapped. "He manipulated you. He stole your code. He adapted it—poorly. He—"

"I should have known what he was doing," she snapped back. "I was asleep at the wheel."

The guilt and shame coursing through her system nearly overwhelmed him.

"And times have changed," she continued. "These days, he doesn't even have to know how to code to launch a successful denial of service attack. It's automated; all you need is a goddamn credit card to buy the tool. Or—" she gestured to the wall-mounted screen "—he can outsource the job." She rubbed her neck, blew out a breath. "He has an undergrad degree in psychology. He's a master at reading body language and facial expressions. He used to take acting and improvisation classes; maybe he still does. He keeps detailed dossiers on all of his targets. He's...a freaking chameleon. He can assume nearly any persona or role, become part of any group, have his victims believing exactly what he wants them to believe." She sagged slightly, like a balloon losing its air. "He was good back then, and from what I've heard, he's only gotten better with time. Do not underestimate him."

Rafe wanted to punch something. "You were her attorney, right?" he asked Jack. "Sounds like this d-bag was behind the whole thing. How—"

"Bailey wouldn't name him as an accomplice, much less the mastermind."

"Why?"

Bailey crossed her arms and didn't answer.

"The judge was influenced by her youth and her clean record," Jack said, "but despite my best efforts, and the fact that the incursion attempt was officially deemed unsuccessful, she still did some time."

Bailey shrugged a shoulder. "Less than a month at a minimum security facility. I met some nice women. Caught up on my reading."

Despite her careless tone, he sensed residual fear jumping in her stomach like grasshoppers. Bailey had some acting skills he hadn't been aware of.

"Thankfully this happened before 9/11, or the outcome would have been fathoms worse," Jack added.

"Wyatt never did get that degree." Bailey smiled tightly. "Pity."

Chico jammed his thumb through the skin of the orange, filling the air with a sharp spritz of citrus. "So, he doxxed you on a message board. He's presumably responsible for the incursion attempts at Sebastiani Labs, and he's the primary suspect for the apartment break-in. What does he want?"

"Other than Bailey? Unknown," Jack answered. "We need more information. He and his friends haven't cracked SL yet—"

"And they won't," Bailey nearly snarled.

"Hey, you have to sleep sometime," Chico said. "When did you start work today?"

"About 3:00 a.m.," she admitted. "I was awake, heard the ping, and drove over so I could give Cheyenne a hand."

She'd been working since three o'clock? Hell, she had to be running on caffeine and adrenaline.

The door opened, and Lukas came back in, popping an antacid from the tube he always carried in his back pocket. "Where are we at?" He didn't explain why he'd left so suddenly, but he looked rattled.

"We were just talking about the 'why'," Jack said. "What's Cooper's end game? What does he want, and why now?" He set the remote on the table. "We have the thread at the message board, a break-in, a stolen computer, and an uptick in malicious incursion attempts at SL. So far, Bailey is the common denominator."

Bailey shifted in the chair, clearly uncomfortable. "We have to assume he's done a thorough physical recon of Sebastiani Labs," she said. "That he has spatial knowledge of the SL campus, its entrances and exits, the roads in and out. Escape routes. He's probably tried to tailgate into the building, chatting with the people taking smoke breaks so he can enter without an employee badge." She paused, staring at Cooper's picture, still displayed on the screen. "People are the weakest link."

Though her voice was steady, she leached self-recrimination. He choked back his feeble, helpless rage. "How do we take this guy down?"

"That's where you come in." When Lukas flipped on the room lights, Rafe saw that every eye in the room was on him. "We need to draw him out."

"How?"

"Jealousy." Lukas glanced at Bailey. "Jack told me about the packages and mail you receive. Cooper's still fixated on you."

His head whipped to where Bailey sat, fiddling with a blue gel ice pack. "He's stalking you?"

She paused, then shrugged. "Nothing actionable."

He shot Lukas and Jack a disgusted look. "You really can't do anything about this?"

"He's smart and he's careful. No handwriting or prints to analyze, no return address, generic printer paper and ink." Lukas looked at Bailey. "Have there been any incursion attempts against your personal accounts?"

"No."

"The condo's clean? No bugs?"

"I swept it as soon as I arrived at Bailey's place and saw the computer was missing," Jack answered. "Whoever stole the computer didn't bother to install anything else."

Bugs? Were they talking about surveillance equipment?

"How about your car?" Chico asked.

Bailey cursed under her breath. "It's been over a week since I checked."

Chico's big fingers flew as he sent a text. Rafe had no doubt that a Sebastiani Security operative would be out in the parking lot checking Bailey's car within minutes.

"Okay, what's the plan?" he asked Lukas.

"Make him jealous. Piss him off. When he makes a mistake, we take him down."

Bailey twisted around in her chair to glare at Lukas. "Are you serious?"

"As a heart attack." Lukas popped another antacid. "Let Cooper see you and Rafe spending time together. Wine and dine. Date and dance." Lukas waved a hand toward him. "Rafe knows the drill."

His eyes widened. What the hell was Lukas up to? "I don't think—"

"Not interested?" Lukas said. "Okay. Chico, how about you?"

Chico grinned, the flash of his teeth rivaling the sparkle of the pea-sized diamonds he wore in both ears. "Sure—"

"Slow down," Rafe snapped. The prospect of someone else masquerading as Bailey's lover sent his temper into the red zone. If anyone was going to do this, it would be him. But… "Maybe we can kill two birds with one stone."

"What do you mean?"

"I have deadlines and work commitments of my own." He glanced at Bailey. "My gallery show next month…you've seen the direction my work is going. I might make better progress if we spent more time together."

Color flushed into her cheeks as she eyed him, considering. Desire and guilt—she couldn't hide either reaction, from him or from his siblings. Antonia watched them with unabashed interest.

"Okay," Bailey blurted.

She'd said okay.

Chico's mini pinged softly. He swore as he read. "Bailey's car's been tagged." He quickly dialed, speaking tersely to the person on the other end. "Don't remove it. Check every car in the lot." He hung up. "I'll pull our security videos, see if the tracker was planted while you were parked here, but…"

"Who'd be that stupid?" Antonia finished.

"Your family's cabin," Bailey suddenly said, going pale as a ghost. "Whoever planted the tracker might have the coordinates to your family's cabin." She raised a fist to her stomach.

Chico's mini pinged again. He read, pursing his lips. "Trackers on all your cars—including Rafe's."

Okay, that was creepy.

Jack cursed. "Probably planted when we were all at Bailey's place last night."

"So the cabin's okay."

Bailey was more concerned about preserving the location of a cabin than her own safety? Lukas had been right about guilting Bailey into moving into the penthouse with Sasha.

Lukas thumbed off another antacid, popped it in his mouth. "Let's leave the trackers in place for now. I want him to know exactly where you two go."

"What if he's got this parking lot under surveillance right now?" Antonia said. "He might know we've found the trackers, and are choosing to leave them in place."

Lukas smiled grimly. "Let him wonder why."

A feint within a feint within a feint. All this surveillance and counter-surveillance crap was exhausting, especially on only one cup of coffee.

"Chico, can you let Jenny know she should sweep her car? And Rafe, I'd like to double-check the security at your place."

He nodded at Lukas. His building's walls were made of brick, but that didn't mean the place was impervious. Yeah, it had to be done, especially if he and Bailey were going to spend time together there. Hours and hours of time together.

Anticipation welled like a Yellowstone geyser.

Bailey stood. "Are we done here? I need to touch base with Cheyenne."

"Go on," Lukas responded. "Jack, Chico and I will—"

Her mini chimed. She quickly plucked it off the table and read. "Crap. Another Denial of Service attack at Sebastiani Labs. Gotta go." She left without saying goodbye.

Before they could make plans.

"Damn it." Lukas exchanged a worried glance with Jack.

"Damn it is right," Rafe bit out. "She's exhausted."

"Yeah," Lukas agreed. "Thanks for making time for this, Rafe. I honestly think it's the fastest way to bring this to a head. Bailey's running on empty, so I'd prefer to work quickly."

He nodded. Apparently his brother had a better awareness of Bailey's limits than he'd thought.

"Do you have a minute to talk?" Lukas asked as he rose from his chair. "My office?"

"Yeah." Lukas left, but Rafe grabbed another cup of coffee before he followed. If Lukas thought he'd be dictating how this 'wine, dine, date' thing would work, he had another think coming.

Lukas might have put him on the chessboard, but now his brother had to step back and give him room to move.

CHAPTER FIVE

Cheyenne and her team shut down the DDoS attack almost as quickly as it started. Rather than go back to the meeting, Bailey slipped into Jack's elegant office, closing the door behind her.

The space smelled like him. Jack may have moved from the California coast to landlocked Minnesota to accept Lukas's job offer, but his cologne carried the scent of the ocean. After another quick glance back at the door, she hurried to the framed photograph hanging on the wall separating his office from Lukas's—a picture of Mavericks, the legendary northern California surf break, on a calm day. Most visitors to Jack's office, upon seeing the print, commented on the beauty of the placid, navy blue water, but had no clue that when the right, rare conditions arose, the water heaved itself six stories into the sky, maiming and killing with its snapping jaws. Bailey had always found the picture very telling.

Standing on tippy-toes, she patted the top of the narrow black picture frame and found the key to Jack's locked desk drawer. Scurrying back to the huge slab of desk, she knelt on the floor behind it. No one walking down the hall could see her through the narrow slice of window if they happened to glance in.

What she was doing wasn't wrong, exactly, but she didn't want to try to explain to Jack, or anyone else, why she was helping herself to a healthy supply of his pheromone intoxication meds.

The cool metal desk key seemed to burn her fingers as she slid it into the slot on the lower right drawer, opening it. Ruthlessly organized, with no clutter—not a paper clip or battery dared stray out of its assigned space—she quickly found the airtight storage container, picked it up, and peeled off the cover. And there were the pills, innocuous white tablets with a slight yellow cast, stored twenty tablets per tiny Ziploc bag. Though the experimental drug had been developed by Sebastiani Labs to help humans resist the effect of incubi and succubi pheromones, Jack was currently the only person who used them. Until a year ago, when she'd been brought into the fold, Jack had been the only human alive who knew that humanity shared their planet with species of extra-planetary origin. As a voting member of the Underworld Council, and managing partner and public face of Sebastiani Security, it was important that Jack's judgment be unimpaired by the pheromones that incubi and succubi emitted as naturally as they breathed.

She pursed her lips as she peered at one of the tiny sealed bags. How much of the drug did Jack take, and how often? She'd taken a tablet on one previous occasion, the night of Scarlett Fontaine's homecoming show at Underbelly last year. In all the scurry and flurry of that day—learning that First Contact had occurred millennia ago, that no one at Sebastiani Security except Jack was human, and that they needed her to pitch in on an undercover security op because Scarlett was in danger—no one had remembered that she'd be as susceptible to incubi and succubi pheromones as Jack would be. By the time Rafe had gotten her up to Sasha's office, she'd been well under the influence, but the tablet he'd slipped under her tongue had worked very quickly. She'd known *exactly* what she was doing when she'd wound her arms and legs around him, pressing tiny, biting kisses into the open V-neck of his crisp button-down shirt. Licking his delicious skin.

Him, licking hers.

"Shit," she breathed. What had she been thinking, agreeing to model for him? Nude?

How could she not?

She was pretty sure Rafe had split a pill in half before slipping it under her tongue. Being that Jack was slightly more than double her weight, she'd do the same. Given how quickly the pills worked, she could take them as needed rather than keeping herself dosed at all times.

How many pills should she take from Jack's supply? Even sharing a conference room with Rafe this morning had scrambled her thoughts, made her fight not to squirm against the conference room chair. How much time would they need to spend together? Holding up a bag, she considered. The Wyatt Cooper she remembered had very little patience, anywhere except the bedroom. They might have this thing shut down, one way or another, before Rafe's gallery showing next month.

One month, up close and personal, with Rafe Sebastiani. She shoved a single filmy packet in her back pocket.

"Hey," Antonia said from the doorway. "What are you doing?"

It took some effort to open a door that quietly. "Just checking some cabling," she replied, quickly casting her thoughts to firewall architecture. Antonia could read emotions as well as her brothers could, but even succubi couldn't see through solid wood. As she rose, Bailey palmed the desk key and nudged the desk drawer closed with her toe. "What's up?"

"Does Cheyenne need help?"

"Nope, she and her team have it covered." Rounding the desk, she followed Antonia into the main hallway, closing the door behind them. She'd have to put Jack's desk key back on the picture frame later. "Back to The Bunker, then," she said cheerily. "Want to reverse-engineer a Distributed Denial of Service attack? I'll explain why our countermeasures worked."

"Cool."

She glanced into Lukas's office as they walked by. Rafe lounged in Lukas's leather guest chair like he didn't have a care in the world, his blond hair lying loose and soft against his rust-colored sweater. Lukas, facing the hall, swigged directly from a bottle of Pepto-Bismol.

The desk between them blocked Lukas's view of Rafe's clenched fists.

Antonia waved her hand in front of her nose. "The testosterone is getting kinda thick in here. What are they arguing about now?"

"Come on," she said, tugging Antonia by the arm. She was pretty sure she knew.

✳

"So, let me see if I understand this." Rafe struggled to rein in his temper. "You're pulling me in on this op so I can—how did you so charmingly put it?—'finally get laid?'"

"That's not the only reason, but I thought it might be a nice little side benefit." Lukas took another swig from the antacid bottle, wiping his mouth with his wrist. "You've spent the last year moping around like a love-sick teenager, and Bailey hasn't been any better. I'm just giving you a push."

"I think I can handle my own sex life, bro."

Lukas snorted. "You're not handling it very well—unless you mean 'hand' in a literal sense. Though come to think of it," he said, narrowing his eyes, "your energy is better since you came back from the cabin. Did you and Bailey—"

"None of your business."

Smiling slightly, Lukas leaned back in his oversized leather chair.

So, Bailey had been acting like a love-sick teenager, too? From their time up at the cabin, he knew Bailey wanted him physically, but…the possibility that his own fledgling feelings might be reciprocated, might have a chance to spark and grow, swam through his system like a shot of Everclear.

But…the op? He was nowhere close to the best person for this assignment. He could handle himself in a fight if he had to, but Chico Perez was lethal. Even knowing this, Lukas had allowed Rafe's knee-jerk rejection of Chico's offer to stand.

"Enough emo reverie," Lukas said. "We have work to do."

Heat flushed his face. "You started it."

"And you can finish it, on your own time."

Finish it? Yeah, right. He couldn't conceive of a finish line. It would take a lifetime to cycle through his ever-growing list of fantasies, most of them so debauched that—

A lifetime? Jesus, where had *that* come from?

Lukas laughed out loud. "If you could see your face." Folding his hands, he rested them on his flat stomach, looking supremely satisfied. "It feels really uncomfortable sometimes, but it's not a fate worse than death."

"What isn't?"

"Falling in love."

His breath caught at Lukas's softly spoken words. Was he? Falling in love? He had no idea, but he…wanted a chance to find out. He wanted what his brother had with Scarlett, and what his father had found with Claudette—a fighting chance at it, anyway.

"But she's not like your other women."

"My other women?" If Lukas had any idea how long it had been since he'd been on a date, much less slept with someone…

"She's not like the women you've dated in the past. She doesn't do hit and runs." He frowned. "I don't think."

Hit and runs? His brother made his sex life sound so unsavory—more unsavory than he deserved. "Lukas, every woman I've ever slept with has known the score."

"Yeah." Lukas leveled a glance at him. "You let them know right up front that you're only interested in a mutually satisfying physical relationship."

"And friendship," he said defensively, shifting in his chair. "I'm good friends with almost all my former lovers."

Lukas held up a weary hand. "You're right. Of course you're right. I'm making a mash of this. All I'm trying to say is that any relationship with Bailey will be…complicated."

"Tell me about it," Rafe muttered. "Just when I think I have a piece of her figured out, she does a one-eighty on me. She made the oddest comment when we were up at the cabin." How to describe this? "We were kissing—"

"Great start…"

"But after you interrupted us—" Rafe glared at Lukas "—there was this distinct whiff of guilt, you know?" From the expression on his face, Rafe got the impression that Lukas knew *exactly* what he was talking about. "When I asked her what was wrong, she waved it off, saying guilt was pretty much her baseline emotion." Rafe picked a piece of lint off the forearm of his sweater. "I know about her felony conviction, and she told me she's a preacher's kid, but—"

"Do you know who her father is?"

Rafe shook his head.

"Come over here for a sec."

Unfolding himself from the chair, he walked around and peered over Lukas's shoulder at the flat-screen monitors dominating his brother's desk. With a quick clack of keys, Lukas accessed a website.

"What is this?" Rafe leaned in more closely. "'The Way, the Truth and the Light.'"

Over the next several minutes, a very slick media presentation showed thousands of people streaming into one of the biggest, whitest buildings he'd ever seen. An attractive couple, their heads close together and gold bands conspicuously glinting, shared a beverage in a cheerful on-site coffee shop. In another picture, a dozen or so well-scrubbed children sat in a circle at the feet of a bearded man who had Bailey's eyes. "Is this one of those mega-churches?"

"In the sense that their bigotry and hate speech is constitutionally protected? Yes." Lukas held up an apologetic hand. "Sorry. But check out some of these videos, and you'll see what I mean."

Lukas clicked—and the longer they watched, the more Rafe's jaw dropped. Bailey's father didn't go quite so far as to say "God Hates Fags" from his pulpit, but…close enough. He turned his head away, sick to his stomach. Bailey had come from that? Escaped from that? He sank back into his chair with a sigh.

"Her parents were MIA during her trial," Lukas said. "They completely cut her off, told her that she'd sinned, and that her behavior reflected negatively on them and their church family."

"So much for the virtue of forgiveness," he grumbled. With family like that, who needed enemies? "Thankfully she had Jack."

Lukas nodded.

"Does she have other family?"

"I know she has occasional contact with her younger sister, Melanie—email, phone calls, that kind of thing. The parents? Nothing. I don't think she really misses them," Lukas mused. "Jack said she'd once described her relationship with her parents like having an amputated finger. You're aware it's missing. There's a gap, an occasional phantom pain, but after a while you learn how to live quite well without it."

"Wow." When their mother died, he'd felt torn limb from limb, wondering why no one could see bloody streaks as he stumbled through the aftermath. He'd used his mother's purple satin bathrobe as a blanket for months. Losing all contact with his father, with him still alive, was inconceivable. "Okay, I get it. She has some issues, sure, but—"

"Issues? The woman has enough baggage to fill a cargo ship." Holding up his hand, Lukas ticked off on his fingers. "She's human. A preacher's kid. A convicted felon. A workaholic. She has intimacy issues up the wazoo."

"So if you think a relationship between us is such a lost fricking cause, why are you shoving us together like this?"

"I didn't say it was a lost cause. I just wanted to remind you that she's…complicated. We both know that you've never had a serious romantic relationship." Lukas glanced at the ceiling again. "It's damn hard work."

Annoyance spiked. Lukas made him sound like an unfeeling man-whore, and nothing could be further from the truth.

"All I'm saying is, if she's just another lover to you, don't even start."

He uttered his biggest fear aloud. "Maybe she just wants me for my body."

Instead of responding—instead of denying it, like he'd hoped—Lukas cursed at the ceiling and snagged his wastebasket with his foot.

"Scarlett still has the flu?"

"What?" Lukas swallowed heavily.

"When you left the meeting, you went upstairs to check on Scarlett, right? Is she feeling worse?"

Lukas jammed his hands into his hair. "I didn't ask you here to talk about Scarlett."

"Actually, you ordered me here, but I let you get away with it because it served my purposes, too. What's wrong with Scarlett? Is she seriously ill?" Shit. The top floor was too far away for him to get a good read on her.

"She's not sick. Not really." Lukas took a deep breath. "She's…pregnant."

Rafe's jaw dropped. "Are you serious? Congratulations!" Shooting to his feet, he walked around the desk again, yanking Lukas to his feet for a hug. "No wonder you're acting like such a dick." His big, brawny brother was scared shitless.

After a slight hesitation, Lukas arms tightened around him. "Scarlett is going to kill me," he muttered. "She made me promise not to tell anyone, and it took me all of fifteen minutes to break my word."

"You know it's impossible to keep a secret in this family."

Lukas rolled his eyes in agreement. "But please try," he asked as they both sat down again. "She wants to keep the news private until—" he shrugged uncomfortably "—you know."

Rafe nodded. Several of his friends had kept the news of their pregnancies to themselves until they were past their first trimester, when the risk of miscarriage dropped. He eyed his brother, noticing the tense lines bracketing his mouth. Risk assessment was Lukas's forte, but left to his own devices, Lukas would torture himself with rare 'what if's' throughout Scarlett's pregnancy. "Scarlett is disgustingly healthy," he reassured Lukas. "She'll be fine." She was healthy now, at any rate. A year ago, when she'd come home from a grueling tour, she'd been stressed out and frighteningly thin. He'd take a swing upstairs before he left today, and have a cozy little chat with his brother's bondmate. He'd drop some subtle hints about Lukas's stress level, and make sure she was eating right, taking the best possible care of herself. "Is there anything else I need to know right now? I have some work I have to catch up on."

"Touch base with Chico. He's coordinating physical security. You and Bailey need to make some plans that get you out in public."

And every time they stepped out in public, they'd be followed. Creepy. "So much for romance."

"If the team is doing their job well, you won't even notice they're there."

Team? They?

The computer chimed softly. Lukas glanced at his monitor and swore. "Time for my next meeting." Carrying the wastebasket with him, he headed for the door. "Don't take the tracking device off your car, and get Chico over to your place sometime today. If Bailey's going to be spending any time at your studio, we need to make sure it's as safe as possible."

He couldn't argue with that sentiment, and Lukas damn well knew it.

✴

Wyatt was walking along Nicollet Mall, enjoying a Subway sandwich, when two suited men suddenly flanked him. "Mr. Cooper." The men crowded closer, grabbing him by the elbows. His meatball sub dropped to the slushy sidewalk. "Please come with us."

Something jabbed into his ribs, hard enough to sting through layers of winter clothes. The man's voice sounded oddly polite for someone threatening him with a gun.

He glanced around. Corporate lunch hour had come and gone, and the pedestrian mall was nearly deserted. Anyone seeing them from the skyway or their office windows would think he'd been unexpectedly joined by two old buddies.

Held up in broad daylight. So much for Minnesota Nice. "My wallet is in my back right pants pocket."

The men didn't respond, just kept hustling him down the slush-covered sidewalk. When they reached Eleventh Avenue, Frick opened the back passenger door of a black limousine idling at the curb. "Ten minutes of your time, Mr. Cooper."

That was the second time they'd used his name.

Frack wrenched his arm up and behind, lifting him to his toes. One centimeter higher and his shoulder would snap like a chicken wing. "Shit, okay. Okay!" The pressure eased, just the slightest bit.

What the hell did they want? The limo was new, and freshly washed. Despite Frack's expert moves, the men didn't look like hired muscle. Intelligence snapped from their eyes, and they both wore winter-weight trench coats over dark business suits. They were dressed to blend—like *he* would dress if he were to accept a similar job. So, what *was* the job? Someone must want to speak to him pretty badly if they'd risk plucking him off the street in the middle of the day, in an area crawling with surveillance cameras.

"Come in out of the cold, Mr. Cooper," a man invited from the back seat.

The gun bit into his ribs again.

Every profiler or self-defense expert worth their consulting fee would advise him to disobey. To *not* get in the car. To fight—hard—to stay in a public place. His odds of survival would be better being shot at close range for disobeying than they would be if he was transported to a secondary site.

Easy for a profiler to say.

"Please."

So polite.

The limo was visible and obvious. He tipped his face up to the nearest surveillance camera in case this so-called ten minutes turned into a body dump, then slid onto the limo's rear-facing seat.

He was immediately cocooned in leather-scented warmth. The door closed solidly behind him, abruptly cutting the street noise to negligible. The car rocked slightly as Frick and Frack climbed into the front seat, and the window separating the front seat from the rear rose with a low-pitched electronic hum.

The door locks thunked, trapping him inside.

Blinking as his eyes adjusted to the dimmer light, he studied the man sitting in the facing seat. He was…round. Round face, chubby cheeks, his round head bald as a cue ball, and wearing circular silver wire-rimmed glasses that picked up the flecks of gray in his fussy handlebar mustache. His suit, though expensive and perfectly tailored, couldn't disguise an advanced case of middle-aged spread, or the gun he carried in a shoulder holster. Physically, he looked like the Buddha, or a jolly old elf, but the expression in his eyes was flat. Dead.

Dangerous.

"Mr. Cooper. Your phone, if you please," the man said politely, resting his hand on the holster.

Wyatt reluctantly handed it over, not touching the skin of the man's soft, pudgy hand. The man quickly broke the phone into components, pocketing the battery and SIM card, then setting the stripped-down carcass on the seat beside him.

Shit.

"Mr. Cooper, I'd like to speak to you about…a mutual interest."

"I don't do business with strangers—or with kidnappers, for that matter."

The man leaned back. "This isn't business. This is blackmail."

"What?"

"I believe you heard me the first time," Buddha said. His benevolent smile sliced like a machete.

He tensed as the man reached into a leather briefcase he hadn't previously seen. Instead of a weapon, he withdrew a digital tablet protected by the same sleek black leather as his attaché. He flipped it open, flicked with his fingers, and spent the next several minutes reducing the last decade of Wyatt's extracurricular work history to bullet points, complete with the prison time he'd rack up for each gig should he be arrested, tried, and convicted.

All the way back to grad school.

Panic crashed over him, a giant wave pounding him down and holding him under. It would be utterly worthless for him to brazen it out, to say, "You have nothing on me," because the man obviously did.

"Several days ago, you came into illegal possession of a computer belonging to—" *flick, flick* "—Bailey Brown." Buddha shook his head pityingly. "Still not over our fascination with Dr. Brown, are we?" A wisp of amusement slipped into the limo's overly-warm air. "Quite understandable. She is a fascinating young woman."

"You know nothing about my relationship with Bailey," he snapped.

"Don't be so sure." The man's gaze went distant, and then sharpened again. "I know you launched a failed Denial of Service attack against Sebastiani Labs this morning. Mr. Cooper, please. We have no reason to believe you will ever succeed."

Wyatt let the slur against his abilities slide. Who was 'we'?

"So, here's how this is going to play out," Buddha continued. "I represent a consortium of people who also have an interest in Sebastiani Labs. Your social engineering skills are exceptionally strong, and have a certain targeted utility. You will use those skills to help us gain access to Sebastiani Labs. You have two weeks."

Whoever 'they' were, they'd tried and failed, too— otherwise they wouldn't need *him*. Sebastiani Labs was a high-value corporate espionage target, but...two weeks? The place was locked down tight. In the end, it might be easier to break into Fort Knox. "And if I decline?"

The man indicated the tablet. "I'll randomly choose one of your many crimes—" *flick, flick* "—and supply some information to the proper authorities." Buddha smiled benevolently. "Before you decline, you might want to consider how long your mother would be able to stay at that gorgeous assisted living facility in…where is it again?" *Flick, flick.* "Arizona? Without you footing the bill."

He wanted to smash the tablet over the guy's head.

"The first crime I report, of course, would be your role in the hack that led to Bailey Brown's felony conviction."

His breathing stopped.

"Given today's hypersensitive cyber-security climate, you'd never see daylight again." The casually lobbed threat lay between them like an unexploded grenade. "I'll contact you for a progress report in three days, Mr. Cooper."

The limo braked to a stop. When the door opened, he blinked against the sudden brightness. "Who are you?" he blurted.

"Mr. Cooper?" Frack said from the sidewalk. "Please exit the car."

"How do I contact you?"

"Mr. Cooper," Frack repeated with more muscle in his voice. He shifted his trench coat, revealing his holstered gun.

He stumbled out of the car and onto the curb. Frack got back into the limo, and Wyatt stared at its tail lights as they disappeared into the stream of traffic, until a honking horn and a splash of cold slush against his pants legs captured his attention. He was in Dinkytown, near the U of M. For all the driving they'd done, at least they hadn't left him at the ass end of nowhere. Hailing a cab, he collapsed into the back seat for the short ride home.

Trying to figure out what the hell to do next.

✳

"Do you get to do that all the time? Like, every day?" Antonia asked as they rode the elevator up to the penthouse.

Uh oh. Maybe that practice hack hadn't been a very good idea after all.

After Cheyenne had finished cleaning up after the failed DoS attempt, Bailey had opened up a video chat between Sebastiani Labs and The Bunker, and she and Cheyenne had spent some time with Antonia, explaining why their security architecture had withstood the particular attack vector Wyatt had used. Finally, to blow off some steam and to reinforce the lesson, they'd done a targeted hack, with Cheyenne on defense, protecting a cache of documents, and Antonia on offense, trying to access them. Though she'd planned on observing from the sidelines, she hadn't been able to resist jumping in, pushing Cheyenne to the limit. Finally, with some help from her, Antonia had penetrated, successfully stealing the documents and crashing Cheyenne's computer.

Good times.

Her wrist was throbbing, but the diabolical questions Antonia had asked during their debrief made Bailey think of an enhancement she should make to the security suite sooner rather than later. A quick meal, some ice for her wrist, and she'd be ready to work again.

When they reached the top floor, the elevator doors opened with a quiet ding. Straight ahead, on a long, narrow table, a Tiffany lamp spilled light on sorted stacks of mail, one for each of the penthouse's residents. The scent of oregano, garlic and onions made her stomach rumble.

"Dad's making lasagna," Antonia breathed.

The door to the girls' unit opened, and Sasha came out, wearing black yoga pants, a baggy dance studio sweatshirt, and slippers. "Hey, Dad and Claudette invited us to their place for dinner."

Slinging her heavy backpack under the table, Antonia veered to her father's door without another word.

Bailey hesitated. One glass of wine from Elliott's excellent cellar, and she might be too tired to log back on and finish her work.

"Come on."

"Okay." She followed Sasha, carrying her computer bag with her out of long habit. No way would she ever leave her computers unattended in the foyer, no matter how good the security was. Sometime before dinner was over, she'd swipe and hide Antonia's backpack. Let her sweat about its location for a couple of days.

Better she learn this lesson now rather than later.

Setting her bag inside the door and placing her dripping boots on a mat next to Antonia's, she looked around without trying to be too obvious about it. Though she'd worked with both Elliott and Claudette for over a year, she'd never been in their home before. Sasha had told her that Elliott's unit was a mirror image of hers, but any resemblance stopped with the layout. Where Sasha's sense of décor leaned toward Scandinavian modern, with bright colors and more than a dollop of kitsch and quirk, Elliott's home, with its rich colors and textures, communicated a relaxed sort of elegance. The money was obvious—in the thick carpets, the framed paintings, the no-doubt-priceless antiques and *objets d'art*—but the latest Stephen King paperback lay on the soft sectional couch that dominated the sunken living room, with a pair of funky red reading glasses folded atop. Even with her responsibilities as the Siren First and the President's bondmate, Claudette somehow managed to keep up on her recreational reading.

Sheer curtains were drawn over the floor-to-ceiling windows, but during the day, sunlight must pour into the room like lemonade. When was the last time she'd seen the sun? She lived like a mole rat.

Male voices murmured from the kitchen. "Rafe's here," Sasha said.

Of course he was. She took a fortifying breath, and then followed Sasha through the swinging doors that led to the kitchen. Antonia was in Rafe's arms, gleefully messing up his hair.

"You annoying little gnat." Rafe batted at her hands. "Stop it. I'll drop you right on your ass, don't think I won't." Antonia squealed in delight as he tipped her backwards, faux-staggering and seeming to lose his balance before righting them again.

She glanced at Elliott, busy by the oven. Sasha walked over to help Claudette gather plates and glasses. No one seemed at all concerned by the sibling roughhousing.

Rafe, despite his mussed hair, looked delicious in a pair of well-worn jeans that clung in all the right places, and a cream cable-knit fisherman's sweater that made his shoulders look a mile wide. He wore his clothes so elegantly, and his body was so perfectly proportioned, that he didn't give an impression of size—especially compared to Lukas and Jack. But he handled Antonia's leggy weight with ease, like she was as light as the gnat he'd called her. Watching his leg muscles tense and flex as he held his sister caused some essential internal muscles of her own to do the same.

Grabbing Antonia around both knees with one arm, Rafe let go with the other. Bailey gasped as Antonia fell backwards with a gleeful shriek, her body pivoting on Rafe's arm like a pendulum. Rafe took a few steps, swinging Antonia back and forth so her long, black hair swooshed against the spotless hardwood floor like a mop. "This floor could really use some cleaning."

"Eww, gross!" Antonia kicked her feet, narrowly avoiding Rafe's groin.

"Okay, enough." Elliott picked up hot pads, opened the oven, and pulled out a pan of garlic cheese bread.

"Hey, cheesy bread." Rafe lowered Antonia until she supported her own body weight, then unceremoniously dropped her, leaving her sprawled on the floor. He walked to the butcher block table, snatched two pieces of bread, and came over to her. "How's the wrist?"

She hid it behind her back.

"That good, huh?"

"It's been a long day, and yeah, it's a little sore."

Rafe frowned. "Maybe you should get some X-rays after all."

"No need."

He set the bread on the nearby counter, and gently pulled her hand out from behind her back. Cradling it between his, he gently poked and probed, checking the slightly swollen injury site, moving her fingers this way and that. Her breath caught as his fingertips stroked her sensitive inner wrist.

The fingers paused. "Hurt?"

"No." Her response was more breath than sound. *This* was why she'd put her hand behind her back. His touch made her melt like chocolate, made her blood flash to steam. Her bones were softening, not providing their usual support, and all he'd done was touch her hand.

What would happen when they were finally alone, when they had nothing but skin and sheets between them?

"Tomorrow night."

"What?" It was like he'd read her mind. When she glanced across the kitchen, she saw that Elliott, Claudette, Sasha and Antonia were busy setting the table, studiously ignoring them—not that they were missing a thing.

Rafe cleared his throat. "Can we work tomorrow night?"

Antonia snorted with laughter. "Is that what the kids are calling it these days?"

"Shut up," Rafe replied without looking at Antonia. No, he kept looking at her, and his pupils were so dilated that she could barely see his tawny irises.

Her stomach flopped like a fish in a landing net. When had 'work' become such a loaded word? "What did you have in mind?"

"Dinner out first, to see if Cooper tips his hand," Rafe said. Did he realize he was still holding her wrist? "Then, back to my place? To my studio, I mean?"

"To see his etchings," Antonia whispered loudly to her sister. Sasha elbowed her so hard she stumbled into Elliott, who almost dropped a water glass.

"Girls, that's enough," Claudette said, trying to hide a grin with little success.

Rafe tugged her out of the kitchen by her good hand, setting the doors swinging. He stopped next to the windows, as far away as he could get from the kitchen without going into a bedroom or bathroom. "Sorry."

"It's okay," she said with a smile. "I have a younger sister. Being a pest is just part of the job. She's—"

"Right. She's right."

Her stomach jumped. "So you don't want to work?"

Glancing at the kitchen, he stepped closer, until a mere hand width separated their bodies. "Yeah, I do. But after we finish working, I'd like to...play. For a very long time."

She let out a breath she wasn't aware she'd been holding. Finally. Finally, there would be an end to this endless, aching need. "Yes." He raised a questioning brow. "To everything—but I can't shake free until Friday night." She and Cheyenne had made plans to roll out a firewall and encryption layer enhancement over the next couple of nights. It was important work that she couldn't blow off, no matter how much she might want to.

She…really, really wanted to.

His slow, expectant smile curled her toes.

"Rafe? Bailey?" Claudette called from the kitchen. "Dinner's ready."

Taking a deep breath, Rafe stepped back. "Be right there," he called back. "Quick. Dinner plans. Have you ever been to Haute Dish?" His voice was a low rumble, stroking her without touching.

"How about Chadden's?" she countered. He scowled slightly, as if going to one of the best restaurants in the Twin Cities was a chore rather than a pleasure. "I think it makes sense for us to go to a restaurant we're both familiar with."

"Okay," he grudgingly agreed. "I'll pick you up here—"

"Better make that at work." She had a Friday afternoon meeting that had a distinct possibility of going long. Then she had to get ready for their date, and most of her clothes were at Sebastiani Security, downstairs in the locker room.

What the hell was she going to wear?

"I'll call for a table."

"A Friday night reservation, on such short notice? You'd better let me. Chadden might tell you he's booked until May just to yank your chain."

He nodded. "Please bring whatever you need to stay overnight." His slightly rough fingertip stroked along her cheekbone. "If you want to."

She inclined her chin, acknowledging his invitation but not committing one way or the other. She wanted to, all right, but she probably shouldn't get used to cozy overnights with Rafe Sebastiani. "Anything else I should bring? For *your* work, I mean?"

He winked. "Just your skin. Let's go eat."

CHAPTER SIX

It was barely 5:30 a.m., but Crackhouse Coffee was doing its usual brisk business. From his position near a parking lot pillar across the street, Wyatt had a clear view of the readers, the writers, the insomniacs, and the club-going hipsters who'd closed down Underbelly a couple of hours ago and simply moved the party next door rather than brave the elements. Now, the first day-shifters and corporate drones were arriving, anxious for the hit of caffeine that would power them through a long commute and an even longer workday.

Twin lights sliced through the darkness as a black SUV pulled to the curb half a block away. There she was, right on schedule.

Hitching his black canvas messenger bag onto his shoulder, he stepped off the curb, wincing as the icy wind slapped his cheeks. A car horn beeped at him as he jaywalked. Holding up an apologetic hand, he trotted across the street to the brightly lit oasis, just in time to hold the door for the trim werewolf female. He stepped into line behind her, studying her from the rear. She wore business-like dress pants and black boots, but her Pocahontas hair spilled luxuriously over her turquoise down coat. She carried a heavy leather computer bag and one of those weekender-sized purses on one shoulder, seemingly unaware of the weight.

The guy searching her SUV right now wouldn't find her computer in the car, but he hadn't expected to snag such a huge a prize this early in the game. No, Cheyenne Winterbourne, network architect and the woman he'd pegged as his most promising vector into Sebastiani Labs, was *way* too smart to make such a rookie security mistake—but on the other hand, he'd been following her for well over a day and she hadn't made him yet. He usually outsourced physical surveillance tasks, but not on this job. He couldn't trust this one to anyone but himself.

"Your regular, Chey?" asked the barista, a burly guy with flame tattoos licking at his wrists.

"Yes, please."

The barista turned to prepare Cheyenne's drink, a large, non-fat caramel macchiato. He'd watched her order the same thing yesterday, from the overstuffed chair in the corner.

"Excellent taste," he said.

She turned her head. "Sorry?"

Dusky skin, snapping dark brown eyes, slashing cheekbones. None of the pictures he'd seen came close to doing her justice. His appreciative smile was genuine. "I said, excellent taste."

"Hi, Wyatt," said the female barista who'd served him yesterday. "What can I get for you today?"

He pointed to Cheyenne's drink. "I'll have what she's having." As the woman flashed two fingers at the tattooed guy, Cheyenne Winterbourne looked him up and down, taking in his khaki pants, leather belt, pressed cotton oxford worn open at the neck with no tie, his slightly chunky shoes, and the faux employee badge hanging from his right pants pocket by a zip clip. Upwardly mobile technology worker, male division. She'd assess the entire package subliminally, in a split second. He'd left nothing to chance, right down to the touch of keyboard monkey slouch in his posture.

He gave her a friendly smile, interested yet not threatening. "I'm Wyatt."

She extended her hand. "Cheyenne."

She'd initiated a physical touch. It was a good start.

As they shook hands, he saw her give his computer bag a second look. It bore a discreet logo from The Wiretappers Ball, a surveillance technology conference he knew she'd attended last year. Between the ID badge and the bag, his pretext of working as an internet security professional should hold.

"I recently moved here. Work transfer." He'd learned over the years not to provide too many specific details to his targets—fewer things for him to forget, and people tended to mentally fill in the blanks anyway. He gestured to the plate-glass window, to where a man walked down the sidewalk backwards, his back to the snow-spiked wind. "Have you lived here long? Maybe you can tell me what people do for fun during the months people can't stand to go outside." Minnesotans loved talking about their irascible weather. The way she answered his question would tell him a lot about her thought patterns, and help him adjust his vocabulary for maximum effect.

"I've lived here all my life. You get used to it," she replied with a laugh, confirming what he already knew. She lived about ten blocks away, in a funky, upscale condo complex just off Hennepin Avenue that catered to single professionals. Every weekday morning, she stopped here to pick up a cup of coffee, which she drank during her long commute to Sebastiani Labs' corporate campus in Chanhassen.

"Have you checked out the St. Paul Winter Carnival yet?"

He shook his head no. He'd lived in the Twin Cities off and on throughout his adult life, but the annual winter festival celebrating all things ice and snow simply didn't appeal.

"Oh, it's a blast." Raising her voice to be heard over the hissing espresso machines, she told him about the ice sculpture contest that drew artists from all over the world, the medallion hunt with its $10,000 prize, about the legendary enmity between King Boreas and Vulcanus Rex. Her vocabulary crackled with texture and movement.

Probably a kinesthetic thinker.

They continued chatting until the tattooed guy called their names. As they picked up their drinks, she admired his scarf. "It looks so soft, and it's almost the same color as my coat."

More texture language. "Thanks. It *is* the same color, isn't it?" He'd noticed her striking coat yesterday, and had bought the scarf to match. Every little connection helped.

She took a half step closer to him, probably without realizing it. Within five short minutes, he'd blown through her subconscious protective barricades at top speed, but despite his tight timeline, he knew better than to get greedy. He wouldn't be surprised if one of the customers peering at an open laptop across the restaurant wasn't reporting his every move to the big man in the limo. He glanced out the window with a sigh. "Well, this weather isn't going away. I'd better get going."

"Tough commute today, with all the ice on the roads."

He inhaled subtly but deeply. Curiosity and sexual attraction, both were there, and the combination bubbled into him like a froth of champagne. He'd have to be careful about the curiosity; Cheyenne Winterbourne hadn't achieved her current position of responsibility because of her stunning good looks. Despite the attraction, her expression was neutral and pleasant. There wasn't a whiff of desperation about the prospect of never seeing him again. She had a great game face—and her nose had clearly been broken a time or two in the past, and never surgically repaired. Scrappy. He filed this away for future reference.

"Have far to drive?" she asked.

"No, not really."

Neither of them moved. Finally, with a slightly awkward laugh, he reached into his computer bag and withdrew a fake business card. "Here," he said. "In case you find yourself at loose ends some night, and in the mood to take pity on someone new to town."

She shot him a deadpan look and took the card. "Oh, I doubt you'll be lonely for long." She tucked the card into her computer bag without looking at it. After rooting around for a couple of seconds, she found a card of her own, but instead of handing it to him, she tucked it in his jacket's chest pocket. "See you around, Wyatt Cooper."

She walked to the door without a backwards glance.

He reached into his jacket pocket and withdrew her card, the card she'd touched his body to give him. Cheyenne Winterbourne, Network Architect, Sebastiani Labs. There was Sebastiani Labs' stylized globe logo, slightly raised and glinting with blue and gold. Underneath, in a smaller version of the same architectural font, were her corporate email address and three phone numbers: desk, work mobile and personal mobile.

He grinned like a kid opening presents on Christmas morning.

He had his 'in.'

✳

"I don't see our tail," Rafe said to Bailey as they followed the maitre d' past the busy bar and into Chadden's restaurant.

"You're not supposed to."

That didn't stop him from wondering which of the many sets of eyes currently watching them might belong to operatives from Sebastiani Security. He was used to drawing a certain amount of attention—his family was high-profile, and he wasn't stupid enough to deny that women found him attractive—but tonight, the attention felt creepy.

He'd felt creeped out ever since Bailey's apartment had been broken into, and damn it, it was justified. It wasn't normal to have one's car tagged by a GPS device, or have your home swept for surveillance devices. Chico's work had been professional and thorough, and he'd upgraded his security system on the spot. On the positive side, the subdivided building's shared walls had passed inspection, with no signs of infiltration.

Infiltration? Such a prospect had never entered his mind, but now that it had, it wouldn't leave. The stories that Chico had regaled him with during the long hours of work had him looking up to the corners and over his shoulder more often than he wanted to admit.

Sure, given his family's prominent position in their culture, he took reasonable precautions, but he'd opted out of Underworld Council matters a long time ago—and the one and only time he'd gotten involved in a Sebastiani Security operation had been the night of Scarlett's homecoming concert, a little over a year ago.

The night he'd taken advantage of Bailey.

"Relax. They've got us," Bailey said, reaching back for his hand as the maitre d' took them on a winding route through the packed restaurant.

Part of the act or not? He'd take it, either way. She'd reached back with her injured hand, and she didn't seem to be favoring it anymore. Clasping it carefully, his eyes couldn't help but stray to the subtle shift and sway of her slim hips under a pair of forest green wool dress pants. She was wearing heels tonight, a pair of stiletto boots that had been worthless in the snow, but did amazing things for her posture, tilting her hips forward—

"Here we are," the maitre d' said.

Bailey had made the reservation, and whether by choice or by chance, they were being seated at his favorite table—the cozy back table for two, close to the fireplace, and tucked away behind a partial wall of reeds, cat tails and pussy willows jutting upright from a base of brushed steel.

He held Bailey's chair as she sat.

"Thank you." When she crossed one leg over the other, her pants leg rose slightly, exposing the fetish-worthy arrangement of straps and buckles adorning her boot. Clearing his throat, he quickly sat down. There was no tablecloth, but the table itself would disguise his body's reaction better than his trim, flat-front dress pants would.

"Enjoy your evening," the maitre d' said, withdrawing with a tiny bow.

He hadn't had a chance to even open the wine list when a smiling waiter appeared at their table carrying two leather-backed menus tucked under his arm, two wine glasses in one hand, and a bottle in the other. "Bailey, so nice to see you tonight! And you too, Mr. Sebastiani," he said with a respectful nod. "Welcome."

The waiter held a bottle of the Sonoma Coast pinot noir Jack had told him was Bailey's favorite. Chadden obviously knew they'd arrived.

"Hi, Wade." Bailey grinned up at the waiter. "Have you gotten any email from your grandma lately?"

The waiter rolled his eyes good-naturedly as he set down the bottle and wine glasses, and handed each of them a menu. "Almost every day. Dozens of pictures of puppies and kittens. The emoticons! And the animated GIFs! Oh, the humanity."

As Wade withdrew the cork from the bottle with deft twists of his wrist, Bailey explained to him that Wade's grandma had recently bought her very first computer. "She's in that phase where she emails everyone everything she thinks is cute."

"Well, thank you for the laptop recommendation," Wade said. Not bothering with the tasting ritual, he poured her wine.

"Glad to help."

"Mr. Sebastiani, would you like a glass, or would you prefer to make another selection?"

"Share, by all means." He watched the waiter pour, feeling slightly out of sorts. No, he was feeling…downright emasculated. Romantic tête-à-têtes were his forte, but tonight? Almost every aspect of the evening, other than his choice of clothing, had been completely out of his control. Bailey had chosen the night and made the reservation, scoring the best table in the house. Here was her favorite wine, delivered to the table before he could order it for her, impressing her with his knowledge. It had taken some fast talking on his part to convince her that they should drive to the restaurant together rather than simply meet there. And now, instead of holding her hand, twining their fingers together, and murmuring over the appetizer selection, Bailey was talking to their waiter about his grandma, her eyes occasionally straying to the mini-comp lying on the table next to her salad fork.

She'd handed him an overnight bag when he'd picked her up at Sebastiani Security earlier, but whether she'd actually *stay* overnight after they finished working was still an open question.

"Rafe? Want to taste?"

He started at the sound of Bailey's voice. "Oh, sorry." He took a quick sip of the wine, narrowing his eyes as plums, oak, and berries stroked over his tongue. Dark and sensual, it went down like a velvet sunset. "Very good."

"Excellent." Wade turned back to Bailey. "Chef wants to know if you're willing to try an appetizer he's experimenting with."

"Sure."

Rafe scowled as the waiter departed. Chadden never offered *him* anything that wasn't on the menu. He studied her as she glanced at the phone again. Just how close were Bailey and the debauched vampire chef de cuisine? He knew Bailey had met Chadden for the first time the night of Scarlett's concert, when she'd been heavily under the influence of the incubus pheromones that had saturated Underbelly like chloroform. Sasha, recognizing her impairment, had come to her rescue, placing Bailey in *his* care.

And he'd had sex with her not fifteen minutes later—before he was certain the pills he'd dosed her with had actually taken effect.

Bailey looked up from her phone. "We picked up a tail when we left Sebastiani Security. Late-model black Accord, parking now. It's almost show time." She picked up her glass of wine, her knuckles white as she clutched the delicate stem. "If Wyatt is running true to form, he has a team working the physical side of the job, doing surveillance, tailing, break-ins and such. He usually doesn't take those risks himself. He doesn't have to. He's very skilled at evaluating people's motivations, at giving them what they want, so he gets what he wants."

A whiff of guilt again—there, then gone. What was she thinking about that put such a pensive look on her face? Exactly what had Wyatt Cooper given and taken from Bailey all those years ago? In all the years since?

"He usually pays his people with jacked passwords, stolen credit card numbers, or compromised Social Security numbers."

"How…"

"His technical skills aren't the strongest, but with the right contacts and tools, obtaining them is a fairly straightforward matter." She suddenly smiled. "Have you ever heard of DEF CON? The hacker conference?"

"Hackers have conferences?"

"Oh, yeah. Great fun. There are workshops, meet-ups, hook-ups, and you can see all the new toys." She leaned forward, her eyes sparkling with mischief. "You're under siege from the minute you enter the hotel. You'd better be carrying an RFID wallet, because every card you own is at risk. Room keys repeatedly lose their programming. Don't even think about using the lobby ATM, because someone's already compromised it. There's a lot of gamesmanship and one-upsmanship, with people looking to make their reputations, or win some bragging rights. You have to assume that everyone you interact with, no matter how nice, has ulterior motives. They can and will screw with you." Laughing, she leaned back against the chair again. "It's a mental workout like you can't believe."

He assessed her across the candlelit table. Even during their time together alone at the cabin, he hadn't heard her string so many words together without a break. Something seemed to spark inside her as she talked about her work.

"In a matter of minutes, someone installs a sniffer on the hotel's network. Next to the conference registration desk, hotel guests' email addresses, passwords, credit card numbers, and other personal information intercepted by the sniffer streams by on a huge monitor. The data is partially redacted before it's displayed, but—" she shrugged "—people very quickly get the point." She grinned suddenly. "The last time I went, a family values politician was busted ordering pay-per-view porn. Good times."

His thoughts raced. How many times had he used his computer at a hotel thinking his transactions were private?

"I couldn't go to the conference when I was on probation. I imagine I could now, but…"

"Your profile is a little too high."

She gave a tiny half-shrug of acknowledgment. "Yeah. I'd be targeted left and right. I find out what goes down every year, but—" a slightly wistful expression crossed her face "—I miss it."

She pulsed with an odd excitement, more intellectual than physical. A frightening thought struck. "You want him to come for you, don't you?"

"What?"

"No need to deny it." He tapped his nose. "You want to go head to head with Wyatt Cooper."

"What I want is to protect the Sebastiani and Underworld Council networks from malicious incursion. If he's stupid enough to try? And I take him down?" She shrugged as if she didn't have a care in the world, but she didn't quite pull it off. Her eyes blazed, and her chin jutted aggressively, like she was about to march into the ring and take on all comers. "Bonus round."

He took another sip of the wine, considering her. Antonia had told him that for all Bailey's technological acumen, she used technology very sparingly when she wasn't in full control of the transaction. She trusted the mini-comp lying on the table because she'd personally developed the security and encryption layer, but out in the world, she paid with cash, refusing to generate credit card transactions that could be used to track her purchases or movements. She thought paying bills online was for suckers. Before spending the day with Chico—hell, before hearing her talk about hacker conference hijinks—he might have thought she was paranoid, but he was coming to realize she assessed technical risk in ways that most people couldn't begin to conceive.

Bailey glanced at the phone again. "Where the hell is he?"

"You seem really excited about this." He wanted to take a bite out of her pugnacious little chin.

"I'm not excited, I'm anxious," she snapped. "I just want to end this, once and for all."

A hush suddenly descended in the room. The reason why walked toward them, wearing a black chef's jacket and a red bandana lashed around his head, greeting diners along the way yet not stopping. Chadden carried two plates. Apparently Chef was delivering his experiment personally.

"Hello, Tidbit." Placing the plates on the table, Chadden leaned over and kissed her on both cheeks. "I'm so glad to see you, regardless of the riff-raff you're with."

Rafe gave him a deadpan look. "Hello, Chadden."

"Sorry to interrupt."

No, he wasn't—not if the unholy glee on his friend's face was anything to go by.

Bailey brushed the vampire's blood red bandana with a teasing fingertip. "Is that sweat I see? Caught you actually working."

"Guilty as charged." Chadden playfully nibbled on her wrist. "What's my punishment?"

Rafe fought to stay in his chair. Chadden was a notorious flirt, a cheerful libertine, and completely without personal boundaries. Erasing the lines of propriety was one of his favorite hobbies, and…damn it, his teeth were *way* too close to Bailey's delicate veins. "That's enough," he said as mildly as he could manage.

"Not in the mood to share today?" Chadden said with a mocking smile. "Pity." With a theatrical sigh, he gave Bailey's wrist a smacking kiss and gestured to one of the plates. "You might find these useful."

Rafe looked at the beautifully prepared plate. Tiny oysters on the half-shell. The son of a bitch had brought them aphrodisiacs. His death glare bounced harmlessly off the vampire's back, because he was talking to Bailey again, not caring a whit whether his insult had hit its target. Bailey listened as Chadden described the basil-infused grapefruit gastrique he'd made for the oysters like a suitor reciting a love poem.

At the next table, a woman sighed. The man she was with shot Rafe a glance of frustrated communion.

Chadden lifted one of the pearly shells, but Bailey turned her head away, wrinkling her nose. "You know I don't like oysters."

How, exactly, had Chadden come by this knowledge? Had he plied Bailey with aphrodisiacs in the past, at his private table back in the kitchen? Had Bailey shared her body—her blood—with him?

He sat up straighter in his chair, felt his chest expand.

"See if you like these, darling. It's a tiny one. Just a bite."

With a wince, Bailey slowly opened her mouth. Chadden placed the rim of the shell on her lower lip, tipping the oyster in her mouth. She didn't chew, just held it in her mouth. Finally, with a violent full-body shudder, she gulped it down. "Eww. Sorry." She shuddered again, reaching for her wine glass.

"Such a Philistine," Chadden said with a shake of his head. "Here, try some walleye cheeks instead." Quickly swapping plates, he placed the oysters in front of Rafe with a knowing grin. "Enjoy."

Heat crawled up his neck. One night, during a boozy pub crawl, he and Chadden had agreed that eating oysters was the closest thing they knew to tasting a woman's most intimate flesh. "Thank you." Taking one of the shells between two fingers, he tipped it into his mouth. A blast of citrus bathed his taste buds then quickly receded, letting the brine of the oyster take center stage.

Bailey stared at his mouth. Her pupils dilated, fathomless pools of green-rimmed black.

Chadden straightened reluctantly. "Well, this has been amusing, but I have to get back to the kitchen."

"Sorry about the oysters, Chadden." Bailey shrugged apologetically.

"I'll find a preparation you like. Someday."

Not if he had anything to say about it. "Thank you, Chadden. Goodbye, Chadden."

"Never mind my hurt feelings," Chadden said with elaborate, injured politeness. "Really. I'll be fine."

Kissing Bailey on both cheeks again, and once on the tip of her nose for good measure, he finally left.

They sat there for several humming seconds. Bailey cleared her throat, picked up a fork, and speared one of the succulent pieces of fish. When her phone vibrated, the fork clanked back onto the plate. Picking up the device, she read. "He's here."

He forced himself not to look for the other man. "Where?"

"He just sat down at the bar." Though her expression didn't change, the needle on her emotional barometer took a wild swing as she sent a quick text back. The response came back almost immediately. "Winnie said he's got a sightline." She looked at him. "Showtime."

He reached for her hand, twining their fingers together. She'd painted her nails a pale mermaid green. "It's not a show. Every touch, every stroke, every look. Whether he's here or not, I want to eat you alive."

Her sea-witch eyes locked onto his. "Same goes. So let's get this show on the road."

Wade appeared back at tableside as if by magic. They ordered their entrees. His food, when it appeared, could just as well have been sawdust for all he tasted it; he was too busy watching Bailey enjoy hers. He fed her bites of Lake Superior Trout from his plate, and she offered him lobster on the fork her butter-slick lips had touched. He completely forgot about Wyatt Cooper, and if the other man entered Bailey's mind at all during their meal, he couldn't sense it.

He could sense nothing but her dark, humid need.

Wade removed their plates and offered them the decadent dessert menu. "Crème Brulee? Chocolate Raspberry Bombe?"

"None for me, thanks," he said. "Bailey?" If she wanted dessert or a cappuccino, he'd find the self-control to sit through more torturous edible foreplay. Somehow.

"No thanks. Just the bill, please."

Wade smiled and shook his head. "Compliments of the chef. May I call the valet for you?"

"No, thanks. I'll take care of it." A short delay in the restaurant's foyer while they waited for the Jeep to be driven to the door would give him a chance to get his hands on her—and for Wyatt Cooper to observe it personally. After Wade left, he slipped a hundred dollar bill under the empty wine bottle, and walked with Bailey to coat check.

"Don't look into the bar," Bailey reminded him after he handed the Jeep's claim ticket to the valet. They walked to coat check, and he helped her into her long wool jacket. "Remember, we're completely oblivious to him."

Not really. Something he couldn't ignore tugged at the edge of his consciousness. After slipping on his own coat, he escorted her to the entrance. Not caring whether Wyatt Cooper had a sightline or not, he lowered his head and kissed her, softly, so softly…a prelude to the evening to come.

Her eyes drifted closed as she sank into the kiss. "Your place," she whispered against his lips. "Let's go."

As he whisked her out the door, he chanced a look back. Wyatt Cooper sat on a barstool, chatting up a woman with his back to the door, but their eyes met in the mirror hanging the length of the busy bar.

A jolt of recognition speared through him.

Wyatt Cooper was an incubus.

CHAPTER SEVEN

"An incubus," Bailey muttered. The Jeep was dimly lit, but not so dark she didn't notice how often Rafe glanced at her—probably to see how she was reacting to the bomb he'd dropped as soon as they'd closed the car doors at Chadden's.

Wyatt, an incubus? It explained so much.

As he drove, Rafe took slow, deep breaths, probably trying to read her. His elegant nostrils didn't dare flare, but she could see his chest expand and contract, even under the heavy layers he wore. Not long after Lukas had received the Council's permission to share the secret of their people's existence with her, he'd also started teaching her how to identify potential members of their species through observation.

She choked back a bark of wild laughter. *Better late than never.*

"Are you okay?" Rafe reached for the visor, pressing a button on the automatic garage door opener clipped to its underside. A block ahead and to the left, a garage door slowly rose on a beige brick building.

"Yeah." She'd known Rafe lived on the West Bank—she'd Googled his address long ago—

but…Chico was right. Once you turned off Cedar, drove away from the bohemian pubs, cafes, art galleries and clubs, the neighborhood turned a wee bit sketchy. Chico had mentioned that upgrading the security in Rafe's tall, thin slice of the subdivided building had been a fairly straightforward matter because of its layout: private garage on the first level, studio space on the second, and living area on the third and fourth.

He could afford to live anywhere—could rent, buy, or build studio space to meet his needs—yet he lived and worked here, in this diverse neighborhood that had more than a nodding acquaintance with poverty. There was more to Rafe Sebastiani than met the eye, not that what met the eye wasn't pretty damn fine. How was she going to keep from jumping him the minute the door closed?

"Really?" he asked.

"Yeah, I'm okay." And she really was. Oddly, learning Wyatt was an incubus had somehow lifted a huge weight from her shoulders, leaving her feeling light enough to levitate off the Jeep's heated leather seat. She'd spent years beating herself up for her weakness, for not being able to resist Wyatt's sexual pull. For mistaking sexual attraction for love.

Pheromones.

But this time would be different. This time, she'd be fully in control. She just had to get away from Rafe long enough to slip one of Jack's pills under her tongue.

Rafe pulled the Jeep into the narrow, triple-deep garage. "Wait a sec." In a move that had Lukas's training all over it, he watched the garage door close in the rear view mirror, waiting until it hit the cement with a soft ka-thunk before unlocking the doors and getting out. Reaching into the back seat, he grabbed her overnight bag. "Ready?"

"Yes." For anything. Everything. Snagging her purse by the strap, she slid off the passenger seat. If it turned out she had just this one night with him, she was going to make it count.

Rather than take the stairway, Rafe ushered her toward an industrial elevator whose doors he opened and closed by hand. Once inside, he pressed the button for the third floor.

So, they weren't going to the studio. "Aren't we working tonight?"

"Yes, but it's too chilly in the studio for the kind of work I want to do tonight. If I'd been thinking, I would have turned up the heat before I left. Do you mind if we do this upstairs?"

"No, but you have to give me a tour of your studio sometime."

"Will do."

Neither of them spoke as the elevator slowly and clankily ascended, her tension rising along with it. Rafe looked straight ahead, his clenched jaw sending his cheekbones into relief. His knuckles tightened on the handle of her overnight bag. His delicious scent darkened, intensified, swirling around them.

She leaned toward him, shivering as her cheek brushed against his hair. *So soft.* Before the night was over, she'd comb it with her fingers, tug it with her fists—Shit. She had to get to those pills in her purse, pronto.

The elevator stopped moving. "Still okay?" he asked.

"Yeah." An embarrassed laugh escaped. "Just a little nervous. I've never been an artist's model before."

"Nothing to it." He shot her a cheeky wink as he opened the doors and escorted her from the elevator, helping her off with her coat and hanging it up in the entryway's closet. "You can put your boots there." He pointed to a tray lying on the closet floor as he took off his own coat. "Need anything before we start? Something to eat? How about a drink?"

Nope, she just wanted to get the work part of the evening done so they could play. Resting a hand on his arm for balance, she lifted her pant leg and unzipped one calf-high boot, and then the other. The sound of the zipper teeth separating seemed unnaturally loud, and went on forever. "Nothing, thanks." Just a moment of privacy so she could take that pill. "Where will we work?"

"Upstairs. In my bedroom." He cleared his throat as he kicked off his own shoes. "There's not enough room for the pose I want down here on the couch. Is that okay with you?"

"Sure," she said. "Let's go." She couldn't wait to see his bedroom.

They padded up the stairs in their stocking feet. Rafe flipped a light switch when they reached the fourth floor, and she stutter-stepped in surprise. She'd half-expected his bedroom to look like a sultan's harem or an opium den, but instead, it was bare and sparsely furnished, with an almost monk-like asceticism—until you took a closer look. His bed was a simple king-sized platform with no headboard, but covered in an exquisite quilt, a work of art that exploded with all the subtle shades of the desert. Next to the bed stood a metal lamp, its base and stalk comprised of too many twining bodies to count. Across the room from the bed was a full wall of floor-to-ceiling mirrored panel doors that must hide closets, shelves and storage. No pile of clothes, not a single stray sock, marred the perfection of the glossy wood floor.

"Finally, a flaw."

"What?"

"You're one of those neat freaks."

"No, I'm not." He grinned. "Believe me, those sliding closet doors hide a multitude of sins."

And she'd open them and snoop the first chance she got. "So, how does this work?" She fingered the collar of her sweater. "Do I just take my clothes off? Lay down on the bed?"

"No, of course not. Follow me."

They walked to a darkened doorway she hadn't noticed before. Rafe reached inside and flicked the lights on, illuminating a gorgeous bathroom that made her think of shifting desert sands. "I need to run downstairs for a minute," he said, setting the overnight bag on the slab of granite supporting a beautiful vessel sink, unmistakably his own work. "Put your clothes anywhere you want. There's a bathrobe on the hook on the back of the door." After a slight hesitation, he rested his hands on her shoulders. For some reason, his touch steadied her, settled her nerves. "Take your time." Lifting a hand, he caressed the hair at her temple. "We have all night."

Her lower abdomen clutched at his words, but before she could touch him back, he turned and left.

She huffed a nervous breath. *All righty then.*

She took Rafe at his word that she could put her clothes anywhere she wanted. Returning to his bedroom, she slid back one of the sliding mirrored closet doors. Dozens of pairs of pants hung on clamp hangers, arranged by color gradation from lightest khaki to darkest black. Two beautiful suits hung at the end of the row, next to what was clearly a woman's bathrobe—heavy purple satin with a shawl collar, fit for a queen, and no doubt left by a former lover. She found an empty hanger, slipped off her own pants, and hung them next to a pair of faded-out cargo pants that looked like Army surplus. Behind the next closet door was a collection of shirts that would make a male model gasp. When she opened a third, she grinned. Instead of the retail precision she'd expected, his sweaters were a jumbled mess. Habit, or nerves? Either brought a sense of relief. She picked up the cable fisherman's knit sweater he'd worn a couple of days ago and lifted it to her face. Her eyelids drifted closed at the spicy scent, at the drugging, musky essence that swept every intelligent thought away.

The pills.

She put his sweater back where she'd found it and stripped off her own, leaving her standing there in her panties, bra and fuzzy knee-high socks. Shooting a quick glance at the stairway, she scurried back to the bathroom. If the bedroom had surprised her with its asceticism, this room met her every preconceived notion and then some. There wasn't a bathtub because the walk-in shower with its multiple shower heads and seating for two took up almost half of the room. The plush, oversized towels hung on heated rods, and the sand-colored tile floor was Caribbean-warm under her feet. Her toes wriggled in pleasure.

"Bailey? You doing okay in there?"

Damn, she hadn't heard him come up the stairs. "Yeah, give me another second."

A pause. "I'm going to change. Take your time."

"Okay," she sang out. Reaching into her purse, she pawed around until she found her brightly colored "C'mon Get Happy" pillbox. She flipped it open with her thumbnail, plucked a half-tablet out of the box, and slipped it under her tongue. As the bitter pill dissolved, she could hear clothes rustle in the other room. Rafe was changing, and she did the same, slipping out of the periwinkle bra and panty set she'd so carefully chosen. She caught a glance of her naked body in the huge mirror and sighed. The panties' elastic waistband had carved visible creases into her skin at the hips.

Well, it wasn't anything he hadn't seen before. As a sketcher of naked women, and as a lover with a reputation, the visible indignities that corsets, pantyhose, underwire bras and Spanx left on a woman's body were certainly no secret to him.

Picking up her mini, she took one final look at her messages. According to Winnie, she and Rafe hadn't been followed home. Wyatt had left Chadden's a couple of minutes ago, and the surveillance team had managed to tag his car while he was inside. Turning the mini to vibrate mode, she threw it in her purse.

No more tech tonight. Tonight was for her.

For them.

She slipped into Rafe's navy terrycloth bathrobe, tying it at the waist and rolling up the sleeves as she left the bathroom. It smelled like him, too—the hint of desert spice, the delicious, drugging musk—but she could tell that the pill was already working. She still felt knee-knocking need, but with the meds on board, her thoughts were so clear she could practically feel her synapses snap. Reaching back to turn off the light, she walked into the bedroom. She might even manage to let Rafe work for a while without jumping his bones.

Or maybe not. Rafe had changed, all right, into faded jeans and a plain white T-shirt that was almost translucent from countless washings. His arm muscles bunched and flexed as he twisted his hair into a sloppy knob at the back of his head, securing it with an elastic band.

Her mouth went dry. Holy Mother, how many men were secure enough in their masculinity to wear their hair in a freaking bun? She wanted to tug on it, mess it up, feel his hair spill over her skin.

"What?" he asked, glancing at her over his shoulder as he pulled back the quilt, exposing showy white sheets.

"Nothing," she croaked. A tray sat on the bedside table, holding a bottle of red wine, a corkscrew, a carafe of water, a couple of tumblers, and a sleeve of Girl Scout cookies—Trefoils, if she wasn't mistaken. She swallowed back a nervous giggle as she approached the bed. "Um, so how does this work?"

He fussed with the pillows, making a cozy-looking nest. "I'd like to sketch you reclining against these pillows, if you don't mind."

"Nope." The bulge straining the button fly of his ancient jeans sent her confidence flying. Opening the robe, she let gravity take it to the floor. "Where do you want me?"

Rafe's eyes widened slightly as he gazed at the skin she'd just exposed. "Right up here is fine," he said, clearing his throat as he gestured to the pile of pillows. "Go ahead and get comfortable." As she climbed onto the bed, she saw him mouth a curse.

She barely bit back her grin.

As he poured a tumbler of water from the carafe and drank, she tried to find the body position that would provide maximum pillow coverage. If she casually hugged one of the bigger pillows, it would cover her…no. She took a deep breath. No. If she was going to sleep with the man, she could scrape up the courage to pose for him first.

What would he see with his artist's eye? Other than elastic marks on her hips?

The mattress dipped as he knelt on the bed. "Do you mind if I shift you a little?" The expression in his eyes reminded her of a tawny jungle cat—a hungry one. "There's a particular body line I'd like to work on tonight…"

"Sure," she squeaked.

He started moving the pillows around, disturbing her nest. "What I'd like you to do is lie on your back, with your upper torso supported by the pillows."

She eyed the pillow pile. "Where does my head go?"

"On this side. Tipped back, here."

The slightly arched position would jut her breasts to the sky. Embarrassment flashed, but quickly receded. Rafe had never given her any reason to think he found her meager breasts inadequate. In fact, the position he'd requested suggested he found them visually interesting indeed. "Okay." She moved onto the pillows, and lay back. Though his touch was nothing but professional as he helped her move into position, her nipples pebbled, and gooseflesh sheeted her skin.

"Cold?" He made a minute adjustment to the angle of her chin.

He was kidding, right? "No. How long do I need to stay like this?" *How long until I can jump you?*

His nostrils flared slightly. "Ten minutes?"

Could she last that long? The pose was…diabolical. She was stretched on a rack of soft, down feathers, displayed for his pleasure. She wanted to writhe, to shift against the sheets, to get some relief from the achy desire coalescing between her thighs.

"Doing okay?" There was the slightest wisp of amusement in his voice.

He knew exactly what he was doing to her, damn it. Well, two could play the tortuous foreplay game. "I'm fine," she said, shifting her shoulders slightly on the pillows to draw his attention to her breasts again. She flicked a pointed glance at his groin. "How about you?"

Swearing under his breath again, Rafe reached for his sketchpad and charcoals. "This shouldn't take long."

But it did—longer than she wanted it to, anyway. He sat cross-legged on the edge of the bed, in her line of sight, but tantalizingly out of reach. As the minutes passed, as the charcoal scratched and stroked against the paper, he looked at her over and over again, but there was a distance in his eyes, as if he looked both *at* her and *through* her to some internal vision that only he could see.

He certainly had no difficulty focusing on his sketching with an erection that, if anything, had grown larger rather than subsided. Occupational hazard? Maybe, maybe not. All she knew was that she was having a devil of a time fulfilling her sole responsibility: lying perfectly still. It was all she could do not to squirm, to writhe, as the charcoal whispered against the paper, as the air stroked her skin with a touch so light it tortured rather than soothed.

"What's that cute little pout for?" he murmured, smudging a shadow onto the paper with the pad of his thumb. From this angle, his cheekbones looked as sharp as skate blades.

"I'm not pouting." *Much.*

"If you could only see the expressions chasing across your face." After one final glance, Rafe gave a satisfied sigh and closed his sketchpad with a snap. Uncrossing his long legs, he leaned over. She heard him set the pad on the bedside table and toss the stubby stick of charcoal on top. A delicate glissando echoed in the room as a glass was filled with liquid. As she stretched her arms overhead, she couldn't quite find the muscular will to turn her head to see whether he was pouring water or wine.

Work was over. It was time to play.

The bed shifted with his weight, and he was back at her side. "Good, you're stretching," he said. "Let me get rid of these." With a series of one-handed tugs, he pulled all the pillows out from behind her back, tossing two up to where the head of the bed met the wall.

She shrugged and rolled her shoulders to loosen her tight back muscles. What a relief to lay flat again! Modeling—holding a single position, whether nude or not—was a lot tougher than she ever imagined. When she rolled her own neck as she'd seen Rafe do, there was an audible snap.

Rafe winced. "Sorry. Here." He handed her a glass—he'd poured the water—and gestured for her to drink. "That took longer than I anticipated."

Propping herself up on an elbow, she took several sips of the cool water. "Thanks." After handing the chunky glass back to him, she lay back down, settling back against his sinfully soft sheets.

Mr. Smooth looked a little startled. Come on, had he really expected her to reach for the bathrobe, lying in puddle on the floor? To hide under the covers? Her stomach twisted, and her pulse kicked up a notch. Should she? Was she being...too slutty?

"Bailey? Look at me." Rafe stretched out on his left side beside her, propping his head on his hand and cupping her cheek with the other. "This doesn't go any farther unless you want it to."

His words were soft and even, but his tawny eyes were hot, molten. His posture was ultra-casual, but his muscles were tense. His nipples were tiny, hard pebbles under the threadbare T-shirt. If anything, the bulge behind his fly was bigger now than it had been when he'd been sketching her.

He wanted her.

She released the breath she wasn't aware she'd been holding, the tension hissing out like the air in a balloon. She wasn't being too slutty; he was simply making sure she wanted this.

How could he possibly misinterpret her outrageous need?

"Bailey?"

Her fingers itched to cup the hard treasure hidden by those ancient jeans, but right now she wanted his hands on her bare skin even more. Taking his hand in hers, she raised it, pressing it between her breasts. His breath hitched as they touched, sending her confidence soaring. "You're so warm," she whispered. Singling out his charcoal-stained thumb, she drew it the length of her sternum, transferring a dusty smudge to her skin.

Rafe tried to pull away. "Shit, I should have washed my hands…"

"No." She took his hand on a meandering journey, dragging it over her collarbones, up her neck, under her chin, up to her lips. His greedy gaze mapped every inch of the route.

Opening her mouth, she captured his thumb and bit.

The mattress shifted as he rolled, levering his upper body over hers. His tawny gaze bored into hers, hot and needy. When she wrapped her tongue around his finger, Rafe exhaled sharply, his abs bunching and clenching against her stomach. She tasted charcoal dust, hot skin, and the slightest hint of herb-infused hand soap.

Her legs shifted restlessly against the soft sheets. She was frantic to feel his hard hands, his lips and mouth, his heavy, long-limbed frame pinning her to the bed. But first…

She reached behind his head, found the elastic band holding his hair back, and tugged. The soft, blond waves spilled down, brushing gently over her breasts. "Ah, God," she gritted out. Reality felt better than any fevered fantasy.

She threaded her fingers into his hair at the temples, looking up at his lush lips and clenched jaw, the rampant masculine beauty of his face shadowed by sheaves of wheat-toned hair. The juxtaposition of hard and soft made her core give a voracious, greedy clench. "Kiss me, Rafe. Please."

His lips crashed down on hers with absolutely no finesse, his tongue pushing for immediate, desperate entry. She couldn't open her mouth quickly or widely enough. His hands clamped onto each side of her head, holding it in place, but her hands were free to move. She frantically clutched at his shoulders, his back, his hips. She needed the delicious weight of his body on top of hers, needed to feel that outrageous ridge of flesh cradled between her legs.

Groaning into her mouth, he complied, swallowing her moan of pleasure as their hips aligned, locking together like two puzzle pieces. She twined her legs around him, and his hips gave a single, languid roll.

"Sorry," Rafe said against her lips.

"For what?"

"I'm too heavy."

When he tried to shift his weight, she simply clutched tighter. "Don't move. You're perfect."

The T-shirt caressing her breasts was soft as a cloud, and the drag of denim against her inner thighs felt deliciously naughty, but she wanted to feel his skin. She grabbed two fistfuls of T-shirt and tugged upward, exposing his lower back. Snaking her hands back down, she burrowed them under the sagging waistband of his jeans.

Nothing but skin.

Rafe groaned aloud, pushed up on his arms, and levered himself to an upright position straddling her hips. Gazing up at him, she tried to freeze-frame what he looked like at this precise moment: eyes glittering with need, his chest heaving, his long hair messy and tumbled from her hands. His unruly erection strained against the button fly of his jeans.

He dragged his T-shirt up and off, yanking it over his head and tossing it away. His chest was…Holy Mother, his chest was sheer perfection. Tawny skin stretched over defined muscles and heavy bones. His pecs were lightly dusted with silky blond hair several shades darker than the hair on his head, and his nipples looked like caramel kisses. South of his cobbled abdomen and belly button, a slightly darker trail of hair disappeared into his waistband. Reaching out, she followed the trail with her thumb.

He covered her hands with his own. "Keep doing that and this will be over before it starts," he said disgustedly.

The thought that Rafe Sebastiani, hedonistic sex demon, might lose control at her touch sent a shockwave rocketing through her.

"Look at you. Here in my bed, where I've wanted you forever," he murmured, taking his long fingers off his own body and finally putting them on hers. He stroked her hipbones with his thumbs, smiling when she sucked her stomach concave at his touch. "So delicate." He inhaled as he stroked her blond pubic hair. Her breath locked in her lungs, but he didn't linger, instead taking a teasing, meandering route upward, stroking the pale scar where her appendix had been removed when she was a teenager, and dipping his pinky into her belly button.

If she was a hair trigger away from orgasm because he touched her surgery scar, what would happen when he finally touched—

"There's that pout again," he teased. "What do you want?" His eyes bore into hers, dark with heat.

He knew exactly what she wanted, but there was nothing stopping her from taking it on her own. Grasping his wrists, she pressed his palms to her breasts. Her helpless gasp at the electric contact combined with his groan. Time dragged by in milliseconds as he mapped her scant curves.

"You're so sensitive," he whispered next to her stiff nipple, his voice sending diabolical vibrations through the violently aroused flesh. He touched the tip of his tongue to her nipple, tasting her, teasing her, before latching on, finally giving her the rougher touch she craved.

Now it was her turn to hold *his* head in place, to not let him move. He seemed to know just how to touch her, alternating tender laps of his tongue with tugs that held more than a hint of teeth.

"Rafe..." She tugged at his fly, and the buttons slipped their moorings without a fight, spilling the thick length of his cock into her hands. His body jerked, and his grunt of reaction around her nipple thrilled all the way to her greedy, empty core. She delved one hand into his gaping fly. She'd just reached his silky balls when her wrist gave a warning twinge.

She needed more room. "Take these off," she ordered.

She felt him smile around her nipple. "Your wish is my command, babe."

Babe. He'd called her that once before, up at the cabin. Maybe he called all his lovers "babe" because it was easier that way, but she sure liked the sound of it slipping from his tongue.

She liked it too much. And he wasn't taking off his pants.

Pushing at his shoulders, she sat up and started working on the jeans herself. He surrendered her nipple and lay back on the bed, eyes glowing as he watched her tug and pull. Helpfully shifting and lifting his hips, she finally yanked the ancient denim over his knees and narrow, elegant feet. Finally, he was completely nude, sprawled for her gaze. If he felt the least whit embarrassed that she was devouring him with her eyes, he didn't show it. No, if anything, his beautiful penis, already outrageously hard, grew longer, harder, and prouder.

He was fantasy personified, and she was…holy shitkittens, she was wildly out of her league. What had ever made her think she could satisfy him?

"Hey." He grasped her around her hips, lifting her up and setting her down on his stomach. "You okay?"

Though his cock nudged impatiently against her backside, his hands were gentle, and the care in his gaze made her eyes sting. Gulping, she opened her mouth and closed it again without saying a word.

"Come here." Wrapping his arms around her, he drew her down until their chests met, until they were skin to skin. He stroked his hands down her back, gentling her for endless moments, making no demands whatsoever. Until she felt really, really foolish.

Okay. I want this. I can do this.

When she shifted her hips against his, an understated but unmistakable roll, his hand stilled.

"I'm sorry," she murmured against his chest.

"For what?"

"Being such a spaz." She nuzzled his chest hair with her lips until she found his nipple. "I'm thinking too much."

He smiled gently.

"I really want this, Rafe."

"Then take it. Take what you want, what you need…however you want it or need it." He lay there patiently, his expression accepting and relaxed, but behind her, his penis pulsed, seeking and stiff. And she wanted it—wanted him, desperately.

Rafe suddenly cursed. "Hold that thought." Hanging on to her with a heavy arm slung around her waist, he reached over to the bedside table, opened a drawer, and withdrew a strip of condoms.

Thank God, at least one of them was thinking about practicalities. She'd been taking oral contraceptives for a long time, more to regulate her cycle than anything else, but if they started exchanging sexual histories right now, they'd be here all damn night without even getting to hers.

The condoms were here. The discussion could wait.

"Let me." She tore one of the Magnums from the strip, ripped open the packet, and rolled it onto his penis.

She nearly snickered. He was definitely bigger than Wyatt.

The snicker turned to a moan as his long, callused fingers trailed up her tender inner thighs, delving into her soft, scalding heat.

"You are so wet," he murmured as he explored her drenched folds. His finger circled around the entrance to her body, teasing ever so softly, pressing but not entering.

A wave of sexual hunger slammed into her, stronger than she'd ever known. Lifting herself up on her knees again, she scooted back slightly, positioning herself over the erect rod of flesh. Wrapping her hand around the base of his shaft, she locked eyes with him and lowered herself.

Rafe hissed as the broad head pressed in, stretching her wide. He clenched his teeth, letting her control the pace. "Ah, God," she gritted out. The pleasure was going to split her in half.

Nostrils flaring wide, he grabbed her hips, stopping her downward slide. "Too much?"

"Not enough."

Relief, and a whisper of a grin, washed over his face as she slowly lowered herself onto him, enveloping his flesh with a long, languid glide. Rafe growled when she rested her full weight on his hips, with him fully seated in the intimate clasp of her body. She stared down where their bodies were joined, to where their pubic hair tangled together. When she reached down to touch, Rafe's hand was already there. Before long, his fingers stroked upward, to where her tender folds joined in a tiny kernel of flesh.

"Ride me," he said starkly.

Resting her hands on his chest, with his hands on her hips, she did as he asked, rising and falling, up and down, slowly, then gaining speed, until they both leaped into oblivion.

CHAPTER EIGHT

Bailey pulled into the Sebastiani Building's underground parking ramp as the sun rose over the horizon. Loaded down like a pack mule with her computer bag on one shoulder and her overnight bag and purse on the other, she strode to the lobby, approaching the last elevator in the row as quickly as her high-heeled boots and wobbly knees would allow.

She looked at the wall blankly. No call button. Where was the... "Crap." Setting down her bags, she pawed in her purse for the matte black key card granting her access to both the penthouse elevator and Sasha and Antonia's top floor apartment. Finding it, she waved it over the security pad, and after several seconds' delay, the doors opened. Nudging the overnight bag onto the elevator with her foot, she heaved her computer bag with both hands, transferred it into the lift, and immediately set it down again.

Her wrist stung like a bitch.

She averted her eyes as the elevator began its upward climb, refusing to look at herself in the elevator's mirrored walls. She'd seen quite enough in Rafe's floor-to-ceiling bathroom mirror not a half hour ago. Her damp hair was slicked flat against her head, her lips were puffy, and one side of her neck was scraped raw by Rafe's morning beard. One of her earlobes was very slightly red from where he'd suckled on it in the night. According to Rafe's heated murmur, she had adorable earlobes. "Like an elf."

Who knew?

She gave her sweater's neckline a useless upward tug. With any luck, Sasha and Antonia were still asleep, because there was no way in hell her succubus roommates would miss the fact that she'd just gotten well and truly laid. The sexual satiation had to be rolling off her in waves.

Rafe had insisted he'd be a poor host indeed if he didn't give her a personal tour of the shower before she left.

Her face heated as she remembered him, sauntering into the bathroom, tousle-haired, sleepy-eyed and wearing nothing but skin, sporting a boyish grin, a night's growth of beard, and an erection that wouldn't quit.

In the end, it had been the grin that made her intention to quickly bathe and then leave evaporate like hot steam. She could have steeled herself against a studied seduction attempt, but lazy anticipation? Boyish delight? His unconscious sigh of pleasure as he'd joined her under the water cascading from the showerheads, content to simply hold her, to savor the touch of the hot liquid sluicing over their skin? She'd stared as ropes of his wet hair sent rivulets trickling down his long, lean form. Finally, his artist's hands had slicked abstract patterns over her wet body as if she was a live canvas before lifting her easily in his arms, supporting her weight against the tile wall as he flexed his hips into hers, again and again…

No, she had not been able to resist.

And now she was going to be late for breakfast with Jack. She plucked her mini out of her purse, noting the time. After scanning for messages— nothing from Jack saying *he* was running late, of course—she sent him a text saying she'd be slightly delayed. Maybe sometime between now and then, her blissed-out expression would fade slightly. No way would Jack miss it; he was simply too observant.

Out of long habit, she quickly checked the status messages thrown by the Sebastiani Labs and Sebastiani Security networks overnight. Nothing out of the ordinary. Maybe they had the woman Wyatt had been chatting up at Chadden's bar last night to thank for the lack of malicious activity.

The elevator slowly drew to a stop, and the chime announcing her arrival at the penthouse level sounded unnaturally loud. Bending, she picked up her bags. When the elevator doors opened, there stood Rafe's father, his own leather computer bag hanging on his shoulder, eyes glued to his mini.

Shit.

"Bailey," Elliott said with a wide smile. "Good morning." As she stumbled off the elevator into the penthouse foyer, he took her heavy computer bag. "Long night?" he asked, kissing her on both cheeks in his courtly way.

"Um, yeah," she mumbled. *Thanks to your son.*

The elevator doors closed—without Elliott on board. He was setting her bags next to Sasha's door.

Damn.

And she'd worried about facing Sasha and Antonia? Elliott Sebastiani, inventor, CEO of Sebastiani Labs, and President of the Underworld

Council, had scythe-sharp perceptive skills. No way he'd miss his son's scent on her body. She, a mere human, could smell it herself.

Yep, there it was, the most subtle flare of Elliott's patrician nostrils as he studied her, assessing and absorbing her emotional energy. It was all she could do not to raise her hands to her burning cheeks. She could practically see him sorting her snarled feelings into mental buckets—embarrassment, confusion, exhaustion, satisfaction—and at the moment, embarrassment was duking it out with satisfaction for dominance. The pills she'd taken seemed to have worked as designed, keeping her thoughts clean and crisp—all the better to marvel at the way Rafe pulled responses from her body that she'd never imagined were possible.

Was that a wisp of amusement flitting across Elliott's face? If so, it quickly disappeared. "I don't like those dark circles under your eyes." He frowned down at her the way Lukas frequently did. "You're not getting enough sleep. Make sure you delegate everything you can to Cheyenne and her team."

She nodded. If he wasn't going to mention Rafe, neither was she. "I'll catch a nap this afternoon."

He was looking at her too closely. His steely eyes saw way too much. "Good," he finally responded.

There was a quiet digital blip, the sound of water dropping. Elliott looked at his mini with a sigh. "My ride is here."

There was no mistaking his annoyance, but the fact that he *was* annoyed meant he probably didn't plan on giving his security team the slip this morning. He did so occasionally, and it drove Lukas nuts. She pressed the elevator call button, and the doors whisked open. "Don't work too hard."

"Remember to take that nap." He held her gaze for several long seconds, smiled, and gently kissed the top of her head.

She swallowed hard as her throat filled, as her eyes stung with unexpected tears.

Sasha's apartment door suddenly opened, and her black and fuchsia-haired head poked from behind the fortified slab. "Hey, Dad. Bailey, I thought I heard you out here. Anyone in the mood for breakfast?"

Shaking his head, Elliott stepped onto the elevator. "Thanks, sweetheart, but I ate with Claudette. My ride's here, and I'm keeping the driver waiting. Have a good day, girls." He waved as the doors slowly closed.

She sighed in relief. All things being equal, she'd rather deal with Sasha than Elliott. "I'm sorry, Sasha, I can't either. I'm supposed to meet Jack for breakfast, and I'm running late." Her mini pinged, announcing an incoming text message. "Hang on a sec?" At Sasha's nod, she quickly read. It was Jack, asking if they could get together later that afternoon at Sebastiani Security instead of meeting for breakfast. "Jack needs to reschedule." After sending a quick reply, she tucked the mini into her pants pocket. She was tired of carrying the thing. "Something's come up."

"Probably his penis."

For someone who claimed to have no interest herself, Sasha sure was interested in Jack's sex life.

"He's supposed to be your best friend," Sasha continued. "Ditching you for another woman is tacky and rude."

She'd seriously considered ditching Jack herself so she could laze about in bed with Rafe. "No biggie. I'll see him later this afternoon." Good for Jack if he'd had an overnight guest. These days, he was wound *way* too tight.

Weren't they all?

"Shit, the bacon!" Sasha blurted. She disappeared, leaving Bailey to follow.

Entering the apartment, she ditched the bags, hung up her coat, and unzipped her boots, setting them next to Antonia's platform Doc Martens. She padded in her stocking feet to the bright, kitschy kitchen, where Sasha transferred the rescued bacon from a pan to a napkin-covered plate. The dainty wrought iron table was covered by a red and white checked tablecloth, and a cheerful pot of out-of-season violets served as a centerpiece.

There were two place settings of black Fiesta ware on the table, not three. "Where's Antonia?" Setting the mini on the table, she snitched a slice of bacon off the plate Sasha had set next to a Pyrex pan of broccoli egg bake.

"Not home. It's just you and me this morning." Sasha about-faced, went back to the countertop, and pumped two cups of Crackhouse Blend from an air pot covered in whimsical Holstein spots. "Have you seen Antonia's tablet? She tore the place apart looking for it last night."

"Geez." Had it really taken Antonia three freaking days to notice it was missing? Explaining to Sasha what she'd done and why—and that Rafe had taken the tablet home with him after dinner earlier in the week to help teach Antonia a lesson—she popped the rest of the bacon into her mouth and chewed. "All the malware and virus protection in the world won't help if she can't keep physical control of her equipment."

"Here. Have some coffee."

"Thanks." Accepting the mug, she took a grateful gulp while Sasha settled into the adjacent chair.

"So, you and Rafe finally did the deed."

She coughed, slapping her hand over her mouth so she wouldn't sputter coffee all over the table.

"Thank you for putting him out of his misery, by the way," Sasha added. Half-standing, she served them both a small portion of egg bake. The delicate scent of herbs and garlic danced into the room. "So, how was it?"

Jesus. After one final series of barking coughs, she glared at Sasha and took a careful sip of coffee, following it with a soothing gulp. "No comment." *Put him out of his misery? What the…* She narrowed her eyes. "Is that my T-shirt?" Under Sasha's unzipped fleece jacket, *The Big Bang Theory*'s Dr. Sheldon Cooper said, "Bazinga!"

"It's a roommate thing," Sasha informed her with a wave of her hand. "Roommates borrow each other's clothes, shoes and make-up, and dish about their sex lives." She settled back in the delicate ice cream parlor chair. "So, dish."

She wrinkled her nose. "I'm not going to talk to you about having sex with your brother. That's…really skeevy." And she had no clue how she'd describe the experience using mere words.

"Not in a family of incubi and succubi," Sasha said with a shrug. "Haven't you ever, you know, compared notes with girlfriends?"

"No." The girls she might have made friends with when she was a child had been too intimidated by her father, and skipping several grades several times certainly hadn't helped her establish a peer group. She'd been the only woman in her grad program, and after she'd met Wyatt, he'd become the center of her world. They'd worked together, studied together, lived together, slept together. Wyatt's wants and needs had been paramount. Her own hadn't even been on her radar.

And she'd let it happen.

"Hey." Sasha's impish face settled into more serious lines. "Talk to me."

She bit her lip, tempted. Rafe's sister or not, maybe a succubi's point of view was exactly what she needed right now. Though Sasha might tease, she'd never judge. And they *were* friends. How odd it was that her first real girlfriend wasn't even human. "So." How to say this? "Say a human's decided to have a—" she cleared her throat "—mutually satisfying physical relationship with an incubus." 'Satisfying'? What an inadequate word. "How do you know which feelings are produced by pheromones, and which ones are real?"

Sasha set her fork down with a clank. "All of your feelings are real. They're real because you're experiencing them."

"But how do you keep what's physical from blurring into the emotional? How do you keep your emotions out of the mix?"

"You don't." Sasha reached for the salt shaker. "Pheromones exacerbate physical desire, but they can't create emotions out of thin air." She salted her eggs with a flourish. "Say you meet a great-looking guy at Underbelly, so hot he smokes. Under the influence of pheromones, you might be more likely to act on that lust, but your feelings are your own."

And if the guy was smoking hot *and* emotions were involved? How would she manage to sleep with Rafe and keep her heart safe? "When I was with Wyatt, I didn't know which way was up or down."

"Who's Wyatt?"

"Wyatt Cooper, my first serious boyfriend." Her *only* serious boyfriend. How utterly pathetic. "He's the guy I was dating when I was arrested." She gave a self-deprecating laugh as she speared into the eggs with the heavy, triple-tined fork. "Correction, he's the guy who let me take the fall alone, but that's water under a very long bridge."

"Classy dude."

She couldn't help but laugh. "Yeah. We—Lukas, Jack and I—are almost certain he's the one behind the recent incursion attempts at Sebastiani Labs."

"This old boyfriend of yours. Is he stalking you?"

Did leaving romantic cards and beautifully wrapped presents at her hotel room door when she traveled for work qualify as stalking? Mailing things to her condo? Using generic email addresses to ask if she'd enjoyed his gifts? She'd always been too ashamed of how her relationship with Wyatt ended to ask for help, even from Jack. Wyatt had always been her problem, not Jack's—until recently, that is. Now he was everyone's problem. That, too, was her fault. "He knows where I work. He knows where I live. The last time I was at my place, with Rafe, Jack and Lukas, he tagged everyone's cars with surveillance devices."

"Sounds like he might be escalating."

He probably was. "He followed Rafe and me to Chadden's last night. When we were leaving, Rafe saw him." She paused. "He said Wyatt's an incubus."

"Wait, your first lover was an incubus?" Sasha set her coffee mug on the table. "How long ago was this relationship?"

"In grad school. Over a decade ago."

"Before you knew we existed. That son of a bitch. But on the other hand…" Sasha brought a forkful of eggs to her mouth, chewed, and then swallowed. "Want more coffee?"

Bailey looked down in surprise at her near-empty mug. "Sure. On the other hand what?"

Sasha popped out of the chair and brought the pot to the table. "A human who's had not just one, but two incubus lovers? You lucky, lucky girl."

Lucky? Another snort of laughter escaped. During the time she was with Wyatt, she'd felt like the prettiest, smartest, and—yeah—luckiest girl in the world. Until the day the FBI had slapped cuffs on her wrists.

"Scarlett once said that when your first lover is a sex demon, it's all downhill from there," Sasha added with a grin.

How true. Wyatt had been the lover that her paltry few subsequent partners had been measured against. They'd all come up short. Until last night. Rafe hadn't just raised the bar, he'd shattered it.

She dropped her head into her hands. She'd known that Rafe Sebastiani would be a once-in-a-lifetime lover, but she hadn't thought their relationship through to its inevitable conclusion. The relationship wouldn't—couldn't—last.

Once in a lifetime. It *was* going to be all downhill from there. "Hell."

"Bailey." Sasha set her cup down with a click. "Incubus or not, Wyatt Cooper sounds like he's a major league asshole who manipulated a young, inexperienced human, and then broke the law. Don't blame Rafe for another man's actions."

"But—"

"Remember, pheromones only exacerbate physical desire—and yeah," she acknowledged, "you might make some really poor decisions based on that desire. Been there, done that. But your emotions? They're yours. They're always yours."

Which meant she had only herself to blame for falling in love with Wyatt in the first place.

Coffee hissed into Sasha's mug as she pumped the lever on top of the air pot. "So Rafe told you Wyatt was incubus, not Lukas?"

An interesting point she hadn't previously considered. This extremely pertinent fact *had* to have come up during Lukas's investigation. Why hadn't she been told? Did Jack know? She raised her knuckles to her suddenly stinging stomach.

Did everyone know about Wyatt except her?

No. It had to be an oversight. "Lukas was in and out of the conference room during the meeting," she mused. "Scarlett wasn't feeling well."

"Was Lukas sick, too?" At her nod, Sasha grinned. "I wonder if Scarlett's told him she's pregnant yet."

"Scarlett's pregnant?"

Sasha nodded. "And Lukas has morning sickness. Side effect from his genetic glitch." She giggled without a whiff of sympathy. "Classic, huh?"

"Wow." Two sitting Underworld Council members were having a child together? Krispin Woolf, the bigoted WerePack Alpha, was going to throw a clot when he heard the news. She'd been at the Council meeting where Elliott and Claudette, the Incubus First and the Siren First, had announced they'd become bondmates. Their happy news had sent Woolf into a rage, and Valerian's serene confirmation that there was nothing in their charter prohibiting such a relationship hadn't helped.

No wonder Scarlett was keeping the news to herself for a while. "What did you mean earlier about me finally putting Rafe out of his misery?"

Sasha wriggled her nose like Samantha on *Bewitched*. "Succubus, remember? Sexual energy's my specialty, and his has been piss-poor since he stopped sleeping with Lorin."

She slumped in her chair as if someone had surgically removed her spine. Lorin was tall and lean, statuesque and stacked. Visually, she and Rafe were a perfect match, except the pairing hadn't lasted. Lorin had chosen Gabe Lupinsky, had bonded with him, instead.

Rafe must have been devastated.

"You kept him dangling long enough," Sasha said. "Nicely played, though it made him absolutely miserable. It's about time someone made him break a sweat."

Her face heated. Rafe had broken a sweat last night, all right, and it had looked fabulous on him. "I didn't keep him dangling." Or if she had, it hadn't been a conscious decision.

Sasha leaned closer, inviting her to spill her secrets. "So, how was it?"

She couldn't hold back the grin. "Fantastic."

An obnoxious trilling sound blared from her mini. Plucking up the device from the table, she silenced it and quickly skimmed. Network incursion at SL. First layer compromised, second layer penetration underway. "Damn. Gotta go."

She stood quickly, dialing Cheyenne on the run. After a quiet night, Wyatt—or his minions—were making up for lost time.

✸

Rafe paced his studio with a phone clapped to his ear, listening as his agent and business manager subtly—or so she probably thought—conveyed her concerns about his pace of production. "Brooke," he interrupted, gazing at his work in progress, "things are going well—or they would be, if I could get off the damn phone and get back to work." Bailey's gorgeous legs extended from the damp clay in a graceful, sated bend it had taken him hours of painstaking focus to achieve. The rest of her body was still in the block, waiting to be exposed.

Memories of the previous night sizzled and burned. He'd never have enough time to sculpt them all. He felt frantic—as frantic now as he had last night.

Last night, he, who usually reveled in spending long, languid hours pleasuring a woman's body without a single thought to his own, had wanted to push, shove, hurry…to do everything in his power to banish the shadows under Bailey's eyes as quickly as he could.

He had to get a grip here. He had an avalanche of work to do.

"Brooke," he said more forcefully, interrupting his tiny bulldog of an agent. She was probably chain-smoking right now, thinking that her husband didn't know.

"Okay, calm down, honey," she soothed.

The endearment lost a little something in translation when uttered in her cement mixer voice. "Brooke, I'm working. Let's talk again next week—" The first-floor door buzzer rudely interrupted. *Fuck me.* At this rate, he'd never get any work done. "Someone's at the door," he said to Brooke. "I really have to go. Yeah. Bye." Ending the call and tucking his phone into his pocket, he glanced at the security monitor. Chadden stood under the awning, protecting his face from the morning sun with an upraised hand and not much else. "It would serve you right if I let you fry," he called into the speaker before slapping the button that unlocked the door.

As Chadden clumped up the stairs, Rafe scurried around, making sure his sculptures were covered. No way did he want Chadden to run his connoisseur's eye over Bailey's naked form, even if it was only rendered in clay.

"Hey," Chadden said as he opened the door.

"Hey. What do you want? I'm working." It wasn't unusual for Chadden's visits to stretch for hours on end, but not today. Images of the night with Bailey flickered in his thoughts like flame. He had to get them down before they fizzled out.

Chadden sauntered over to the mini fridge and extracted a can of Coke. "Want one?"

"No." Despite his answer, a red can sailed toward his head. He caught it one-handed.

Chadden sprawled on the red velvet sectional couch and cracked open a can of his own.

Rafe glanced at the clock. Though his friend looked supremely relaxed, ready to settle in for a long, cozy chat, he'd have to leave for the restaurant soon. Though Chadden's capable sous chef handled the Saturday lunch crowd, Chadden would be cooking that evening. Hyper-persnickety about his *mis en place*, he'd spend hours preparing the ingredients he'd need for the evening's special.

Chadden glanced up at the ceiling. "Is she still here? Mind if I say hello?"

Setting the unopened can down on his long worktable, he crossed his arms, saying nothing.

"A little testy this morning, are we? Did the romantic evening not go as planned?" Chadden arched a black brow. "Too bad. Things were looking so promising when I left your table."

He opened his mouth to snap back a denial, and then closed it. He wasn't going to talk about his night—and morning—with Bailey. It was...private, too special to share. Finding her in the shower earlier that morning, apparently preparing to leave without even waking him, had made his stomach clutch. "What do you want?" he repeated, shifting his weight from one leg to the other. "I'm working here—or trying to, anyway."

Ignoring him, Chadden looked around the studio, taking in—ah, shit. He hadn't covered two finished pieces over on the shelf, and Chadden had locked onto them like a fighter pilot on an incoming missile. Rising, he sauntered to the shelf and picked up a rendering of a stretched-out Bailey, cradling it in his long-fingered hands. "Very nice."

"Give me that." There was no lasciviousness in his friend's voice or touch, just a quiet appreciation, but it was all he could do not to yank the sculpture from Chadden's hands. His hypersensitive nostrils flared, picking up the slightest hint of…was that envy? About what?

"You will treat her well." The underlying threat was all the more pronounced for how softly Chadden's words had been spoken.

"Of course." An expression he couldn't read clouded his friend's face, and his pulse kicked up a notch as a horrible thought struck. "I—are you interested in Bailey, too?" Not that he'd step back if Chadden said yes. And he would not share her. Could not. Seeing another man's hands on her, even Chadden's, would send him around the bend.

Chadden strolled back to the couch and sat, wearing a smile that was a little too wicked and nostalgic for Rafe's peace of mind. "Settle down," he finally said. "Have I ever told you about the first time Bailey and I met?"

"I know how you met," Rafe retorted. "I was there." Yes, he'd been at Underbelly the night of Scarlett's last public performance. He'd watched Bailey, under the influence of second-hand pheromones, cuddle right up to Chadden. Luckily, Sasha had been right beside her, because Chadden's definition of 'behave yourself' tended to be…flexible. Rafe had volunteered to bring Bailey upstairs to

Sasha's office so she could take a dose of pheromone intoxication meds, and…

Yeah, look how *that* had ended up. Bailey might have been safer with Chadden after all.

"She's entirely too innocent for me, but perfect for you, I think." Chadden gave a theatrical sigh. "So, I need to find a new carousing partner, eh?"

Rafe shrugged, and let him draw his own conclusions.

Chadden cocked a thumb up to the ceiling, gesturing to the bedroom. "You're… compatible?"

"You might say that," he muttered.

"I'm happy for you, my friend."

"Don't celebrate yet," Rafe cautioned. Thanks to that asshole Wyatt Cooper, she was skittish about any relationship, much less one with another incubus. If it hadn't been for her experience with Cooper, Bailey might be able to simply enjoy the sensations the pheromones produced, and not have to think so damn hard. Bailey was as responsive as a dream, her skin sensitive to the slightest touch, but he'd still noticed her thinking, assessing, much more frequently than he would have liked.

Chadden left the couch again, pulling back the tarp he'd draped over a completed sculpture. His gaze was frankly admiring as he eyed Bailey's lithe form, as he stroked a finger down the line of her smooth, glazed back.

Her nude back. "No touching." Shouldering Chadden away from the table, he draped the figure again, hiding it from his assessing gaze.

"Can't blame a guy for looking."

"Yes, I can." Rafe quickly walked to the stairwell door, and opened it with a flourish. "Go away. I have work to do."

"Sculpting naked women. Nice work if you can get it."

"I have." He pointed at the stairs. "Go. Now."

"No, no, really. Don't beg. I really can't stay." Chadden joined him at the door, wrapping one long arm around his shoulders, pulling him in for a hug. "Imagine. Rafe Sebastiani, off the market. An era is ending—" he grinned suddenly "—leaving more women for me."

"Don't say anything," Rafe warned. "She's skittish enough without becoming a fixture on the damn grapevine."

"You think you're not already there? Get real." Chadden stepped over the threshold, but turned back one final time. "I wish you luck, my friend—and let me know if you need some oysters."

"Get out." Rafe closed the door and locked it. Chadden's final smile had been more than a little wistful.

Maybe Chadden had had enough with variety, too.

CHAPTER NINE

Bailey sat upright on the futon, wiping her bleary eyes, squinting at the security screen mounted on the wall next to the door. Someone was coming into The Bunker.

Jack.

She plowed her hands through her hair and winced. Her wrist stung like a bitch.

What time was it, anyway? She'd taken the nap she'd promised to Elliott, but only after hours of grinding work, tag-teaming with Cheyenne and several members of her team. They'd spanked Wyatt's clever little worm, but it had taken serious effort. Wyatt had rounded up some stellar talent to assist him with this gig. She still had no idea what his end goal might be. One way to find out would be to allow the worm to penetrate, to watch where it went and analyze its behavior, but that course of action was far too risky. After coding and testing a patch to shore up their infrastructure, she'd left deployment to Cheyenne, sent everyone on the Council a quick status update, then had stumbled to the futon and crashed.

Her stomach stung as badly as her wrist did.

"Hey." Jack walked in, juggling a large white take-out bag and two bottles of water in one hand, and a flexible ice pack and an elastic bandage in the other.

"Hey." Yawning, she stretched her arms overhead, wincing at the sharp pain gnawing at her stomach lining. She glanced over to the table, where Jack unpacked two clear clamshells of green salad, paper napkins, and plastic silverware from the take-out bag. While his back was turned, she scrubbed at her stomach with her knuckles—not that it helped.

"I've got a bone to pick with you," Jack grumbled.

She barely managed to drop her hand before he turned. "Likewise."

"But let's get that wrist on ice first. I can tell it's swollen from here." Carrying the gel pack and Ace bandage, he joined her on the futon, and within a couple of minutes, her wrist was efficiently wrapped. As he walked back to the table to retrieve the salads, she saw that his khaki pants and oxford shirt still looked country club crisp, even this late in the day. She was still wearing last night's date clothes, and the nap hadn't done her wool pants any favors.

"Dinner is served."

"Thanks." She looked at the beautiful spinach salad he'd handed her, trying to muster up some enthusiasm. Most food just didn't sit very well these days. She hadn't had anything to eat since breakfast with Sasha. "What time is it?"

"Just after eight," Jack replied. "You've had a long day."

"Yeah." One more day where she hadn't seen sunlight, not that there were many hours of sunlight to be had in the dead of a Minnesota winter. As they ate, she filled him in on the day's work. "We're clear. Until next time."

"Why Sebastiani Labs? What's he after?"

"Who the hell knows?" she said with a sigh. "I just know that I'm tired of his shit. And speaking of which…did you know that Wyatt Cooper is an incubus?"

Jack's eyebrows rose. "What?"

So that answered *that* question. He hadn't known. "Wyatt followed Rafe and me to Chadden's last night. Rafe could tell he was an incubus as soon as he saw him in person."

"Why didn't Lukas say something at the meeting? That's odd."

"He did leave the conference room for a moment," she said.

Jack unscrewed the tops off the water bottles, handed her one, and drank from his own. "He's going through antacids like crazy."

"I don't think they're going to help," she said ruefully. Scarlett's pregnancy wasn't her news to share—and for that matter, it hadn't been Sasha's to share with her, either—but if the communication lapse about Wyatt's species was due to pregnancy-induced brain fog, Jack should know so he could compensate for Lukas if he needed to. "Scarlett's pregnant."

Jack's grin nearly split his face open, but he sobered quickly. "Krispin Woolf is *not* going to be happy."

"Two sitting council members, having a half-breed baby?" She put air quotes around half-breed with her fingers. "No shit." She half-heartedly twirled her fork in the salad, picking up a chunk of bleu cheese on the white plastic tines. "On the other hand, if he strokes out hearing the news, his death would clearly be from natural causes. Sometimes it's all I can do not to strangle the guy."

Jack snorted with laughter, but then sobered. "So what's your bone?"

Bailey gave an embarrassed half-shrug. "I thought you knew that Wyatt was an incubus and hadn't told me."

He shook his head, his jaw tight. "Somebody needs to knock that son of a bitch out cold."

"I appreciate the thought, but we have to catch him first." She poked at the salad, snagging a slice of hard-boiled egg. "So what's yours?" She was almost afraid to find out.

Jack reached into the front pocket of his khakis and withdrew a familiar-looking Ziploc bag.

She froze.

"Yeah, you should look nervous," Jack said, scowling. "I received a refill from Sebastiani Labs yesterday. Imagine my surprise when I discovered my count was off."

She'd remembered to put the desk key back, but she should have figured that he'd count his pill supply. "Damn it."

"That's pretty much an admission of guilt," Jack muttered. "It's Rafe, of course. Are you being careful?"

Her jaw dropped. "Are you asking me about safe sex?"

"No, silly. The drugs. What dosage are you taking?" He eyeballed her body, pursed his lips. "You're a little less than half my body weight. Half a tablet? Maybe a third. You'll have to experiment."

Jack was handling this much better than she thought he would.

"How many pills have you taken so far?"

How many times have you had sex with Rafe? She knew Jack wouldn't judge her, but that didn't stop her cheeks from turning lobster boil red. "Half a tablet. Once."

"Any wooziness? Lightheadedness?"

"No." She remembered every wonderful, debauched thing she and Rafe had done with crystal clarity.

"Watch out for it, especially if you're around people who smoke." He paused, and then gave her a long sideways glance. "I wish you would've asked me for the pills instead of taking them."

She eyed him back. How could she explain? They didn't discuss their sex lives in detail, but they didn't avoid the topic, either. "Wyatt was an incubus, Rafe is an incubus. I just wanted a little insurance." She paused. "I'll enjoy him, but it's a short-term, physical deal."

A muscle ticked in Jack's cheek. "Did Rafe say that?"

"No," she said, annoyed. "This is my decision, Jack. I'm allowed to have a fling. One might say I'm overdue."

"Well, we should tell somebody at SL Pharma that you're taking the pills so they can collect data and provide some oversight. I'm the only guinea pig they've got so far."

Bailey nodded. The pheromone intoxication meds were still highly experimental, so she fully understood the importance of collecting data and keeping tabs on her physical reactions and responses. "What data do you report? How, and to whom?" She'd collect it herself, and turn it in after her relationship with Rafe was well and truly over.

Jack gave her the name of a contact. "Wyland also gives me a check-up once a quarter or so," he added. "Basic physical, blood work, and so on."

Wyland was annoyed enough with her right now that she wasn't about to let him anywhere near her with a needle. "I'll touch base with him." Much, much later. She wasn't about to reveal to anyone but Jack that she was taking the meds so she didn't stupidly fall in love with Elliott Sebastiani's stunning younger son.

"You done here?" He'd finished his salad, but she'd only eaten a quarter of hers. Thankfully, he was used to her bird-like appetite. "Let's shut it down for the night."

She nodded, not looking at the futon. After Jack left, she'd catch a quick nap, then get some more work—

"I'll walk you out."

Making sure she actually left. Damn it, he knew her too well.

"Any chance of you not working tomorrow?" he asked. "The Council meeting's not until Monday afternoon."

Which was why she had to get some work done tomorrow. Dealing with Wyatt's shenanigans had pulled her attention away from the dozens of balls she juggled, and some were about to drop. She and Wyland would have to spend most of Monday morning closeted in a conference room at SL as it was, pulling together a coherent status report on the archiving project for the Council meeting. If she didn't put some time in tomorrow, she'd be completely unprepared.

"Bailey?"

"I'll try."

He shook his head, but didn't press. "Meet you at the front door in ten."

"Okay." After Jack left, she collected the equipment she'd need to work from Sasha's place. Maybe if she closeted herself in the bedroom, she could put some flesh on the bones of the idea she'd gotten during the power outage up at the Sebastiani family cabin about how to access the tech unit Lorin had found up at the Isabella dig last year.

Technology was pretty much ubiquitous these days, but if she could find a place so remote, so unpopulated, that there'd be no ambient network for the tech unit to attach to…yeah, the idea had some legs. Too much scientific research was being done in Antarctica, but north? Canada, Alaska, the northern Rockies? Definitely some possibilities there.

She'd discuss the idea with Wyland on Monday, scoping the work so she could accomplish it solo. She'd need something productive to do after Rafe decided it was time for him to move on.

✳

Wyland lifted his gaze from the laptop screen. "Very…intriguing."

She'd just walked him through a draft of the proposal she'd knocked out yesterday. After hours of research, she'd found three feasible locations on the

North American continent where she could work—locations so remote there'd be no technological infrastructure for hundreds of miles—and her wild-assed idea to create a rolling Faraday cage out of a tricked-out RV had some definite possibilities. She'd also spent the evening watching part of a *Buffy the Vampire Slayer* marathon with Antonia, so if Jack happened to ask, she could tell him she'd relaxed without it being a complete and total lie.

"A couple of weeks ago, I was up at the Sebastiani cabin when the power went out. No electricity, no network access. I was limited to battery power, working completely local. The idea came from there."

She and Wyland were working in one of the smaller conference rooms near Elliott's office, which meant they'd had had hours of uninterrupted time, all the privacy they could want, and thanks to Willem Lund, Elliott's executive assistant, an endless supply of coffee—or she had, at any rate. Wyland had made do with parsimonious sips of water all morning.

He flipped the proposal back to the first slide. "The individual who performs this work would be alone for months, with little to no communication with the outside world. No internet, no phone…"

"Wyland, until I can get at the device's innards, I can't know what kind of tech it can compromise. Given what I saw when it was out of the box at Sebastiani Labs last summer, we have to assume that all technology is susceptible."

"So your only technology, under this proposal, will be a couple of laptops?"

She nodded. "Loaded with my tooling. Strictly local access." She'd be kicking it old skool.

"What if you had an emergency? How would you get help?"

Yes. If Wyland was poking holes in her plan, he'd accepted it in concept. She—they—would not walk into today's Underworld Council meeting empty-handed.

"Which reminds me." Wyland stood and walked towards the door.

"We're not done working yet, are we?" They hadn't even started talking about the archiving project.

Wyland closed the blinds on the narrow slice of window, stepping out of the room momentarily. When he returned, he was carrying a black doctor's bag.

Shit.

"If you won't go to a doctor, a doctor will come to you," Wyland said. "Let's start with your wrist. Extend both arms, please."

She pushed back both sweater sleeves with a put-upon sigh. He eyed both wrists before focusing his attention on the left, carefully flexing the wrist and fingers, pressing on her ligaments and tendons, watching for any sign of guarding or wincing. "I'll have you know that I used voice recognition software for work yesterday." For some of it, at any rate.

"Good. Are you remembering to use ice?"

"Yes, doctor." Her sarcasm had no effect. His initial training may have occurred before the War of 1812, but he was, indeed, a doctor.

"Hop up on the table."

"What?" she squawked.

"Right here." He patted the end of the table they weren't using for their work. "I want to check out that ulcer you're brewing."

"So, my appetite's a little off. It's just stress." She glared at him. "I'm experiencing some boundary issues with my work colleagues."

"Up on the table."

Fuming, she climbed onto the table, and lay flat on her back. Before she could huff another annoyed sigh, Wyland's chilly hands were under the hem of her sweater, professionally palpating her abdomen. She held back a hiss of pain as he pressed just south of her sternum, but just barely. He narrowed his icy blue eyes. "Try to relax," he said, pressing again before unbuttoning and unzipping her dress pants so he could continue his examination of her lower abdomen. "Look how loose these are," he admonished. "Are you having regular periods?"

Her jaw dropped.

"Bailey, I'm a doctor."

"Not *my* doctor," she snapped.

"Well, if you'd go to yours, we wouldn't be here, would we? Up," he said, helping her into a sitting position before digging in his bag for a blood-pressure cuff and stethoscope. Pushing the sleeve of her sweater even higher, he wrapped the cuff around her upper arm and rapidly squeezed the flexible black bulb. The cuff tightened, its Velcro fastener gnashing its tiny teeth, before air left the cuff with a relieved hiss. "Slightly elevated."

"Gee, I wonder why. I'm half-stripped in a conference room, and a vampire's asking me questions about my menstrual cycle. Can I zip my pants now?" She didn't wait for his permission, zipping and buttoning her pants with emphatic motions.

"It's a wonder they stay up. You're losing weight you can't afford to lose."

"I—"

"Probably have an ulcer," Wyland finished matter-of-factly. "I'd like to run some tests to confirm my diagnosis." Whipping out his mini, he started tapping. "I have an open block at 2:00 p.m. Thursday. How about you?" He waited until she grudgingly grabbed her mini, opened her calendar, and looked at Thursday. Finally, something positive about back-to-back meetings all day long. "Sorry. I'm slammed." She probably could shift some things around if she wanted to but...she didn't want to.

"Friday morning, 10:00. Change of location. "He swiped and tapped. "Incoming."

She and Wyland met weekly, Fridays at 10:00 a.m., to work on the archiving project. With a standing meeting time, they were able to get a couple of hours of work in per week on the long-running and long-suffering project, the job Lukas had originally hired her to do. Unfortunately, the project had received a miniscule slice of her attention because she had so many competing projects.

When her mini blipped, she read his update. That wily bastard. This Friday's meeting was now taking place at Memorial Hospital's endoscopy lab.

"We might want to make this our regular meeting location," he mused. "With a scope snaked down your throat, I might finally get a word in edgewise."

Had the chilly vamp just made a joke?

"In the meantime, please eat non-spicy food, and try to push some calories. You're no good to anyone if you're sick."

There was a soft tap at the door. "Come," Wyland called.

Willem poked his head inside. "Lunch is set up in the boardroom if you're interested." The council members usually shared a collegial meal before their meetings. Now that the conference room door was open, she could smell lasagna.

Her empty stomach audibly growled. "We done here?" she asked Wyland. "I could choke something down."

"Make sure you do."

She didn't miss the look the two men exchanged. She had a feeling that between the two of them, she'd eat whether she was hungry or not.

✳

Sprawled face down on his bed, annoyed by the cheerful morning sun, Wyatt couldn't find the energy to move. Yesterday, on a jagged, euphoric high as he watched SkoolHaus's clever worm bore its way through SL's outer security layers, he'd called Nicola, the yoga-toned admin he'd flirted with at Winston, Inc., to see if she was available for lunch. They'd met at Wisteria, a quiet, posh restaurant on the ground floor of an equally quiet and posh boutique hotel, but they'd barely ordered drinks before she suggested they have their meal delivered to a room upstairs. Then, alone and back at his place that evening, slapped in the face by failure yet again, Cheyenne had called, asking if he wanted to get dinner and a pint at Kieran's. In no mood for a noisy pub and pleading the need for a quiet night in, he suggested they share takeout at his place instead.

He'd been the beneficiary of her voracious sexual appetite—and, ironically, at least some of her euphoria had come from beating back *his* failed hack.

Why had he let so much time pass since he'd had a werewolf lover? Cheyenne positively lit him up sexually; she was strong, raunchy, and generous, up for anything. He hissed in a breath as he remembered her adventurous tongue, lapping at his most sensitive flesh—flesh that was, at this very moment, flexing and stretching awake. He snaked his hand under the covers—

"Mr. Cooper."

He lurched to a sitting position, his hand fumbling for the handgun he kept in his bedside table drawer.

"You won't be needing that."

His eyes darted around the empty room. He didn't hear footsteps, or anyone rustling around out in his living room, kitchen or office. Where...

"Finally awake, I see."

A familiar, chubby face beamed at him from the screen of the laptop he kept on the desk in his bedroom.

Crap. His entire setup was likely compromised. Had Cheyenne...no. Last night was the first time she'd been to his place, and she hadn't touched any of his equipment—nothing that wasn't attached to his body, at any rate. He'd personally escorted her to the door several hours ago.

But now Buddha had tipped his hand, speaking up when he could have lurked, quietly collecting information. He wanted something. Throwing back the covers, Wyatt stood, fully naked, and unhurriedly reached for the gray sweatpants Cheyenne had stripped off him last night. It was past time he found out who the hell he was dealing with.

"No need for pay-per-view with this set-up, is there?" he drawled. "Free porn. Quite the job perk."

An expression of distaste tightened the man's face. "Mr. Cooper, there has been no progress. You may not be the right man for this job."

He didn't respond, waiting.

"Very good," the man finally said. "You're not completely without skills. But perhaps it's time to admit, just between the two of us, that your technical abilities might not be up to this task."

"Whose are?" he said with a shrug. The safeguards that Bailey had put in place at Sebastiani Labs had shut his Dream Team down cold.

"You are barely competent technically, but—" Buddha's eyebrow rose, lifting a roll of forehead fat "—when you employ your social engineering skills, your success rate improves significantly." A dark-suited man handed him a sheaf of papers, which he quickly flipped through. "With some delightful side benefits, I see." He held up a picture of Cheyenne, riding him, her long dark hair streaming down her back. "You're a very busy man."

His stomach clutched as he assessed the camera angle. Had Buddha reversed the webcam, or had he installed cameras of his own? "Who *are* you?"

"You may call me 'Sir.'"

"Give me a name," he snapped.

"Mr. Cooper, you aren't in a position to ask any questions, or make any demands." He indicated the window he was speaking from with his chubby hand. "Do you have any doubt whatsoever that I have all of the data and resources I require to incarcerate you for the rest of your natural life?"

No, he didn't doubt it at all—but all things being equal, he'd rather take his chances with this guy than with the Council and Lukas Sebastiani.

Were all things equal? He had no idea.

Anger grew—anger at himself. He'd gotten cocky. Buddha, or his dark-suited minions, had found his condo, infiltrated his equipment. He'd been operating so blithely, so successfully, for so long, it hadn't crossed his mind that he could be the target of the same schemes he used on others. Despite the sweat pants, he suddenly felt stark naked. Padding across the room, he pulled a thick sweatshirt off the top shelf of his closet.

"Mr. Cooper."

"I'm getting dressed," he said, scouring the corners of the room for surveillance equipment while he was out of the man's sightlines. As soon as this conversation was over, he was going to rip the place apart from top to bottom.

"Mr. Cooper, there has been a troubling lack of progress thus far."

And the guy hadn't hung up yet, made any threats, or arrested him. Yes, he needed something. Stepping into his slippers, he took a seat at the desk, facing Buddha businessman to businessman.

"Your worm managed a miniscule degree of infiltration before it hit a brick wall. What happened?"

He wanted to know the answer to that question, too. SkoolHaus had taken the failure personally, and was tearing his code apart at this very moment. But damn it, he would *not* be lectured like a schoolboy who'd failed a test. *They'd* come to *him*. They'd approached him for a reason, even if he didn't yet know what the reason was. Time to push a little. "Each failure reveals something about their infrastructure. Perhaps you could tell me what you've already tried." *Analyzing your failures might help me discover a feasible attack vector more quickly.*"

On-screen, Buddha stopped flicking through pages with his chubby finger. His face was completely blank, but menace throbbed across the ether. If they were meeting in person, Wyatt might very well have hands around his throat right now. He swallowed as stomach acid tried to crawl out of his throat.

"I'll take your request under consideration."

Wyatt's confidence surged at the concession. "Thank you. The information would be very helpful. To your earlier point about social engineering, I'm making progress. The woman in the photo? Her name is Cheyenne Winterbourne, and she's the network architect at Sebastiani Labs."

"Spelling?"

"What?"

"How is her name spelled?" As Wyatt rattled off the letters, Buddha turned his head to speak with one of the suits behind him.

The minion bent closer to listen, bringing his head into the frame.

Wyatt watched his lips.

"Yes, sir, Mr. Ba—" The guy turned away, scurrying to do Buddha's bidding.

Crap. A partial name was all he had.

"Carry on, Mr. Cooper," Buddha said. "I'll be in touch."

The screen went black.

Damn it. Leaning back in his desk chair, he released a shaky breath. "Mr. Ba." It wasn't much, but it was something. He'd tap some contacts, put out some feelers—*after* he tore his apartment apart, eradicating any surveillance equipment he found, and installing some safeguards of his own.

CHAPTER TEN

Given how many other options there'd been for her to choose from, she couldn't begrudge the Council members their spicy lasagna. Chadden's tomato basil soup had been delectable, but the creamy risotto had gone down like a dream. She hadn't had a full stomach in ages. "Push calories," she grumbled under her breath as she took a seat at the boardroom table next to Jack. Okay, maybe her pants *had* gotten a little loose—no need to make a big federal deal out of it—but if she made it through this meeting without her stomach stinging like a thousand paper cuts, maybe she'd ask Chadden to make her some more risotto. It might be easier on her stomach than his ultra-rich pasta.

"Quiet, please. Let's come to order," Willem requested from his seat near the head of the table. He waited for the chatter to subside. "Security shades engaged?"

"Engaged," Lukas seconded. The tell-tale blur let in natural light minus the UV, and also blocked the view of anyone who might be trying to look in from the outside.

Willem dimmed the room. "Voice and data recording initiated."

Establishing secure storage for the Council's highly confidential records had been her first assignment as a Sebastiani Security employee.

As Willem displayed the agenda on the large screen mounted on the wall at the end of the oblong room, she verified that her mini was set to vibrate and placed it on her lap, where it would be available for some surreptitious back-channel communication. Settling into the large leather chair, she looked around the room she privately called the Holodeck. Valkyrie First Alka Schlessinger was still on sabbatical, but otherwise it looked like they had a full house. Valerian, recovering from a bout of pneumonia, was attending the meeting holographically. No doubt Wyland had recommended that he not expose himself to germs by attending the meeting in person.

She bit her lip. She'd intended to ask Wyland about Valerian's health at their meeting earlier, but it had completely slipped her mind.

The Underworld Council's make-up was species based, with two representatives, a First and a Second, attending each meeting. Lukas had mixed things up a couple of years ago by abdicating his seat as the Incubus Second to focus exclusively on security and technology risks. Antonia had assumed Lukas's position as Second, to Rafe and Sasha's everlasting relief.

Starting with Elliott, they circled around the table, with everyone stating their name and affiliation. "Elliott Sebastiani, representing incubi and succubi."

Low-key and ego-free, Elliott definitely had a tendency toward understatement. "Elliott Sebastiani, Incubus First and Underworld Council President, present and presiding," Willem stated for the record.

"Claudette Fontaine, Siren First."

"Scarlett Fontaine, Siren Second." Scarlett, looking a little pale, nibbled on a saltine cracker. Lukas, sitting next to her, gave a hard swallow, but the trash can he'd gotten into the habit of carrying around with him at Sebastiani Security was nowhere in sight. Krispin Woolf, the WerePack Alpha, would swoop in like a crow on carrion at the slightest sign of weakness.

"Lukas Sebastiani, Security and Technology First," he said, thumbing a tube of antacids.

"Jack Kirkland, Security and Technology Second."

It was her turn. "Bailey Brown, Security and Technology subject matter expert."

Seated across the table, Krispin Woolf straightened. "Point of procedure. I request we clear the room of any attendees not explicitly sanctioned in our charter."

"Right on schedule," she muttered under her breath.

Jack jabbed her leg under the table.

She sat back in her chair, arms crossed. Every month, Krispin tried to get her booted from this meeting, and every month he was voted down.

"Voice vote," Willem stated. "All those in favor of clearing the room of subject matter experts, please say Aye."

"Aye," Krispin said.

"Opposed?"

A chorus of opposed votes filled the room, including one issued by the WerePack Beta, Krispin's son Jacoby.

"The opposed votes carry," Willem said.

She leaned over toward Jack again. "As a point of procedure, we should finish taking attendance before taking a vote."

"Shh."

She hated to admit it, but Krispin had a point. Somehow, over the last year, she'd gone from being a subject matter expert who attended fifteen minutes of the meeting and then left, to not leaving at all. She flicked a glance up to the agenda. First up was a discussion about the qualifications of yet another candidate to fill the Humanity Chair, a position left vacant by a deceased human scientist whose name they never said aloud, for his own family's protection. Lorin sometimes joked that they should just offer *her* the Humanity Chair and be done with it already. Hopefully the Council would come to a decision soon. Bailey wasn't at *all* comfortable with her opinions being taken as a proxy for all of humanity, even if Jack was at her side.

Lorin introduced herself for the record, explaining that her mother, Alka, was enjoying her sabbatical and had just taken a very interesting side trip to the Nazca lines in Peru. When she glanced up, Elliott scrutinized her from his seat at the head of the table. She leaned back in her chair, using Jack's body to block his steely gray gaze, only to find Wyland, across the table, watching with his unimpeded sightline.

"Jacoby Woolf, WerePack Beta." Jacoby's motorized scooter was positioned a chilly three feet away from his father's chair, a visual reflection of the fractured relationship between Alpha and Beta. Last year, Jacoby had voted with the majority against his father's highly risky proposal to accelerate research on one of Lorin's most intriguing archaeological finds: a capsule, nearly two feet long, made of the same unknown alloy as the unusual lockbox, containing dozens of vials of organic material—material Woolf the Elder had wanted to use for an ill-conceived gene-splicing project. Though the vote had occurred months ago, there was still a rift between father and son. If the men had exchanged a single word since they'd arrived, she hadn't seen or heard it.

"Krispin Woolf, WerePack Alpha." He flicked a dismissive glance at Lukas, seated across the table from him. "I see from the agenda you're proposing yet another candidate for the Humanity Chair."

To say Krispin Woolf disliked Lukas would be an understatement. Having lost his bid for Council presidency to Elliott Sebastiani some years ago, Woolf had expanded the scope of his enmity to include the younger generation. The fact that his slings and arrows rarely injured his targets enraged him.

"Not my candidate," Lukas responded.

Woolf looked startled, and opened his mouth to respond.

"Let's finish taking attendance, please," Willem interjected smoothly.

She felt sorry for Willem. Keeping this powerful, unruly crew on-task was an impossible job.

"Wyland, Vampire Second."

"Valerian, Vampire First," Valerian said. Always an eccentric dresser, today the elderly historian looked like Hugh Hefner hosting a party at the Playboy mansion in his heavy silk pajamas and bathrobe. She picked up her coffee cup and sipped to hide her tiny smile. When you were over nine hundred years old, you could wear what you damn well pleased.

"I'm glad you could join us, sir," Willem said before stating his own name for the record. "Our first item today—"

"Whose candidate is it?" Woolf interrupted.

Bailey exhaled heavily. 'Imperious' was the WerePack Alpha's default affect. The diplomatic Willem always had his hands full herding this particular cat.

"Whose?" Woolf repeated.

"Mine," Claudette answered.

Okay, *that* took the wind out of Krispin's sails.

Lukas had proposed the three previous candidates—Michio Kaku, Neil deGrasse Tyson, and Brian Cox—any of whom, in her opinion, had more than the right stuff to shepherd humanity through the complex array of issues that would arise when people learned that, not only were they not alone in the universe, they'd shared their planet with so-called 'aliens' for thousands of years. In Krispin Woolf's opinion, each candidate had possessed a fatal flaw: being human. Though Lukas's proposal to begin an active search to fill the Humanity Chair had been accepted by the Council long ago, Woolf continued to undermine the process. None of the candidates had been completely knocked out of the running yet—she thought Brian Cox would be an absolutely perfect choice—but the search, and the political in-fighting, continued.

She looked at Lukas, sitting with a neutral expression on his face. That faker. He knew perfectly well who this candidate was. Even before Elliott and Lukas had bonded with Claudette and Scarlett, the incubi and sirens had been strong political allies.

"Willem, if I may?" At Willem's affirmative nod, Claudette rose. As she made her way to the front of the room, a picture and resume filled the large screen.

She recognized the candidate. Not a cosmologist, astrobiologist, or a theoretical physicist this time, but a diplomat…one with unimpeachable peacekeeping bona fides. Three years ago, Torsten Boateng's negotiations with vicious Somalian warlords had been instrumental in allowing food and medical aid to reach previously inaccessible areas of sub-Saharan Africa.

"Torsten Boateng," Claudette confirmed, her cinnamon-and-sugar bob swinging as she pivoted to face them. "Graduate of Yale and Yale Law. Rhodes Scholar, with graduate work in history and economics. Multiple diplomatic assignments, primarily in Africa. He now works as a troubleshooter for the United Nations."

As Claudette hit the high points of Boateng's public and not-so-public accomplishments, Woolf stared stonily at the screen, saying nothing. There really wasn't much he *could* say. It was rumored Boateng had been on the shortlist for the Nobel Peace Prize last year.

She sent a text to Lukas: *Nicely played.*

Two seats down, Lukas glanced down to his own lap and read. One corner of his mouth quirked in acknowledgment.

Elliott steepled his fingers together, a pose he adopted when deep in thought—a complete ruse, because there was no way that he, Claudette, Lukas, Scarlett, and probably Jack hadn't already talked the pros and cons of Boateng's candidacy into the ground. He wouldn't have been presented as a candidate otherwise. "His government and intelligence contacts could be very useful to us in the event our existence is revealed to humanity."

Well, that was all well and good, but did Boateng have enough of a scientific background to accept even the possibility of their existence? What did they know about his spiritual beliefs? She'd ask Lukas after—

"Bailey?" Elliott said. "Something to add?"

Every member of the Underworld Council looked at her expectantly. The heat vents chose that moment to take a break, and the silence was absolute.

"Please." Woolf waved a sarcastic hand. "We await your subject matter expertise."

Lukas straightened in his chair. "You're out of line."

"Gentlemen…" Claudette tried to calm things down with her powerful siren's voice.

"This is the first proposed candidate who doesn't have a cosmology, astrobiology, or theoretical physics background," Bailey quickly interjected. "Is there anything in Boateng's background that indicates he'd accept even the possibility of your existence?"

"Good question," Claudette responded. "Spiritually, he identifies as agnostic, and throughout his career, he's demonstrated an ability to suspend judgment until he assesses all available data." She suddenly smiled. "One moment, please." She strode back to her place at the table and retrieved something on her laptop with graceful taps of the keys. "May I?" she asked Willem.

Willem passed control of the meeting to Claudette. A couple of seconds later, the professional headshot and resume blinked away, replaced with a different picture: a younger Boateng, boarding a plane, carrying a copy of a familiar-looking book.

Bailey bobbed her head in acknowledgment. An interest in the work of the person who'd previously held the position was a damn good start.

Claudette sat down. "He appears to have the mix of skills, experience, and gravitas we require."

She nearly snorted. If gravitas was a job requirement, she was safely out of the running.

"Are there any other concerns or reservations to discuss at this time?"

At this point in the proceedings, Krispin Woolf usually pulled an obscure procedural delay out of his back pocket.

No objection came. "The candidate advances," Willem said.

The tension in the room noticeably dropped, and the heat vents kicked in again with a heroic huff. Other agenda items passed in a blur, until Lorin presented an update on the items she and her bondmate Gabe Lupinsky had discovered at the Isabella archaeological site last summer. Preparations for the upcoming dig season were underway.

"Are there any updates about Paige Scott?" Elliott asked Lukas.

Last summer, a grad student had disappeared from the dig, accompanied by a mysterious vamp Lorin suspected of having used Paige to gain access to the site. The guy had attacked Lorin, holding an otherworldly weapon to her head that had singed her skin on contact. She'd kicked away the weapon and had been fighting for her life when Gabe had tipped the balance, shifting to wolf form and shredding the vamp's calf with his teeth. The vamp had been bleeding like a stuck pig when he and Paige had evaporated like smoke, disappearing right before their eyes.

"No news," Lukas said curtly. "We're still looking."

At her side, she heard Lorin sigh in frustration.

Bailey surreptitiously eyed her tall, sturdy form, casually clad in jeans, suede boots, and a many-pocketed canvas field jacket. An exotic scarf, an explosion of color, draped around her neck in casual loops, but she made no attempt to hide the scars that the vamp's weapon had seared into her skin. She carried more muscle than Rafe's usual lovers, but she definitely shared their supermodel height, long hair, and killer cheekbones.

What the hell was Rafe doing with *her*?

"Gabe confirmed that the weapon we recovered is made out of the same alloy as Pritchard's—as *the*—lockbox," Lorin corrected herself. Though the evidence was tantalizing, no one was quite ready to conclusively state that the unusual box Lorin had excavated last summer belonged to Noah Pritchard, pilot of the legendary, doomed *Arkapaedis*, whose crash, according to their oral histories, had marooned their ancestors on Earth in the middle of a brutal Minnesota winter.

The piece of the puzzle that just might connect the dots? The tech unit—but not if she couldn't figure out how to crack the damn thing.

Wyland rose. They were up.

He quickly and succinctly gave his archivists report. The preservation and digitization project he was spearheading was behind schedule. Most of her work on the project—estimating storage needs, and building out and securing the infrastructure—was complete, but the capacity calculations needed monitoring and occasional fine-tuning. While he described the painstaking care the preservationists were taking as they worked with the fragile, priceless documents—some nearly a thousand years old and largely written by Valerian—she considered the tech unit. Sleek and sexy as anything you could buy at the Mall of America's Apple Store, it had been found in the lockbox, buried underground, resting next to wild rice kernels dating back almost three thousand years.

Three thousand year old digital data. What a glorious mind-fuck. How could she even begin to verify the data's age? Would she even recognize a date notation if she saw one? In terms of file structure, did the thing even use bits and bytes? Ones and zeroes? It was an unparalleled opportunity to assess the efficacy of digital as a long-term storage medium, not that she'd ever be able to publish her findings—

"Bailey?"

"Yes?"

"Could you talk about your idea for accessing the tech unit?" Wyland asked. "It's…rather ingenious."

Remaining seated, she described the high points—haul a bare-bones research lab to a geographic location so remote there'd be nothing for the tech unit to latch onto, no ambient technology for hundreds of miles. "I'm thinking of Alaska, the Arctic Circle, northern Canada," she said. "The idea is not fully fleshed out yet, but—"

"That *is* ingenious," Lorin said. Lorin and Gabe had been there, working with her, when the tech unit had latched onto Sebastiani Labs' network despite her careful precautions.

The admiration in her voice was a comforting balm. Bailey gave a one-shouldered shrug. "I was up at a cabin in northern Minnesota a couple of weeks ago, and we lost electricity for a couple of days. No electricity meant no internet, conserving battery power, working on paper…" And it had been quiet, so quiet. Being cut off from the outside world, from all its chatter and distraction and interruption, had soothed her thrashing brain, quieted the static. She'd focused deeply and well for the first time in recent memory. The ice and snow, the crackling fireplace, and Rafe, stretched out on the couch, not hiding his hunger as he drew her… Smothering a sigh, she focused on the matter at hand. "I started thinking about ways to build out a mobile lab that was completely self-contained, unconnected to the outside world, away from technology's reach." She shrugged. "Sometimes, to move forward, we need to turn back the clock."

She looked around the table to see people's reactions. Wyland, though not smiling, looked satisfied and pleased. Krispin Woolf's face was blank, but his eyes were burning. Pissed off as usual. Lukas took quick notes on the pad in front of him.

If Lukas was already in logistics mode, it was as good as a provisional 'go.'

Then questions flew like bullets.

"Far northern hemisphere, that means working in the summer," Claudette said. "It's January now. That's a tight timeline for such a complex project. You *are* thinking this summer, right?"

She nodded. Yeah, Rafe would probably have moved on by then.

"Budget?" Jacoby inquired. "Who's heading this up?"

Elliott stepped in before anyone could respond. "I recommend a cross-functional project, funded by the Council and Sebastiani Labs, with Security and Technology in the lead, and working with Physical Sciences and Archiving to flesh out the plan. Any objections?"

No one spoke.

"Willem, please put this at the top of the agenda for next month's meeting." Elliott gave her an approving nod. "Nicely done."

She nodded back, proud but barely holding back a tired sigh. One more fast-track project. One more plate to keep spinning and not let fall.

As Willem pulled up the presentation for the next item on the agenda—ugh, financials—Lorin scooted her chair closer. "Who's we?" Her eyes danced with amusement.

"What?"

"You said, 'we lost electricity.' Who's 'we?' Were you up north with Rafe, by chance?" Lorin nudged her with her elbow. "Very romantic."

At her furious blush, Lorin's smile grew.

Though she didn't feel like she needed Lorin's approval to sleep with Rafe, she wondered if she'd just received it.

She sat back in the big leather chair, tuning out the discussion of balance sheets and investment performance so she could focus on Project Arctic Circle. So much work to do, in so little time—and at the same time Wyatt and his crew were swarming over Sebastiani Labs' network like ants at a picnic.

Christ on a cracker, what had she done?

What she needed to do—no more, no less. Straightening, she wrote "June 1" on the pad in front of her. Circled it with hard strokes of her pen.

Her relationship with Rafe now had a nice, tidy end date. Though time was at a premium, she would enjoy what little remained.

With a vengeance.

✳

"Thank you, thank you, thank you!" Antonia hugged the tablet Rafe just handed her like it was a long-lost lover instead of a digital gadget she'd not seen for several days.

"You're welcome." He'd leave it to Bailey to deliver the lecture. Speaking of lovers… "Is Bailey around?" He'd gotten a lot of work done since they'd seen each other last, but exchanging the occasional harried text wasn't cutting it anymore.

Antonia smiled knowingly. "Come on back."

He followed her through a maze of cube walls to the back corner, to an unmarked steel door that looked strong enough to survive a good-sized nuclear blast. Antonia slapped her hand against the security pad mounted at the side of the door. He heard a very quiet chime, followed by a louder click as the heavy door's lock disengaged.

Antonia held the door open, but didn't enter herself. "I think she's still asleep," she whispered. "Don't do anything I wouldn't do."

Evil little imp.

A bump of lust elbowed him forward, into a room that was unquestionably Bailey's domain even if he couldn't see her yet. Computers dominated the décor, racks and stacks of them, their tiny lights blinking red, amber and green. Over a dozen monitors squatted on tables, and flat-screens hung on the walls, as precisely positioned as museum paintings. Over in the corner, she'd made herself a snug little dorm-like den, with a futon piled with blankets, a small side table, and task lighting. The room smelled like warm plastic, reams of paper, and stale pizza, overlaid with an oddly pleasant metallic sting he'd come to associate with her signature emotion: intellectual curiosity. Sometimes, he thought he could smell her very thoughts, feel them snap, slice and spark.

There was a soft snuffle from the futon, and the pile of blankets suddenly shifted. He grinned as Bailey turned over, revealing a sleep-lined face and a shock of blond hair. A tiny pair of reading glasses he didn't know she wore slipped to the floor.

Stepping around accordion-pleated green and white striped paper, a sleeping laptop, a white Styrofoam clamshell, and a can of Diet Coke, he made his way to the futon and knelt at her side. She snuggled more deeply into the blankets, tucking her injured left hand under her chin.

She was pale, so pale, and there was no disguising the dark circles under her eyes. Picking up the tiny glasses, he set them on the table, on top of two invitations: one for a wedding, and the other for his gallery show. The half-empty bottle of Pepto-Bismol bumped up against the invitations must be responsible for the chalky pink residue staining her chapped lips.

Damn it.

Leaning over, he kissed it away—softly, so softly—before quietly standing up. No matter how badly he needed to kiss her, she needed sleep more. He lightly stroked the hair at her temple, the whisper-soft touch completely at odds with his growing anger. When was the last time she'd seen sunlight? Had she left this room since they'd seen each other last, or had she been holed up here like a rat in a cage?

His brother was about to get served an extra-large piece of his mind.

He wound his way through the maze back to the main hallway, the heels of his heavy boots banging against the carpeted floor. The vibrations radiated up his legs. When he reached Lukas's office, he shoved the door open. "Lukas, damn you. I—"

Empty. He was talking to thin air.

About-facing, he stalked back into the hallway. Next door in the break room, he heard the murmur of Antonia's voice, and Lukas and Jack laughing in response to whatever she'd said. How dare they amuse themselves, relaxing and having fun, when Bailey was running herself ragged?

He strode to the break room, stood in the doorway and stared. Antonia, still cuddling her tablet, saw him first. "Uh oh. Someone's pissed."

"Gee, ya think?" He glared at all of them, but pointed at his brother. "Your office. Now." He went back to Lukas's office, clenching and unclenching his fists. Though he was a pacifist by nature, he knew how to throw a decent punch—and one of his fists just might connect with his brother's face pretty soon, gallery show be damned.

He paced the small space as he waited. So many computers, so many blinking lights. Lukas's office was pretty much an Emergency Command Center, with the largest of the monitors on his desk displaying the Hot Sheet. Yellow and green rows scrolled by, each one representing a call received by their police force. The minute a Code Red hit the Hot Sheet, Lukas went to the crime scene. His brother's ability to tie a taste to an emotional signature, courtesy of his genetic glitch, sometimes supplied a key clue or a lead that Gideon and his team could then follow up.

Lukas walked into the office, closing the door behind him with a snap. "What's your problem?"

Blood pulsed in his temples. "What's the problem? Are you fucking kidding me?"

Lukas eyed him carefully, his nostrils flaring. "Throttle back so we can talk." He gestured to his visitor's chair.

Fuck that. "I'll stand. Have you seen Bailey lately?"

"Please, sit down." Lukas walked to the other side of his desk. "I think she's in The Bunker, taking a nap."

"She's practically passed out!" He paced, purposely knocking into Lukas with his shoulder as he passed. His brother's lips tightened, but he didn't reciprocate, damn it. "She's exhausted."

"Aren't we all." Lukas dropped into his oversized desk chair. "Will you sit, damn it?"

He threw himself into the chair Lukas had indicated. "What the hell is going on here? Have you all lost your bloody minds?"

Lukas's eyes flicked to the Hot Sheet.

Did he even realize he'd done it? His brother was always on duty, but that didn't mean Bailey had to be, or that she should even try. Her little body just couldn't handle it.

"Blame Wyatt Cooper," Lukas said wearily.

Having worked for nearly three days straight, Rafe was operating on next to no sleep, catching catnaps in snatches and food on the fly. Even hearing Cooper's name on Lukas's lips worked his last frayed nerve.

"Bailey and Cheyenne are getting pinged around the clock." Lukas reached for the large plastic bottle of antacids that sat on his desk, shook three tablets out with a clatter, and popped them in his mouth. "She was woken up again last night, and got pulled out of a meeting a couple of hours ago." He crunched on the tablets and swallowed them. "I swear he's toying with her, but Bailey says not. According to her, Cooper and his hired guns are in a reconnaissance phase, poking around the edges of the network but not actually making a serious attempt to penetrate."

"If they're not trying to penetrate, why does she need to respond so urgently?"

"She says she can learn how to fight them by watching what they poke, and how. But so far she hasn't gotten a handle on them—other than to confirm that Cooper can't possibly be working alone."

So she hadn't gotten any decent sleep in days, since she'd left his bed. Well, she'd damn well be back there, and sleeping, before the moon rose tonight if he had to carry her out of there himself.

Lukas leaned back and stared at the ceiling, the big leather desk chair creaking alarmingly. "If he's using human accomplices, building the case against him is going to be tricky."

His brother was already looking ahead to Cooper's arrest and eventual prosecution, and humans were out of their justice system's jurisdiction. The thought of Wyatt Cooper doing some serious time, and finally paying for what he'd done to Bailey so many years ago, was satisfying, but he had more immediate concerns. Bailey simply couldn't keep up this pace; she was burning out before their eyes. "Lukas, how would you manage all this work if Bailey wasn't here?"

"I don't want to even think about it."

Yeah, there was more than a whiff of panic there. "If she doesn't get some rest soon, you're going to have to," he said. "Haven't you noticed that she's about to drop? Working around the clock isn't a long-term solution—for anyone."

Lukas looked at him. "Life must be pretty comfortable over on that side of the desk."

The comment hit him like a grenade. He absorbed the shrapnel, felt it slice deep. Growing up in Lukas's shadow had been a challenge and a half, but he'd honed his own skills and talents, forged his own path, outside the so-called family business. This was the first time Lukas had ever—

"Strike that." Lukas held up a weary hand. "I didn't mean—"

"I think you did, and fair enough."

"No, it's not. And I'm sorry." Lukas raked his hands through his hair.

Rafe nodded, accepting his apology. The edgy defensiveness was gone, replaced by guilt and true remorse. Lukas's emotions were whip-sawing all over the place.

"I owe you a free shot."

The corner of Rafe's mouth tugged up in a grin. When they were young and shared a bedroom, they'd play a game where they'd trade punches, with the first to make an audible sound of pain losing. It hadn't mattered that the winner didn't actually win anything. "I'll bank it, thanks." His smile slowly disappeared. "When I leave here today, I'm taking Bailey with me."

Lukas snorted a laugh. "Like she'd actually get any sleep."

Rafe shot to his feet. "Do you really think I'd disregard her exhaustion just to get laid?" He slapped his hands on the desk, leaning over and glaring down at Lukas. "If great sex was all I wanted, I could get it anywhere, have it with anyone, and you know it."

"Rafe—"

"Do you really think that I'm incapable of deeper feelings? That I don't want the type of lasting relationship, the happiness, you have with Scarlett? That Dad has with Claudette?" He straightened. "That I couldn't find it with her?"

The door suddenly opened. "Half the floor can hear you yelling," Jack said.

About how he could have great sex with anyone he wanted. Rafe pinched the bridge of his nose with thumb and forefinger. "Sorry. We—I'm out of here." He felt the weight of Jack's hard stare as he walked to the door. When he reached it, he glanced back at Lukas. "You do us both a disservice."

He closed the door behind him, leaving Lukas to deal with Jack.

Antonia stood in the hallway, watching. "You okay?"

"Yeah," he said with a sigh. "Can you get me back into The Bunker?"

"I can do better than that." She indicated the tablet she still held cradled in her arms. "Follow me."

When they arrived at the fortified security door, she gestured to the matte black palm pad. "Hold your hand there until I say drop." He did as she asked, holding his hand against the pad while she swiped and tapped. Finally, the tablet chimed, the door clicked, and the tiny light switched from red to green. "And *voila!*" she crowed. "Access is yours."

He stared at her. The little twerp had given him access to a secured area with a couple of taps on a tablet, and without asking anyone for permission.

"Let's test it out."

Stepping back, Rafe waited for the door lock to engage again, for the light to turn back to red, and repeated the sequence. The door clicked, the light turned green.

"After palming in, you have a seven second window before the locks re-engage."

"Okay."

"Rafe…" She hesitated. "Cut Lukas some slack. He's wrong, and he knows it. He's under a lot of stress right now."

And so was she. "Come here." He hugged her, scrubbing his knuckles against her head, kissing the tip of her nose. Lukas was right about one thing. He and Sasha were able to pursue their own interests because of Lukas's and Antonia's skills, interests, and abilities. Hell, he'd be sitting in the Incubus Second chair right now if not for his little sister, the diabolical genius. "Thank you," he said.

"No problem." She grinned. "It was really easy."

He'd let her think he was thanking her for getting him into The Bunker for now. "Okay. Bailey is officially off the clock until 9:00 a.m. tomorrow morning. If you call her, ping her, text her, email her, instant message her, or attempt to contact her using any mechanism currently known to man or beast, I'll shave you bald."

"You'd have to catch me first."

"Try me."

Nostrils flaring, she assessed him. Her right eyebrow rose, Spock-like, before she nodded.

He kissed her nose again. "Now scoot."

She turned and walked away with an emphatic flip of her long hair, but her approval followed him through the door to The Bunker.

✳

"Mmm." Bailey didn't have to open her eyes to know exactly who brushed snowflake-soft kisses against her lips, barely a touch before melting away.

Rafe. He'd awakened her with a kiss, but unlike those chaste Disney princesses, she didn't have to wake up, marry the prince, and rule the kingdom. She could simply enjoy. "Come back here," she murmured, threading her fingers into drifts of hair to pull him closer.

The moments stretched and pulled as their lips clung and separated. He tasted like exotic tropical fruit, or coconut-spiked rum. Sunny, sunny Rafe, her wicked, cheerful sunbeam, warming her in winter, the sunlight to her shade. She reluctantly opened her eyes and focused. Rafe was smiling down at her, his hair curtaining their faces. "How did you get in?"

"Antonia."

He was kneeling beside the futon, his upper body leaning over hers. She wanted to feel his weight, have him press her back into the plush fabric. When she lifted a hand to cup his cheekbone, he leaned into her touch like a sleek desert cat, voluptuous pleasure tightening his features.

She glanced at the door, willing it to stay closed. How much weight would the futon hold? Maybe she could talk him into staying for a while, taking a break.

She'd barely finished the thought when Rafe gave her a pursed-lipped smooch. Pushing to his feet, he took her hands in a gentle grasp and tugged her to a seated position. The bundle of blankets dropped to her waist, revealing her threadbare New Kids on the Block T-shirt. "Come on," he said, jerking the blanket away. "This is a jail break."

"What?" she squawked. "I can't leave." She looked, wild-eyed, at the piles sitting on tables and chairs around the room. She had so much work to do. A draft of the proposal that Elliott had requested they fast-track lay on the floor at Rafe's feet; she'd been fleshing out the technology infrastructure section when tiredness had overtaken her. She and Wyland had narrowed the location to three specific sites, and a very unhappy Chico was leaving next week to check them out in person. In a little less than five months, she'd probably be in Alaska, living in a trailer. Alone, for months on end.

Screw her work. Thoughts of Alaska's midnight sun were no match for Rafe's liquid sunshine gaze. "Okay, let's go."

Rafe looked surprised.

Clearly he'd expected her to put up a fight. *Nope. Not this time.* "Your place?"

"Sure." His eyes searched hers as he pulled her to her feet, probably waiting for the 'gotcha'.

It was all she could do to not step closer to his heat, to hold on tightly to his lean, muscled frame. She stepped back, ignoring the pinch in her heart. "Give me a few minutes to tie up some loose ends." Tonight, she'd follow Elliott's delegation advice with a vengeance.

Rafe sat on the futon she'd just vacated, suspiciously eyeing the piles of paper. "You can follow me home in your car." He picked up her reading glasses. "Will you put these on for me? Please?" He wiggled his brows lecherously.

"You're nuts." She snatched them from his hand, folded the bows, and set them next to the computer she was about to use. By the time she dropped onto her rolling stool, she was already deep in thought. After a quick email to Cheyenne, she'd be ready to go.

Cheyenne would have to handle Wyatt's shenanigans without her help tonight.

CHAPTER ELEVEN

When he'd called Cheyenne to ask if she wanted to go out, Wyatt had envisioned a night at Underbelly or First Avenue, or maybe sharing some wine and appetizers at an intimately-lit downtown restaurant. He *hadn't* envisioned holding a flashlight for Cheyenne as she knelt in a mound of snow, digging at the base of a tree with a gardening trowel in the dark. "People actually find this enjoyable? Worth $10,000?"

Cheyenne didn't look up. "Yeah. Look around."

Even though it was after eight p.m. on a weeknight, they were far from alone. Apparently hundreds of other people thought that today's Winter Carnival Medallion hunt clue, when added to the clues that had already been published, added up to Como Park. The park had a festive tailgate feel, crowded with singletons, couples, families and groups laden down with blankets, backpacks and Thermoses. Everyone was digging in the snow, using implements varying from bare hands to the biggest snow shovel Wyatt had ever seen.

The bank thermometer across the street read an ungodly -5 F., and the scent of cheerful competition hovered like visible breath.

This was nuts.

Cheyenne threw a side-eye at two nearby men, and started digging harder. "It's here. I can smell it. Look at all the media trucks, all the cameras." She indicated the local news station vans parked along the street with a jerk of her head.

"I hope you're right," he said, teeth chattering. "It's freezing out here."

"I'll warm you up later."

"I'll hold you to that." He looked around, pretending interest in his surroundings. The crawling sensation at the back of his neck had nothing to do with the temperature.

They were being watched.

By whom? From where? They were surrounded by trees, bushes, buildings, milling people and random foliage. The possibilities were endless. Well, whoever was freezing their ass off spying on them in the dark would see, and report back, exactly what he wanted them to see—him, cozying up to Cheyenne Winterbourne.

His cell vibrated in his coat pocket. Plucking it out, he glanced at the screen, gave it a couple of taps. Bailey's car was on the move, and so was Rafe Sebastiani's. He stared at the two red dots, slowly traversing the city streets. Both took a turn that would lead them to the West Bank.

They were on their way to Rafe's place. Together.

Finally.

Bailey's car hadn't moved from Sebastiani Security's parking lot for days, except for the time when a tough-looking Hispanic dude had moved it for the snowplow. Despite his fun-time reputation, Rafe Sebastiani had spent the last few days alone, his car not moving from his garage. The only sign of life had been the second floor studio lights, burning for two days straight.

He'd used the time to supervise his team's careful and methodical exploration of Sebastiani Labs' network from a safe, virtual distance. Though he fumed at the glacial pace, he recognized it as necessary to achieve their ultimate goal. While the techs did their work, he'd done his. His detailed analysis of Sebastiani Labs' entrances, exits and escape routes revealed them to be largely theoretical, because actual entry, exit or escape would be nearly impossible to achieve. There was no lobby receptionist to flirt with. When he entered the building and approached the desk, a monitor on the desk blinked to life, and a sophisticated, androgynous avatar had politely asked him who his appointment was with. He'd blurted out Cheyenne's name, but she hadn't answered her phone. He'd left the campus, made a quick clothing change, and, disguised as a satellite dish repairman, installed surveillance equipment outside Rafe's living room and bedroom windows. He'd had his equipment upgrade story all ready, but Sebastiani hadn't even noticed him.

He couldn't wait to access the bedroom feed, to mentally superimpose his face over Sebastiani's as Bailey's lithe, nude form writhed beneath him.

A sudden cheer went up from across the park.

Cheyenne threw down her garden spade in disgust.

A little girl wearing a pink snowmobile suit, hat, scarf and mittens, and so bundled up she couldn't lower her arms to her sides, held the medallion in one hand and a White Castle burger wrapper in the other. She jumped up and down in her tiny matching boots.

"A kid found it? In a Slider box? You're freaking kidding me," Cheyenne muttered. Nonetheless, she stood, brushed the snow off her knees, and joined in the clapping. Reporters and their camera crews rushed to the little girl and her beaming father, catching the cuteness for the ten o'clock news. "Not enough time for reconnaissance, damn it." She wrapped her arms around his waist, but he could barely feel it through layers of heavy coats and clothing. "They published the clue in this morning's paper, but I couldn't get away from work any earlier than I did." She sighed, her breath a misty white cloud. "Busy day today."

Yeah, his team had kept her hopping all day long. He probably should make it up to her. "My place?" he invited, brushing a whisper-soft kiss on her lips.

She increased the pressure, sending pleasure streaking down his spine. Cheyenne wanted him, and wasn't afraid to show it.

He liked that in a woman.

"How about mine instead? Cool white wine, hot whirlpool tub?" She grinned. "I did promise to warm you up."

"Sounds great." After they collected her gear, he took her by her mittened hand and started the long walk back to her SUV, their boots crunching against the snow.

He wouldn't stay the night. After he got home from Cheyenne's, after he slaked his initial hunger, he'd settle in and watch some home movies.

*

"Delicious." Bailey scooped the last of the wild rice soup out of a chunky pottery bowl Rafe had likely made himself. "You could give Chadden a run for his money with this recipe."

Sitting across the butcher-block island, Rafe snatched another breadstick from the basket. "Someone else already did. It's from the Byerly's cookbook."

She nodded as he named the beloved local grocery store chain. She had the same recipe book packed away in a box at her condo someplace.

"I made a double batch last Saturday, after you left, and I've pretty much been living on it ever since." Setting down his wineglass, Rafe reached across the island and took her left hand, stroking his fingers over her ligaments and tendons, shifting her wrist to check her range of motion.

Her brain stutter-stepped. How could such a gentle touch sizzle so much? "You've been eating nothing but soup for days? That's not enough fuel for a big guy like you."

He picked up the Chianti bottle, refilled their wine glasses, and took her hand again. "I'd say we're both overdue for a meal and a break."

Though he looked more relaxed now than he had when they'd left The Bunker, the bright kitchen lights revealed how tired he was. The skin under his eyes was smudged with shadows, but seated across from her, wearing jeans, a white T-shirt, an ancient V-neck sweater with a hole in one elbow and sleeves pushed up on his forearms, he still looked tasty enough to gobble up with a freaking spoon. With his hair pulled back into that saggy, ridiculously sexy bun again...

Holy flying monkeys, no wonder he had to beat lovers off with a stick.

"Did I hurt you?" He loosened his grip on her hand. "You just tensed up."

"Nope. I'm fine." She made a conscious effort to relax, to stop her feeble mooning. Pretty soon she'd be writing their names together in a hand-drawn heart, dotting her i's with smiley faces.

"Your hand is shaking."

"So it is." Giving into impulse, she twined her fingers with his, fighting back a smile at a miniscule bit of clay she saw underneath his thumbnail. For some reason, the tiny imperfection felt like a gift. "So, when am I going to see this studio of yours?" She was dying to see where he worked.

"Are you sure you've had enough to eat?" He lifted their joined hands to his mouth and nibbled on the tip of her index finger, turning her knees to noodles.

She nodded. "You?"

"Of this?" he mumbled around her finger. "Never." He gave the fingertip a sharp nip that sent a bolt of lightning up her arm, then released her. Rounding the island, he picked up their wine glasses. His luscious scent made her dizzy, made her think of him striding across the hot desert sands, his white robes flapping in the wind… Rafe of Arabia.

She'd popped half a pill during the drive over. Why hadn't the thing hit yet?

"You might want to put on your shoes," he said as they walked to the door leading to the stairwell. "The studio floor will be cold." When he turned, slipping into a pair of clay-specked suede moccasins, she rooted around in her purse, grabbed another half a pill from her pillbox, and slipped it under her tongue, trying not to wrinkle her nose.

At some point, she'd tell Jack's Sebastiani Labs contact that the pills tasted like ass.

Stepping into her own short boots, she followed Rafe one flight down. The combined scents of chemicals, glazes, paints, and damp clay grew stronger, more pungent, as they approached the fire door leading to the studio. The aromatic stew was…oddly pleasant.

Rafe watched her carefully. "Let me know if the smell gets to be too much for you." At her nod, he opened the door, walked in, and beckoned her to follow.

Despite his earlier comment about the lack of heat, the shadowy, cavernous space felt comfortably warm. When he flipped on the huge overhead lights, her preconceived notions about what an art studio looked like—austere and antiseptically clean, like a gallery— were flipped upside down.

It was messy, with metal shavings and blobs of clay on the floor. Stiff rags were thrown on the floor next to an industrial-strength washing machine, and the dryer sat with its door ajar, clean rags at the ready. There were sketchpads and easels, and wadded-up pieces of paper, and what looked like a portable blowtorch unit sitting in the corner. Chico had told her that Rafe had his own kiln, and that there were blocks of stone and sheets of metal stored down on the first floor. The shelving units held a healthy collection of paints and glazes. Metal picks, wooden dowels, and other tools stood upright in containers.

Though she was curious about the plastic-shrouded figures, she couldn't resist walking over to the potter's wheel in the corner. How many women had he seduced re-enacting that famous scene from *Ghost*? Patrick Swayze and Demi Moore had turned throwing a pot into slick, slippery foreplay, an expression of love that even death could not deny.

He wrapped his arms around her from behind, his tall frame cuddled against hers. She shivered as his wine-warm breath sheeted across her neck, and she shifted her hips in welcome. His cock was as hard as the concrete floor where they stood.

He cleared his throat. "Let me show you what I've been working on."

As he led her to the floor-to-ceiling shelving unit dominating the entire north wall, she glanced down at his groin. Wyatt had always treated a hard-on like a Sev 1 showstopper, an issue that needed immediate attention. But Rafe not only walked, he spoke in full, coherent sentences, describing his work process as he uncovered the sculptures.

A man who could think with both heads at one time. She snickered, an unladylike sound that would no doubt horrify her mother.

"What's so funny?"

"Nothing." Her eyes widened as she took in the figures he'd unveiled. "Are all these—"

"You? Yes."

It was her, all right—her nude body, in various poses, oozing frank sexual satiation. She slapped her hands to her sizzling cheeks.

He raised a finger to his lips and assessed the sculptures he'd uncovered. "I'd like to work in something other than clay, but I don't have a lot of time before the showing. There are so many other poses I'd like to capture."

A primitive thrill shot through her as she stepped closer to the shelves. Instead of feeling exposed, or even self-conscious, she felt an odd sense of pride. Of power. Her father would call it sin. "Can I touch?"

He nodded.

She reached out and stroked the nearest figure—of her, stretched out on her back, one knee raised, arms thrown overhead and head tossed back. The individual features of her body were abstracted rather than realistic—no pubic hair at the juncture of her legs, and her nipples were suggested rather than specifically sculpted—but in the lines of the sculpture, he'd captured exactly what she'd been feeling at that moment: the abandonment, the freedom, the utter sense of release. Uncanny. "It feels like leather," she said, stroking again.

"It hasn't been fired yet." He wrapped his arms around her from behind again, his hair-roughened forearms resting just under her breasts. His breathing was faster, rougher, as his lips caressed the tender patch of skin under her ear.

She locked her knees so she could remain standing. "Can I tell you a secret?"

"Anything, sweet girl."

She swallowed, grabbing onto her courage with both hands. "Sometimes I think of you here, all alone, skimming and gliding your hands over the clay. Over an inanimate me." She paused. "It turns me on. A lot." Heat bloomed between her thighs, made her slicken with need.

She wanted to drag him down to the nearest horizontal surface. Now.

Against her back, Rafe's chest expanded and contracted. "Whatever's going on in that big brain of yours, I really like it." His hands moved north, cupping her breasts. A tiny noise escaped from his throat. "You're not wearing a bra."

She shrugged. "It's not like I need one."

"Jesus, you're killing me." Stepping back, he looked at her closely. "Are you sure you're okay with me showing this work publicly? I don't want to cause any problems with your family."

Like her family would care. Well, Mel would care, but her sister would think it was freaking awesome. "It's not as if anyone will know it's me."

Rafe's dark, sensual chuckle stroked over her like heavy silk. "You keep telling yourself that, honey."

She shrugged one shoulder. "The people who know us, who know we're—" she swallowed, hard "—sleeping together, might figure it out, but..." She took the two steps that brought their bodies together again. Tipped her face up to his. "Thank you," she whispered. "Thank you for making me look—feel—so beautiful."

He cradled her face in his hands. "I sculpt what I see."

She glanced back at the sculptures. They were unmistakably sensual—even sexual—but somehow not lewd. His ability to capture an emotional moment, to express it in clay, was uncanny. Despite what Rafe said or thought, no one would ever guess that she'd been his model—or if they did, they'd marvel at his genius for seeing the extraordinary in such ordinary raw material.

Imagine. Her, Bailey Brown, an artist's muse. A *sex demon's* muse. The idea was deliciously naughty, as intoxicating as his drugging scent.

Had the other pill hit yet? Her thoughts were razor blade sharp, perfectly able to register and appreciate the precise level of havoc Rafe's hands, body, and mouth wreaked on her hungry body. She could write a scientific paper on the subject. She giggled as Rafe dragged his lips along her jawline, behind her ear, nibbling along the precision-cut border where her hair met the nape of her neck.

"Have I ever told you how much I love your hair?" he murmured.

The vibration of Subject A's lips against Subject B's skin stimulated Subject B's autonomic nervous system such that—

"Hiding those ears would be criminal, and the nape of your neck is a bloody poem."

Subject B exhibits classic autonomic response. Galvanic reaction causes body hair to rise. Mammary papillae are erect. Shivering is noted. "I'll pass that along to my stylist," she responded.

She could barely talk. He was melting her down from the inside out. *Touch of Subject A's lips against Subject B's ear causes a rhythmic clenching of pubococcygeus muscles. Increased blood flow engorges the vaginal walls, producing sexual lubrication…*

She almost snickered aloud. Would she have to produce her damp panties for peer review?

"Tickle?" Rafe murmured, lifting his head slightly.

"A little." Suddenly craving a firmer touch, she lifted his hands to her breasts again. She felt his groan of reaction, the unconscious roll of his hips. Reaching behind him, she grabbed his ass, tugging him more tightly against her.

A shudder wracked his body. "Bailey…"

Her need was feral, frantic, clawing for release. "The couch." Overstuffed and upholstered in bordello-red crushed velvet, it looked completely out of place, yet somehow utterly right. She could already feel its soft nap against her bare skin.

"I like how you think."

They made their way to the couch, groping, tasting, unfastening buttons and zippers along the way. His sweater and T-shirt, her hoodie and T-shirt, were unceremoniously stripped off, thrown out of the way. They both kicked off their shoes. Rafe lay down on his back, pulling her to lie on top of him.

Barefoot and bare-chested, sprawled on the couch, he was the most decadent treat she'd ever had the pleasure to sample. Lifting his head slightly, he tugged at the elastic band, releasing his long hair from its messy knot with an unselfconscious shake of his head.

Her breath stuttered at the juxtaposition of long, soft hair and hard cobblestone abs, just flat-out locked in her lungs.

His eyes were so hot they burned.

"What?" His voice was low and rough.

"I love your hair." Talk about the understatement of the decade. Shifting her weight, she perched on the edge of the couch, sitting next to his hips, so she could better see him. "Your dad has long hair, and Lukas is growing his back out again. Is long hair an incubi thing?" Wyatt had worn his hair on the long side, too.

"Our necks, shoulders and upper backs are erogenous zones," Rafe responded, cupping her bare breasts again. "We grow out our hair to—"

"Turn yourselves on?"

His answering grin was beyond wicked. "Don't knock it till you've tried it."

She was all too familiar with that particular activity, thank you very much. "I'm never going to be able to look your father in the eye again."

"So uptight," Rafe teased. Releasing her breasts, he pressed her hands into his pecs. His tan nipples were pebbled, as erect as hers were, but surrounded by a silky, tawny pelt. "You really want to talk about my father right now?"

"Your father's very attractive, but… no." Not when she had over six feet of lean, hedonistic debauchery spread out like a buffet before her. "I have plans for you."

The fire in his eyes flared. "Tell me more."

"Not telling. Showing." She had to touch him, taste him. Take him, over and over again, as often as she could while she still had a chance.

Rafe stilled when her nose touched his chest hair, gasped as she followed the whorl of its growth pattern with her tongue, groaned when she latched onto his nipple. His jean-clad legs shifted restlessly as she suckled. His abs clenched as she stroked her hands south, following the narrow trail of hair below his navel, slightly darker and more wiry than the hair on his chest. When she reached the waistband of his low-slung jeans, he sucked in his breath, his stomach going slightly concave.

Creating more room for her hands. Her mouth.

She lifted her head, releasing his nipple with an audible pop. Stared at him as she tugged, releasing the buttons on his fly. Pride—yes, pride—flooded through her. She'd put that tight, wild expression on his face.

She dipped her head again, licking her way down the same path her hand had just taken. His hands cupped her head, his fingernails scratching into her scalp. Her gasp of reaction gusted onto his stomach.

With a groan, his hips rolled toward her mouth.

He'd read her mind.

She looked at his open fly, framing his erect penis and his tidy nest of pubic hair. Did he ever wear underwear? She nudged the thought aside. Why cover such beautifully-formed flesh? She reached out to touch, running her finger down the underside of his long shaft. Ruddy and heavily veined, silky smooth yet hard to the touch…he was warm, so warm. She could barely see the heavy globes of his testicles, lightly furred with golden hair.

The jeans were in her way. "Lift," she said, tapping his hipbone with her forefinger. Dropping his hands from her head, Rafe did as she asked, and she quickly tugged the ancient jeans over his hips, down his legs, and off, tossing them over her shoulder.

Holy Mother. He was a mind-blowing juxtaposition of beauty and brawn—brawn she could better appreciate now that he lay naked before her. His lean muscles were a work of art, cut and honed as if Michelangelo had carved him with his chisel. And that hair, tumbled in such abandon, a heavy hank slipping over the edge of the couch… Jesus. Though she possessed zero artistic ability, she yearned for a camera, for a sketchpad, for the skill to capture even a fraction of his splendor.

Her memories would have to do.

His nipples and chest hair were damp from her mouth, and his folded hands rested low on his stomach, almost touching his penis. What she wouldn't give to see those long fingers wrapped around his own flesh, showing her exactly what pleased him.

"Bailey." His sandpaper voice rasped over her. His eyes glittered, predatory and hot. "Lose the pants."

She glanced down, surprised to find herself still half-dressed. Her boyfriend jeans sagged nearly to her hip bones, exposing the elastic waistband of her red Wonder Woman underwear.

It figured.

He lay on his back, but the patient pose was an illusion. She could see the coiled power in his muscles, ready to be unleashed at the slightest provocation.

Power flooded into her. Steadied her. She was going to provoke him, all right—right up to the edge.

And over.

Standing just out of arm's reach, she tugged at the button fastening the waistband of her jeans. She heard his breath catch as the jeans sagged a couple of millimeters and then stopped. She fiddled with the tab of her zipper, slowly dragging it down tooth by tooth.

One corner of his mouth kicked up when he saw her underwear, but he didn't say anything. The hands so patiently resting on his own stomach shifted south, tantalizingly close to his twitching penis.

She swallowed, hard. Stared, helplessly.

"Why did you stop?" he asked.

"Why did you?"

Heated approval glowed in his eyes. He inhaled deeply, his face tightening with pleasure at whatever he smelled, whatever he sensed. Eyes on hers, he wrapped the fingers of his right hand around his penis and gave a slow, languid stroke.

Her brain emptied, just poured its contents out like water onto the ground, but she somehow managed to take off her pants, watching him watch her, as electricity arced between them. When she slipped out of her underwear, Rafe's jaw clenched, but he kept his pace slow and steady, using a firmer touch than she'd ever dare. The plump head of his penis was a dusky, ruddy rose, and slick with moisture.

She dropped to her knees beside the couch and covered his hand with hers. Twining their fingers together, she took him into her mouth. His dark, salty taste crashed onto her tongue like a storm at sea. She suckled strongly, trying to get more of his wild, primal essence.

With a growl, he surged upright, grabbing her around the waist and twisting her. Soon she was lying on her back, sandwiched between crushed velvet and his hot, heavy body. His eyes were wild, glowing gold, his teeth bared like a pirate on a looting spree. His chest heaved as he dragged breath in and out of his lungs, choppy and rough. His erection pulsed between her thighs.

She'd done this. She'd driven him to this. And she needed him inside her, rolling and pounding.

Now.

"Rafe—" She couldn't articulate what she wanted, couldn't put her outrageous, yawning need into words. But somehow he knew—knew she wanted his weight, his heat, his body surging into hers.

"Hang on a sec," he whispered, getting off the couch. She barely had time to shiver, much less protest, before he was back again, donning a condom with efficient motions. Then his heavy body covered hers again, her hips forming a natural cradle for his. Supporting his upper body weight with his forearms, his hair curtaining their faces, he watched her with an expression she couldn't read.

With a hard swallow, eyes on hers, he rocked his hips, the broad head of his penis barely nudging her damp opening. He flexed back, inhaling deeply. Threading his fingers through her hair, he rocked again, pressing but not entering.

"Please," she strangled out, wrapping her legs around his hips with all her strength.

Mouthing a curse, he drove into her—a long, blinding glide that made her eyes roll back in her head. "Jesus." When she could focus again, she saw Rafe staring down at her, jaw clenched as he held himself motionless, giving her a chance to adjust.

"Okay?" His voice was like gravel.

"God, yes." She tightened her legs around his hips. "More."

She almost heard his control snap, a sail flapping in the wind. His hips rolled, surging into hers, over and over again, for long, timeless minutes. She could do nothing but skip over the waves with him, racing the wind, over the crests and through the troughs. She could do nothing but ride out the storm, lashed to the mast, until they were tossed onto shore with a final, furious heave.

CHAPTER TWELVE

"This isn't a fish house, it's a fish mansion," Bailey muttered to Jack the following Saturday as they watched Sasha trot out to meet the guy who'd driven onto frozen White Bear Lake to deliver their pizzas. The weather was sunny and cold, the sky a painful, cloudless blue, and they'd both been invited to join the Sebastiani family in what was apparently a long-standing family tradition: entering the St. Paul Winter Carnival ice fishing contest. Not that anyone seemed to be fishing except Lukas.

All had been quiet on the Wyatt front for a couple of days, so she hadn't felt like she could turn down Lukas's invitation to join them—not without incurring Wyland's wrath, at any rate. He'd overheard Lukas issue the invitation, his supercilious eyebrow raised as she'd mentally cast about for a good reason to refuse.

Because Rafe would be there, and she needed time to think.

The pills didn't seem to be working very well anymore.

Ever since she and Rafe had made love—had had sex, she ruthlessly corrected herself—in his studio, she'd found her thoughts drifting far too frequently to how crushed velvet felt against her breasts as Rafe rocked into her from behind. How his cock dragged so exquisitely in and out of her violently-aroused flesh, filling her to bursting. How his long fingers had bit into her hips, holding her in place to receive his thrusts.

She shivered at the memory.

"Cold?" Jack asked.

She made a vague humming noise, which she hoped sufficed. She was dressed for the weather, and had stayed active enough in the vaguely rectangular area the Sebastiani family had staked out on the busy lake with their parked cars, trucks, and SUVs. Over by the fish house, Elliott and Claudette tended a charcoal grill. The scent of sizzling hamburgers made her stomach rumble—whether in hunger or protest, she didn't know. Scarlett sat in a sling chair next to Lukas while he fished, drinking hot chocolate and paging through the latest issue of *Rolling Stone*. Rafe and Antonia played catch, flinging a rock-hard football over Lukas's head a good distance away from where she and Jack stood.

Pheromones shouldn't be a problem, but…they were. It didn't matter what Rafe wore; she mentally stripped it from him, exposing the frame and flesh beneath. Even today, wearing a pair of black ski bibs and a fleece jacket, she wanted to tackle him to the ground and take him.

She couldn't seem to get enough of him, and it wasn't like she was sex-deprived. Without her quite realizing how it happened, she'd gotten into the habit of driving to Rafe's place after she was finished with work for the day rather than go to Sasha's and Antonia's. They'd prepare and share a simple meal, and then go down to the studio, where she'd strip to her skin and pose on that red velvet couch. Rafe would work for a couple of hours, then wash the clay from his hands and join her, teaching her what her body wanted, what it craved, encouraging her to explore her sexual boundaries. To ask for anything, without shame.

The man could make a mint as a sex therapist. Or a gigolo.

A wave of heat washed over her.

Across the clearing, Rafe looked at her, fumbling the perfect spiral Antonia had just thrown.

"Rafe?" Antonia snapped her fingers to get his attention.

Every head swung to Rafe, then to her, back and forth, like they were watching a match at Wimbledon. It had been like that all afternoon.

"This thing is as hard as a brick," Rafe grumbled.

Antonia grinned. "That's what she said."

"Smart ass." Rafe tackled Antonia into a nearby snow bank.

Face flaming, Bailey turned away from Antonia's shrieks of laughter and went into the custom-built fish house Lukas had borrowed from a friend. It was an odd mix of rough and luxe, with heat, seating, a kitchen with table, and satellite TV. It had not one, but two skylights, and a drop-down bed that was stored in its upright position, hooked to the wall. There was even an indoor bathroom of sorts—a five gallon pail with a snap-on toilet seat, placed in a curtained-off alcove—with biodegradable toilet paper and hand sanitizer sitting on a nearby ledge. The urn of coffee perking on the table had kept her using the facilities far too frequently.

Retrieving her purse from the pile of belongings in the corner, she quickly found her pillbox, took a full tablet instead of a half, and popped it under her tongue. She was going through the pills at an addict's pace, but she had to do *something* to combat the way Rafe distracted her.

There was a knock on the door. "Yes?"

"Can I come in?" Sasha called.

Swirling her tongue, she willed the horrible-tasting pill to dissolve more quickly. "Sure."

Sasha pushed the door open with her shoulder, carrying five pizza boxes, letting in a wedge of bright sunlight before closing the door again. Setting the boxes on the table, she unzipped her fuchsia snowmobile suit to its belted waist and shrugged out of the arms, letting them hang. "I need coffee. Want some?"

Bailey shook her head. "I'm cutting myself off." If she had one more cup of the amazing brew, her stomach's non-violent protest would escalate to something far more dire.

She'd blown off her appointment with Wyland yesterday. Like a coward, she'd texted him instead of calling, using Wyatt and his minions as an excuse. Wyland must have kept the information to himself, because neither Elliott nor Lukas had read her the riot act this morning.

After filling her cup, Sasha set it down on the table next to the pizza boxes, locked the fish house door, whisked back the bathroom curtain, stepped inside, and closed it. There were whishing and whooshing sounds as she lowered the one-piece garment enough to use the facilities. "Haven't seen much of you this week, roomie," she called from behind the curtain as liquid tinkled into the bucket.

Bailey started setting out the things they'd need for lunch: paper plates, napkins, silverware, hamburger buns and condiments. Why did having a conversation with someone peeing behind a thin, fabric curtain feel so much more invasive than talking with the same person from a bathroom stall at work?

The tinkling stopped. Toilet paper rustled. "If you wanted to stay with Rafe instead of with us, all you had to do was say so."

Had she hurt Sasha's feelings? "Sorry."

"No need to apologize." Behind the curtain, elastic snapped. More rustling as Sasha pulled up whatever she was wearing under the snowmobile suit. A zipper fastened with a soft gnash of teeth. When Sasha whisked the curtain aside, she was rubbing her hands together. The scent of antibacterial cleanser stung her nostrils. "Let's get these pizzas set up."

Transcribing the scrawled hieroglyphics on the pizza boxes—sausage, bacon cheeseburger, Hawaiian, hot Italian sausage, and one veggie mix—they arranged the boxes on the table.

Someone pounded on the door. "You disappeared with the pizza."

Rafe.

"I'm going to the bathroom!" Sasha hollered. Dropping her voice again, she continued speaking like Rafe hadn't said anything. "Will you be staying with Rafe, then?"

I have no idea.

"Sasha!" Antonia yelled. The doorknob rattled. "Unlock the door."

Sasha didn't even blink, just continued to look at her with eyes that saw too much.

"I'm sorry. I should have called and let you know my plans had changed." She looked away, fiddling with the napkins, arranging them in a decorative fan. "We're kind of taking it day by day."

More pounding. Sasha shot an annoyed look at the door. "No need to apologize, you dolt. I haven't seen Rafe this content, this relaxed, in ages. Whatever you're doing, keep on doing it."

Her thoughts flashed to the red couch. To Rafe's bed. To his shower. Her cheeks flamed, hot as the grill outside.

"Sasha?" Elliott's voice. "The hamburgers are done."

"Coming!" Her expression turned from teasing to serious. "You're good for each other, you know. Enjoy yourself."

"While it lasts," she said softly.

Sasha opened the door. "Everything come out okay?" Antonia said crabbily, elbowing past her sister on her way to the pizza boxes.

"Yes. Thank you very much for asking."

Rafe entered, eyeing them cautiously, like an animal sensing odd vibrations before an earthquake.

"That veggie pizza smells fabulous," Scarlett said. "I'm starving."

Lukas urged her into a chair. "Sit. I'll bring you a piece."

Scarlett looked like she was about to protest, but she sat down instead, letting Lukas serve them both. The look they exchanged was filled with secrets.

"Veggie pizza, right?" Rafe said, suddenly at her side. "We need to push some calories."

"Um—"

He filled her plate with pizza, some green bean casserole, and a small pile of sliced apples drizzled with caramel sauce.

Everyone filled their plates, took them outside, and settled into the chairs placed around the bonfire. While she ate, Rafe watched her—too closely, and with eyes that stripped her naked.

⁕

After finishing his meal, Rafe laid the grill's removable grate in the snow and attacked it with a scrub brush. What was up with Bailey? Though she laughed and smiled, her laughter was brittle around the edges, and both Sasha and Jack were shooting him the side-eye. Jack's accused him of being the source of Bailey's stress, and Sasha's urged him do something about it.

He hadn't gotten a second alone with Sasha to ask what she'd said to upset Bailey during their private fish house chat.

There was still too much food left on her plate, though he'd watched her eat most of the green bean casserole, nibble at broccoli florets she picked off the pizza, and clean the caramel sauce off the apples with maddening swipes of her tongue. Now, gathered around the bonfire making s'mores for dessert, she seemed content to talk to everyone except him.

Sasha sidled up next to him. "We need to talk."

"What did you say to her?" he hissed.

"I don't know!"

"Look at her." Rafe jerked his head to where Bailey and Jack sat, unwrapping chocolate bars, their heads close as they talked. Prior to today, he hadn't known what jealousy felt like. He knew better than to be jealous of Jack, but he *was*—jealous that she'd feel safer with the other man than with him. "She's as skittish as a vamp standing on the equator at sunrise."

"I teased her about how we never see her, told her that if she wanted to stay with you instead of us, all she had to do was say so."

Bailey was pretty much living with him, a state of affairs he should find odd and unsettling, but didn't. After the first time they'd made love down in his studio, it was as if a switch had been flipped in their relationship. Her sexual confidence had grown by leaps and bounds. Watching her face light with wonder and discovery as she rode them both to oblivion made his chest puff with pride.

It also broke his heart. Her sanctimonious father had a lot to answer for. But she was part of *him* now, part of *his* family, whether she recognized it or not.

Whether he convinced her to stay with him forever or not.

And there it was. Removing his aviator sunglasses, he rubbed at the bridge of his nose with his thumb and forefinger.

He'd met his mate.

"Rafe?" Sasha rested her hand on his forearm.

Of course his sister knew exactly what he was feeling.

"I told her to enjoy herself, to enjoy you. You know how she answered?"

"Do I want to hear this?"

Sasha stared across the clearing to where Bailey and Jack were sitting. "She said, 'While it lasts.'"

"What?"

"Your reputation precedes you. You have some work to do, Romeo."

"I'm sick to death of hearing about my so-called reputation." Rafe glared down at his sister. "Before she and I connected, I hadn't slept with anyone in over a year—and even *that* time was with *her*, the night of Scarlett's show at Underbelly."

Sasha's eyebrows rose. "Okay, that explains a few things."

"So, yeah," he said defensively. "She's moved some clothes over—"

"You gave up closet space? It must be love," she teased.

"We cook together, we hang out, we shower together, sleep together, jostle for sink space as we brush our teeth together in the morning. We all but live together—as much as she lives anywhere, that is." Her nomadic existence drove him nuts. He wanted her to have a home.

"Quite the little love nest you've got there."

"What's wrong with that?"

"Nothing," she reassured him. "Nothing, sweetie. But—" she gestured to the others "—does everybody else here know how serious this is? Does *she* know?"

"How can they not? They can smell it on me." He'd tried, for her sake, to maintain a minimal sense of decorum today, to not gobble her up with anything but his eyes.

"Rafe. *We* can smell it on you, but Bailey can't." She glanced at the two humans again, then quickly away. "Have you said anything, done anything, to show Bailey that this relationship is more than fun and games for you? Does she know that you love her?"

The sun was too bright, the sky too blue, the air too thin. Sound receded, and the only thing he could hear was his own thumping heart. By hoarding every minute of their time together for himself, had he made her feel like he was ashamed of their relationship? That she was his short-term little secret?

"Hell." He handed his sunglasses to Sasha. "Hold these." Taking a deep breath, he crossed over to where Bailey and Jack talked about somebody named Mel's upcoming wedding. "Bailey, a minute?" He didn't wait for her to respond. He grabbed her uninjured hand and tugged her to her feet.

"What?" she asked, exasperated.

And then he kissed her like they were the only two people in the world, instead of standing in the thick of his cheering, clapping, obnoxious family.

✳

Glaring at his computer screen, Wyatt assessed the guy coordinating the technical aspects of the Sebastiani Labs hack—what little of him he could see, at any rate. Though they'd worked together before, Wyatt still didn't know what the guy looked like. SkoolHaus focused his web cam on his chest, refused to meet in person, and took payment for services rendered using a numbered offshore account. The guy had been spouting excuses long enough that Wyatt could identify stains from three major food groups adorning the other man's signature Schoolhouse Rock T-shirt. "So, you're telling me you can't fulfill the contract."

"That's not what I'm saying at all." SkoolHaus rattled off a litany of technical roadblocks they'd encountered, most of which flew right over Wyatt's head, but the bottom line was that, despite a week of digital poking and prodding, of all-nighters and endless orders of expensed pizza, SkoolHaus and his crew still hadn't found an in to the SL network. Adding insult to injury, Bailey had pretty much moved in with Sebastiani. Last night, he'd watched them cook a cozy, romantic dinner together, brushing up against each other at every opportunity. If what he'd observed from the bedroom feed was any indication, the incubus was a very satisfied man. In the last decade, Bailey's sexual repertoire had grown by leaps and bounds.

"Dude. Consider what we're doing here, who we're going up against. She might be a white-hat corporate sellout, but she knows what the hell she's doing." There was more than a hint of admiration in his voice. "We need more time."

Wyatt glared at the ceiling. More equipment? Sure. More money? Okay. But time was a commodity in extremely short supply. He could feel the rope of Buddha's deadline tightening around his neck like a phantom noose.

There was a knock on SkoolHaus's side, which the guy blithely ignored. "What do you want to do?" One thin shoulder rose in a half-shrug. "We can exploit their hiring process, get someone inside, but—" another shrug "—it'll take some time." There was another knock, louder this time. "Go away!" SkoolHaus hollered.

Wyatt heard a loud crash, the sound of wood splitting, cracking apart. Bodies swarmed into the room, filling the screen.

"Hey!" SkoolHaus yelped as someone yanked him out of his chair by the waistband of his saggy jeans.

A piece of folded paper dropped on the table. "Warrant."

Shit shit shit. Wyatt jabbed the power button, crashing his machine.

Shoving up out of his own chair, he stared in disbelief at the dark, taunting screen. How long would it take a forensics expert to track him back, to find out exactly who SkoolHaus had been talking to?

Not long at all.

Were the cops who'd served the warrant local, state, federal? International?

His cell phone rang, the soft, melodic chime sounding as loud as a bullhorn. He stared at it, not moving. Two rings. Three. As the fourth died down, he looked at the display. An unknown number, but he knew exactly who the call was from, damn it. Swallowing down the lump in this throat, he picked up the phone and answered. "Yes."

"Mr. Cooper." Buddha's voice sounded especially cheerful. "How are you today?"

He didn't respond. The silence lingered for long seconds.

"Oh, Mr. Cooper, this is only a temporary setback."

Who the hell did this guy work for? The fear constricting his throat was replaced by a seething rage. "Temporary? You just took out my lead developer—"

"It was a multi-jurisdictional effort," Buddha said. "A piece of data here, an informant there…and just this morning, a financial analyst found an offshore account that tied everything together in a pretty little bow."

His stomach clutched.

"Not one of your accounts—not yet, anyway," Buddha chortled. "It'll take some time to unravel all the skeins, and once they do, they'll have bigger fish to fry than you, my friend. But that's neither here nor there."

Silence yawned on the line, except for the soft rustle of paper, pages being flipped. Probably looking at his file.

"I've got something in progress," he blurted.

The pages stopped flipping. "Please. Enlighten me."

With a mental apology to Cheyenne, he started talking.

CHAPTER THIRTEEN

"This shouldn't take more than a minute." Bailey shot Rafe a guilty glance from the passenger seat as he pulled the Jeep into a reserved space in the Sebastiani Building's underground parking lot. She'd managed to dodge Wyland's calls since yesterday morning, but he'd just done an end run around her, calling Rafe, who'd handed her his phone without a second thought when Wyland asked to speak to her. "Wyland, I—"

"Don't care about your health? Don't care about wasting time and resources?" His voice gave her freezer burn. "I *will* have the hospital bill you for the missed appointment."

The guilty feeling redoubled. "Fair enough. Sorry."

Rafe put the Jeep in Park and turned off the ignition.

"Pick up your phone, look at your calendar, and give me a time. Now."

"Wyland, it's Saturday night." Glancing furtively at Rafe, she chose her words with care. "No one is scheduling appointments on a Saturday night."

"They'll schedule one for me." Wyland's voice sounded hard enough to chip rocks.

He was probably right. Underworld Council member? Check. Vampire Second? Check. Licensed physician with full practicing privileges? Check. Whoever picked up the phone when he called Memorial would trip over themselves to do his bidding.

Crap.

With an exasperated sigh, she plucked her mini out of her purse, tapping it to retrieve her work calendar. Meetings, meetings, meetings, all week long. She'd hardly have time to pee, much less take a trip to the hospital for a medical procedure. Over in the driver's seat, Rafe patiently waited—or maybe not so patiently. His long fingers tapped the leather-wrapped steering wheel.

No clay in his fingernails tonight. They were going out on a real date—an actual date, at Underbelly. Rafe was dressed to kill, wearing a pair of perfectly draped pants and a bronze oxford shirt that should have looked ordinary but didn't. Despite the heat burning in his eyes when she'd walked out of the bathroom wearing a pair of Sasha's leather pants and a duo of silk camisoles, she felt like road kill in comparison.

"I'm waiting."

She jerked her gaze back to the mini. "I'm looking, damn it." At her side, Rafe's eyebrow climbed.

She scanned her calendar, honing in on the early morning hours, before her workday officially started—not that she hadn't been on call 24/7 for months now. She gazed at Rafe's long, lanky form, folded behind the wheel. An evening appointment was absolutely, positively out. "Tuesday morning, 6:30 a.m. Take it or leave it."

"Taking it."

Damn it.

"I'll email you the prep instructions. Nothing by mouth after—"

Rafe plucked the phone from her hand and brought it to his ear. "Goodbye, Wyland." Hanging up, he set the phone on the dash.

Her jaw dropped. "You...hung up on him." Rafe had hung up on the Vampire Second.

"He can monopolize your time on Monday. Tonight..." He reached over and caressed her tender inner wrist. "Your time..." He brought the wrist to his lips. "Is mine." After a quick, teasing nibble, he returned her hand to her lap and got out of the Jeep. Once at the passenger side door, he helped her from the seat, much as he had the night they'd gone to Chadden's restaurant. Tonight, she wore flat black boots rather than heels, and there were no snow banks for her to slip on, but she enjoyed the sensation of Rafe's hand at the small of her back nonetheless.

"I can hear the music already," she said as they navigated the busy underground parking ramp. The concrete under their feet practically vibrated. As they entered the vestibule where the elevator and stairs were located, they passed posters of Underbelly's coming attractions. The club featured an eclectic mix of acts in all musical genres—both live bands and DJs—and was a favored venue for unannounced secret shows.

"I think Sasha's in the booth tonight," Rafe said.

"Is that good news or bad news?"

"Depends on what she plays." Dropping a soft, clinging kiss onto her unsuspecting lips, he waited until the vestibule emptied before escorting her into the private elevator that would allow them to enter the club between the kitchen and the back bar, bypassing the line out front.

"Hey." Flynn, the club's night manager and mixologist extraordinaire, greeted them as they approached, but didn't lose focus as he draped what looked like a curl of grapefruit peel on the rim of a tall, sugar-rimmed glass. A trio of regulars sat at the bar. Two of the women avidly watched Flynn, but the third had eyes only for Rafe—or rather, Rafe's hand, and how it rested lightly on her hip.

If looks could kill.

"Rafe," the woman said—just his name, but her tight expression and flaring nostrils said everything else. Succubus, and definitely pissed.

"Shane." Rafe smiled politely, but his hand tensed.

The low-grade churning in her stomach kicked up a notch. Obviously he and the beautiful redhead had some history.

"I haven't seen you here in a while." The woman took a sip of smoke-colored liquor from her lowball glass.

Rafe's hand slipped down to her hip. "I've been busy."

"Work, I imagine," the succubus said, glancing at her dismissively. "When will you be sending the invitations to your gallery show?"

She'd received hers weeks ago.

"I'll ask Brooke to make sure you get one."

The woman's eyebrows beetled together. Incubi and succubi were pros at subtext, and the exquisitely made-up Shane clearly did not like what she was hearing.

"Where's Jack tonight?" asked the short, curvy brunette sitting next to Shane. "He owes me a dance."

Rafe glanced at Bailey. She shrugged in response. She used to know what Jack was doing on Saturday nights, and with whom.

Flynn set two Greyhounds in front of the women with a flourish. Wiping his hands on a snowy white towel, he stepped out from behind the bar and wrapped her in a hug. "Hi there, sweet stuff. Long time no see."

She hugged him back, giggling when Flynn pretended to nibble on her neck. "I've been busy."

Rafe stiffened. "Careful with those fangs."

His scent strengthened, intensified, wrapping around her like a cashmere shawl. He didn't sound like he was joking.

Flynn lifted his head, released her, and took an obsequious step back.

"Do you know where Sasha is?" Rafe scanned the room. "We should probably say hi to her while there's a break in the action."

The music had stopped? She hadn't even noticed. Pheromones drifted through the air like sweet chloroform. She'd taken a pill before they left Rafe's place, but...

Flynn activated outgoing audio on his headset. "Sasha? Rafe and Bailey are at the back bar." A pause while he listened to her response. "Okay." He flicked it off again. "She'll be right here. Can I get you something to drink while you wait?"

Rafe glanced at her inquiringly.

"Malibu and pineapple juice, please. Very light on the Malibu." She didn't know whether her stomach would appreciate the libation, or reject it—violently.

"Rafe?"

"How about a Guinness."

"One Malibu pineapple and one Guinness, coming up." As Flynn turned to make their drinks, Rafe drew her away slightly, wrapping his arms around her. "Don't mind Shane," he said quietly. "She's—"

"A former lover?"

A very interesting shade of red started creeping up Rafe's neck. He inhaled, relaxing slightly when he realized that she wasn't pissed off. How could she be? Two beautiful sex demons, having sex. It was as logical as IF-THEN-ELSE.

"We...enjoyed each other's company for a short time, a long time ago," he said. "It wasn't serious."

Bailey looked at the other woman. "I think she begs to differ."

"Not my problem." He laid his forehead against hers. His loose hair stroked over her bare shoulders, and she couldn't control a reflexive shiver.

"Has he ever fed from you?"

"What?"

Rafe jerked his head towards the bar. "Flynn. Has he ever fed from you?"

She burst out laughing. "No. What makes you ask?"

His hands, looped around her waist, drifted several inches lower. His long fingers flexed into the leather. "You looked really comfortable for a woman who had vampire fangs so close to her jugular."

"His fangs were nowhere in the vicinity," she scoffed. A wild thrill jolted her. "Are you jealous?"

"Yes," he rumbled, so softly she could barely hear him. "Jealous of any man who touches you."

Sound collapsed on itself. Laughter and conversation hushed, and the clink of glasses and bottles receded into silence. But she heard their rough breathing, and the rasp of his fingertips against her sensitive scalp as he tipped her head up, and lowered his lips to—

Rafe's body suddenly jerked. "Damn it." He whirled around to where Sasha stood behind him, grinning. He rubbed his right butt cheek. "When will you outgrow the pinching?"

"Bailey can kiss it better," she responded wryly. "I've been standing here for almost a minute, but you were so busy playing caveman that you didn't notice." Sasha's thigh-skimming trapeze dress, worn with black shadow-striped tights and platform Doc Martens, barely covered the essentials. "Those pants fit you really well," she said, giving her an approving glance. "I thought they might."

"Thanks for the loan." The butter-soft leather felt wonderful against her skin, and rubbed just the right way against the lacy La Perla thong she wore underneath. Over the last few days, her underwear collection had near-doubled in size, the new lingerie more silky, slinky, and decadent than she'd ever buy for herself. When she'd asked Rafe for an explanation, he'd blamed it on underpants gnomes.

The gnomes had exquisite taste.

"Are you here to dance?" Sasha asked them. "What are you in the mood for?"

"You know," she said with a vague wave of her hand. "The kind of music you usually play here on a Saturday night." Slow. Melodic. Throbbing. The kind of music that caused people to pair up, to cling together, to drift into the shadows along the edge of the dance floor for something more than dancing.

Sasha grinned. "Got it."

And she did. The music Sasha played over the next hour was everything she'd asked for. Moving her feet was completely unnecessary; a sway was movement enough. Rafe's chest was warm, the fabric of his cotton shirt not quite as crisp as it had been when they entered. They were plastered together from chest to hip, Rafe anchoring her to his body with one hand against her back, and the other draped on the northern slope of her ass. Under the soft drape of his pants, he was more than half-erect.

She inhaled deeply, dreamily. It wouldn't take much effort at all to bring him to full, raging hardness. One, maybe two, strokes of her hand. Or her mouth. She glanced past Flynn's bar to the Employees Only door. Right back there. Or maybe the private elevator… "Whoa." She wove on her feet. The room was cloudy with pheromones—Rafe's, and everyone else's. "I need to take a bio break."

She needed to take another pill.

Holding her hand, Rafe led her off the dance floor and back to Flynn, who'd tucked her purse under the bar for safekeeping. She left the men talking and made her way to the ladies' lounge, the music hushing as the door closed behind her. The opulent oasis, painted a deep, plummy purple, made her think of pitted fruits and harem tents. Over at the makeup mirror, a woman blotted freshly-applied lipstick. Shane's friends sat, chatting, on one of the pomegranate red settees. Nodding to them, she entered one of the small private stalls, each individually and lavishly decorated and with a heavy door that went all the way down to the floor. Closing the door and locking it behind her, she sat on the tiny upholstered stool and rooted around in her purse.

Finally locating her pillbox, she plucked out two half-tablets, popped them under her tongue, and waited, cursing at the fiery sting in her stomach.

Yeah, she probably had an ulcer.

No doubt the prep for Wyland's procedure would involve dietary restrictions of some type…nothing by mouth after midnight or some such thing. How would she pull that off with Rafe around? He seemed to have appointed himself her personal dietitian, making sure she ate healthy meals for dinner and didn't leave the house in the morning without eating breakfast first.

Grimacing as the pills slowly dissolved, she dragged lightly-scented air into her lungs, waiting for the mental clouds to disappear.

The pill sure was taking its own sweet time. She looked down at the hot pink pillbox, still open in her hand. After a slight hesitation, she reached for another sliver of pill, slipping it under her tongue before the others completely dissolved.

And she waited, rubbing the sore spot just below her sternum.

"Hey." There was a soft knock. "You okay in there?"

She'd fallen in love with a sex demon, and someone was chipping away at the inside of her stomach with a goddamn ice pick. She was just peachy. "Yeah, thanks." Giving her stomach one final, comforting scrub with her knuckles, she opened the door. The inevitable ladies' room waiting line had formed, and a woman with a face full of piercings brushed past her to get in the stall. Shane's friends were still there, chattering away.

How long had she been sitting in the stall? She'd better get back to Rafe.

Tugging on the door, she was smacked by a wall of fast-paced, raucous sound. Death metal? Celtic thrash? Sasha was the expert, but…damn. During the time she'd been in the bathroom, Underbelly's vibe had undergone a radical transformation. The atmosphere felt slimy and vile. A mosh pit had formed, and dozens of muscle-bound men careened off each other in a testosterone-fuelled scrum.

Up in the DJ booth, Sasha, holding her headset so it covered one ear, glared down at the dance floor, where her brother danced with Shane—if you could call their near lack of movement dancing. The lithe succubus twined around Rafe's body like a stubborn Kudzu vine.

He saw her, and his guilty expression was a sucker-punch. She about-faced, stalking back to the lounge, her boot heels rapping angrily against the floor.

"Bailey!" she heard him call from behind her. "Wait!"

Ignoring him, she shoved the door open with her shoulder. "Whoa, Speed Racer," Shane's brunette friend said, quickly stepping back.

"Sorry," Bailey muttered, chancing a quick look back.

Rafe was right behind her, his broad shoulders filling the gap left by the open door. "Ladies," he greeted the room as he entered, not looking at them.

His eyes were locked on hers—concerned, and very pissed off.

Her simmering anger threatened to boil over. What right did *he* have to be pissed off?

"Hey, Rafe," someone at the makeup mirror sang out.

Bailey rolled her eyes. It figured that no one was the least bit surprised to find Rafe Sebastiani in Underbelly's ladies' lounge. Hell, he probably had a favorite stall for his assignations.

"Can we have a moment?" he asked the women.

The brunette shook her head, murmuring, "Shane strikes again." Shooting Bailey an apologetic glance, she touched Rafe's forearm as she left.

Bailey was so angry she could scream. To think that she'd almost— She whirled, turning her back on him. A sob tried to escape, but she gulped it back.

Rafe opened all the bathroom doors to make sure they were alone. She heard a loud click as he locked the entrance door from the inside. Felt his body heat as he came up behind her. "Bailey, that wasn't what it looked like."

She turned to face him. "And what, exactly, do you think it looked like?"

An uncomfortable expression skittered across his face. "I can imagine. You left, I was standing there talking with Flynn, and she was suddenly...there. On me. Dragging me out to the dance floor. I didn't want to be rude, but she..." He jammed his fingers into his hair with a frustrated sigh. "Sasha tried to help by changing the music," he said tiredly. "I was trying to figure out how to extricate myself as gracefully as possible when you came out and saw us."

"Yeah, you looked like you were struggling, all right." She focused on a whorl of wood on the door instead of him. The sight of the other woman winding herself around his body had sent a stake through her heart. "I get that you're an incubus, Rafe, but how many lovers do you expect me to be able to handle?"

"She's not my lover!"

She shrugged with what she hoped was a modicum of sophistication. "Sex partners, then."

Rafe snorted a laugh. "If you only knew."

"Knew what?"

"Bailey, I haven't slept with anyone but you in over a year."

Whatever she'd expected him to say, that wasn't it. "You're shitting me," she blurted.

"I wish." He turned toward the wall of mirrors and crossed his arms over his chest, his lips twisting with something other than humor. "It's entirely your fault, you know. No one else will do." He swallowed, his Adam's apple bobbing in his throat, before he turned to face her again. "Bailey, I'm falling in love with you."

She goggled at him. Rafe Sebastiani, love a human? Love *her*? She couldn't believe it. Couldn't let herself believe it.

Could she?

"I love you," he repeated.

Her breath caught. No man had ever looked at her with an expression of such misery and hope before. "Are you sure it's not just—" she waved her hand vaguely "— Operation PDA?"

"Hell, no—though Lukas's reasons for asking us to work together weren't exactly lily-white." He stepped closer. "Why do you think I kissed you the way I did in front of everyone I love?" Another step. Suddenly he was standing right next to her, his luscious lips a hairsbreadth away from hers. "It's you,

Bailey," he whispered. "Not Shane, or Lorin, or any other lover I've had. It's…you."

Could his words be true? Her heart must have thought so, because she closed the distance between their lips and kissed him.

Rafe's groan held more than a smidgen of relief. He slipped his arms around her, lifted her, and set her on the wide ledge of the makeup mirror, delving into her mouth with his agile tongue. He sipped from her, drank from her, like he had a raging thirst that could never be quenched.

She spread her knees apart so Rafe could step closer. They both groaned when she wrapped her leather-clad legs around his hips, when the thick ridge of his penis nudged against her empty core. Need coiled, tight and low.

His face was taut with need, his eyes glittering. He was so beautiful, and he was hers.

A frantic, feral sound escaped from her throat as she reached for his belt buckle, unfastening it with a metallic clank. His cock leaped into her eager hands. He hissed in pleasure at her touch, tipping his head to the ceiling, teeth clenched.

There was a knock at the door. "Bailey? Rafe?"

Sasha.

"There's a line forming out here," she called. "Can you… take this upstairs, to my office?"

Her lips quirked. She had very fond memories of the other time she and Rafe had gone upstairs to Sasha's office.

"Damn it." Reluctantly stepping back, Rafe helped her down from the ledge, making sure she was stable on her feet before letting go. "Just a minute," he called back, carefully zipping his pants over his unruly erection. "I'm going to have to walk outside like this," he said, disgusted, "and it's entirely your fault."

She giggled. "Surely a sex demon with your reputation can't be embarrassed by such things?"

Another knock. "Rafe..."

"Coming."

She snickered.

"Be good," he admonished, dropping a kiss on her nose as he unlocked the door.

So many people, staring right at them. So many knowing looks—including Sasha's—but if Sasha's wicked grin was any indication, she heartily approved.

Though her cheeks burned, she felt oddly proud. She, Bailey Brown, had made out in Underbelly's bathroom with a gorgeous incubus who was temptation incarnate. Who was having difficulty walking.

Who said he loved her.

"Let's go home," she said, taking his hand.

Rafe smiled down at her. "Let's."

CHAPTER FOURTEEN

Cheep cheep cheep.

Rafe stilled, listening. What the hell...? Something had awakened him from a fabulous dream: Bailey, her eyes raining love like a thunderstorm, making love to him with an abandon she'd never exhibited before. Except it hadn't been a dream. She was lying naked in his arms, cuddled up against him, her arm slung possessively across his stomach.

No, it hadn't been a dream at all.

He'd driven from Underbelly to his place as fast as the deteriorating road conditions allowed, her hand wandering his thigh, almost singeing him through the fabric. The minute he'd pulled the Jeep into the garage and the door had closed behind them, the hand moved north, cupping him, measuring every inch of his need with her clever little fingers.

With a perfectly good bed upstairs, he'd almost made love to her right then and there.

Make love? Rafe almost snorted aloud. He'd almost come in her hands. It had been...a near thing. But he'd held himself back, yanked on the reins, and gotten them out of the chilly garage. They'd started stripping each other during the short elevator ride up, losing clothes as they kissed and groped their way across the living room, as they lurched upstairs to the bedroom. By the time they'd made it to the bed, he'd been frantic—frantic to claim his mate.

She hadn't returned his words of love yet—not out loud, anyway—but she'd expressed her feelings with her hands, her touch, her expression, the way she trailed her tongue over his body.

He smiled slightly, looking down at her dear little face. His little PK had shed her inhibitions, all right, making love to him like the little overachiever she was. Her eyes flicked back and forth behind her closed eyelids. Was she having erotic dreams, or coding the solution to some sticky computer problem? He couldn't read her while she slept—not yet, anyway.

That took time. Over time, he'd learn her more subtle emotional nuances—

Cheep cheep cheep.

Ah, he recognized the sound now—her mini, downstairs in her purse. Bailey shifted against him, her brow wrinkling slightly, before she settled again without opening her eyes.

She responded to the damn thing like a mother with a fussing infant. Well, not tonight. It wasn't a crying infant, and she was going to damn well get some sleep.

Moving carefully, he slid out from beneath her, shivering as he left the warm nest of the bed. With a quick glance over his shoulder to make sure she was still asleep, he padded downstairs, almost slipping on the tiny violet thong lying on the second step from the bottom. Her leather pants sprawled on the floor next to the couch, and his pants and belt lay companionably nearby. His T-shirt was a pool of white lying alone on the hickory floor, but a pile of colors tangled together near the door—his shirt, and her candy-colored silk camisoles, lying on top of their coats, taken off first.

Her purse must be under the coats.

Lorin would be amused at his deductions. Rafe Sebastiani, foreplay archaeologist. He flipped on a light so he could—

Cheep cheep cheep.

Damn, the thing was loud, and the purse wasn't under the pile of coats, but lying alongside it, where the heavy fabric couldn't buffer the sound. With a quick glance toward the stairs, he snatched up the purse and opened it, peering inside. How could such a small purse hold so much stuff? Rather than take the time to dig, he dumped the contents onto her coat. A circular container hit the hardwood floor and broke open. Dozens of pills skittered and bounced, a tiny pharmaceutical hailstorm.

"Shit."

The mini pealed again, the trio of cheeps repeating themselves over and over again. Plucking up the mini, he fumbled around, pressing buttons until the thing fell silent.

"Rafe?" Bailey stood at the top of the stairs, gloriously nude, one hand rubbing her eyes, and the other resting on her stomach. "What are you doing?"

"Sorry, babe." He indicated the mini, still in his hand. "I was trying to turn this thing off. I didn't want to disturb you."

Walking down the stairs in her bare feet, she picked his T-shirt up from the floor and slipped it over her head. The thin white fabric settled to mid-thigh, obscuring his vision. When she joined him, he handed her the unit. "Does this happen every night? Because if it does…"

She didn't look at the gadget, or at him. She was staring at the pills, spilled all over the floor.

"Sorry about that. I'll pick up every one, I promise." He plucked up the nearest pill, blew on it, and dropped it back into the hot pink pillbox. "Dust bunny removal is free of charge." Rather than the amusement he expected, tension crept into the room like an insidious fog. "What?"

She opened her mouth, but didn't speak. Her eyes were glued to the pill he held.

He looked at it more carefully, recognition hitting him like an uppercut punch. Yes, he recognized this pill. From that night over a year ago, when he'd given her one in Sasha's office, the night of Scarlett's show.

His breath left his body, forced out by the glacier suddenly sitting on top of his chest.

"I can explain." Kneeling at his side, she hurriedly collected pills.

"Can you?" he said distantly. The explanation seemed pretty clear already. The woman he loved was drugging herself so she could be with him.

She scrubbed her knuckles against her stomach, grimacing. "It's not that I don't trust you, Rafe—"

"Really." Was that his oh-so-reasonable voice, speaking so clearly and lucidly? Like she hadn't stabbed him right through the heart with a freaking ice pick?

Her sudden anger snapped at him like a whip. "Rafe, look at this situation through my eyes for a minute. I'm having just a few teeny, tiny issues here."

"Issues?"

Her eyes bored into him. "Me, being human. You, not. Me, being a preacher's kid. You—" her laugh held no humor "—not. Then, learning my first lover was a sex demon, too?" She threw her hands in the air.

His voice cracked back. "And you didn't think to share these 'teeny tiny issues' with me? Bailey, taking experimental medication is no fucking solution."

"Well, it seemed to be working well enough to begin with," she snapped. "How could we have a relationship, find an equal footing, if I lose all common sense when I'm around you? I needed the safety net." A hand crept to her stomach, her knuckles scrubbing against the soft cotton fabric.

"You didn't trust me with your emotions."

She bit her lip. The knuckles scrubbed harder, faster, but she didn't seem to be aware of it. "It wasn't like that."

"It was exactly like that."

"Well, with your reputation, can you blame me? I—" She suddenly doubled over, both hands clutching at her midsection. "Holy—"

Pain. Lancing physical pain.

Fear flicked the glacier aside like a gnat. "What's wrong?"

She coughed, spraying a mist of blood over his chest. It dripped down her chin, spattering drops on the white T-shirt and the hardwood floor. She collapsed onto the cold wood, her arms wrapped around her stomach, her knees drawn up protectively.

"Shit." Calling 911 was out. She might be human, but the drugs she'd taken were paranormal, experimental. And he could get her to the hospital faster than any ambulance could. "Hang on, babe."

Covering her shivering body with his coat, he jammed his legs into his pants, threw on his shirt without buttoning it, and stomped into his boots. He slipped the pillbox into his front pants pocket. Scooping her up, coat and all, he stepped onto the elevator, trying to shove the fear aside as he mentally plotted the fastest route to Memorial Hospital.

Her body contracted as she coughed again. "Hang on." Her face was speckled with blood, like a vampire first learning how to feed. But Bailey wasn't a vampire, she was human—and that was her lifeblood, seeping into his shirt, staining his skin bright red.

✳

"Hey! You can't park there—"

Carrying Bailey, Rafe shouldered past the night guard. Memorial's lobby was crammed with patients and their worried families, on two legs and on four. Werewolf pups bayed. Babies cried. But he kept walking, straight to Reception, almost bumping into a tall woman bundled up for the weather.

"Mr. Sebastiani?"

She looked familiar, but Rafe kept his eyes on the prize: the closed door leading to the treatment area. He would throw his family's name around so hard and so obnoxiously that they'd bump Bailey to the front of the line just to shut him up—

"Rafe."

"What?" he snapped.

"Annabel Melvin," the woman said. "I treated your brother and Ms. Fontaine when they were attacked last year."

Yes, he remembered her now. A formidable Valkyrie, Dr. Melvin had somehow kept Lukas hospitalized for days longer than his irascible brother had intended.

Dr. Melvin unbuttoned her coat, tucking her hat and mittens into the pockets. "What happened?"

"We were arguing, and she clutched her stomach and coughed up blood." So much blood, and she'd spit up more three blocks away from the hospital. He didn't know whether her closed eyes meant she was exhausted or unconscious.

"You were arguing?" Melvin asked.

Ah, hell. He probably shouldn't have mentioned the argument—not when the inside of his Jeep looked like a crime scene.

Melvin quickly examined Bailey's face, peeled back her lips, and looked at her hands and nails. Glanced at his.

Rafe's breath flash-froze. Did she really suspect him of—

"Bailey Brown, right? She works for your brother." Rafe could almost see her shifting puzzle pieces around, turning them this way and that, trying to complete the picture. "Human."

Rafe nodded, relieved. "She's been having stomach problems, but I don't know what kind."

"Could be a perforated ulcer," she said. "Come with me."

They walked toward the door leading back to the examining rooms, the soft soles of Melvin's winter boots squeaking against the linoleum floor. Melvin badged them in. "Page Penn," she called back to the person behind the reception desk. "What's open?"

"Exam Two."

She nodded. "Please ask the valet to take care of Mr. Sebastiani's car. It's parked out front." She glanced at him. "Keys?"

"They're still in the Jeep." He'd probably left it running. "Um, watch out for the blood…" he called weakly. But the worker was already scurrying to obey Melvin's directive. Ah, screw it. The valets here probably dealt with leaking body fluids every day of the week.

"Follow me." Melvin quickly strode down the hall.

"Sure is busy here." He shifted Bailey's slight weight in his arms.

"Full Moon Saturday night."

He followed her into a small room painted what was probably supposed to be a comforting shade of sage green, but instead reminded him of the pea soup that Regan had puked up in The Exorcist. Gleaming medical instruments were mounted on the walls, sharing space with cheerfully framed posters reminding parents of the benefits of vaccination, and advising wolves of the proper placement of their tick medication. Sample-sized bottles of VampScreen sat in a basket on the desk. While Melvin tossed her long winter coat onto the visitor's chair, Rafe set Bailey on the examining table. Her skin looked white as the paper sheet covering the bed, and despite the jostling, her eyes stayed closed. There were no blankets, so he covered her with his coat again.

Dr. Melvin quickly checked Bailey's vitals, wrapping a blood-pressure cuff around her upper arm. It hissed and pumped as Melvin rhythmically fisted the bulb.

Bailey lurched up, coughing, spraying blood on his coat and Melvin's yellow silk blouse. Melvin grabbed a small plastic pan and placed it in Bailey's hands. "Let's take a minute."

While Bailey coughed, sputtered and spit, he supported her with an arm around her shoulders. Finally, she settled, quieted—and her eyes stayed open.

"Do you have a history of ulcers or gastrointestinal problems, Ms. Brown?"

Bailey looked at Melvin's blouse with dismay. "Oh, God. Look at the mess I've made."

"Never mind that," he said. "Just answer the damn question."

"Can I have some tissues, please?"

Rafe plucked three or four sheets of institutional-grade tissues from a light blue box and handed them to her. She spit into the tissues, wiped her mouth, and then crumpled them. "Where should I—"

Rafe plucked them out of her hands. "Answer the question."

"Would you like Mr. Sebastiani to step outside?" Melvin asked Bailey.

Ah, hell.

After a slight hesitation, Bailey shook her head. "My stomach's been sore for, oh, three or four months now."

Before they started seeing each other. For some reason, the thought brought him the slightest bit of relief.

"I know I've let it go too long." She shot Rafe a guilty glance. "Wyland scheduled some diagnostic tests for early Tuesday morning."

Not an early-morning meeting, then. She'd lied to him.

"Do you know which tests?" Melvin asked patiently.

Bailey shook her head. "The details are on my phone." She glanced at him again. "Did you happen to bring it?"

He shook his head. He hadn't thought to bring the infernal phone with them, but…reaching into his pants pocket, he withdrew Bailey's pillbox. "She's also been taking these."

Melvin took the container from him and quickly flicked it open. "Prescription?"

"Experimental—and confidential," Bailey answered, shooting him an annoyed glance. "Developed by Sebastiani Labs. They counteract pheromone intoxication in humans."

Melvin took in his barely-buttoned shirt, and Bailey, naked under his T-shirt. A couple more puzzle pieces probably clicked into place.

There was a token knock at the door. "Come," Melvin said.

The door opened, admitting a harried-looking man sporting a heinous case of bed head. His badge, clipped askew on the pocket of his wrinkled white jacket, identified him as Dr. Adnan Penn, MultiSpecies Trauma.

"Sorry to wake you, Adnan," Melvin said. "I'd appreciate a consult." Melvin quickly ran down the particulars. Several words and phrases jumped out in bold: possible perforated ulcer. Experimental drugs, possible OD. Human.

"You brought me a human?" Penn said as he peered down Bailey's throat with a handheld scope.

"The pills she's taking were developed to reduce the effects of incubi pheromones on humans," he snapped. "I wasn't about to take her to Hennepin County."

Melvin patted his arm. "Calm down, Rafe. She's in good hands." She looked at Penn. "Endoscopy?"

Penn nodded back. "We'll know more about the right course of treatment once we know exactly what we're dealing with." He looked at Bailey. "But I think it's likely you'll need surgery tonight."

Bailey dropped her head onto her upraised knees.

"Relax for a moment while we make some arrangements." Melvin spoke to Bailey, but her hand was on his, steady, stable and reassuring. "We'll need to do some blood work, and I'll send a nurse in to help you clean up." She glanced at Rafe. "We also need more information about the medication she's taking."

"Call Jack," Bailey rasped. "I want Jack."

Pain lanced through him at her words, but he rested a comforting hand on her back. "I'll get him." She was shivering. "Could you ask the nurse to bring some blankets?"

Melvin nodded. "She's a little shocky. The blood loss doesn't help."

Rafe stood sentinel while the phlebotomist battled Bailey's tiny veins, filling too many vials with blood she couldn't spare. A faerie nurse came in next, carrying towels, washcloths, and a hospital gown. Waves of Jamaica lapped in his voice, low and comforting, as he filled a basin with hot, soapy water. When the man helped Bailey out of Rafe's T-shirt, now stiff with dried blood, it was all he could do to not step in and take over.

"Now, what happened to you, hon?" The slim man's voice was warm and caring, but his emotions and touch were entirely professional. Nonetheless, Rafe stayed until Bailey was clean and warm, shivering with pleasure under the weight of two heated blankets.

"She's dozing off," the nurse said with a gentle smile. "Why don't you step out for a moment and get something to drink, take a break? There's coffee and tea in the family rooms off the lobby. I can show you—"

"I know where they are, thanks." He and his family had spent endless hours in the family rooms last year, waiting for news about Lukas and Scarlett after they were attacked. "Will you stay with her?" He didn't want to leave Bailey alone, not for a single minute, but he had some phone calls to make.

The man studied him, and nodded.

"Thank you." With a quick kiss to her cheek, he made himself leave the examination room. On autopilot, he found the family room where he and his family had spent the most time last year. Decorated in Early Institutional Living Room, with several stiff couches and chairs, there was a full-sized refrigerator, an aquarium, a coffee maker that ran twenty four hours a day, a door that closed, and a landline phone. He made two calls, to Jack and Lukas, telling them that Bailey was having stomach problems, that they were at Memorial, and that she'd probably need surgery before the night was over. He'd fill them in on the details when they arrived.

Hanging up the heavy black handset with a clatter, he sat back on the couch, staring at the colorful fish as they darted through a castle play fixture, unaware of time passing until he felt a warm weight on his shoulder.

Lukas's hand.

"Is she okay? An ulcer, right? Damn it, I should have hauled her little ass to the doctor myself."

Rafe almost smiled. Lukas's case of bed head was worse than Dr. Penn's. Dressed in a pair of army green pants, barely-laced steel-toed boots, a black T-shirt, and no jacket, Lukas looked like he was going to war. He noticed his brother assessing his garments just as carefully, especially his bloody shirt, chest and hands. "She had an appointment with Wyland for Tuesday morning," he said, defending her. "Her stomach was a little more impatient than that. Taking those damn pills didn't help."

"What pills?"

The door opened again as Jack arrived, looking so alert that Rafe suspected he hadn't been to bed yet. Maybe he'd interrupted a hot date with his phone call.

"What happened?" Jack asked.

Rafe filled him in.

"What pills?" Lukas repeated.

Jack's lips tightened.

"You knew?" Rafe glared at him.

"She promised me she'd be careful with the dosage, that she'd talk to somebody at SL."

"What pills!" Lukas bellowed.

"She's been taking pheromone intoxication meds for weeks," Rafe said. "Gobbling them like candy."

"Why would she do that?"

Rafe turned away, staring at the fish tank again.

"To keep her thoughts clear while she worked so closely with Rafe," Jack answered.

Jack's answer was nowhere close to the whole story, but it would do for now.

Lukas jammed his hands into his hair. "That little idiot."

"Who's your contact at SL?" Rafe asked Jack. "Melvin wants to talk to somebody about the meds."

Lukas dropped his hands. "Melvin's her doctor?"

"One of them, yeah. Penn's doing the tests, and if she needs surgery for a perforation, he'll do it."

A flush crept up Lukas's neck, turning it a ruddy pink.

"So she's seen your junk," Jack said, rolling his eyes. "Get over it."

"I've seen a lot of men's junk," Dr. Melvin said as she entered the room, a wry sparkle in her eyes. "Mr. Sebastiani, I hope your testicles have fully recovered? You never did come back for that follow-up appointment. Hello, Mr. Kirkland. Good to see you again."

Melvin had changed her blouse. Instead of blood-spattered yellow silk, she now wore dusty purple cotton under a starched white jacket. Her winter boots had been exchanged for practical black flats.

It appeared she planned on staying a while.

"Bailey's given me permission to fill you in on what we know about her condition." She perched on the edge of the stiff couch. "She's on her way to the Endoscopy suite with Dr. Penn. He'll confirm the perforated ulcer, see if there are any other areas we need to be concerned about. If he's right—and I think he is—she'll be taken directly to the OR from there."

"Is she conscious, able to consent?" Jack asked. "I've got her power of attorney if you need it."

Of course he did. Resentment burned like a brush fire, but he managed to fight it back. Given Bailey's strained relationship with her family, Jack was probably the closest thing to next of kin that she had.

"She's tired, but awake and alert," Melvin responded. "Is there anything about the experimental medication she's taking that might compromise her thought processes?"

Jack shook his head. "If anything, her thought processes would be sharper."

"Fascinating," she mused. "You've taken this medication yourself?"

He nodded.

Melvin was looking at Jack's big, healthy frame with obvious interest. "Do you have information about their composition? I'd like to ensure there's nothing in them that might interfere with anesthesia, or interact poorly with other medication we might need to use during the course of her treatment."

Jack looked at Lukas, who nodded back. The decision to reveal confidential information to Melvin had just been made by Council members, not friends. "I have the specs in my office at Sebastiani Security," Jack said. "I can be there and back in ten minutes."

Melvin glanced at her watch. "Excellent." She stood, and once again rested her hand on Rafe's forearm, smiling reassuringly. "She's young and otherwise healthy, Rafe. She should be fine."

As soon as Melvin left, Lukas and Jack huddled together, talking in bullet-point bursts and pressing buttons on their minis.

Rafe looked away. He was sick to death of those damn gadgets. His brother, and everyone who worked for him, were tethered to the damn things like dogs on leashes. "I need some air."

He needed to wash Bailey's blood off his hands.

Lukas halted his conversation. "Rafe?"

Rafe held up a hand, shook his head, and slowly walked out of the room.

CHAPTER FIFTEEN

Bailey.

The voice in her head was like a paper cut, stinging more than it should for its size. Maybe if she kept her eyes closed, whoever was bothering her would just leave...leave her to float, under the waves, above the pain.

She knew she was in a hospital. Crisp white sheets, the scent of institutional cleansers, and the soft mechanical beep of monitoring equipment circled around the perimeter of her consciousness, but she was calm under the waves, submerged yet breathing, occasionally breaking the surface to sip some air before slipping back under again.

Bailey. Wake up. Now.

Her eyelids flew open so quickly the bed spun like a whirlybird. Gasping, she threw out an arm to steady herself, and found Wyland standing by her bedside.

"So, you're finally back with us."

She scowled up at him. "That's some bedside manner you've got there."

"Whatever works."

"Christ on a cracker." She dropped her head back onto the too-flat pillow. If that was what a vampire thrall felt like, she was glad he hadn't unleashed it on her before. He rested his palm against her forehead for several seconds, and then his cool fingers were at her wrist, taking her pulse.

"How do you feel?"

It was a fight to keep her eyes open, but she quickly assessed. There was a slight pain in her stomach, a distant sting, but nothing like the flamethrower burns she'd felt at Rafe's.

Where was Rafe? He'd been here; his scent still lingered in the room.

"I'm…okay," she finally said. "A little nauseous. I guess I blew like Krakatoa, huh?"

Wyland's thin lips twitched. "I hear you left quite a path of destruction in your wake."

She'd spewed like a volcano, all right—all over Rafe, Rafe's coat, his car… She closed her eyes and groaned. "Dr. Melvin's beautiful blouse."

"Comes with the territory." He tapped at a tablet, updating records and swiping others out of the way. The illuminated screen turned his already pale skin as white as parchment.

"What time is it?"

"Ten minutes before sunrise, Sunday morning."

So she'd only been out a couple of hours. Outside her window, dawn painted the sky a watercolor pinkish gray. "Looks like you might be stuck here for a while."

"Again, it comes with the territory."

She bit her lip. "I'm sorry I blew you off on Friday. If I'd kept our appointment—"

"You probably would have needed surgery tonight." Wyland said with a shrug. "Maybe without the dramatic cleaning bills, but you would have needed surgery just the same."

"I don't have time to be sick."

"Penn repaired the perforation laparoscopically, so your recovery time should be relatively short." He eyed her. "But if you don't do something about your stress level, you'll be back in this bed again in no time."

Someone knocked softly on the door. Jack poked his head in. "Can we come in?"

We? Was Rafe here?

"For a few minutes," Wyland said. "She needs to rest."

Lukas followed Jack into the room. The door closed behind them.

Where was Rafe? He was the one she really wanted to see. But if he showed up right now, what the hell would she say to him? He'd been so angry, so hurt, but given the same set of circumstances, she'd make the exact same decision: take the pills.

Damn it.

Wyland glanced at one of the monitors standing on the pole at her bedside. "Your blood pressure is up. Are you in pain?"

She shook her head. "Could I get a drink of water? I'm parched." Her mouth felt as dry as dust.

"Just a sip," Wyland said.

Ice cubes rattled as Jack poured a couple of stingy ounces from a blue plastic pitcher dripping with condensation. He unwrapped a straw, placed it in the cup, and held it to her lips. Her incisions twinged as she sucked in the cool liquid, but the pain level was nowhere close to what she'd somehow gotten used to living with.

"How are you feeling?" While she drank, Jack stroked her stiff, sticky hair off her forehead with his big hand.

"Stupid. I'm feeling stupid." Wyland was right; she'd let her stomach go untreated too long. She blinked back angry tears—or tried to, at any rate. Jack's worried expression made them spill over.

Jack set the cup down and gathered her in his arms, holding her while tears elbowed each other out of the way for the privilege of falling first. He held her for timeless minutes, murmuring nonsense words while tears leaked all over his dress shirt. She snuffled against his chest. "Can you hand me a Kleenex?" She was probably trailing snot, too.

Lukas, looking a little green around the gills, handed her white tissue. For him, simply being in the hospital was tough enough—all these second-hand emotions, all these smells and tastes—but with second-hand pregnancy hormones in the mix, his sensory system must be about maxed out.

Raising the tissue to her nose, she honked. Jack cracked a smile, his first since he'd entered her room. "Ouch." She raised a hand to her stomach.

Wyland flicked a finger across the tablet. "Let me see when you're due for pain meds."

Lukas was staring at her. "What?" she asked. "Do I still have blood on my face or something?"

"It's my fault you're here in the first place. I knew you were brewing an ulcer."

"No, it's not. It's my fault. Mine alone." With a sigh, she lay back against the pillows. "Has anyone seen Rafe?"

Lukas and Jack exchanged a look.

"I found him nodding off at your bedside when I first came in," Wyland responded. "I told him I wanted to examine you, and that he might want to use the opportunity to clean up, eat, maybe catch a short nap."

Had he gone home, or was he still here in the building? Somehow it seemed too desperate a question to ask aloud.

"It's probably a good idea to let him to cool off a little first." Lukas glared down at her like a displeased giant. "What the hell were you thinking?"

She closed her eyes. "So he told you."

"Damn right he told me, though apparently Jack knew about this half-assed scheme of yours as well, and didn't shoot it down like any reasonable person would have."

"Leave Jack out of this."

"He shouldn't have let you—"

"Let me, nothing," Bailey snapped. "I took the pills from his office—stole them—without his knowledge. He noticed his pill count was off and called me on it. I explained my reasoning. He gave me the documentation set—" which she still hadn't read "—and described his own experiences before we discussed dosage. But puh-leeze. He had nothing to do with my decision to take them. Permission was not his to bestow."

"The drug might have exacerbated a pre-existing medical condition," Lukas said. "It...complicates matters somewhat."

Yeah, it probably did. "Does Dr. Melvin think that's what happened?"

"Let's not jump to conclusions," Wyland said. "The perforation's timing could be entirely coincidental. At any rate, Bailey's experience provides valuable data. I understand you took the medication on one occasion last year, with no adverse effects?"

'On one occasion?' What on earth had Rafe revealed about their one-night stand, and to whom? She hesitantly nodded.

"We also know that ulcers are exacerbated by stress," Wyland added. "That's an issue we can do something about."

"We have to report this to SL Pharma," Lukas said.

"Already in motion," Wyland said. "Melvin, Penn and I will work up some case notes and present them to your father." The tablet Wyland held chimed softly. As he read, one of his white-blond eyebrows climbed.

"What?" she asked.

"Excuse me." With no further explanation, Wyland left.

Bailey pointed at the door as it slowly swung shut. "See what I mean? That's what it's like to work with him."

"Never mind Wyland," Lukas said. "Why did you find it necessary to take the medication in the first place?"

"Lukas." Jack's voice, though quiet, commanded attention. "Have you ever given any thought to what it's like to be human, to be subject to pheromones, vampire thralls, and empathetic faerie mind melds on a day-to-day basis? What it feels like to have your personal will, your sense of self-control, erode under your feet? To not be able to trust your feelings and emotions?"

Yes, Jack understood.

"Don't tell me that you're taking those pills, too," Lukas said. "When we're not working, I mean."

Jack laughed. "When aren't we working?"

"Jack."

"I take them…infrequently."

Bailey suspected those infrequent occasions had a lot to do with Sasha Sebastiani. "Lukas, you've probably figured out by now that Rafe and I are…involved," she said. "I figured that taking the pills would help me remember that the euphoric feeling most humans mistake for love is chemically induced."

"But it is love," Lukas argued. "Rafe loves you."

"How can you know?" she pressed. "How can I—how can anyone—trust their feelings, knowing that pheromones are a factor?"

"My brother loves you."

"How nice to be able to sniff emotions out of the air. If you remember, humans can't." Though, to be fair, Rafe had told her, using words, that he loved her. Gah, she was so mixed up. "Lukas, Wyatt Cooper jerked me around like a fucking puppet. I had to try to level the playing field a little."

"You're really going to compare your relationship with Rafe to the one you had with Wyatt Cooper?"

"They're both incubi! How can I know the difference?"

The only sounds in the room were the soft beeping of the monitor, and a breakfast trolley rattling down the hall on the other side of the closed door.

"So why did you start taking more medicine?" Lukas suddenly asked.

"What?" She punched a button to silence the annoying beep. She could feel her pulse pounding perfectly well, thank you very much.

"You told Melvin that you'd recently increased dosage. Instead of taking half a tablet, as you and Jack originally discussed, you started taking full tablets instead. Why?" His gaze pinned her to the bed.

Good question. "The euphoria wasn't going away. It was getting worse."

"Yet your thoughts and decision-making processes were unaffected?"

She nodded.

"Bailey, the medicine was working just fine. The euphoria you're feeling? It's coming from you."

His soft words hit her like sniper fire.

"You love my brother. My brother loves you." Striding to the door, he glanced back over his shoulder. "Now you have to decide if you have the guts to do something about it." Lukas left the room. The door snapped behind him, a tiny, attention-getting slap.

She leaned back against the bed with a wince, resting a hand just below her sternum. "I don't think my guts are quite up to it at the moment."

Jack sat down in the chair beside her bed. "You realize you can't take the meds anymore, right?"

She nodded. Yeah, she realized that. But what she didn't know was what the hell she was going to do next.

✳

Rafe paused outside Bailey's hospital room door. Keep your cool. Just keep your cool.

The short time away from the hospital should have done him a world of good. After he'd scrubbed the mess off his hardwood floor, assembled a frightening bundle for the dry cleaners, and showered Bailey's blood off his body, he'd eaten something, collapsed onto the bed, and slept like the dead for a couple of hours. Unfortunately, seeing Bailey's blood spattered across the interior of his Jeep in broad daylight brought it all back again.

He was pissed. And hurt. And angry. And miserably, miserably in love.

Taking a deep breath, he tapped on her door with his knuckle.

"Come in," she called.

When he entered, he saw a split-second shaft of relief cross her face before it clouded up again. He inhaled surreptitiously. Her energy was better, healthier, but emotionally, she seemed to be a mixed bag—just like he was. With her freshly washed hair wet, parted on the side and combed flat, she looked achingly young. All traces of blood were gone, except for the bagged pint hanging off the IV rod, filling the tubing snaking into her wrist. She still looked pale as skim milk. The neck of the pastel blue hospital gown gaped, exposing her delicate collarbones. Hidden under the gown were three small abdominal incisions covered by gauze. He'd studied them while she slept, staring at them, ready to holler for help if they started gushing blood.

"Hey."

"Hey." He cleared his throat awkwardly. "You look so much better."

"I feel better, too." She picked up the remote control and hit the mute button, eyeing the bags he carried.

"I brought you a few things. Some fleece jackets, long-sleeved T-shirts, yoga pants." He'd also brought a bottle of the shampoo they'd taken to sharing, and several pairs of the delectable panties he'd bought for her. Yeah, dirty pool, but he'd come to realize that this game would not be won by ordinary means—and he meant to win.

Setting the duffel down by the single stingy closet, he walked to the bed with her purse. Her tiny nostrils flared.

Was she trying to read him? How freaking adorable.

"Hello," he said softly, searching her face as he slowly lowered his head, giving her every opportunity to avoid his kiss if she wanted to. When she reached up, cupping his face and lifting her lips to his, relief shimmered like summer sheet lightning. Supporting her head and neck with his hands, he touched his mouth to hers, softly, so softly. A tiny noise escaped her throat, and she deepened the kiss, her fingers threading through his hair, the scrape of her nails against his skull a tender form of torture.

This was getting out of control fast. He reluctantly lifted his head.

She slapped her hand to mouth. "God, my breath must be horrible."

He smiled, shaking his head. "But you could use some lip balm."

"Yeah," she replied, digging into her purse and somehow coming up with a tube of ChapStick on the first try. "There's no checkbox for 'human' on your hospital's admission form, but dry air is universal."

"You're dehydrated. Want some water?" He didn't wait for her response before picking up the pale blue plastic glass with a straw in it, and holding it up to her mouth.

She drank deeply, emptying the cup.

"More?"

"No thanks." She sat back against the pillows propping her up against the upraised head of the bed. She wore one blanket around her shoulders like a shawl, and he could barely see the outline of her legs under the rest of the pile. Bringing her fleece clothing had been a good idea.

She pawed through the purse. "Where's my mini?"

Damn it. "I gave it to Lukas for safe-keeping. You'll hardly need it here, while you're recovering, will you?" Okay, that came out a little surlier than he'd intended.

Stare down. Her anger was a slow-burning fuse, but he wasn't backing down from this one. He gestured to the purse. "You have other phones if you need to make any calls. Your only priority while you're here is to recover, to get well."

Under the blankets, her left foot jiggled. "You had no right to do that."

His own simmering anger boiled over. "I have every right," he snapped. "I'm the one who watched you puke blood like a geyser."

She raised a hand to her largest incision. "I'm hardly about to forget, but—"

"Hundred-hour work weeks," he barreled on. "Not enough sleep, eating unhealthy food, no fresh air. And now those pills." He laughed harshly.

"You're making some really poor choices right now, babe."

"They're my choices to make."

They were, damn it, but… With a sigh, he sat on the bed, setting the purse aside so he could take her hands. The mattress flexed under his weight. "Bailey, those pills probably punched a hole through your stomach lining. What the hell were you thinking, taking experimental medication on top of an ulcer?"

She yanked her hands away. "I was thinking I couldn't allow another incubus lover to jerk me around like a dog on a leash!"

"A dog on a leash? Are you serious? Does Scarlett look unhappy and controlled? Does Claudette?"

"They're sirens. They have some natural defenses." She sagged back against the upraised head of the bed like her bones wouldn't support her anymore. "What do I have? Nothing."

So sad, so lost. And so, so exhausted. Jesus, what was he doing, fighting with her while she lay in a hospital bed, less than a day out of surgery? Remorse threatened to swamp him. Maybe he was as big an asshole as Cooper after all.

"Bailey, is it fair to make me pay for another man's crimes?" His words produced a whiff of guilt, and he chanced taking her hand again. Her pulse bumped under his thumb. "And you're wrong, you know."

"About what?"

"About not having natural defenses—"

Lukas burst in without knocking, carrying Bailey's computer case and her chirping mini, his own screeching a duet. Jack followed close behind him, fumbling at the unit clipped to his waistband.

Ignoring him, Lukas slapped Bailey's mini into her hand like a nurse handing a surgeon a scalpel. "Incursion at Sebastiani Labs," he rapped out. "He's in."

"Damn it." Fingers and thumbs flew as she read, swiped, and clicked tiny keys. Rafe stepped away from the bed as Lukas unzipped her computer case and booted up her workhorse of a laptop, the one she'd told him was loaded with her own tooling, and the souped-up suite that allowed her to tunnel anywhere she damn well pleased.

She peered at the mini. Swore. "Looks like an inside-out."

"What's that?" he asked.

"One of the basic tenets of network security is to protect the perimeter, but the whole approach is built upon a sometimes erroneous assumption—that all outsiders are bad, and all insiders are trusted." She stared at the mini. "Someone launched this attack from the inside."

Lukas looked pissed off enough to chop wood with his bare hands. "How the hell did he—"

"I don't know yet." There was a different chirp as Bailey received a phone call. "Cheyenne. Cheyenne, calm down. What..." As she listened to what the other woman said, her eyes narrowed to dangerous slits. "Tell me what he looks like." After several seconds, she closed her eyes momentarily, mouthing a silent fuck. "Hang on a sec." She covered the mouthpiece with her thumb. "Guess who Cheyenne's been dating." She banged her fist against the bed, stretching the IV tubing taut.

"Jeez, be careful—"

"Wyatt pretexted her," she said, disgusted. "Classic approach. Start dating Sebastiani Labs' network architect, maybe exchange some pillow talk, build up some trust, and…"

"How the fuck did he get in?" Lukas asked.

"Apparently she told him that she could really use a massage. He sent her an email at work containing a link to a spa coupon. First twenty responders get fifty percent off kind of thing. She trusted him and clicked on it. The link brought her to a website he'd set up, with an embedded, malicious—" She made a slashing motion with her hand. "Never mind the details. Bottom line, he's seen and recorded everything she's done at work for at least a day. Passwords, architecture, source code, contracts."

"Next steps?" Lukas bit out. "Your call."

Her eyes glittered. Adrenaline filled the room; he couldn't help but absorb it. She was as jacked up as Lukas or Lorin got when they sparred. This was a different kind of battle, but it was a battle nonetheless.

As Bailey spilled a stream of acronyms and jargon to Cheyenne, Antonia burst in, wearing painted-on jeans, skyscraper heels, and too much makeup. "My mini is blowing up."

Bailey kept talking to Cheyenne, but pointed at her laptop, gesturing for Antonia to finish setting it up.

The door opened again. "What in the world is going on in here?"

Uh-oh. The charge nurse, with her tightly-permed gray curls and even more tightly pursed lips, was a tiny termagant. He and Lukas had taken to calling her The Admiral during the time Lukas was in the hospital. To say she ran a tight ship was a massive understatement.

"I don't care what your last name is, or how much money your family donates to this hospital," she snapped, hands on her polyester-clad hips. "You will follow the rules. You will keep to two visitors at a time. You will keep those infernal devices on vibrate or turn them off so they do not disturb other patients." She shot Rafe a suspicious glance. "And none of your shenanigans, either."

Rafe reddened. She'd busted him flirting with one of her nurses, a gorgeous faerie, back when Lukas was a patient. Despite her accusation of shenanigans, the encounter had gone nowhere fast.

The nurse hadn't been Bailey.

Lukas nudged Jack toward the charge nurse, unabashedly throwing him under the bus.

Annoyance sparked into the room, but Jack's expression was buttercream-smooth as he engaged the charge nurse in conversation, spilling James Bond charm as he led her from the room.

While Jack did his thing, Lukas turned his back to the room and dialed a number—probably their father's—and reached for a tube of antacids. Antonia brought Bailey the laptop, now sprouting antennas and peripherals he didn't recognize, kicking off her shoes and settling on the bed cross-legged. Bailey put Cheyenne on speaker so she could use the keyboard two-handed. Her fingers glided and danced, setting her IV tubing swinging.

When Rafe quietly left the room, no one noticed.

CHAPTER SIXTEEN

"You're kidding me. I feel fine!" Bailey glared at Penn and Melvin, who'd just dragged her away from the VIP suite's reception area—where she'd set up a makeshift but functional computer lab—to her hospital room. Between her, Cheyenne and Antonia, they'd contained the worst of the damage, but there was still so much work to do.

Not calling Rafe back when he'd walked out of her room last night was one of the hardest things she'd done in a very long time, but duty called. Since then, he hadn't been anywhere in the vicinity. She yearned for him. Burned for him.

It hadn't been the pheromones, after all.

And now these doctors were informing her that they didn't want to release her, not quite yet. She glanced at the clock mounted next to the hospital room door. "I have a meeting in five minutes."

"Let me check your incisions." Penn gestured to the bed, still as crisply made now as it had been last night because it hadn't been slept in.

With an impatient sigh, she obeyed.

"You've had a textbook recovery so far," he said, lifting her turquoise fleece pull-over and tank top and gently pressing on her stomach, "but there are a few additional tests we'd like to run."

"What tests?" When she tried to sit up, Penn stopped her with a hand on her shoulder. He then performed the most thorough physical exam she'd ever had without completely disrobing first. He moved his cold stethoscope over her heart, lungs, stomach, and intestines. He checked her eyes, ears, nose, and throat. He probed her neck and throat with careful fingers before moving on to the lymph nodes in her armpits. He double-checked her pulse again, checked her blood pressure, and took her temperature.

Finally, she shoved his hand away. "What's this all about?"

Penn and Melvin exchanged a glance. "We have your full blood panel back," Penn said. "Your hemoglobin levels are low normal. White count low normal. The experimental meds you took were apparently very fast-acting, and cleared your system within hours. But we found—" Penn paused "—an anomaly we'd like to investigate further."

Her stomach jumped. "What? What's wrong?"

The doctors glanced at each other again. "Nothing's wrong," Penn said. "Per se."

Melvin pushed him aside. "Adnan, your bedside manner is atrocious. Bailey, the pre-surgical workup we ran yielded some unexpected results."

"What? Tell me."

"You appear to have succubus lineage."

"What?"

"Just the slightest hint," Penn hastily added. "Greatly diluted."

Melvin helped her sit up—which was good, because the bed was spinning. As her balance steadied out, an odd calm fell.

Succubus lineage. Wow. Maybe she had some natural defenses, after all. "Why hasn't this…anomaly been picked up before?"

Melvin shrugged. "We all have a lot to learn about the genetic code, but needless to say, human medicine isn't looking for evidence of other branches on their family tree."

"You could go to a human hospital for a serious health issue today and they would never know," Penn assured her. "There's no need for you to worry about exposure—"

"Yet," Melvin cautioned him. "Don't make any assumptions about how long their ignorance might last." She fiddled with her badge, hanging around her neck from a beaded lanyard. "Bailey, you're the first human patient we've treated at this hospital. These results made us realize that we've been presented with an amazing opportunity: to research the degree to which our species' DNA has crossed into the human population. We know it happens, of course, but—"

"We'd like your permission to sequence and study your full genome," Penn said.

There was a soft knock on the door. "Bailey?" After a slight pause, Antonia poked her head around the jamb, a white hospital blanket wrapped around her shoulders. She'd discovered the blanket heater in the small but well-stocked supply room down the hall, declared it awesome, and said she was going to order one she could use at home. "Everyone's here."

Penn frowned.

Antonia frowned back.

"Adnan." Melvin put her hand on Penn's forearm. "Bailey, give it some thought. Let us know if you'd like more information."

She would, after she cleared some space in her brain. "Thank you."

What do you know, Dad? Sex demons in our family tree.

Bailey followed Antonia to the family room located on the other side of the VIP suite's reception area. Jack, Lukas and Cheyenne were already seated at the small oak table. Cheyenne still wore her winter coat, and cupped a mug of hot coffee between her hands.

"I want a piece of him," Cheyenne said to Lukas, her voice filled with gravel. "That asshole."

Lukas was watching her carefully. Was Cheyenne fighting a shift?

"I should've known something was off." Setting down the mug, Cheyenne yanked at the jacket's neckline. The snap closures released in a fast sequence, sounding like she'd emptied a clip in the small room. A couple of feathers flew.

"How far are you willing to go?" Antonia asked.

All heads swung to where they stood by the door. "There you are." Cheyenne looked Bailey up and down. "For someone just a day out of surgery and still in the hospital, you look disgustingly healthy."

"Yeah." Entering the room, she sat in one of the uncomfortable upholstered armchairs, touching Cheyenne's shoulder in communion as she passed.

"What do you need me to do?" Cheyenne asked Antonia. "Name it."

"Are you willing to keep sleeping with him, act like nothing's wrong, to buy us some time?"

Bailey jolted. Whoa, that was cold. "Antonia—"

"Yes." Cheyenne shrugged, a little too casually. "No hardship; he *is* really good in bed, right?" She glanced at Bailey as if for confirmation before flashing a vicious smile. "Maybe I'll tie him up. Break out the whips and chains. For the greater good, of course."

"As a humanitarian gesture," Antonia agreed, grinning.

Bailey snorted with laughter as she imagined Wyatt trussed up like a Thanksgiving turkey, a ball gag in his mouth.

Lukas looked at them like they were all crazy as loons. Across the table, Jack sat quietly, observing. This was probably the first time he'd ever heard her laugh about Wyatt Cooper.

"We need to stop playing his game," Antonio stated, all laughter gone. "He acts, and we react? Screw that. We need to go on the offensive. Play the player. Socially engineer the social engineer." Her tiny smile was somehow far more frightening than Cheyenne's toothy snarl.

As Antonia laid out her devious plan—God, her ability to so completely immerse herself in someone else's mindset was truly, truly frightening—the energy in the room changed. A fire sparked to life, the flames fed fuel as Lukas, Jack and Antonia authorized a remote incursion of Wyatt's computer system. Jack translated Antonia's thoughts to an action plan, complete with resourcing and timeline. Lukas wrangled risks, controlled the burn.

And she was already designing the incursion in her mind.

"Okay," Jack said, "I think we have a plan."

If the plan worked, it was entirely possible that Wyatt could be out of her hair—out of *everyone's* hair—for good, in a matter of days, but there was a hell of a lot of work to do between now and then. Antonia would finish the last bit of cleanup on Sebastiani Labs' network, freeing up Cheyenne to keep Wyatt occupied. "Well-occupied," she drawled suggestively. Lukas would run the plan by his father and obtain his authorization. Jack's job was to mock up the faux 'highly confidential' documents at the center of the plan, making sure they looked authentic enough to keep Wyatt reading while the malware she'd embed in the documents slithered into his system.

Elegant. Efficient. Deadly.

"I feel so stupid, being taken in by him." Cheyenne stared down at her lap. "This is my fault."

Bailey shook her head. "No, it's mine. I should've realized that he'd try something like this when he couldn't penetrate from the outside. I should have warned you."

"He's good," Cheyenne said with reluctant admiration. "The 'accidental' meeting at Crackhouse Coffee. The fake employee badge, the spoofed corporate email address. The hot, lonely transfer, trying to make friends in a new town." Cheyenne's lips tightened. "He played me like a freaking violin."

"Don't blame yourself. Wyatt makes you feel like you're the only woman in the world. He says everything you want to hear. He knows what you want before you do. He's really good at this." All the more reason to take him down—and with this plan, the shoe would finally be on the other foot. This time, *she'd* be the one to lure *him* in, dropping dollops of data like chum for a shark. And then, she'd circle in for the kill.

Once she got rid of Wyatt once and for all, she'd figure out what to do about Rafe, and the rest of her life.

Lukas stood. "Bailey, do you need more equipment?"

She shook her head. "Not if I work at The Bunker. Let's pack it up." If Penn and Melvin wouldn't spring her, she'd leave against medical advice. Cheyenne was right; she felt disgustingly healthy.

Except for her sore heart.

The meeting broke up, with Cheyenne hurrying off to scheme against Wyatt. Lukas and Antonia each took equipment with them when they left. With Jack following her, she returned to her barely-used hospital room to pack up her things.

"You didn't stand a chance, either, you know."

Opening a drawer, she removed yoga pants and wispy panties, stuffing them into her duffel bag.

"Think about it," Jack continued. "As a human, you had even fewer natural defenses available to you than Cheyenne does. Plus, you were a teenager—a socially stunted one, at that."

Now probably wasn't the time to mention her succubus blood to Jack—especially when she didn't know what, exactly, that meant yet—but some reason, knowing about those few scattered chromosomes made her feel much more confident about her ability to deal with Rafe.

If *he* still wanted to deal with *her* when all this was over.

"I, for one, would love to put Cooper away for using his incubi pheromones to influence your behavior back when you were in school."

She sighed. The fact that she had succubus lineage would undoubtedly complicate their case. "I'll do my best to get him to confess." Because that was the final stage of the plan—her, talking with Wyatt one on one, and recording the conversation. A laugh slipped out. "Do you ever think about how utterly weird all of this is? We're both human—and they're not—but with them, I feel more at home, more a part of things, than I have for a long time." Stuffing the last pair of cobweb-thin underwear in the duffel bag, she gave it a vicious zip. "I should feel more concerned about how set apart I feel from humanity. But—" she shrugged "—I'm not."

"Friends are the family you choose."

True. Somehow, the Sebastiani family, and her work colleagues at Sebastiani Security and Sebastiani Labs, had become her family—the family she'd chosen. And Jack had simply always been there.

"Have you talked to Rafe today?" he asked quietly.

"And say what? I don't think Rafe wants anything to do with me right now." Or maybe ever, but she couldn't think about that right now. "Come on." She handed him the duffel. "Let's blow this pop stand."

"Aren't you going to check in with Melvin and Penn?"

"Nope."

Jack raised a brow. "Leaving AMA? Pretty gangsta."

Linking her arm with his, she thought about the long hours of code-slinging to come. "Dude, you ain't seen nothin' yet."

✴

Rafe closed the bamboo blinds with a whoosh. The sun, hard and bright, hurt his tired eyes. He closed them and rubbed, which had the added benefit of blocking out the view of his tiny tyrant of a business manager making her second meandering lap around his studio, examining his work.

Tearing open a vein would be less painful.

His gallery show was less than two weeks away, and they'd finalized some last details: choosing the wine and champagne, selecting the hors d'oeuvres, and thankfully Brooke had located more of the fabric he needed to drape the pedestals with. They'd finalized plans to transfer the sculptures to the gallery, an intimate space on Hennepin Avenue, where he'd personally oversee the installation.

In less than two weeks, Bailey's nude body would be on public display, on red crushed velvet, for every critic, invited guest, and family member to see.

Brooke's sensible shoes tapped an erratic pattern against the concrete floor. She was starting her third lap, stepping back occasionally, holding a finger to her lips as she considered. He barely held back a sigh. His deadline loomed like a tsunami wave, several miles offshore but visible, and making its ominous, inexorable approach. If he didn't get back to work soon, it would crash down on his head. But Brooke was his first, best, and most exacting critic—and damn it, now she was moving the sculptures around. He bit back a yelp as she separated the series he mentally called the Shower Sequence: Bailey's arms, gracefully reaching overhead toward the stream of water. Her hands as they slipped through her own hair, then his. Her body, leaning weakly against the tile as he, on his knees, bathed her most intimate flesh with his tongue.

He couldn't stand it any longer. "Brooke, you're moving them out of order."

The tiny faerie glanced at him with bird-black eyes. "Just trying something." Her frizzy head, her hair dyed an improbable red, barely came up to his chest. She was as short as Bailey was, but more than made up for her lack of stature with her outsized personality. Her loud caw of a laugh could clear a room.

"Could you get me a Coke?" she asked. "None of that diet crap, either."

He sighed. Chadden had consumed the last can in the studio's mini-fridge, but he had more upstairs. If he left, she'd move more sculptures, but he could always put them back in their original order. "Sure. Be right back."

He hurried up the stairs and opened the refrigerator, but didn't see any red cans. "Shit." He had a case in the pantry. Retrieving it, he poured a can of the room-temperature beverage into a glass, added a few ice cubes, and trotted back downstairs again. He felt like a parent rushing home after leaving his infant with a babysitter for the first time.

He handed her the glass, and she took a sip. "Thank you, hon." Stepping back, she gestured toward the sculptures she'd arranged on the long center table. "So, what do you think? Take some time."

He did as she asked, slowly assessing her progression. Circling back, he repeated the circuit. "Damn it," he finally muttered under his breath.

Brooke, her eye honed by decades as an art scene insider, had discerned something he hadn't. He gave a single, curt nod. Her arrangement *was* better. It said more, revealed more.

Of him, damn it.

The first grouping of sculptures featured Bailey alone—standing, sitting, reclining. In the next group, there was something in the curve of her legs, or a subtle depression in her skin, that suggested the presence of another body.

His.

"Now, this." Brooke walked past the most erotic grouping to the end of the table, to get a better look at the sculpture he'd started working on last night. "This is interesting. It doesn't feel like the others."

Probably not. His hands disembodied from his conscious brain, he'd molded the lump of clay into a figure of the two of them together: her, on her knees and writhing in pain, and him, cradling her in his arms. Thankfully only he could see the blood. He'd never be able to scrub the image out of his mind.

Brooke covered his hand with hers—to comfort, or to stop him from slamming his fists down on the still-damp clay? "You have a week to finish the cycle."

"What cycle?"

The hand smacked him on the shoulder, and then gestured to the first sculpture, the one he'd worked on at the cabin. "There, she's alone. Alone, but...you've captured a glimmer of awareness, an almost innocent sensuality. Here—" she pointed to the next sculpture "—awareness dawns. She's...poised. Waiting. And this sculpture here?" She indicated one of the reclining poses, with Bailey's head thrown back in abandon. "You've obviously just slept together for the first time. And here? The emotional tone shifts. Notice here, in the curve of her hip, the slightest depression—like an arm is draped over her, but there's no arm? Just a suggestion. Very clever." She slowly walked down the row, pointing to a sculpture of Bailey sitting atop an abstract male form. "And here's where you appear for the first time." She flicked him a cheerfully lascivious glance. "Though you might have rendered yourself in greater physical detail."

"I think I feel violated."

A caw of laughter. "I'm bonded, not dead, Bubbeh." She paused. "It's a turning point in the relationship, for both of you. Do you really not see it?"

Of course he saw it. He'd completed the sculpture the day after they'd made love on his crushed velvet couch, right across the room.

She followed his glance. "So that's the place, eh?"

His cheeks heated. She saw too damn much. No doubt she'd connected the dots between the couch's upholstery and the fabric he'd insisted she locate for the pedestals.

She walked back to his work in progress, *Bailey, Bloody*—a horrible, horrible name, but he couldn't scrub it out of his head. "Here's another turning point, and this time, there's a lot more emotion from you than from her. You're frightened. Frantic."

Damn right he'd been frantic. Turning away from Brooke, he jammed his hands into the hair at his temples. Would everyone at the show see his emotions, spilling like he'd been gut-shot? Now he knew how his models felt.

"So, what's next?"

He thought back to their shouted words, to the uncomfortable discussion they'd left unfinished, to the way Bailey hadn't even noticed he'd left her hospital room. "I wish I knew." Yesterday, Lukas had let him know she'd left the hospital. There'd been no communication from Bailey herself, so he'd buried himself in work.

"Well, you can't leave the cycle unfinished."

He glared at her. "Maybe it's an existential statement about how relationships inevitably hit the wall and become utter fucking train wrecks."

She lifted her hands to his cheeks—then pinched, hard.

"Ow!"

"You don't believe that, and neither does she."

He dragged an impatient hand over his three-day beard. "Maybe you see something I don't, Brooke." Maybe he'd sculpted what he wanted to see instead of what was really there.

"What's wrong with your nose, hon? You love her. She loves you. So, where will this turning point lead?"

"I have no bloody idea."

"Well, where do you *want* it to lead? Communicate that in three or four sculptures."

"Oh, that's all," he said sarcastically. Complete four sculptures in a week? At the quality level he insisted upon? He'd be working around the clock, with no time for anything or anyone else—not that Bailey would even notice. "How the hell do I communicate eternity in three or four sculptures?"

Brooke patted him on his cheek. "You'll figure it out. I can't wait to meet your little human." She narrowed her eyes. "I don't think she's returned her RSVP card yet."

"She probably won't." If the flurry of activity he'd seen back in her hospital room was anything to go by, The Queen Bee's hive was a-buzzing. "I wouldn't count on her."

Brooke glanced at the sculptures and smiled. "And I wouldn't count her out."

CHAPTER SEVENTEEN

Slow up. Calm down.

Though it was dark and had been for hours, Wyatt paused in the shadows half a block away from Crackhouse Coffee. Less than an hour ago, Bailey's car had finally moved from Sebastiani Security's parking lot to the Sebastiani Building's underground ramp, and his surveillance team just reported in that she and Antonia Sebastiani had gone downstairs to the coffee shop.

He'd be able to verify for himself that she was okay.

The night Bailey had gotten sick, he'd been at home, updating dossiers and writing his final report for Winston, Inc., when the real-time feed had popped to life.

So much blood, and so little information.

Why had Sebastiani taken her, a human, to Memorial? It was very odd. And even hospitalized, she'd somehow managed to shut their hack down cold. Cheyenne, who'd assisted her, had been absolutely voracious last night. This morning in the shower, he'd noticed a distinct imprint of her teeth in the skin just above his cock—acceptable payback given he'd mentally superimposed Bailey's face over hers all night long.

Déjà vu struck as he scanned the coffee shop's windows. The evening rush hour was over and the place was absolutely packed, which had its pros and cons. He'd have a better chance of blending in with the crowd, but his preferred table, partially tucked behind a wooden beam, probably wouldn't be available.

A sheet of long, black hair caught his attention as Antonia Sebastiani gracefully rose from the leather love seat next to the fireplace. Carrying two heavy mugs, she went behind the counter to get refills—no waiting in line for a member of the Sebastiani family. Curled up on the other side of the love seat, Bailey stretched her arms overhead, rolling her head to work the stiffness out of her neck muscles. A heavy black three-ringed binder lay open in her lap, and the coffee table in front of the love seat was littered with books, papers, and the stack of magazines provided by the restaurant for guests to read. She looked tired, but beautiful. Whatever health problem had sent her to the hospital seemed to be resolved.

He knew she hadn't seen Rafe Sebastiani in days.

He tugged his black knit skullcap down to his eyebrows. Between the hat, two days' growth of beard, his baggy pants and a beat-up Trollhaugen Ski Patrol hoodie, he shouldn't rate a second glance.

He waited for Antonia to sit back down with the steaming mugs before entering, shivering in pleasure as the heat leached through his clothes. Over near his preferred table sat several couples on dates, a woman typing on a laptop, and two guys dressed a lot like him. A group of laughing women crowded around at the table for eight, empty plates and full coffee cups sharing space with e-readers and well-thumbed paperbacks. Behind the book club, his usual table was open.

Nodding at the women—they'd provide excellent camouflage—he sat down, plucked up a menu, and opened it. Over at the fireplace, Antonia read *Dissecting the Hack*. Bailey scribbled something in a spiral notebook and showed it to Antonia, who narrowed her eyes, nodded, then tapped something out on her tablet.

Had The Queen Bee found a protégé? Was she teaching Antonia? Using her? Both?

Was Bailey working a very long con?

"Hi, there. Are you ready to order?"

His stomach jumped. Just his luck that Sasha Sebastiani was working the coffeehouse side of the family complex tonight. "Um, yeah."

She smiled down at him, stylus expectantly poised over a handheld gadget. Her manner was professional, friendly. She didn't know him from Adam. Suddenly he was starving. "I'll have two eggs over hard, an order of bacon, hash browns, and a lightly toasted English muffin, please."

She tapped almost as quickly as he spoke. "Anything to drink?"

"Large coffee."

"Leaded or unleaded?"

"Caffeinated, please." He had hours of work ahead of him tonight. His most important task? Figuring out the fastest way to get one of his guys hired at Sebastiani Labs. Buddha hadn't been at all forthcoming about the specific information he wanted. "Just get me an in," he'd said.

With SkoolHaus out of commission, it was easier said than done.

His food arrived quickly, delivered by some dude, not Sasha. Picking up his phone, he popped in a pair of ear buds, pretended to select some music, and eavesdropped on the bawdy conversation at the next table while watching Bailey and Antonia. As he crunched into his last piece of bacon, he saw Bailey smother a yawn, snap the binder closed and start gathering her belongings. Antonia stood and stretched, exposing a vulnerable slice of belly. A small object fell from her lap, bouncing off the hardwood floor, coming to rest just under the love seat.

A USB stick. The Incubus Second had dropped a thumb drive.

Jackpot.

He held his breath while Antonia chattered away, stuffing her things into a backpack so heavy that slinging it over one shoulder pulled her momentarily off-balance. Giggling, she righted herself, stepped into her discarded flip-flops, and tugged Bailey off the couch. Talking quietly, they left through the coffee shop's inside entrance, no doubt heading for the private elevator leading to the penthouse.

Leaving the USB stick behind.

Dropping money on the table, he walked across the coffee shop, carrying his mug with him. He made it to the leather love seat before anyone else sat down.

"Let me clear this up for you," Sasha said, picking up the empty mugs and crumpled napkins Bailey and Antonia had left behind.

He pulled out an ear bud. "Thanks. The fire feels wonderful tonight."

"Doesn't it?" She treated him to a gamine grin that had a distinct sexual pull. "Can I get you a refill?"

He glanced at his half-full mug, then back at her. "No thanks. I'm set."

"Enjoy."

"Thanks." Dropping down on the love seat, he picked up the latest City Pages from the pile of newspapers and magazines lying on the coffee table, opened it with a crackle, and pretended to read. After a couple of minutes, he reached for his coffee mug, fumbling the paper. Several pages of the pulpy newsweekly fluttered to floor.

Right next to the stick Antonia had carelessly dropped.

With an exasperated sigh for anyone who might be watching, he bent down, picked up the pages, and scooped up the hot pink Hello Kitty USB stick at the same time.

Hello Kitty. He nearly rolled his eyes.

Neatly reassembling the paper, he set it back on the table, finished his last ounce of coffee, and left.

Behind the counter, Sasha smiled, picked up her phone, and dialed.

✳

At the Bunker the next morning, Bailey lifted her hands off the keyboard and flexed her stiff wrists. "I think we're in business."

"Undetected?" Lukas asked.

"So far, so good." According to Chico, who was upstairs monitoring audio from the bug Cheyenne had managed to plant in Wyatt's bedroom, the shower had just stopped running, and Wyatt was getting dressed. Bailey glanced at the clock. Wyatt was running late—so late he might not notice she was jacked into his laptop.

As she'd predicted, Wyatt had hit Antonia's USB stick as soon as he'd gotten home from Crackhouse last night, spending hours sifting through the supposedly confidential documents the youngest member of the Underworld Council might carelessly carry on her person. With each click, with each document he'd opened, she'd surreptitiously slithered in, crippling his security apps and replacing them with her own, blowing his system wide open and giving her full control. After countless hours and endless cups of coffee, her brain and body were about to shatter apart, but she was in.

She had root, so she was God.

When she stretched her arms overhead, her hands brushed against Lukas's chest. Whirling on her stool, she purposely clipped him in the shin with her boot. "Will you quit looming?"

The kick didn't have any obvious effect, but Lukas, carrying his morning sickness trash can, stepped back anyway.

Her foot jiggled as she glanced at the clock. If the calendar Cheyenne had stolen a quick peek at was accurate, Wyatt had an on-site meeting with a customer in Woodbury this morning. Between the round-trip commute and the time it would take for Wyatt to tour the customer's manufacturing facility, she'd have a three-hour window to work unobserved—if he didn't take the damn laptop with him. The wait was killing her. "I need more coffee."

"Stay put." Jack rose from the futon he shared with Antonia, who'd drifted off to sleep a couple of hours ago. "I'll get it."

"That's okay. You've been bringing me coffee all night long." She stood and stretched again, joints audibly popping. "I need to stretch my legs."

Lukas and Jack exchanged a glance.

"What?"

"Nothing."

An ugly suspicion dawned. "I'm drinking decaf, aren't I?"

Jack shot her an exasperated look. "You just had surgery for a freaking ulcer."

Her shoulders sagged. No wonder she was so damn tired.

Lukas's mini blipped. "Okay, he's out of the apartment and on his way to his car."

She glanced at her screen. Her programs were still running, which meant he'd left his laptop on the desk in his bedroom rather than take it with him. Showtime. "I can't think with you hovering over my shoulder." Nudging Lukas aside with her elbow, she sat back down again and fired up a crawler script that would suck up files like a Hoover, quickly copying them to an external drive attached to her computer. One copy of Wyatt's hard drive would be taken into evidence untouched, but she'd tear other copies apart personally.

"Guys? Seriously. Back off."

"Come on." Jack tugged on Lukas's T-shirt sleeve. "Let's give her some space."

The futon creaked ominously as Lukas sat down. Jack left the room. Sounds receded as she stared at the screen, visualizing the architecture, the bits and bytes flying, the ones and zeroes streaming between programs. She superimposed a mental map of her bore routes, and the precise damage they'd wreaked along the way.

After a quick check of her own equipment, she started exploring Wyatt's hard drive. They needed information, and fast. "Music, videos, pictures, contracts, spreadsheets, tax documents," she muttered as she clicked. "He's auto-logging his instant messages, the dumb shit." She'd read the chats later; right now, time was at a premium. Where were his client files, his dossiers? Who'd hired him to infiltrate Sebastiani Labs, and what were they looking for?

"See anything we can use?" Jack was back with more coffee.

"Not yet." She kept clicking. "Here are the documents we planted on Antonia's stick—ah, here we go." Dozens of folders and files, going back years. She saw big brand names, multi-nationals, NASDAQ companies, and start-ups. Not every folder had a copy of a contract—a big tip-off that the work might not be strictly legal—and none of it was encrypted or password protected. "Christ on a cracker, a new law school grad working their first case could connect these dots before breakfast." She grabbed the thermal mug and took a big slug of the decaf. Maybe she'd get some placebo effect from its scent, taste and warmth.

Lukas came up behind her and peered over her shoulder. "What's this?" He pointed at a folder named ASSOCIATES.

She clicked on it, her eyes widening. Wyatt had used people's hacker handles as filenames? This was a prosecutor's wet dream. "What an idiot, leaving all this information lying around where anyone can get at it."

"You're hardly anyone," Lukas said. "Accessing this information took some…unique skill."

"All someone has to do is break into his apartment and steal the damn laptop," she scoffed. "If the hard drive falls into the wrong hands, he—and they—are screwed." She skimmed the list. "This guy's doing time. So is he." Further down, she recognized the name of a young woman who'd hacked her abusive father's pacemaker, permanently incapacitating him. And there was Andy, who'd been quickly and quietly fired from his automotive industry job. Though his intentions had been good—he'd only meant to expose vulnerabilities in the vehicle's onboard computer system—remotely disabling the car's brakes during a high-speed test drive probably hadn't been the smartest move.

Any device connected to a network—cars, medical devices, phones, gadgets—could be hacked, and most of the associates on Wyatt's list had the skill to do the job.

Jack pointed. "There's your name."

And Rafe's, right underneath it. What the hell… She sorted the files by date. Four dossiers had been updated within the last twenty-four hours—hers, Rafe's, SkoolHausRok's, and someone named Buddha. She wiggled her cursor over SkoolHaus's file. "I've heard of this guy—solid skills—but this Buddha? Haven't heard of him." She clicked, opening the file. As was his habit, Wyatt had written his dossier with the most recent entry at the top of the document. She did a quick search on 'Sebastiani

Labs.' Multiple hits. "Jackpot," she bit out. "Who are you, Buddha, and what do you want?"

Lukas pulled up a chair—much better than having his six-and-a-half foot frame looming behind her like Frankenstein's monster. Antonia sat on his lap.

For several minutes, the room was silent, except for the whirring fans keeping the room cool. "Blackmail?" Antonia suddenly said, pointing toward the bottom of the screen. "Cooper claims he's being blackmailed by this Buddha guy."

Bailey read the paragraph Antonia had gotten to before anyone else. "If Wyatt doesn't penetrate Sebastiani Labs and turn over any and all information to this Buddha, Buddha turns him in to the authorities."

"Well, that's specific," Antonia said. "Not."

"What information? Whose authorities?" Lukas asked. "Is this Buddha human, or one of us? And why Sebastiani Labs?

"Espionage?" Bailey said with a shrug. "A privately-held company like Sebastiani Labs has its fingers in a lot of very lucrative pies. It doesn't compete for contracts, keeps out of the media…"

"Cooper's thoughts, Cooper's perceptions," Jack muttered. "There's no hard evidence here. Any IMs from this Buddha guy?"

Bailey accessed Wyatt's instant message logs. "Nope, nothing." She took another sip of her cooling coffee, and then set the cup down. Taking a deep breath, she clicked on the largest file—hers, or rather The Queen Bee's—and scrolled to the bottom of the document to find the first entry. "Whoa." Written on the day she'd been convicted, not that the son of a bitch had actually been at the courthouse to support her.

"He's…careful with his language," Jack noted as he read along. "Terse, factual. Nothing that's quite incriminating."

She scrolled up, skimming quickly. "Here's the first reference to a gift…but he doesn't say he left it."

"The tone is changing," Lukas observed.

He was right. Emotion was starting to creep in.

"Look." Jack pointed at the screen. "San Francisco, a couple of years ago. A description of what you're wearing, and his reaction to it. Same thing here. Miami. He seems to be fixated on a Hermès scarf."

"That gorgeous scarf I found on the floor in front of my hotel room door?" She'd given it to the concierge, thinking someone would surely return for such an exquisite lost item.

"He'd probably clued in to the fact that you were throwing his wrapped gifts away without opening them," Jack said.

"Now I feel extra-virtuous for turning it in to the Lost and Found, and not just keeping it."

As they read, it became clear that Wyatt had followed her, and had hired others to follow her, for years. That bastard.

"Whoa," Antonio suddenly said.

"What?"

Antonia pointed to an entry. "This just turned into the Penthouse Forum."

"What do you know about Penthouse Forum?" Lukas asked, frowning.

"Please."

As brother and sister bickered, she read what Wyatt had written. A slice of real life, the first time they'd slept together…highly embellished and emphasizing his prowess, yes, but certain key details were uncomfortably accurate. "Dated last year? We weren't…what the hell…." She looked at the date. "He wrote this during last year's Black Hat conference."

"Did you attend?" Antonia asked.

"No, but he did." Her coffee tried to crawl up her throat.

"Keep scrolling," Jack said.

She did as he asked. The entries came more frequently, were longer, and much more imaginative. She recognized a few real-world details—the time they'd sneaked into the computer lab for a quickie with a professor's voice droning just outside the closed door; the hot kiss they'd shared on a Ferris wheel—but the entries clattered into straight-up fiction territory pretty darn quickly.

Lukas studied her. "Are you okay?"

"Yes." Her skin wanted to crawl off her body, but she had to keep going. She needed every lick of data she could get her hands on before meeting with Wyatt in person.

"Rafe," Antonia suddenly said.

"Huh?" Her head whipped to the door.

"Sorry. Here." Antonia pointed to the monitor. "He mentions Rafe."

She read the most recent entries, swallowing back a coffee-flavored sting. Wyatt's erotic descriptions were…uncomfortably accurate. Ribbons of dread fluttered in her chest as understanding slowly dawned. "He has a camera at Rafe's."

Jack swore.

She whirled toward Lukas. "Please tell me you have a tail on Rafe."

"We have a team out front at his building," Lukas assured her, but he shifted his wastebasket to the other arm and quickly punched buttons on his mini. "Chico, status check on Rafe?" Lukas kept his gaze glued to hers as he waited. Listened. "Okay. Okay, thanks. Tell the team to stay on him." He ended the call. "Rafe hasn't left his place since he got back from visiting you in the hospital earlier this week. His business manager visited him yesterday, and his studio lights have been burning ever since."

"Last confirmed visual?" He could be injured, bleeding, unconscious—

"Less than an hour ago," Lukas reassured her. "He's fine."

Wyatt had a way of turning allies into enemies. "Is his business manager trustworthy?"

"Completely." Lukas laid his big hands on her shoulders. "Rafe's fine. I'll send Chico over to Rafe's place to locate the cameras, but…you realize we can't remove them yet."

She nodded curtly. Tipping Wyatt off that the cameras had been discovered would serve no purpose, but she seethed on Rafe's behalf. He didn't deserve this, and neither did she. Damn it, neither did she. "Bastard," she whispered.

The cursor blinked invitingly. She was dying to leave him a personal message, right here in the document, letting him know his system had been compromised, but that was her ego talking. It might completely screw up the case. "Can someone bring me my purse?"

In seconds, Antonia plopped it in her lap.

Pawing through its contents, she quickly pulled out a disposable phone. Opening a text message box, she considered, and then keyed: *Chadden's. Tomorrow night. 8:00 p.m., you asshole.*

With a sigh, she backspaced, replacing the last two words with *-TQB.*

"What are you doing?" Lukas asked.

She jerked her finger back from where it hovered over the Send icon. "Am I authorized to use a burner phone to send an anonymous text message to Wyatt?"

Lukas, Jack and Antonia looked at each other. Nodded. "You'll need to enter the phone into evidence," Lukas added.

"Sure." After a pause, she hit Send. Handing Lukas the phone, she grabbed his trashcan and heaved.

CHAPTER EIGHTEEN

When Bailey walked into Chadden's restaurant the next night, Wyatt was already there. The nervousness she'd shoved into the background elbowed to the front of the line.

Settle down. You can do this.

"Hello." The chef himself greeted her at the door, kissed her on both cheeks, and escorted her to coat check despite Lukas's request that he stay out of the way. "He's been here about fifteen minutes," Chadden said. "He ordered seltzer water, and he's getting twitchy."

Wyatt had arrived early, and she was exactly on time. The first point was hers. "Is everything ready?"

Chadden nodded, and then gestured to the door with his thumb. "How about out there?"

"All set." She'd seen the slush-splattered surveillance van parked down the block. Lukas, Jack and Chico were a reassuring thirty seconds away. She glanced over Chadden's shoulder to the busy bar. Almost half of the crisply-dressed waitrons were Sebastiani Security operatives. "Where are Gideon and Jenny?"

"Commander Lupinsky and his partner are in the restaurant." Chadden helped her remove her bulky coat, taking a leisurely tour of her body before giving her a near-silent wolf whistle. "Look at you."

She'd paired a pair of black skinny jeans with a simple black silk blouse worn over nothing but skin. Glancing down at her pebbled nipples, she bit her lip. "Is it too much?"

He shook his head. "Delectable, darling. Unfasten one more button."

"Really?" She already felt underdressed and overexposed.

"Trust me." When he reached for the button, she slapped his hand away and unbuttoned it herself. She wrapped her arms around her chest as cool air wafted over the slippery fabric, but Chadden gently pulled them away. "Chin up, shoulders back," he advised. "You look delicious."

She looked down at the calf-hugging boots she'd zipped over the pants. After Sebastiani Security's faerie profiler had finished reading Wyatt's dossiers, she'd suggested Bailey exploit a possible submissive streak she'd sensed by wearing some leather. She and Sasha had spent nearly an hour flipping through the dizzying collection of leather pants, skirts, dresses and vests in Sasha's closet. When Bailey spotted the boots—black leather, over-the-knee, and blessedly flat—they'd built the rest of the outfit from there.

She'd trade every item of clothing she wore for her mini comp, which Lukas had deemed too risky for her to carry. Without it, she felt utterly naked.

"Bailey, any information you get will help," Lukas had said. "There's no pressure." No pressure? Ha! Not only would she have to hold her own against Wyatt, against the pheromones that had intoxicated her so thoroughly and completely when she'd been younger, but thanks to that damn ulcer, she'd have to do it without drugs.

Her stomach jumped like minnows in a bait bucket—how apropos, given she was about to go on an epic fishing expedition. They needed to learn more about this Buddha. "Okay, enough stalling," she muttered to herself. "Let's get this show on the road."

Chadden's eyes locked onto hers. "You're strong. Powerful. Stunning."

His voice caressed her, echoing strangely in her head. Her spine straightened, and her confidence soared.

Vampire thrall.

He kissed her on both cheeks. "Go kick his ass."

When she walked into the bar, Chadden stayed at coat check.

She was on her own.

The wait staff had seated Wyatt at the round table in the corner, closest to the hidden surveillance equipment that would record every word of their conversation. After testing the sound levels earlier in the day, she'd asked that 'Reserved' placards be placed on several nearby tables. Hopefully having fewer people near them would reduce both the background noise and Wyatt's suspicions.

He'd dressed for a date, wearing trim black dress pants, black leather belt and shoes, and a gorgeous shirt that matched his blinding blue eyes. As always, his dark bangs flopped disarmingly over his forehead. When he rose to greet her, his eyes skimmed her body, widening ever so slightly as they reached her chest.

Chadden had been right about the extra button.

"Bailey." He stepped closer.

She steeled herself for his touch.

He wrapped his arms around her, pulling her against to his body, giving her what had to look to others like a very enthusiastic greeting between lovers. His scent twined around her as his hands stroked her shoulders, her back, her sides, under her arms. He whispered kisses against both ears. Her waist, hips and outer thighs didn't escape his touch. He was patting her down, checking her for earpieces and wires, but the knowledge didn't stop her nipples from beading, or her womb from giving a hungry, reflexive tug.

She fought to stand still under his wandering hands, cataloging her physical reactions distantly, clinically, as if she was a doctor observing someone else's physiological response rather than experiencing it herself. Wyatt was, by any rating scheme, a gorgeous man, and he had first-hand knowledge of her personal erogenous zones. Of course her girly bits were dancing an Irish jig. Her body might be dancing to his tune, but her thoughts were uppercut sharp. It was all she could do not to knee him in the balls.

His hands finally dropped. "How nice to see you again. Shall we sit?" Smiling urbanely, he gestured to a ladder-backed chair in the corner. Sitting there would trap her behind the heavy table, and keep her within easy physical reach.

So that was the way he wanted to play it? Asshole.

As she sat, she channeled the persona she'd concocted for this meeting: her own personality overlaid with a helping of Lady Heather, the classy dominatrix who'd given *CSI*'s Gil Grissom so many uncomfortable moments, a smidgen of Sasha's sexual confidence, and Julian Assange's chilly arrogance.

Remember your succubus blood. "Nice to see me? Unfortunately—" she pointedly brushed her hand down her arm, as if wiping away his touch "—I can't say the same. I'll cut to the chase." She glanced around, lowering her voice. "This is my gig, Wyatt. Back the fuck off."

A slow, sly smile bloomed on his face. "I knew it. You're working a long con."

She sat back in the chair, hoping she appeared relaxed. Inside, a trap door had opened, dropping her stomach to her knees. Okay, he'd nibbled on the bait. Now, she just had to be a good enough actress that he'd swallow the story they'd all concocted hook, line and sinker.

His lips twisted. "I suppose I have you to thank for the wild goose chase earlier today?"

She smiled but didn't respond. It had been a simple matter to spoof the GPS device Wyatt had installed on her car, sending whoever was assigned to follow her on a scenic drive to Duluth when her car hadn't moved from the Sebastiani Building parking lot.

A waitress suddenly appeared at their table. "Welcome to Chadden's. What can I get for you this evening?"

It was all Bailey could do not to goggle at Sebastiani Security's most senior female undercover operative. Tonight Winnie wore the same trim black slacks/white shirt/black vest combo as the rest of Chadden's staff, adding makeup and a huge pair of hammered silver earrings she usually couldn't get away with when she was working. "Um, I'll have a glass of the Sonoma pinot noir."

"And you, sir?"

Wyatt indicated his empty glass. "Another seltzer water, please."

Winnie nodded. "I'll be right back."

Winnie's presence nearby settled her stomach slightly—which was fortunate, because Wyatt was studying her like a bug pinned under a microscope. "You clever, clever girl," he said admiringly. "You have everyone fooled, don't you?" Under the table, he grasped her hand. It was all she could do to let him. "Is Kirkland in on this?"

She let a tiny smile creep onto her face. Let him think she'd burned her best friend, that she was using him, and everyone else, to get access to... everything.

"And sleeping with Sebastiani?"

It took a lot of effort to let the smile twist, to give a cynical shrug. "Would you pass up a chance to sleep with a man like that? Please."

His eyes went vague. What kind of debauched fantasies swirled in his brain, and exactly who had the starring role? Did she really want to know?

He focused again. Took a deep breath. "You've changed."

She shrugged. "So have you, I imagine. It's been a long time."

He acknowledged her point with a nod. "And I see you've picked up some pretexting skills along the way. Using Antonia Sebastiani to drop that USB stick? Brilliant."

So, he'd figured out her hack vector. It didn't matter. And...use Antonia? As if.

"Grooming the Incubus Second, teaching her the tools of the trade? Infiltrating Sebastiani Security? That takes epic balls." The sideways glance he gave her was half-admiring, half-horrified, and he fiddled with her index finger like he still had a right to. "I couldn't figure out why you'd close a successful consultancy and go work for someone else, but I think I'd close my business to focus full-time on a score that large, too—though heaven help you if Lukas Sebastiani figures out what you're doing."

"Let me worry about Lukas." It was all she could do to keep Assange's vaguely interested, mildly superior expression on her face. Wyatt's admiration turned her stomach.

"You have access to all Sebastiani Security and Sebastiani Labs assets. You attend Underworld Council meetings. Depending on the day, you live either with Rafe Sebastiani, or on the penthouse floor of the Sebastiani Building. It's taken you a little over a year to go from completely outside to the pinnacle of power," he marveled. "How the hell did you—"

"Wyatt." She pulled her hand from his. "I'm not here to share war stories. I need you and your Island of Misfit Toys to back the fuck off." She hardened her voice. "You're costing me time and money."

"Maybe I can assist."

Did he have someone on the inside yet? It wasn't outside the realm of possibility that he'd gotten a plant through Sebastiani Labs' hiring process, but it wasn't likely, either. He was probably delusional enough to think Cheyenne was still under his thumb.

"We—you and I—were a good team once."

Anger suddenly roared like the engines of a jumbo jet at takeoff. "A good team? You're kidding me," she snapped. "You don't know the meaning of the word, Wyatt. Class move, by the way, letting me take the fall alone."

He glanced around the bar. "Quiet down." Wyatt leaned closer, taking her hands, speaking so softly she wondered whether the surveillance equipment would be able to pick up his voice. "What good would it have done for both of us to be arrested and charged? Given your youth and family connections, I was fairly confident Kirkland would be able to get you off with a slap on the wrist."

Reasonably certain? A slap on the wrist? It was all she could do not to slug him. "You're pretty blasé about someone else losing their freedom."

"Come on, you were only incarcerated for a month."

She clenched her fists until her knuckles turned white. Only a month. As if years of stress, shame, family estrangement, loss of privacy and autonomy, closely-supervised probation, damage to her reputation, and a permanent criminal record were negligible prices for someone else to pay to ensure his continued freedom. Rage rose like a flash flood, threatening to drown her.

"Is Kirkland in on this too, or—"

"Enough ancient history," she interrupted. "Right now, just once, just between you and me, I want to hear you admit that you stole my code. That you modified it—poorly—without my permission, and then used it for a purpose it damn well wasn't designed for." She flicked him a scornful look.

"Believe me, I paid a price, too."

"What price?"

"You think the real story didn't get out? My reputation was shot, my credibility destroyed. It took a very long time to build it back up again."

"I lost over a decade of my life. I lost a career. I lost my family, my friends, my…" *I'm losing it.* She throttled back a decade of pain and rage. "Screw your precious credibility, Wyatt."

"Fair point," he hastily acknowledged. "You're right. I'm sorry." His voice was syrupy with apology, but if she was supposed to be lapping it up with a spoon, it wasn't working.

It wasn't working.

Her body might be responding to him, but her brain was firmly in the driver's seat, even without the drugs. And…he looked at her like she was his savior, like she had answers he didn't. He was dying for her to take this over, to take control—and she would, just not in the way Wyatt might want. "So, Wyatt. You seem to have gotten yourself into a bit of a mess." She looked at her watch. "This Buddha. Tell me about him. What does he want?"

Words spilled from him like a dam had been breached: how he'd been plucked off the street and shoved into a limo by gun-carrying goons. How he was certain the man knew everything, absolutely everything, about his extracurricular work. "He knows it all, every gig, large and small, from the time we worked together until now. He's threatening to turn me in."

She let the 'we worked together' statement slide. "Turn you in to whom? Who does he work for?"

"I…don't know," he admitted. "I get a whiff of law enforcement from him, and he obviously uses top-of-the-line tech, but—" he wiped away a bead of sweat trickling down his temple "—the guy is creepy. I overheard one of his minions call him something that began with the letters B-A. Whether it's a first name, last name, or a title, I don't know." He lifted his seltzer glass halfway to his mouth before noticing it was still empty. "Where the hell is that waitress?"

Keep him focused. "Why is he so interested in Sebastiani Labs?"

"I don't know. I haven't been able to penetrate yet, so I don't know what's there to interest him."

You can't begin to imagine. "Is he human?"

"I don't know. You could find out. *We* could find out." He leaned in, eyes glowing like they were lit from within. "Team up with me again, Bailey. Help me get this guy off my back. And after that? We could be lovers again, business partners again—partners in every sense of the word."

His pheromones bloomed, filling the air between them with dark, luscious musk. His eyes locked onto her lips. When he slowly leaned closer, it was all she could do to not recoil, to not back away. A small sound escaped her throat as he brushed his lips over hers, back and forth in a soft, testing touch that firmed when she didn't pull back. He opened his mouth slightly, deepening the kiss, nudging her lips with his tongue and inviting her to reciprocate.

Perfect technique, really, but the kiss tasted of mint and manipulation, and left her utterly cold.

Over Wyatt's shoulder, she saw Lukas, Jack and Chico enter the foyer. Gideon Lupinsky, Jenny Williams, and a couple of his cops closed in from the restaurant.

Wyatt pulled his head back slightly. "Your technical abilities, combined with my pretexting skills?" he murmured against her mouth. "We could rule the world."

She jerked away, wiping her lips with the back of her hand. "That's the difference between you and me, Wyatt. I don't want to."

"Cooper." Jack's voice was flat and cold.

Wyatt looked around and saw he was surrounded. "You bitch." He lurched to his feet, knocking his chair over with a clatter, shoving the table so the empty seltzer glass fell and shattered on the floor. He bolted toward the entrance, dodging and weaving, but Jack caught him, slamming him against the wall. A gorgeous piece of art crashed to the floor, sending colorful pottery shards flying.

The spacious bar suddenly seemed too small to hold so many large, jostling bodies. Behind her, she heard Jenny and Winnie clearing the room.

"You fucking bitch," Wyatt snarled at her.

Jack plowed his fist into his face. There was audible crunch. Blood sprayed, and Jack followed through with a hard knee to the groin. Wyatt sagged against the wall, but Jack jerked him upright, holding him up with a hand at his throat.

"Jesus." She scrambled out from behind the table.

Jack brought his face close to Wyatt's. Whispered something she couldn't hear. Wyatt's color bleached to white.

"Jack." She pulled on his arm. "Stop it."

Jack kept whispering until Wyatt gave a short, jerky nod. Stepping back, Jack let him wilt to the floor. Gideon moved in, rolling Wyatt to his stomach and jerking his arms behind his back. He efficiently lashed Wyatt's wrists together with zip cuffs.

"What was that all about?"

He smiled tightly. "My fist slipped."

As Gideon and Lukas yanked Wyatt out the door by his elbows, Chadden joined them. Over in the corner, his employees were already straightening the table, picking up the fallen chair, and sweeping up shattered glass. "Okay, that got a little rowdier than you said it would," he said to Jack.

Jack flexed his fingers. "Bill me."

"Believe me, I will." Chadden gestured to the entryway between the bar and restaurant, where dozens of patrons craned their necks to see what was going on. "The next round's on you. And that?" He pointed to the yellow and blue pottery shards lying on the floor. "That was one of Rafe's earliest pieces. It's gonna cost you."

Reaching down, she picked up a bug she'd affixed to the back of the work earlier in the day—and remembered an important question she'd forgotten to ask Wyatt. "Damn it."

"He'll make me another one," Chadden assured her. "After he gets done with your nudes, of course."

"Shut up," she said without heat, handing the bug to Jack. "I didn't get a physical description of Buddha." Wyatt had distracted her with his goddamn lips.

"We'll work him in interrogation." Jack wrapped his arm around her shoulders, pulling her in for a hug. "Good job, kid."

Thank God the entire conversation had been recorded, because right now she couldn't remember a single detail to save her life.

"You worked him like a lion tamer cracking a whip."

"I was pissed. That helped." It also helped that she hadn't been overcome by his pheromones. Her body might have responded, but in her mind, she'd felt more like a Method actress, giving the performance of her life. She hadn't drowned in him. Hadn't wanted to.

She wanted Rafe.

Jack reached for his vibrating mini and read the tiny screen. His knuckles were scuffed and speckled with blood. "Cooper's secured in the van. They're on their way to Holding."

Given the severity of the charges Lukas planned to lodge against him, it wasn't likely Wyatt would be allowed to roam free while his attorney mounted his defense. She allowed herself a tiny smile. Wyatt would *not* be pleased with his new accommodations.

"Gideon wants us to meet Jenny over at Wyatt's apartment."

She nodded. She was dying to get a look at his set-up.

"I'll have to recuse myself when this case comes before the Council," Jack muttered.

"That's what you get for physically assaulting the suspect." She'd no doubt be called upon to testify—an extremely unappealing prospect.

"Come on," Jack said. "Let's go."

A short time later, they pulled up to Wyatt's high-rise apartment complex. Dozens of residential floors were stacked above multiple floors of retail, parking and office space. Smack-dab in the middle of downtown, there would be a lot of activity, at all times of the day. "He'd be able to come and go at will here, with hardly anyone the wiser," she said as they entered the building. "Easy to blend in with the crowd."

Jack indicated the cameras, staring down from the corners where wall met ceiling. "Decent security system." They took the elevator to the twenty-first floor, the doors opening onto unremarkable white walls, gray industrial-grade carpet, and the scents of sauerkraut and spaghetti sauce. Jenny Williams waved to them from a door down at the end of the hall.

Bailey pointed. "There she is."

When they arrived at the door, Jenny hesitated for a moment, letting Jack enter, but blocking her way.

"What's wrong? What have you found?" Oh, Jesus. "Cheyenne…" She tried to shove past Jenny, but the sturdy Valkyrie held firm.

"No one else is here. Cheyenne's fine." Jenny held her shoulders, and gave her a little shake. "Cheyenne's fine."

She sagged with relief.

"But we found some things you might find upsetting. I want to talk to you—"

"That son of a bitch." From inside the apartment, Jack's curse bounced off the walls.

"Let me go," she said to a grim-looking Jenny. "I've dealt with Wyatt before. Nothing he could do would surprise me." When the other woman reluctantly stepped aside, she entered Wyatt's apartment.

Man cave, six-figure salary division. The living room was dominated by an L-shaped leather couch, aimed at a huge, wall-mounted flat screen TV coated with so much dust she couldn't imagine anyone actually being able to see the picture. The coffee table was littered with 'zines, newsletters, thumb drives, the last three issues of *The Hacker's Quarterly,* and empty Red Bull cans. In the galley kitchen, there was a high-tech espresso machine, a four-slice toaster, an open bag of potato chips, and a row of colorful cereal boxes he hadn't bothered to put in the cupboards. The take-out menus wallpapering his refrigerator door hit uncomfortably close to home.

"Two bedrooms?" she asked Jenny.

Jenny nodded. "He uses one as an office, and the other for sleeping. He has computer equipment in both rooms."

She peeked into the office, recognizing the high-end equipment, the black Aeron chair, and the familiar snarl of cables, cords, and surge protectors snaking along the baseboards. This room he dusted, this gear he cared for. Despite the cracked window and a small fan, it smelled warm—too much equipment in too small a space. She nodded to the guy kneeling on the floor—one of Gideon's e-team, taking pictures.

"I can't let you touch anything," Jenny said, "but we wanted you to see his set-up before we dismantled it and took it into evidence."

Four computers—two laptops, and two towers connected to flat screen monitors—and no suspicious-looking peripherals. If she innocently bumped into the desk, it might jiggle the mice just enough to deactivate his screen savers, but no way would Jenny allow her to access his machines, see the tools of his trade: the scripts and bots, the social media sites he mined for information, the bulletin boards, his avatars and personae…thousands and thousands of messages scrolling by, too quickly for any one person to possibly read.

She'd choose a solitary, Red Bull-fuelled coding jag over all that 'socializing' any day of the week.

Wyatt was right. Put the two of them together, team them up, and between them they might form one reasonably normal person. His sociability was one of the reasons she'd been so drawn to him in the first place—a moth drawn to the unfamiliar flame.

Moths drawn to flames inevitably got zapped.

"Do you see anything unusual?" Jenny asked.

"No. Go ahead." Turning away from temptation, she went to Wyatt's bedroom. It smelled citrusy and very slightly damp; he'd probably taken a shower before meeting her at Chadden's. He had a queen-sized bed covered with navy blue linens, a bedside table with a lamp, and another desk holding yet another laptop. On the screen was a paused video or movie that showed a lot of bare skin. Next to the laptop, a half-dozen DVRs fanned out like playing cards.

"Home movies?" She scanned the corners of the room for cameras. "Cheyenne is going to be *so* pissed off."

"It's not Cheyenne," Jack said between clenched teeth. "Look again."

She did—and all the blood in her body crashed to her feet.

Rafe's head, nuzzling between her spread legs. His hair, draped over her stomach and legs as he—

She swayed as black spots danced in her peripheral vision. Wyatt had watched them, recorded them, whacked off to their private—

"Let's sit down." Jack wrapped his strong arm around her waist.

"Not on the bed," she gasped. "Not in here."

Jack led her to the living room, to the couch, and pushed her head down between her knees. She heard the faucet running in the kitchen, and then he handed her a glass of water. "Drink this."

Had Wyatt made copies of the files? Uploaded them somewhere? Had he paid off his minions with amateur porn? A hysterical giggle escaped. She was going to have to scour the dirtiest back alleys of the internet for copies of her very own sex tape.

If her parents hadn't already disowned her, this would probably do it. "Jack?"

"Hmm?"

"I have to quit." She'd known that her presence at Sebastiani Security might draw unwanted attention, but this was ridiculous.

"No, you don't."

"I do. I should've done it a long time ago." She sat up. "We're getting hacked left and right, and now Rafe's privacy has been unconscionably compromised. How much risk do the people I love have to take on because of me? I'm a target, Jack." She sighed heavily. "I'll always be a target."

Resting his hands on her shoulders, he gave her a tiny shake. "I know seeing that recording is a shock. The sense of violation has to be outrageous. But you know better than to make decisions based on emotion instead of facts. You *know* better. Take some time to assess the data, to draw conclusions based on actual information." Another tiny shake. "Use that outsized IQ to find another solution, because this one is not acceptable."

She took a deep breath. "How am I going to tell Rafe? This is all my—"

"No," Jack snapped. "It's Wyatt Cooper's fault." The couch dipped with his weight as he sat next to her. "Bailey, Rafe will be fine," he said quietly. "He loves you."

She shot him a sideways glance. "Yeah, so much that he hasn't contacted me since he walked out the door of my hospital room."

Jack pulled his mini off his belt, pressed and clicked, and then handed it to her. "Read."

She looked down at the tiny screen. Texts, dozens of them, from Rafe. How was she? Was she eating? Sleeping? Being careful with her workload? "Why didn't he contact me directly?"

"I imagine he thought you were ass-deep in alligators—and that you could use some breathing room." He glanced grimly at the bedroom. "I'll have to go over to Rafe's from here to recover the recording equipment and take it into evidence. Why don't you come with me?"

She wanted to see Rafe—too much—but before she could, she had to take a shower, cleanse herself, wash Wyatt's touch off her skin. "I need to clear my head first." If she saw Rafe now, her will would disappear like water down the drain. Jack had told her to find another solution, and the tiniest hint of an idea was sparking to life—an idea that, if carefully nurtured, might solve about eight problems once and for all.

"How are you doing with the pheromones after that kiss? Are you okay?" Jack eyed her closely. "Being in the van while Cooper patted you down gave us all a couple of bad moments."

"They weren't as big an issue as I thought they'd be." She explained how she'd been aware of the pheromones physically, but how her mind had skimmed over them, like a surfer riding a wave.

"Because you love Rafe."

"Yeah," she admitted. In hindsight, Wyatt had done her a massive favor with his unwanted kiss. Between her smidgen of succubus blood, and her love for another man, she now knew she had some very effective natural defenses. She stood, nodding briskly. "Go tear out those damn cameras. I'm going back to The Bunker."

Jack stood, too. "You're sure you won't come to Rafe's with me?"

"Not right now. I…have an idea I want to flesh out."

He eyed her warily. "You and your ideas. You frighten me sometimes."

"That's why you pay me the big bucks." She hugged him, then kissed his nicked-up knuckles. "Thank you, kind sir, for avenging my honor."

"It was long overdue." He kissed the top of her head, and then tapped her temple with his finger. "Don't get all wrapped around the rails in there, okay?"

"Okay."

Jack's mini vibrated. "Lukas and Chico are on their way to Rafe's." He glanced up. "Sure you won't come with me?"

It was tempting, so tempting. "No."

"I hope you know what the hell you're doing." He walked towards the door.

"Jack?" He turned back, eyebrows raised. "Tell him that… tell Rafe I'll see him soon."

"When?"

She thought about everything she had to do. "What day is it?" Between hacks and hospitalization, she'd completely lost track of time.

"Today is Wednesday."

"His gallery show, at the latest."

"You're going?"

"Of course." Even if everyone there would be looking at her nude body. A snort of laughter escaped. If Wyatt had uploaded any of those files, people might already be doing so. Searching for the files was Job One.

"I'll check in with you later," he said, his hand on the doorknob. "Don't do anything stupid."

She jerked her head to the door. "Go."

No, she wasn't about to do anything stupid. Actually, the idea sparking to life might be one of the best she'd ever had.

Now, she just had to find the courage to follow through.

CHAPTER NINETEEN

Rafe stood near the bathroom door, arms crossed, fuming as Lukas leaned out the open bedroom window to shout something to Chico. After explaining everything that had gone down at Chadden's a couple of hours ago—including the fact that Jack had smashed in Cooper's pretty nose—Chico was out on the fire escape removing a small, blocky device from his satellite dish.

Apparently his satellite dish did more than translate airborne signals into subscription-based entertainment.

That fucker. The thought of Wyatt Cooper watching them in bed, catching even a glimpse of Bailey's bare skin, made him want to smash something.

Lukas and Chico talked and gestured, but individual words didn't register. He didn't know what to do with the killing fury streaming through his body, as vicious as the cold front shoving into the region.

Lukas crawled back in again, closing the window behind him with a swirl of snowflakes. "Chico thinks he sees another camera one floor down." His brother was watching him closely. "He'll check it out, and then come in downstairs." Sheets rustled as Lukas climbed off the bed Rafe hadn't used in days. Other than showering, and bolting back a quick meal standing over his kitchen sink, he'd spent nearly every waking and sleeping moment down in his studio.

One positive thing about not having seen Bailey recently? The fucker hadn't gotten any decent film in days. He gestured to the cameras. "Does Bailey know about this?"

"Yeah," Lukas sighed, swiping a hand through his hair. "Come on, let's go downstairs. Jack's on his way."

"But not Bailey."

No answer from his brother. Of course not.

As they walked downstairs, the door buzzed. "I'll let him up," Lukas said.

"Fine." Rafe stalked to the kitchen. If any situation called for a few medicinal shots, finding out his bedroom had been a secret movie set qualified, but he didn't have any hard liquor in the house and a civilized bottle of wine just wouldn't cut it. There was nothing civilized about the primeval rage pounding through his veins. As he assessed the pitiful contents of his refrigerator, he heard Jack climb the stairs with a heavy tread. Lukas greeted him, and they held a low-volume conversation.

He reached into the refrigerator. They'd have to make do with two six packs of Heineken.

"I'll take one of those," Jack said from behind him.

He glanced back. Lukas had buzzed Chico up, too. Twelve beers shared between four guys wouldn't provide anywhere near the oblivion he sought, but Lukas could always go buy more.

Rustling in a drawer for his church key, he popped the tops off four bottles and passed them around. Several drops of blood adorned the chest of Jack's dress shirt, and his knuckles were scuffed and red. He would have preferred throwing the punches himself, but no one had told him about the op—not even Chadden, that son of a bitch. "How is she?" he asked Jack.

Jack shook his head. "She's going to sprain her brain thinking so damn hard."

"What happened?" Lukas leaned on the big island separating the kitchen from the living room, sipping at his beer.

"She gave notice."

Lukas's head snapped up. "Again?"

Again?

"I think I talked her down for now." Despite his words, Jack didn't look certain of success. Bailey could do that to a man.

So, Bailey had tried to quit her job, more than once? Good for her. When were Lukas and Jack going to wake up and smell the burnout?

"I took the tracking device off your Jeep," Chico said. He looked none the worse for the wear after climbing around on his fire escape in a snowstorm wearing nothing but jeans and a shirt.

"Thank you." To be honest, he'd forgotten about the damn thing. "So, tell me how things went down at Chadden's."

Jack described how Bailey had sauntered into the bar, dressed to kill, and played Wyatt Cooper like a fiddle. "She followed the sequence we rehearsed, and got most of the information we needed."

"She was completely chill, a total badass," Chico added. "Even when he kissed her."

Rafe straightened from his slouch. "He kissed her?"

"Not for long." Lukas smiled coldly. "That's when Jack took him down."

"With a fist to the face and a knee to the junk." Chico lifted his bottle in a toast. "Nicely played."

Jack took a sip of his beer. "She distracted him long enough so we could enter the restaurant unobserved and then arrest him."

Distracted him? What the hell did *that* mean?

"She, Jenny and I went to Cooper's place to look at his technology set-up while these guys took him in."

"He lawyered up as soon as we got there," Lukas said. "He's not talking."

Jack's expression was hard enough to chip rocks. "Seeing Cooper's film collection really knocked her for a loop."

"You didn't let her watch them?" he snapped.

"No, of course not. But there was a video paused on his desktop when we walked in, and…" He shrugged. "He had five or six DVDs lying on the desk next to the computer."

"They were taken into evidence? Jesus." The thought of cops, techs and lawyers watching the films—

"Jenny tagged them limited access."

His head was pounding so hard his eyeballs might pop.

"Calm down, Rafe."

He whirled toward Lukas. "*You* calm down." He didn't know what to do with the anger, the sense of violation. The incendiary hours he and Bailey had spent in his bed, lost in each other, were *theirs*, no one else's, damn it.

Was he going to be left with nothing, not even memories?

Jack took a slug off the bottle, his expression grim as he swallowed. "What concerns Bailey most right now is the possibility that Cooper uploaded them to the internet."

"That son of a bitch."

"Throttle back. We don't know that he did. But the thought of it was enough to make Bailey offer her resignation so she could go scorched earth if she had to." Jack looked at Lukas. "She's concerned that her presence at Sebastiani Security poses a risk to the companies, to the Sebastiani family, and to the Council—"

Lukas cursed under his breath.

"—and she's right. You know she is. But risks can be managed. Mitigated. I urged her to find some data, to determine the actual scope of the problem, and then find a solution." Jack finished the last ounce of beer in the bottle. "I have no idea what she's going to come up with, but she wants to be alone to do it."

"She's been alone her whole fucking life!" Rafe yelled.

"It's how she copes," Jack said with a shrug. "It's how she's always coped. She needs time to think, to work things through." Opening the refrigerator, he pulled out what remained of the first six-pack. "Anyone else ready?"

Chico nodded, lifting his empty bottle. Lukas shook his head.

His own bottle was nearly full, and dewy with condensation. The one gulp he'd taken roiled uneasily in his stomach. With a sound of disgust, he set the bottle down on the island.

Jack picked it up and drank. "Bailey said she'll see you at your show Saturday night."

Not until then? "That's just great." He glanced at his key ring, hanging on a hook by the door. He could drive to The Bunker in ten minutes, and be shaking her until her teeth rattled in eleven. Kissing her in twelve—

"She loves you, Rafe," Lukas said.

Jack nodded in agreement. "She told me so tonight. I heard her say the words."

He hadn't heard the words. He walked blindly away from the island, thinking about the sculpture firing in the kiln downstairs, the final work in the sequence Brooke had urged him to envision—him on one knee, asking for her hand in the human tradition.

What would Bailey think—what would she *do*— when she saw the sculpture?

"Hell." He stared out the window, watching the snowflakes swirl. Whether Bailey realized it or not, she was no longer alone. She'd never be alone again.

But the more time that passed without contact, the more nervous he got.

*

Bailey made sure the hushed, darkened hallway was completely empty before slipping into the back entrance of one of the glass-front rooms rimming the balcony of her father's mega-church. The rooms had always made her uncomfortable, reminding her of the high-buck private skyboxes at Target Center or The X, but today, the dark, private rooms served her purpose perfectly. She'd promised her sister she'd attend her wedding in person, but Mel didn't need a big family blowout ruining her wedding day.

As the door closed quietly behind her, she cast a worried glance to the ceiling, half-expecting a lightning bolt to crash down from the heavens. She'd arrived as part of a crowd, and being the day was bright and sunny, the Jackie O. sunglasses covering a third of her face didn't look too radically out of place. The man checking invitations at the door hadn't looked at her twice. Lukas would have fired him on the spot.

She pulled out her mini and sent Mel a quick text message letting her know she'd arrived. Leaving the lights off, she flipped the speakers on, slipped out of her coat, and set it on one of the padded theatre seats. Under different circumstances, she'd be in the East Wing dressing room with her sister and her bridesmaids right now, giggling, sighing, and making last-minute adjustments to Mel's dress before she walked down the aisle.

But circumstances weren't different, and they hadn't been for a very long time.

Sharing this day with her sister was one more thing her father's decision had taken from her, but it was a waste of energy feeling resentful. She and Mel had managed to stay in touch over the years, exchanging birthday and Christmas gifts at restaurants or coffee shops—and if she wasn't mistaken, Mel found the covert contact more than a little exhilarating.

Not so surprising, given Mel also had succubus blood.

Which of her parents had brought a sex demon's libido into their oh-so-pious marriage? She looked at the altar, dominated by the towering pulpit her father mounted every Sunday, so frequently railing against the sins of the flesh.

He must be a very conflicted man indeed.

As the festively-dressed guests socialized down on the main level, she lowered herself into one of the comfortable padded seats with a sigh. She was tired—exhausted, really—but it was a good kind of tired, not the zombie apocalypse type. Since she'd walked out of Wyatt's apartment, she'd been hyper-productive, fielding the occasional question from Gideon's e-Team as they examined Wyatt's computers. As one of the victims in the case, he'd vetoed her direct involvement, but she'd compensated by dissecting her working copy of Wyatt's hard drive. Jenny had informed her that the DVRs they'd taken from Wyatt's desk were blank, which squared with her own analysis. She hadn't found any indication Wyatt had copied the video files, and nothing had shown up online, either. There'd been no snide back-channel chatter about The Queen Bee's new porn sideline out on the hacker boards. Even if Wyatt had planned to make copies or upload them somewhere, he simply might not have gotten around to it.

Who knew? Wyatt wasn't talking—and if his blackmailer had ever existed, he or she had dropped off the face of the Earth.

She and Cheyenne had also hammered out the bare bones of a proposal that, if accepted, would mean a shift in roles for them both. If Elliott and

Lukas signed off on their plan, three people from Cheyenne's team would assume more responsibility at Sebastiani Labs, freeing Cheyenne up to take over some of *her* day-to-day tasks at Sebastiani Security. This, in turn, would allow her to focus full-time on the Council's strategic objectives.

If the proposal wasn't accepted, she'd quit, and make it stick.

She'd also put her condo on the market for a bargain-basement price, never dreaming it would sell in a day. The new owners wanted to move in quickly, so now, in addition to everything else, she had about a month to find another place to live.

She really wanted was to live with Rafe. Would he understand that it wasn't him she'd distrusted, but herself? Had she completely ruined things?

"Hey." Jack's soft voice. "Sorry we're late."

She glanced at the door. Jack and Sasha, together? This…might not end well.

"I wanted to check out this church thing." Sasha removed her long coat. "I've never been to a human wedding before."

"Right." Jack must really be worried about her emotional state if he'd dragged a succubus along as backup—especially *this* succubus. "Jack, how's your schedule Monday morning? I'd like to book some time with you and Lukas."

"How about later today?"

She shook her head. "Monday is fine." She had to talk with Rafe first. After tonight, she'd have a better picture of what her future might hold. If Rafe forgave her—if they had a potential future together—she'd stay in the Twin Cities. If Lukas accepted her plan, she'd remain at Sebastiani Security.

If either man rejected her, she had bigger decisions to make.

"I think the wedding's about to start." Sasha sat next to her, leaning forward on her chair as people took their seats below. The huge sanctuary quieted, and music wafted in from the speakers: *Canon in D*, but with a distinct Celtic twist.

The groom escorted a beautifully dressed couple down the aisle to the front right pew, kissing them both before proceeding to the altar. When he turned, she got her first real-world glimpse of Mel's beloved, Daniel O'Brien. A shaggy-haired Irishman wearing a kilt, a tuxedo jacket, and wire-rimmed glasses, her sister's absent-minded professor looked ecstatic, and luminously in love.

Yes, he'd suit Mel very nicely indeed.

She swallowed a lump in her throat as her sister's bridesmaids, dressed in long columns of red, walked down the aisle, escorted by tuxedoed groomsmen. The bridesmaids and groomsmen lined up at either side of the altar. The lump returned as the music swelled, as the guests all rose in unison, looking expectantly toward the back of the church.

She couldn't see Mel until she was about halfway down the long center aisle, escorted by both of their parents. She knew her father would figure out a way to both give his daughter away and officiate at the ceremony, but her mother's presence at Mel's side was a pleasant, non-traditional surprise.

"You favor your mother," Sasha said softly.

"Mel looks more like her than I do." Seen from behind, the two women looked more like sisters than mother and daughter. Down at the altar, her mother was lifting Mel's fingertip-length veil, giving her a sweet kiss. Their father did the same, and then escorted her mother to the front left pew before ascending the shallow stairs with a swirl of white robes, positioning himself under the spotlights in the center of the large altar.

Mel and Daniel joined hands. The look they exchanged was drenched with love.

As her father's spoke the opening words of the traditional ceremony, her mother suddenly turned, looking up to the balcony where they sat. A timeless second passed. Her mother's nostrils twitched, and a bittersweet smile tipped her lips before she turned and faced forward once again.

A sob escaped her clogged throat. She turned her head into Jack's chest and let the tears flow.

CHAPTER TWENTY

Rafe took another sip of Bollinger as the critic nattered on and on about delicacy of line, and sublime sexual and emotional tension. The man was gay and his interest aesthetic, but if he kept talking about Bailey's body in such specific terms for very much longer, he was going to lose his protruding front teeth. Rafe had long ago come to terms with the fact that to be an artist making a living from his work meant showings, critics and reviews—opening your imagination up for judgment, and occasionally taking it on the chin—but right now, this guy made him want to throw a punch or two.

If he felt exposed, how in the world would Bailey react? Hell. There wasn't a person here who could possibly misinterpret how he felt about his as-yet-unidentified muse. The buzz was building, and Brooke was ecstatic.

"Thank you so much for your time, Mr. Sebastiani." The critic closed his notebook, and tucked it into his suit jacket. "I notice there are no prices..."

Because he wasn't sure they were for sale. How could he part with a single one? On the other hand, why keep them around, torturing himself with what he couldn't have? "Contact Brooke next week."

"Ah, you want to maintain the set." The critic gave *Bailey, Bloody* a covetous glance. "Entirely understandable. The sculptures in sequence are as much a part of the experience as any individual work. Museums, then? Who's offered?"

Rafe resisted glancing at his watch. Resisted looking at the door. The showing was half over, and Bailey hadn't shown up yet. "You'll want to speak with Brooke." From the other side of the room, loud laughter lanced through his aching head. He and Brooke had wanted to create a cocktail party atmosphere, and they'd succeeded beyond his wildest expectations.

He hated cocktail parties. What had he been thinking?

Too many people, and most of them strangers. His family and most members of the Council hung out together over in the corner, covertly guarded, but Lorin and Gabe had made a break for it, holding hands near the beginning of the sequence. He'd lost sight of Chico and Winnie, both off duty, who'd raised a few eyebrows by arriving together. Over near the bar, Wyland was in quiet conversation with Scarlett's friend, investigative journalist Tia Quinn.

"Hello, Darby."

His sister. Thank the universe.

Rising on tip-toes, Sasha kissed both of the critic's cheeks. "I hate to interrupt, but can I borrow my brother for a moment?"

"Certainly."

Sasha shot an apologetic smile over her shoulder as she drew him away.

"He's staring at your ass," Rafe muttered.

"Darling, everyone stares at my ass."

He nodded, acknowledging her point. She wore a vintage black velvet riding jacket with peplum over skin-tight leather leggings, paired with sky-high Louboutins. Fashion with an edge, yet not sacrificing warmth—an important consideration on the coldest night they'd had in weeks. The valets outside parking cars were really getting a workout tonight.

She peered around his shoulder. "Where's that creepy dude who asked whether I'd been your model?"

"Gone." Thankfully. Did the man not have eyes in his head? Or if he did, did he actually think Rafe would express amorous feelings for his sister in clay? He shuddered. "People are odd."

"No shit."

He glanced at the door again.

"She'll be here." Taking his hand, Sasha led him to the corner where his friends and family had gathered—coincidentally or not, right next to the last sculpture in the series. He closed his eyes, swallowing hard. The fire opal ring tucked in his left front jacket pocket burned him like a brand.

Claudette separated herself from his father, extending both arms. "Rafe."

He stepped into her embrace. The approval and encouragement she'd embedded in his name comforted him like a balm.

"Beautiful work, Rafe," his father said, resting a hand on his back. "Simply beautiful."

So much said without words. He had his father's blessing. "Thanks," he choked out.

Someone handed him another glass of champagne, and he took a quick sip. Hopefully the tiny bubbles would break up the lump in his throat. His entire family was here, and there was Jack, Bailey's best friend, standing between his sisters. "Thanks, everyone, for coming."

"We wouldn't miss your show for the world." Scarlett toasted him with a mug of frothy hot cocoa. Lukas, hovering protectively next her, drank nothing and looked distinctly green around the gills. "While everyone is gathered, can we share some news?"

"Finally." Antonia rolled her eyes.

"Hey." Sasha nudged Antonia with her elbow.

Scarlett glanced around the circle, no doubt noticing all the knowing glances. "Well." She looked at Lukas, who shrugged in denial. "It seems you all might know our news anyway."

Rafe gestured to a hovering waiter for more champagne. "There's no keeping a secret in a family of incubi and succubi."

"And then there's the fact that Lukas has been upchucking his morning cornflakes for weeks," Antonia added. "Kind of hard to miss."

Sasha stepped in. "Can we let her finish?"

Scarlett clutched Lukas's hand. "We're having a baby!"

During the congratulations that followed, Rafe noticed that Lukas looked equal amounts exhilarated and terrified, and he caught his father and Claudette exchanging a concerned look. While most parents might have vague, sparkling dreams of their child becoming president one day, these parents would have to plan for its near-certainty. Their child would lead, would be groomed to take a seat on the Council.

Lukas and Scarlett would need every wit at their disposal to effectively parent an incubus/siren child who might inherit both parents' extravagant skills.

If he and Bailey ever had a child, what gifts might he or she—

He whipped his head to the entrance. She was here, removing her coat to reveal a lime green cocktail dress that clung to her curves and drew too many eyes—including those of the smooth attendant who'd just taken her coat, gloves and scarf and handed her a claim ticket. Shivering, she stepped away from the entrance, accepting a flute of champagne she probably shouldn't drink.

A tiny, redheaded tornado was on an intercept course. His feet moved, but not quickly enough.

Shit. Brooke would reach Bailey first.

✳

She was overdressed.

There were so many people, a shifting sea of sophisticated, artsy black. She looked down at her bright green dress, with its retro, vaguely *Mad Men* vibe. She'd felt so confident and sexy standing in Nordstrom's dressing room.

Now, she felt hideously out of place.

She considered not handing her coat and gloves to the smiling attendant, but he'd already given her a claim ticket and it was too late for that. "Thank you." She stepped away from the chilly entrance, out of the traffic pattern. Instead of the intimidating, hoity-toity snobbery she'd half-expected, the event seemed more like a party. Black-uniformed wait staff smiled as they circulated, carrying trays of wine, champagne, and hors d'oeuvres. Everyone milled around red velvet-draped pedestals.

Displaying her naked body.

She took a deep breath, and exhaled sharply. *Okay, suck it up. Find Rafe and apologize.* Certainly no one would connect her with *The Dreamer*—for that was what Rafe had called his show—especially if she…just stayed here against the wall, out of everyone's way.

"Champagne?" A hot waiter handed her the flute before she could think about it. Shooting her a flirty smile, he continued on his way.

Should she drink it? Wyland was probably here somewhere; she could ask him, but… "To hell with it." She took a sip, raising an approving eyebrow as the tiny bubbles effervesced on her tongue. There really was a difference between the okay stuff and the really good stuff.

"You look like you could really use that." A tiny woman joined her, holding a glass of white wine. Her exuberant red hair flamed against her simple black blazer, shirt and pants. In lieu of a necklace, a pair of rhinestone-studded reading glasses hung suspended on a silver chain.

"Yes, I guess." Having to look down to speak with someone was a novel experience.

"I'm Rafe's agent, Brooke Kearney." Her voice was pure New Yawk. "And you're Bailey." The bird-like woman skimmed her frame with oddly knowledgeable eyes before shaking her hand. "So nice to finally meet you. Rafe is occupied with his family at the moment. Why don't I take you through?"

Her stomach lurched. "No, that's not necessary. I can wait—"

"Here, in the corner? In that gorgeous dress? Honey, I don't think so." The woman grasped her hand, her French manicured nails digging like talons.

Okay, she was going to get a personal tour of the sculptures whether she wanted one or not.

Soon she and Rafe's agent were standing at the first pedestal, and she recognized the sculpture as the one Rafe had been working on when she'd arrived at the cabin. Yes, it was her nude body, but...abstracted somehow, with breasts more suggested than specifically sculpted. She looked down at the tiny card, which read, simply, "One," in the same spare, architectural font as the sign in the gallery window.

The Dreamer. It was nice of Rafe to at least suggest that the figure—um, *she*—might be sleeping or dreaming instead of waiting to have sex, or recovering from it. But there was no disguising the sensuality eddying off the sculpture in waves.

It wasn't until they'd reached "Nine," and seen that slight depression in her hip from the weight of Rafe's invisible hand, that it clicked. The series wasn't simply a set of erotic nudes. He'd sculpted the physical and emotional evolution of their relationship, laid it bare in clay. He was there in the sculpture with her, present without physical form.

It was genius. It was...uncanny.

They'd reached "Sixteen" before she noticed the hush in the room. She tensed, feeling the weight of dozens of eyes upon her.

Brooke's nails bit in. "Breathe."

She obeyed, drawing herself up to her full height. She had absolutely nothing to be ashamed of.

"That's my girl," Brooke murmured. "You'll do nicely, for a human."

For a human? If she only knew.

"Yes, you'll do nicely."

"I'll do a damn sight better than that, Ms. Kearney." If Rafe gave her half a chance.

The other woman patted her hand. "Please, call me Brooke."

The air at her back warmed. She shivered as she inhaled his scent, as gooseflesh rippled over her skin.

"Rafe. There you are." Brooke released her hand and stepped back.

She turned to face him. Yes, there he was, looking slightly pale and drawn, like a poetic Heathcliff. He wore head-to-toe black like the rest of his guests, and his hair spilled over his shoulders, a waterfall of spun gold.

Their eyes locked.

"Why don't you take over the tour from here?" Brooke patted her forearm. "We'll talk soon, dear." She disappeared into the crowd.

There was an awkward silence. "You look tired," she blurted. Oh, God. She hadn't talked to him in almost two weeks, and those were the first words out of her mouth?

He smiled ruefully, acknowledging her words with a nod. "You, on the other hand, look simply stunning." His eyes dropped to her stomach, then climbed back to her face. "How are you feeling?"

"Fine." What an understatement. Funny how slowing down, not allowing life's white river rapids to simply sweep her along, made her feel better than she had in ages.

He reached toward her, hesitated, and then stuck his hands in his front pockets.

She absorbed the sting, waited for it to dissipate. Even if she'd ruined things between them forever, the next move was hers. "I owe you an apology, Rafe."

"For what?" His nostrils flared—unnecessarily so, because she wasn't about to leave without letting him know exactly how she felt, even if she had to declare those feelings here, in the midst of hundreds of curious people.

And she very well might. Rafe would draw attention anywhere he went, but here, at his own gallery show, wearing those body-skimming clothes and his hair catching the light? He looked like a golden god standing center stage.

She took a shaky breath. "I'm sorry for letting you walk out of my hospital room without stopping you. I'm sorry for thinking you were anything like Wyatt." She swallowed, hard. "I'm so sorry I didn't trust my feelings for you."

He didn't respond, just stood there looking at her. In the silence, she overheard a woman murmur to her friend, "Is that the chick he was with in Underbelly's bathroom?"

He still hadn't said anything, and her heart dropped to her feet with a big, soggy splat. "I've ruined it, haven't I?"

Silence greeted her words.

Well. She had her answer. Now she just had to figure out how to make her legs work so she could get out of here.

"Bailey." Removing his hands from his pockets, he came closer, taking her champagne glass and setting it on the nearest pedestal before taking both hands in his. "I love you so damn much."

He was already lowering his head.

A small, thready moan escaped as she gave herself over to the rush, as their lips touched and she finally tasted him again. It didn't matter that she was over-dressed, or that she could barely balance in her high-heeled shoes, because Rafe was worshipping her with his mouth, holding her steady so she wouldn't fall. Her entire world narrowed to the feel of his lips slanted over hers. Unlike Wyatt's textbook-perfect kiss, Rafe's was hot, hungry, and completely lacking in technique. His arms and hands clamped their bodies together with no smoothness or savoir-faire whatsoever. She couldn't get close enough to him, to his exotic hothouse scent. She wanted to climb into his body, burrow under his skin.

"Rafe." Brooke's voice.

Rafe lifted his head, blinking.

Brooke picked up the glass Rafe had so carelessly placed on the pedestal, wiping away a minute bit of condensation with the hem of her blazer. "You have an audience."

She glanced around, at the too-interested gazes of Rafe's guests, at the Sebastiani family smiling at them from the corner. Lorin grinned and lifted her glass in a tiny toast. Someone with teeth like a chipmunk eyed them with interest, scribbling in a small notebook.

God, he was working. "Rafe, I didn't mean to get into this here—"

"Don't you dare apologize." He dropped another kiss on her lips before reluctantly dropping his arms. She barely had time to miss his touch before he took her hand again. "Would you like to see the rest of the sculptures?"

"I'd love to. They look so different when they're fired and glazed." She gestured toward the nearest pedestal. "I swear I see you...yet I don't."

"Good eye." He rested his free hand on her back, just below her waist—a little too low for propriety. The possessive weight thrilled her, but he was starting to look a little uneasy.

Brooke handed him a fresh glass of champagne. After a muttered "thank you," he raised it to his lips, drained it, and handed the empty glass black.

He tugged on her hand, drawing her toward the next sculpture. Rafe's presence was a little more obvious, if you knew what to look for—and she most certainly did. This sculpture had been inspired by the first time they'd made love down in his studio. She'd climbed on top of him and ridden them both to oblivion. "Why do you get to be an amorphous blob, and I...?" She gestured toward her naked form.

He shot her a grin. "You're much prettier to look at."

"I beg to differ," she said wryly. But she couldn't complain about how she looked—no, not at all. Somehow he'd captured her abandon, and her confidence, in a way that felt artistic and emotionally rich instead of exploitive and porny.

As Rafe led her through the next few sculptures, she noticed that he'd rendered himself with an increasing level of detail. She trailed a fingertip over his clay back, his body half-covering hers as his lips trailed down her stomach. Glancing back at him, she eyed the warm, shallow crater between his collarbones, so alluringly showcased by his open-necked shirt. Licking it drove him wild.

Rafe's Adam's apple bobbed, his nostrils flaring as he absorbed her helpless desire. His body scent deepened, delicious tendrils swirling around them, as he leaned closer.

This—he—felt right. Perfect. Inevitable. She wanted to lick him from stem to stern.

Rafe kissed her, a light caress that ended way too soon. "You're killing me here."

"And you're working. I'm sorry—"

"Don't apologize." He ran his hand down her back, transferring warmth through the satin fabric of her dress. "Let's just get through the rest before I lose what's left of my mind and drag you to the floor."

He seemed to tense up as he drew her towards the last sculptures. She didn't recognize the poses from the time they'd spent together, but the emotion he'd captured—the yearning, the love—made her throat clog with sudden tears.

"The critics are wrong, you know," he said softly. "About *The Dreamer*."

"How so?"

"She's not the dreamer. He is. I am." He led them to the final sculpture, of the man—him—down on one knee before a standing woman.

Her breath dissolved, leaving her lungs empty. Did he understand the human signifi— Yes, apparently he did, because he suddenly stepped back, reached into his pocket, and dropped to one knee before her.

"Bailey?"

She looked down at Rafe, who looked up at her with a face blazing with love, and extreme nervousness. He held a black velvet box. "Oh, my God."

The people around them went silent, unabashedly watching as he opened a small, black velvet box with a flick of his finger.

"Bailey Brown, will you marry me?"

The ring, glorious fire opals set in a wide band of gold, blazed under the gallery lights, but she barely noticed. She looked around the room, at all the people watching them—*oh, my God, Rafe's entire family*—then back down to Rafe's nervous face. A giggle escaped. "Yes," she whispered. "Yes. I love you so much."

Ignoring the ring, she kissed him—a kiss that laid her heart bare. Ignoring the cheering, clapping and congratulations, she breathed him in, forever locking the moment in her memory.

Her head and her heart were finally in synch. He was her home.

She didn't know how much time had passed before she drew away from him, ever-so-slightly. "How about right now?"

"Right now what?" He slid the ring on her finger.

Though the weight would take some getting used to, the ring fit perfectly. Wiggling her fingers, she admired how the opals caught the light. "Let's do it right now." She giggled when his pupils dilated, when his eyes flared with sensual heat. "No, not that— though I can't wait to get my hands on you again. No, I meant let's get married right now."

"You want to catch a flight to Vegas instead of having a traditional ceremony?" He grinned. "Let's go."

He'd marry her in a human religious ceremony if she'd wanted one? A tear fell, and she hastily brushed her cheek. What did she ever do to deserve this man? "In your world, we can marry now, with a single word."

"Bondmates? Are you serious?"

She nodded. She'd never been more certain of anything in her life. "Ask me."

He bent his head so their foreheads touched, creating a curtain of privacy with his hair. "I love you so much."

"I love you, too."

His beautiful eyes glowed. "Will you be my bondmate, Bailey?"

"Yes," she whispered.

And with a single word, an oral contract between them, it was official.

As they kissed, a private celebration in the midst of the party surrounding them, she realized Rafe was wrong, or maybe he was half-right. *They* were *The Dreamers*, partners for life, for better and for worse, in sickness and in health, leading each other into temptation…to wherever their dreams might lead.

ABOUT THE AUTHOR

Tamara Hogan is the award-winning author of The Underbelly Chronicles paranormal romance series. An English major by education and a software engineer by trade, she recently stopped telecommuting to Silicon Valley to teach, edit, and write full-time. Tamara loathes cold and snow, but nonetheless lives near Minneapolis with her husband and two naughty cats.